Innocent EYES

– A Cane Novel –

Charlotte E. HART

Rachel DE LUNE

©All rights reserved. No part of this book may be reproduced without written consent from the author, except that of small quotations used in critical reviews and promotions via blogs.

Innocent Eyes is a work of fiction. Names, characters, businesses, places, events and incidents are either the products of the author's imagination or used in a fictitious manner. Any resemblance to actual persons, living or dead, or actual events is purely coincidental.

INNOCENT EYES – A Cane Novel
©2018 HartDeLune
Charlotte E. Hart • Rachel De Lune

Cover Design by Rachel De Lune
Book design by LJDesigns
Editing by H.A. Robinson and Rox Leblanc
Chapter Illustrations by L.J. Stock, LJDesigns
eBook Formatting: L.J. Stock, LJDesigns

OTHER BOOKS BY:

Charlotte E. Hart

The White Trilogy
Seeing White
Feeling White
Absorbing White

The VDB Trilogy
The Parlour
Eden's Gate
Serenity's Key

The Stained Duet
Once Upon A
The End

Rachel De Lune

The Evermore Series
More
Forever More
A Little Something More (Christmas Novelette)
Surrender to More
More Than Desire
Finally More

Standalone
Reminiscent Hearts
The Break

ACKNOWLEDGMENTS

Rachel's Acknowledgements

Sitting in a bar in York, Charlotte and I argued over planning versus pantsing. You can ask Grace Harper - she was there having a ball!!

And now, I'm writing the acknowledgement for our first book baby. This writing journey has taken me to some super happy places, and writing with Charlotte has been an absolute blast. How could it not be, given her attitude to life and writing. Charlotte, I'm lucky we met all those years ago at our first signing - we have Jo and Rachel to thank for that.

So, thank you Charlotte for letting me put a HEA in, and bringing you as close to a sweet romance as I dare.

To our amazing support team - Lea - you were so enthusiastic about this project. It wouldn't have happened if not for your encouragement. Thank you for always giving so much support. Super hugs to you.

To Rox, Heather, Weezy, Bare Naked Words and Grace (for keeping our secret), Innocent Eyes wouldn't be out in the world without you. Thank you.

And the most heartfelt of thanks to our readers and supporters. We are so grateful for every single one of you.

Hugs

Charlotte's Acknowledgements

Charlotte says all of the above, too, apart from the bit where I thank myself because that would be ridiculous. Instead I'll thank Rachel for being my first co-writing partner, one who I've adored writing with to bring Innocent Eyes into the world. And yes, we did sit in a bar in York discussing planning vs pantsing. It was hilarious, and I still think I'm right about pantstering being the best way to be honest, but I think it's fair to say we compromised on our specialities to come to the perfect combination of both. Including Rachel's HEA.

Slave - that's Leanne Cook - still my superstar. Always will be.

Beta Team - Amazeballs, as usual.

And to all our readers, thank you so much for your continued support.

And the only other person left is my better half, without whom none of this would ever be possible. I love you more than words can say.

x

CHAPTER ONE

Quinn

My fingers roll the dice around as I stare up at the guy, my feet crossed on top of my desk while I lean back in the chair. Fucking idiot. Standing there with his silencer aimed at me as his body quivers and shakes. Threatening me? No one threatens me. No one fucks with me, angers me, or gets inside my head. I'm a ghost of a human, forced that way by a father who built the enterprise I now run.

"You gonna shoot then?" I mumble as I scroll through my phone. I haven't got time for this shit. I've got other meetings to get to, deadlines to deal with. I glance over, taking in his offensive crumpled suit and then travel my eyes to the barrel. "Is it even loaded, Benny?"

Benjamin Mazarono. Low life scum who occasionally runs packages where packages shouldn't be run to. Today, he wants a larger cut of the 20K he's just dumped at my feet. He's not getting it. He can take his chances killing a Cane, see how far that shit gets him when he walks back out onto the streets of Chicago, if he manages to get past Rody on the door. He glances around becoming flustered by my antipathy at his attempted threat.

"Didn't think it through, did you, Benny?" If he hadn't snorted some of my goods up his fucking nose it might have helped him see more clearly.

I kick my feet from the table and pull out the only thing that's going to make this situation fuck off so I can get on with my day. He blanches, his body sidestepping as I round the desk and lift my own slice of heaven at him, the other hand still spinning my dice.

"I just want some more fucking money, man." Man? I'm not his man. Not his friend either. I'm his fucking boss, or his boss's boss. I sneer and aim somewhere near his head.

"Pick a number, Benny."

"What?" he snaps, his hand juddering as he raises the other one to keep the silencer's aim a little more level.

"Two to twelve, pick a fucking number." I step into him, crossing my red carpet and causing him to move backwards towards my office door. My fucking office. Not my father's anymore. Mine. He dares come here into my space with a fucking shaking hand and threaten me? I should suck his heart out for that alone. "Pick a number before I pick one for you."

"Quinn, man. This ain't. I didn't mean..." He scrabbles his legs a little further, the polished wood of my pristine panelling getting closer to him by the second. Two to twelve, that's all he's got now and the meaning of those numbers. When I roll these cubes of ivory in my fingers, fate has its say. If this dick chooses the right number, he gets a reprieve. If he doesn't, game on.

"Quick, Benny."

His eyes widen as he watches me toss the dice, the small white flashes saying so much about his life chances as they go. They all know this is how it works. A flick of the dice and it's all decided. They tumble down and bounce over the floor, little black dots spinning around, ready to make decisions I have no interest in making.

"Four," he splutters to the sound of his back hitting my wall.

I keep watching my dice, waiting for them to stop and give me a direction to travel in, until I hear him lever the trigger. I've pulled mine before he has a chance to finish his stupidity, still watching my little cubes bouncing and tumbling as I listen to the grunt that comes from Benny the dead. The fucking things land on a pair of twos before I've noticed the fat slob slide down my mahogany panelling.

How's that for bad luck and fuck all timing?

"Should've given fate a chance, Benny," I say as I slide the ivory cubes from the floor. "Shame."

The door clicks and opens, Rody finally making an appearance at the sound of a shot. Bit fucking late if you ask me, but he's part of the old team, and I haven't got a hope of getting rid of him unless I kill him myself.

"You okay, son?" The term makes me glare at him, maddened by his continued use of it. *Son.* He lowers his face and looks at Benny's still corpse. "I was out front."

There's hardly any guise of a son here anymore. Brother maybe, carer for my mother, too, but not a son. I lost that accolade when I killed the first client my father told me to. I became a Cane then. A man.

I rub at my scar, remembering the sensation of the knife that dug in around my neck. It still burns, reminding me to always watch my back. No one ever goes behind me anymore, not unless they're strung up and incapable of causing damage.

"It's alright, Rody." It is. He's too old to be protecting me anyway. I should have a new version of him guarding me now, not my father's has-beens hanging around, no matter how much they know the business. "Get rid of him. I've got to get home."

I slip my slice of heaven into my holster and pick up my phone, grabbing my jacket on the way.

"What about his kid?"

"What about him?"

"He's thirteen."

"The dice roll to twelve, Rody."

That's answer enough for me. Twelve or below would have meant something to me, might have given me reason to do something about ensuring he was set up right. Thirteen? Well, that's past those combined numbers. Thirteen is a man, the beginnings of one. Little Mazarono Jnr can go blow dick to eat, or learn a fucking craft like the rest of us had to. Hell, if he came here and asked for it, I might give him his father's job.

Rody frowns at me as I walk to the door, my father's eyes glowering out of his sockets. Screw him. I'm not my father. Times have changed. We live in a world where drugs and computers rule now, not mafia connections and the charm associated with them. It's about time the rest of the old school caught up. Marco Mortoni for a start, whom I have meetings with soon. He should take over like I have, bring his father's enterprise into the 21st century rather than have it linger under decrepit control.

"Son, you…" I stop in front of him, daring him to call me son just one more fucking time. "Quinn. He's a child."

"There's no conscience here, Rody. I'm not my father. You give him something if you're so bothered about the little shit."

I'm unconcerned about the fate of children. There are thousands of them out there. I've got my own shit to deal with—for a start, the routine task of visiting my damned father.

The streets take less time than you'd think. When you're a Cane, rules mean nothing. We're above them. Stop signs? Fuck that. Speed? Fuck that, too. Cops? I snort as one watches me jump a red, the wheel of my Corvette turning in my hands, and then swing the other way undaunted. Most cops are in our pockets. They were there when my father ran the business, and their children and partners are still there now. I pay them more than they'll ever earn legitimately. That's what my business means to me. It has to. Money laundering, drugs, gun running, casino deals, and bent fucking everything. We don't know what straight is. That's my life. Has been since I was fourteen, even before that if you count the private schools my father sent me to from his illicit earnings. It's why these dice keep rolling in my hands, keeping the decisions as easy as that. Conscience and morals mean nothing against keeping this business floating. Decisions do, and I make the hardest ones on the roll of the dice, never letting the outcome affect me.

The phone rings, Jonathan Hannover's name flashing.

"Yeah?"

"We have some problems here, Mr Cane."

"What?"

"For a start, there's a hundred thousand down on a debt. Although, Shifty says he's on that one." Is he? I steer the next streets, listening to the sound of my dice rolling in my hand and thinking of the green fields of home, my real home. I might live in Chicago, but England's where I grew up until Father moved us here, and Cane began in earnest. "Mr Cane?"

"Run the rest off." There's a sigh, followed by the manic tapping of a keyboard.

"The Colbort deal is still up in the air." Preston fucking Colbort, pissing around with the new casino he should be handing over to me in London. The revelation that he's not holding up his end of the deal pisses me off instantly. His family need a reminder of who owes what to whom? "Pinchin's on point. The money is still good there." Drugs. Never a problem to offload. "The boys are still running funds through Stepstone Travil, although that's becoming a tad perilous and I wanted your opinion on what I should do." A tad fucking perilous. The Britishness makes me snort. High-end dicks with their accents, pretending they're not as dirty as we are over here. "One million is a lot to syphon through."

"A tad?" I laugh. He huffs and taps his keyboard again.

"This is quite serious, Mr Cane, it's becoming difficult to manage due to the continued amounts. The CID are investigating locally and I can't see another wash viable. When your father was–"

Fuck my father.

"You're paid enough, find another route," I cut across him, following the gravel drive up to the house and scanning the grounds. "Either that or I'll roll my dice, and you can take your chances like your brother did." The sharp intake of breath proves my point. Do or die. No one lets us down. Your family gets in our bed, it fucking stays there. "What's the hundred K for?" I pull up to the main house and open the door, engine idling ready for the chauffeur to clean it.

"It's a girl. Gambling debts."

Large gambling debts for a girl. The thought intrigues me, but not as much as the idea of Preston Colbort not handing over the casino he offered as collateral for his unpaid debts. Or the fact that the Hannover family can't manage my money correctly.

I walk to the house, my eyes scanned by the security system before I take the steps up to a formal marble entrance, then cross the expanse to Father's home office so I can pull up the spreadsheet Hannover's looking at.

"Where's Colbort?" The laptop's open the second I pull it from the hidden safe, codes already inputted before I've sat down at his highly polished wooden desk.

"He's in London at the moment, planning to travel to Monte Carlo next week for his wife's thirtieth birthday party."

I scan the documents as he carries on telling me of the other 'issues' we have to talk about. Fucking issues. A hundred grand is the least of my problems. My mind works the numbers, spreadsheets and tracking opening up inside me like a cyclone. They're my thing—numbers.

By the time I've processed the fuck ups he's incurring, I've slammed the laptop closed and rolled my dice across the desk.

Seven.

"I'll be on the plane tonight," I snap out, infuriated by his inability to manage the one thing he's supposed to. There's another intake of breath, followed by the sound of him getting up from his too comfortable chair.

"Mr Cane, it's been difficult these last few months."

"Has it?" I couldn't give a damn how difficult his life is. It's about to get a whole lot simpler.

My hand scoops up the dice and I head out of the panelled room, straight for my father who's waiting for his weekly update on my damn money.

"It's the continued amounts, Mr Cane. I can't funnel it anywhere. It's getting messy." I cross the extravagant lobby again and head for the stairs, buttoning my suit jacket and pocketing the dice.

"Set up a meeting with the girl." She'll fuck her debts off if nothing else. Shifty can do it while I eat dinner, entertain me for a while. "And I want to see Mitch Warner of Stepstone at your office. I'll give you a reminder of how Canes do business. Your father understood it well enough."

"Yes, Mr Cane."

The call ends with my finger shutting the phone down. Father doesn't like phones, thinks they're all bugged. This one's not. Nothing I have is bugged, this house included now. The security company we own ensures that with daily sweeps of the house and grounds. Two permanent staff monitor all the extensions and movements, along with the ten other staff who keep their eyes on everything and patrol the grounds. It's fully computerized now, not like the archaic system I inherited when he told me to take over. I'm in control of all this. That's my job here now. I am Cane, regardless of my father's refusal to accept that fact or his old boy's denial. Without me, this whole sordid little enterprise of ours would fold and be burnt to the ground. Stolen from beneath his dying chest. It's me who moves this beast along. Me who steers its next course of action. Me who keeps it as powerful as it is.

I wind my way along the lavish halls, directing myself towards the room I fucking hate and clicking my shoulders ready for the meeting I've got no interest in.

I hate him.

I hate what he did, who he is, and what he made me become because of it. But mostly, I hate that he's made me enjoy it, enough so that I'm far better at it than he could ever have been. Cane was nothing but a small link in a Mafia chain when I arrived and took over. It was bound by constructs and loyalty I no longer care to honour. Now it's a global foundation for deceit, lies, and corruption. Stronger for it. I fucking did that, made us what we are now. Quinn Cane. I can't even blame him anymore.

I fucking despise him for that.

CHAPTER TWO

Emily

"Just hold it there. Eyes right at me." Mrs Banks blinks a few times but doesn't move. I press my finger down and the shutter snaps closed. "Perfect. If you want to lie back now?"

I put my camera down on the box crate in the corner and grab the small stepladder leaning against the brick wall. I drag it into position, retrieve the camera, and gingerly climb the three steps. *God, Jenny. Why today?* The same curse has been running through my head all morning.

Jenny, my receptionist come studio assistant, hasn't turned up to work.

Again.

If she wasn't my best friend, I would have fired her months ago. Even with the friendship status, it's proving difficult to ignore her tardiness and general lack of professionalism.

The shoot today is important. It's my first boudoir shoot, and I need the moral support and help in the studio. Having fun with a family or kids is very different to ensuring a woman looks sexy and alluring for the camera. The client needs to be relaxed, which means I have to put her at ease.

It's more difficult than I had hoped.

"You look gorgeous, Mrs Banks." I lean over and snap the

woman who has propositioned me to do this shoot. Apparently, I took a family portrait of her daughter and grandchildren last year. The results are hanging over her fireplace at home. Then she had the idea for a racy present for her ruby wedding anniversary, and she wanted me to take the photos.

"Can you pull the boa around you slightly? Yes, great." I take a few more shots before stepping off the ladder. Mrs Banks has been a natural in front of the lens. She isn't self-conscious and wants to have a good time.

"Are we done, dear?"

"I'd say so, Mrs Banks. You did wonderfully." I offer her a kind smile and take a small sigh of relief for myself.

I've worked hard over the last five years to develop the studio. It was two years before I could afford my own space, concentrating on outdoor shoots or corporate work in offices. Turning the back room into a courtesan's dressing room has been fun for a change. Perhaps it was just first-time nerves that had my hands shaking.

"If you want to head into the bathroom and get changed, I'll meet you upstairs. Would you like a drink?"

"A cup of tea if you can?"

"Of course. Take your time."

I leave Mrs Banks and head upstairs. The antique desk by the door is still unoccupied, but Cheryl's working at her computer in the back of the room.

"Morning. You're in early."

"Yeah, I had some prep-work to do before later."

"No problem." Cheryl is a freelance photographer who comes in to help when we're busy. She also books the studio for her own clients as long as I don't have anyone scheduled. It's a nice way of earning a little extra cash.

Cheryl's style is edgier than mine. Not all of my clients want the same look for their portraits, so having a second photographer helps me to grow my client base.

As well as our photos being different, our looks are poles apart. Her jet-black hair and sleeve of skull and rose tattoos contrasts vividly with my blond hair and creamy skin. Where she wears heavy Doc Martin boots, ripped jeans, and any shade of black, I choose skirts, dresses, and colour.

The large, open-plan studio is divided into sections. The front is set up as a reception and waiting area, an office space with two computer stations where Cheryl and I work, and an alternative space for shoots behind a curtained-off corner area. The hallway at the back leads to the small kitchen, a room we fitted out for hair and makeup, plus a storage cupboard. Finally, steps descend to the photography studio space in the basement, where lighting, backdrops, and props are set up ready to be used depending on the shoot.

"Do you want a drink?" I ask Cheryl.

"No, ta. I'm good." She barely glances at me, engrossed in the images on her screen. Being work colleagues, I'd hoped that we could grow into friends as well, but Cheryl keeps quiet and to herself.

I make two cups of tea and place them on the low coffee table in front of the leather sofa in the waiting area. Mrs Banks comes over to join me with a beaming smile on her face.

"That was the most fun I've had in months. Thank you, Emily."

"You're welcome, Mrs Banks. Here." I offer her a seat and her tea. "Now, it will be a few days before I'll have the photos processed and edited for you. Then you can come back in, and we can go through the ones you want to be made into the album." I get up and grab my diary off of Jenny's desk. "How about you come back in next Thursday?"

"Can we make it the following Tuesday, dear? I have bridge club on Thursday."

"No problem. I don't have a package specifically for what you've asked. I've based this on my usual family shoot album."

"Fine, fine. I told you. I don't mind paying. I just want to have a collection of photos that will give Harold something to think about." I splutter, barely keeping from spraying tea over myself. Mrs Banks is certainly a character.

"Well, we can go over the details next week." I put the tea down and pencil Mrs Banks into the book.

The tiny bell on the front door rings and I glance up to see who's walking through the door. Jenny sneaks in as quietly as possible. She catches my stare and walks swiftly to her desk. I clench my teeth together and remember that she's my friend, not just my employee.

"The finished album will be ready by the end of next month, won't it? It's my forty-fifth wedding anniversary in December. I don't want to leave anything to chance."

"Yes, that's plenty of time. Don't worry. You'll have a wonderful gift for your husband." I stand and smooth down the front of my dress, holding the diary across my chest. It's an automatic reaction. I cover my breasts every chance I have. My hourglass figure doesn't extend to my hips, and I look woefully out of proportion.

"Jenny, could you fetch Mrs Banks' coat? It's in the makeup room." Jenny looks affronted that I'd consider asking her such a thing, but goes to retrieve the coat.

"See you next week, Mrs Banks."

I show her out and turn my pleasant smile on Jenny. "Care to explain yourself?"

"I'm sorry, I'm sorry. I lost track of time and, well…" Her excuse dies before it's even formed on her tongue.

My mismatched eyes take in her appearance. Her tawny hair looks like a bird tried to nest in it, and her tights have a ladder running up the back. Her skirt and shirt are the same she wore last night. "Did you even go home last night?"

"Yes, thank you." She sounds affronted again, but looking at her state of dress, I can't work out why.

"Were you sober? Because you look a mess, Jenny. You being late is turning into a habit, and I can't afford to keep carrying you like this." I keep my voice soft and calm. The whines of complaint and protest are only a moment away. There's absolutely no use in getting angry at her. Jenny never changes.

"That's none of your business. You're not my mother."

"No, but I am your employer. You can't keep doing this, Jenny. If you're late again, I'll have to let you go. I need someone I can trust and who is reliable."

"I am. Come on. You trust me more than anyone. I'm your best friend."

"Then why don't you start acting like it and show me some respect?" I intend my voice to have more bite. Of course, I can say the words, but I struggle to put any venom or power behind them. The only time my voice holds any strength is when I sing.

"I do respect you. You know I'm having a hard time, that's all. I promise it will get better." And I know it will. For a few weeks, she'll be on her best behaviour. Then it will slip. It's a cycle with Jenny, and I'm still in the dark as to what causes the pattern. At first, I thought it was related to whomever she was sleeping with. But boyfriends or dates don't coincide with her bad behaviour.

"We'll see. You can help me move the furniture back to normal downstairs, and Cheryl has a client in an hour."

"Seriously?"

"So help me, Jenny."

"Fine. Yes, I'll get right to it."

How does she manage to do it? It's her job to assist me, be the receptionist and look after the studio, but if I ask her to do anything, she makes it sound like she's doing me a favour.

"And please tell me you haven't forgotten about Friday evening? I have a rehearsal and need you to mind the studio between four and six. I can't miss it, and Cheryl isn't available."

"Friday? This Friday?"

"Jenny!"

"Relax. It's no problem. I can shift my thing."

"Good." I walk away. Cheryl gives me a questioning glance as I pass her and I just shake my head.

Jenny has been my best friend since secondary school. I was shy and awkward, and she was fearless and popular. She befriended me and made my life that much easier through school. I was the odd girl with the funny eyes, always with my nose in a book or behind a camera. She stood up for me, confided in me. We supported each other.

I thought we'd be friends forever. We were inseparable all through school, and I can't help but look back with a fondness that is ingrained in me. We grew apart when we went off to University. Jenny got in contact after we graduated and we rekindled our friendship. I moved closer to London and started doing what I had always loved.

But Jenny wasn't the same. Something had changed in her, like someone, or something, had broken her spirit. Now I'm the one who helps her, stands up for her and defends her. She's gone through countless jobs, can never stay in the same house or apartment for long. She even lived with me for a few years, but I couldn't have her working for me and living with me.

She's told me she has a flat in Peckham, but she hasn't convinced me she's still renting it.

I hang the feather boa on the chair and go about stripping the bed.

"Here, I can help." Jenny's followed me down into the studio. "I'm sorry. I've had a bad morning, that's all."

"You can't use that as an excuse. We have responsibilities."

"I'd forgotten about the concert. Sorry."

"It's fine, as long as you're here. Please don't let me down." The choir I sing with is performing in a local concert on Friday night. It's our final rehearsal before our debut in front of the paying public. Nerves wrack my body every time I think about it.

I'm comfortable behind the camera, but certainly not out in front for people to see. Now, as well as the notes to sing, I'll be pre-occupied with Jenny.

"Is there anything wrong? You've not been yourself for a few weeks now," I venture in an attempt to settle the tension between us.

"You know I hate asking for help," she mutters, as she helps me pull the sheets off the bed.

"But you can," I press.

"Fine. Can I borrow some money? Maybe get an advance on my wages for the next couple of months?"

"Months? How much do you need to borrow?"

"I'm hoping my parents will be able to help, but I was thinking about five thousand."

My mouth falls open as I stare at my friend. Despite her unkempt appearance, all I can see is the girl who befriended me in school. My stomach churns with worry as to what she needs five thousand pounds for, and although I know I'll likely regret it, I can't help but ask.

"Why do you need the money? Are you in trouble?"

"No. Nothing like that. It's to do with the flat. I got a little behind on the rent, and for me to stay, I need to pay the arrears and advance next month." She bats off my concern, but her eyes don't meet mine. I know she's lying.

"Do you want me to transfer it online?"

"No. No, I mean, that's not what they want. Cash. If you can?" I stare at her for a moment, waiting for her to spit the truth out. She doesn't. She squares her shoulders and stares me down. I know she'll win. She would do this when we were younger. She'd draw on some inner courage to stand up to whoever was in her way. I never thought she'd turn it against me, though.

"Cash?" I give her another chance.

"Yes. If you can."

"Jenny, this is a loan, right? I can advance you some of your wages, but you can pay the rest of it back, okay?"

"Sure. And I'll smarten up. Promise." Her tune brightens when she realises she's won. What does it say about me, though? Am I doing her a favour and helping her out? Or just enabling her problems to grow bigger by not calling her out and forcing her to face them?

"I'll get the money by the end of the week. You can have it Friday."

"You're the best." She steps forward to engulf me in a hug, and she can't hide the smell of stale cigarettes and alcohol from her clothes and hair. I cling to her as she embraces me and pray she isn't getting mixed up in something she'll later regret, or that costs her too much.

"Come on then. This room needs to be back to the basic shell. The drapes and fabrics all need to be put away, and the chair needs to go back upstairs."

"On it." Jenny's enthusiasm returns instantly, a contrast to her initial sulky attitude. Then again, I've just agreed to lend her five grand. She doesn't have the option to argue with me.

* * *

My attire doesn't consist of many black items. A pair of jeans and a shirt are the extent of what hangs in my wardrobe, but black is the uniform for tonight, so I've bought something new. Of course, everything black is slinky and sexy and not the overall appearance I want to give. I finally find a more demure dress that contains my cleavage and brushes the tops of my knees. Capped sleeves and a mandarin collar complete the outfit.

I ease up the side zip and slide my feet into a modest peep-toe heel. Done.

Jenny is at the studio, and I have twenty minutes to get to the church for the rehearsal. All Saints has superb acoustics and suits our chamber choir. Steven, the musical director, wants our first performance to be quite traditional, so the repertoire for tonight includes Bach, Bernstein and the piece I hate to sing, *Ave Maria*. He's been promising for some time to allow us some more contemporary music. Hopefully, after this performance, he'll finally come through.

I bundle up to make the short walk to the church. It might only be October, but there isn't any lingering warmth from the mild autumn we've had. Luckily, All Saints isn't a draughty old church. It's a beautifully restored triple-gabled building with high arched ceilings. It feels warm and light as I enter, which is at odds with my internal images of churches.

I haven't set foot inside a church since I finished school.

"Ah, Emily. Come on, come on. We're going to run through the full programme before the doors open." Steven bustles over to me and moves me into position with the other members of the choir. Ann and Jane, my fellow sopranos, are waiting for me.

I don't have time to pay attention and worry about the nerves rioting in my stomach. Steven thrusts my music book into my hands and takes his position.

Two hours later, we're waiting for the audience to take their seats. My tongue feels too big for my mouth, like I've been stung by a bee and am having an allergic reaction. My saving grace is the lighting in the church is bright and makes it hard for me to see the audience. Steven keeps moaning about lifting heads up, looking out, and projecting. He can't complain in the middle of the performance, though.

There are two other choirs performing tonight. We're on first—the warm up if you like—and I just want it to be over. I love to sing; that's why I joined the choir. Music makes me happy, but performing doesn't. I just have to hold onto every note, feel the energy and joy it gives me, and pretend the people in front of me aren't there.

And it works. My hands grip my music folder like a lifeline, and I focus on an empty seat four rows from the front, but I don't let my anxiety win. I'm confident with the songs and let the delight of the music invigorate my blood.

Even *Ave Maria* can't dampen my enthusiasm.

By the end of the evening, my cheeks ache from smiling so much. I've accomplished something I never dreamed I would. Although I don't intend to repeat it anytime soon, I feel good about myself.

After all the music, it's a gentle melody from one of the other choirs that sticks in my head. Its delicate tune obliterates everything else I've heard this evening and settles into my psyche. It's restful and sweet, and I hum the notes all the way home.

I collapse onto my bed as soon as I lock the front door.

Exhaustion hits me like a freight train, but I hold it back long enough to grab my phone and plug it in.

Displayed on the screen is one text.

No one called. No one visited. Two hours of quiet. I don't see why you had to stay open tonight. I guess that's why you're the boss. See you Tuesday. Jenny.

CHAPTER THREE

Quinn

I walk away from the old man, quietly closing the door and barely holding on to the respect that shimmers above the hate. It's a slither of top lining, just keeping me on-side enough to not smother him. Loyalty to the family. Loyalty to my mother is more appropriate, the same loyalty that brings me to her door every time I'm here.

"Mother?" I ask, my knuckles rapping on her door. Nothing. No fucking sound at all other than the continued wails that hover around her all the time.

I open the door anyway, not waiting for an answer that will never come. She's there, her body curled around the profligate furnishings, legs draped on the floor by the floral couch. Her eyes flick to me, their sneer as deadly as it always is.

"Who are you, pretty boy?" she drawls as she turns to face me. Her blouse opens, then she trips over the length of her scarf as she tries to get up. I move to help, catching her and pushing her back to the couch before she does more damage than the pills already do. "Get off me," she snaps, her fingers slapping out and scratching across my face. "I'll fuck you up like I did them. One fucking touch. You want some, pretty boy?"

"Mother, calm down." She slaps again, her eyes suddenly

wild and untamed. It makes me grab for her, shielding her from damaging herself in the frantic struggle. "Calm, Mother." As usual, calm doesn't descend into this room. It becomes a frenzied attack, her arms thrashing for contact, fear etched into every feature as she keeps coming at me. I shove at her, pushing her back to the couch again until she relinquishes her fight, all the time murmuring words at her to ease this spell. It finally finishes with me holding her down, my arm braced against her chest as she battles for all she's worth, me looking away to the corner of the room.

"Quinn?" she says suddenly, her tone as pretty as I remember when I was four. "Baby? What's happened?"

"Nothing, Mother," I reply, drawing away from her and straightening my suit. She frowns and looks down at herself, her hands working the buttons on her blouse together and then patting her hair down. "Nothing at all." I walk into the bathroom and grab some water, collecting her pills on the way to help ease her back to fucking earth again.

"Who the hell are you?" she yelps as I walk back in. I shake my head and move towards her slowly, offering her the glass. "You're trying to poison me. They tried that once. I'll fucking kill you if you try." I slow all my movements, my pace reducing to that of a snail.

"Pills, Mother. You remember? It's Quinn. Your son."

"I haven't got a fucking son. You're here to rape me, aren't you?" She shivers at that, and then moves, her feet clambering over themselves to get to the door.

I sigh and watch her go, safe in the knowledge that the key is still in my pocket. She rebounds off the door, her hands beating at it as she screams for help. It'll stop in a while. She'll come back, remember me. So I sit and roll my dice again, the water and pills placed beside me on the small table. Remember me? It's fucking pitiful. I don't think she's remembered me properly for years. Maybe occasionally when she looks at me, the touch of her fingers reminding me of lullabies she used to sing all that time ago. She's gone, though. She's been gone for fifteen years. She was murdered. Murdered by this family and the man I call Father. Her life was sucked out and discarded, spat on, and her frame is kept in this room only because he hasn't got the balls to put her out of her misery. Me either.

"Quinn?" she says, a sob catching in her throat as she crumples to her knees and watches the door. She's waiting for me to visit. Her maid, Livia, says she does that. She sits in the window sobbing, waiting for her favourite son to visit her. All fucking day, apparently. Shame she hardly ever shows that to me. "Quinn, baby. Where are you?" She starts talking to herself after that, mumbles and mutters under her breath as she crawls the floor, her eyes searching for something. "Where's my baby gone?" I've gone, too. I went the moment she did and that fucker made me a man. Quinn baby has long since left, his heart removed the moment this job took over and she told me to protect the family. "QUINN?"

She can shout all she wants. There's no point answering until I get a snippet of her back. It's the softness in her eyes—that's what she needs to find me again. The fear and terror etched there won't let her see me. But that's what comes of living this life we're all in. It's what I've hardened to, what she couldn't. But then I haven't been raped for sport, nor pawned off to pay debts. She has. She's endured it all for the Cane family. That's what wives do for their families. That's what he told me, anyway.

I watch her for a while longer, knowing that's the truth. It might be fucked up and indecipherable to the masses, but this isn't the masses. This is a mobster's hold of tyranny. We don't accept anything less than we asked for. Why would anyone else? Opponents. Allies. We're all the same. We do anything to protect what's ours, showing the world we're on top of the power tree. We have to. Integrity isn't a luxury any of us can afford, not that I have any to care about. My only version of that lies in loyalty to this family, her in particular, and the thought that I can change the old ways with time and patience.

The damn tears come next. They're enough for me to stand again and gaze out of the window, partly disgusted with her weakness. I just listen as she starts wailing, my eyes roaming the grounds. Livia's out there walking to the car with purposeful strides as she waves her hand at the driver. They're fucking. Have been for some time. Servants fucking. It's as annoying as these howls of disarray coming from her wretched voice behind me, but then what else is there for comfort when you work for us? Fuck all. You do your damned job and, with any luck, you get a paycheck and keep your life as payment. You don't show us you care about someone or something. We'll likely use it against you. No one comes to work here under any other pretence. It's in the contract. You fuck up, you die.

They drive off, their car passing my brother's as he screams up the gravel, dust flying from his green Ferrari's wheels. Fucking moron. I smile, though, laughing at the move and remembering the small part of me that wishes I was as carefree as he is. Josh has no concerns, nothing to tax the money he spends. He's free to fuck up as much as he likes as long as he comes nowhere near my business. He's too weak for a Cane. Always was. He's explosive, volatile, and fucking drunk most of the time. He says it's because he could never live up to me. I say it's because he's never had to. Silver spoon fed. Everything money could buy given to him as if it was his deific right to have it. He hasn't worked for it like I have, hasn't had to prove a thing. He's just the youngest kid who got the goods that Father delivered, while Nathan and I are the ones who took the brunt of our father's life. I've been made, Nathan's been pulled along, and Josh has simply been allowed to evolve.

It's a pretty fucking useless attempt at evolution.

I follow his movement as he gets out and looks up at me. He can't see me; he's not even looking for me. He's looking for his mom, hoping she remembers who he is and tells him what to do. He lost her at thirteen, just at the point when a man's life is about to be moulded. I'd already been made by then. I was twenty. Already honed as a killer. No fucking going back. And it was too late for Nathan not to follow. He was hot on my heels at eighteen, well on the road to perdition with me, but Josh has been screwing around ever since. No route onwards, no guidance, and all I can do is watch on and pick up the pieces, because I won't let him into the business. I can't afford the disruption to my order. He exists, that's all, with me managing the fuck ups he makes and the money he wastes. It's another one of my jobs. Protect the family, always, irrespective of whether they deserve it or not.

Eventually, the wailing stops behind me and quiet resumes. I turn to watch her crawl to me, her eyes dazed and confused as she scans the floor for answers, her fingers finally biting into my ankle like they usually do when she remembers me.

"Quinn? What happened?" I look down at her there, a certain amount of compassion coming as my knees crouch to her level.

"Nothing, Mother." I grasp hold of her elbows to lift her up, my own hands running the silk of her blouse fully together again. "Nothing at all. You just tripped."

"Did I?"

"Yeah."

"Oh. I don't remember."

I smile at her and help her through the suite, the feel of her soft hands on my arm a reminder of times gone by, and then let her get comfortable on the bed. She lies there, her hair tangled from the yanking she's been doing, her small limbs shifting up to form some kind of comfort for her lacking life. And then she stares around, probably unaware of the room she's in.

"Where am I, Quinn?"

"At home, Mother. Your suite." I wander off to retrieve the pills and water, wanting to give her a few hours peace as she sleeps.

"I don't recognise it. Have we redecorated?"

"Yes, Mother." We haven't. This room hasn't changed for fifteen years. She picked it before we lost her, and finished it three days before Father made her go.

"It's pretty. I bet you chose it. You were always good with colours. You remember the art work you used to do? You should paint again."

"Perhaps another day, Mother," I reply, coming back in to find her looking at me.

The vision of her there, soft eyes I remember gazing at me with that green-blue haze, would have made me hope ten years ago. There's no point in that anymore. I don't hope for anything. Hope is a luxury I can't enjoy. That woman left a long time ago. She left the day Father made her go to pay his debts. She never came home but for these miniscule seconds that show up occasionally.

"FUCK YOU," she spits, her hand suddenly throwing a pillow across the room at me. I sigh again and walk towards her, knowing what's coming and gauging the need to call someone else to help me sedate her. "Don't fucking touch me." She jumps from the bed, both hands up in defence as she backs to the bathroom door.

"Mother, calm down. It's me, Quinn."

"I'm not doing this again. I'm not," she shouts, her feet fumbling over the rug until she falls to the floor. I watch her as I slowly move over to her, the glass placed on another table as I go. "You've taken enough. Leave me alone."

"Mother, you need your pills."

"No. No, I can't do it anymore. Please stop. Don't hurt me again." She shakes her head rapidly, limbs scrambling back away from me. "FUCK YOU ALL." She screams the last of it as my fingers reach for her neck, her chin fitting into them as easily as they always do. "Stop it. Get off me." I tighten the hold, wrapping the rest of her into my grip and forcing her mouth open with my thumb in the side of it. "Oh god, please, no more." She bites down, sending agony through me just like any good Cane woman should, but it's not painful enough for me to stop the insertion of four pills.

She coughs around them as I grab her nose and cover her mouth, more insistent mumbles coming from her as I keep clinging onto her frame and stare out the window. It's just movement from her then—legs kicking out as I hold on, arms trying to push their way free. It's not fucking happening. I've done this too many times. This is what a son does for the woman who brought him into this world. It's my loyalty to her.

The only sense of it I have for any woman.

The fighting recedes slowly as the meds kick in, so I sit for a few moments longer, looking out the window, refusing to think about what happened to her. It's done now. It was done a long time ago. She did what she had to for her family. He ordered it, and because of her, we're all still alive and breathing. There isn't a female on the planet with as much backbone as this woman. No one else deserves the energy I give Mother. That's why I only fuck whores. I fuck them and leave them, no care to the action other than my own satisfaction. There's only one woman I give a damn about and it's the one in my arms. She took everything our world delivers and then she was dumped back on our doorstep—debt paid. It's what happens when you get involved with us, because when this world we're in fucks, it fucks with whatever it needs to in order to get the debt paid, sometimes for the sheer hell of it.

I end up putting her back into bed as I always do, not bothering with the covers. They wake her quicker for whatever reason, make her edgier and more difficult for Livia to manage. And then I turn to leave without a backwards glance, calling for the plane as I lock the door behind me. It's time to visit the motherland, remind it that Canes can cross oceans with the wealth they've accumulated if they need to. Remind it of how it should operate for us.

CHAPTER FOUR

Emily

The weather is ominous, the cold snap in the air chilling my skin despite the layers of scarves and jumpers I've piled on, but I got a few great shots out at Ruskin Park. My only company has been the nameless tune I hummed all the way home on Friday night. It's like the repeat button has been pressed and forgotten. I catch myself lost in the notes half a dozen times. It's a melodic tune that has seeped inside of me, bursting to break free when I give it half a chance.

On Tuesday, Jenny is at the studio before me. The hostility I felt from her last message has obviously been forgotten over the weekend. Or so I think.

"Good morning, Jenny."

"Morning." She's at her desk with her laptop open, and although she's in work, the pout on her face tells me she isn't happy about it.

"Good weekend?" I offer.

"So-so."

No reciprocal enquiry, but then, I should know what to expect. Her mood is as dull as the October rain outside.

I don't have a client booked until later this week, so I start on the edits for Mrs Banks and the Wheeler family from last week. As the morning progresses, Jenny doesn't come out from under her thunder cloud. She doesn't get up to make a cup of tea or take my offer of conversation. Nothing seems to change her tune.

"Come on. I won't apologise for Friday, Jenny. And I've just lent you a lot of money. You could at least try to be polite." My hands have found my hips as I stand in front of her desk.

"Thank you for the money. I'm not trying to be a bitch, but you don't understand what's going on with me, so it's best you just leave me alone."

Her defeatist attitude shakes me. "Then talk to me. We're friends, or so I thought. Best friends."

"We are. But that doesn't mean we share everything. We're not twelve years old anymore."

"Really? I thought we did share our troubles with each other? If you can't even be bothered to tell me what's going on then I give up." I grab my bag and leave to go and fetch some lunch. I'm not going to be a pushover and pander to Jenny as I've already done.

When I return, Jenny hasn't changed her manner. Her face is glum, and I ache to lessen her burden. Instead, I ignore her and concentrate on work.

Jenny's mood swings aren't anything new, but her attitude has been increasingly crap over the last few months. She's never been visibly disrespectful to me before or refused to share her problems. I want to be there for her. But how can I if she doesn't open up and tell me what's bothering her?

I don't believe her excuse for the money. The more I've thought about it, the more concerned I've become. The list of possibilities for what the money could be used for grows longer and longer. Gambling debts, drugs, a loan shark—all as bad as each other.

I try to put my worries for Jenny to the back of my mind, but having a limited number of close friends means it's a hard thing to do.

The last boyfriend I had was over a year ago. Dating websites seem to work for some, but I have no luck. Awkward first dates with men who are after a quick date followed by sex aren't what I was looking for then, or now.

It seems there's a shortage of early-thirty-something-men who are interested in anything close to art or culture of any kind. Even socialising seems a step too far for most. It's not like I'm asking for Jake Gyllenhaal on the criteria.

Jenny doesn't say goodbye at 4:30 p.m. and just gets up and leaves. If I'd said no to lending her the money I might have accepted it, but I haven't. It's getting harder and harder to tolerate her behaviour, and I can't hide the hurt it causes.

I lock up the studio and make the short walk to the tube and the Victoria line. Twenty minutes later, I'm walking the familiar path to Darlberg Road. It's too expensive to rent and build the savings needed to buy in London, and the studio has taken all of my savings. It's still my priority. My goal is to have a successful company. With that will come the means to buy my own house in time. Until then, I'm stuck in the rental market.

For now, I settle for my little slice of heaven in the shape of a one-bed flat in a Victorian terrace in Brixton. The garden clinched it for me. The space is mine to relax in. No judgements, no Jenny, no questions, customers or bills to worry about. I can be alone with my thoughts and pretend the real world isn't still racing past outside.

The drawn-out squeak hasn't magically vanished as I push

the front door open and step into the cramped entryway.

I dump my laptop on the table in the living room before kicking my modest heels to the side and pouring myself a deserved glass of white wine. After taking a sip, I pad into the garden, despite the weather, and sit on the wooden bench looking out on my patch of solace.

The simple flower borders have died back now that autumn is growing cold. The colour has drained from the plants, leaving a mix of mossy greens and browns in their place. The two borders leave only a narrow, paved strip down the centre of the garden. No grass to stretch out on and bask in the sun when, and if, it decides to show itself. But I don't mind. It's my little escape.

As the cool wine hits my lips again, the tension of the day begins to fade into the background of my mind and the random notes of the tune from Friday evening replace it.

I fight the lonely pang that hits my chest at having no one close to share my down time with. I've always promised myself that I don't need a man in my life and that if it were meant to be, then it will. But a small crevice of my heart longs for someone who will support and love me, and share their life with me.

I gulp a mouthful of wine, bringing a halt to my self-induced pity party.

Every few months the same thoughts and desires seep into my mind and take over like an infection. I think of Mrs Banks and her photos for her husband and laugh. If I were married tomorrow, I'd be pushing eighty before my forty-fifth wedding anniversary. There certainly isn't a groom in sight. There will have to be a boyfriend first, and that's proving hard enough.

I shake my head clear, sending my wavy blond hair

scattering around my face. Picking myself up, I leave the garden and top up my wine before changing into a pair of slouchy pyjamas.

The song that has rooted itself in my brain begins to play in my mind, and I hum along to a few notes, unsure of where the melody will take me.

***

The drizzle isn't what I want to walk through on my way to work, but the weather is perpetually bad in London. It makes it difficult to schedule any outside shoots, and of course, those are some of my best work.

I put the kettle on after opening up and take a seat on the sofa in the reception area. I'm distracted by a race of rain drops sliding down the window pane, a desperate battle to reach the window ledge first.

The jangle of the bell as Jenny breezes in spoils my concentration and I don't see which droplet wins.

"Good morning," she chirps. My eyes pop as I watch her tuck herself behind the desk and get set up.

"Good morning," I reply, stunned that this is the same girl from yesterday.

"Before you say anything, I know. I'm sorry about the way I've been treating you. I've been a bitch, and you haven't deserved any of my venom."

"Well, thank you for saying that. Have you got everything… taken care of? You seem happier today."

She pauses for a moment, and a ghost of something crosses her features. The creases around her eyes crinkle for a moment before she glosses them back smooth. "I think I have.

But I sort of need another favour." She smiles as she wrings her hands together.

"Excuse me? Aren't we still in the middle of the last favour I did for you?" I shift back into the sofa and take a sip from my mug of tea.

"This time it's different. You'll like this one." She comes to join me, all excited. "When was the last time you had a date?"

I roll my eyes, horrified she's so blunt. She knows it's been months. "I can't remember. A while," I confirm, not happy about the turn of conversation.

"Well then, this is just what you need. I have a date on Friday evening."

"Yes?" I follow along with her, wondering what plan she's designed.

"And I'd love it if you could go in my place. He's, well, he's a business type, and there's this other guy I've been seeing."

"You've double booked?"

"Kind of. What do you say?"

"Why can't you just cancel? It's a blind date for goodness sake."

"Yes, I could. But this way you get a date and so do I. We both win. This guy sounds more your type anyway. More sophisticated. He's taking me to The Regal, so he's not too shabby. What do you say?"

I stare at her for a moment, reading her face. She's edgy about something, and dread pools in my stomach that she's doing this because he's a total loser.

"Have you met this man before?" I enquire.

"No. It's through a dating app."

"So, what's the problem with cancelling?"

"Fine. I will. It doesn't matter. I just thought you could do with a night off. You've not been with a guy in forever." My defences shoot up, and Jenny's warm demeanour from a few moments ago is now frosty

"Don't be so mean about it, Jenny. Some of us have responsibilities. I'll find a guy when I'm ready."

"I was trying to say sorry and get you to have some fun. That's what friends do, isn't it? Come on, where's the harm?"

I mull over Jenny's offer. I have been grumbling about the men, or the lack thereof, in my life. Perhaps this *is* an opportunity I should take. Jenny's eyes are wide with anticipation. She shifts, edging closer to me, and I feel the silent pressure from her. She's more eager for me to go on this date than she is for her own.

"Fine," I concede. "I'll go, but if he's a jerk, I want an escape plan. You call me after half an hour, and if I answer, you're my excuse. Deal?"

"Okay, drama queen." She smiles a genuine, happy smile, but relief flecks her eyes. Her arms are around my neck, and she pulls me against her in a quick hug. I reciprocate before she pulls away and stands abruptly.

"You're going to have fun. I promise. Thank you," she sings as she claps her hands together.

"It's just a blind date. It's not a problem."

"You might need to pretend to be me. Is that okay?"

"So, I introduce myself as Jenny. Anything else I need to know?"

"No, no. Dress up. Let your hair down. We can sort the finer details during the week." She bounces back to her desk and seats herself, looking content.

47

I let the plans percolate and find that despite the odd circumstances, a flutter of excitement wakes in my stomach. Jenny's right. It has been too long, and I shouldn't give up just because I've been on a losing streak.

Jenny delivers a cup of coffee to my desk mid-morning. The last few days of roller-coaster mood swings are back on an even keel. "Hey, Jenny, is there a profile pic of this guy? And what's his name?" I've found myself imagining him in my mind—tall, ruggedly handsome with intense eyes.

"Sure. His name is Jonathan Hannover."

"Jonathan. Right. And a picture?" I roll the name over in my mind picturing someone who is much older than me. Maybe he's a silver fox, greying at the temples?

"Oh, I wouldn't believe everything people put on their profiles."

"If he's a toad then I'll be excusing myself and running to the bathroom to escape."

"Don't judge a book by its cover, Emily. Looks aren't everything," she scolds.

"I know. I've had a few blind dates in my time. I can handle it."

***

Thursday evening finally greets me, but instead of slumping into my chair and curling up with the latest edition of Practical Photographer as I normally would, I'm rifling through my wardrobe, ready for tomorrow.

My hands run along the rainbow of coloured garments hanging in front of me. I've never had the problem of what to wear before. Most of my dresses are modest and conceal much of my cleavage, or I team a skirt with a top, my attempt at making my figure look more hourglass than it is.

I pull a dress from the haven't-worn-in-forever end and study it. A creamy lace material with embroidered flowers, it has a sweetheart neckline which will only draw attention. I don't want to give the wrong impression on a first date, but the dress is pretty. Cinched in at the waist, it flows down to my knees. It's a summer dress really, but if I wear a jacket, I could get away with it.

I try it on, wrestling my boobs into position, and take a look in the oval Cheval mirror in the corner of the room.

My mismatched eyes make a quick evaluation. The dress is lovely, and it clings to my silhouette beautifully. I shouldn't be ashamed of my assets. Some women would be envious of my chest. I just always feel uncomfortable in my own skin. Being teased at school for having boobs didn't help. And not just small, developing breasts, I had full on D cups by the time I was fourteen. Boys would stare, and girls would call me names behind my back. Until Jenny caught them. It was just another thing people would tease me about. The self-confidence they knocked from me won't magically reappear anytime soon. I twirl in front of the mirror and take a breath.

This man, this Jonathan, is a complete stranger. It's a blind date. It might go horribly wrong, and I'll never have to see him again. Or, he might be gorgeous, and this could be the start of a whirlwind romance. I should wear something I like and feel good in. I can wear what I like. I've seen plenty of women flaunt their assets in public. And in a rare moment of courage, I hang the dress up, ready for tomorrow evening.

CHAPTER FIVE

Quinn

London

It's cold here, has been since I stepped off the plane this morning, but I can't suppress my need to amble around taking it all in. The last time I stepped off a plane, other than to get me back to Chicago, was in Columbia.

Hardly the same effect.

I tug my scarf closer and watch the traffic pile up as I cross the road. Fucking cars are never ending in this city. I'd almost forgotten how close it all is, the streets cluttering up on each other, ceaseless noise careering around. It makes me chuckle after a while, memories of my youth coming from somewhere in my mind.

Youth. It seems so long ago. It makes me glance over the women milling around, watching their hustle and bustle, children hanging off their arms as they keep going into the night. I've forgotten that, relegated it to a place best kept for the less criminally minded. Youth has no place in my life; neither does the imagery associated with it. Josh still lives in that world. I don't.

I turn the corner, allowing the cold to creep into my bones and remind me of this city. These back streets are as gritty as I remember them—dirt littering corners, dilapidated buildings crumbling above the whores who patrol their territory. I smile and pull my collar up, shaking my head at another advance from one of them as I keep moving with no destination in mind.

"Come on, baby," she calls after me. "Hundred quid, anything you want."

Anything I want. One hundred pounds wouldn't compensate her for the amount I want. Cheap fucking whore. I'd forgotten how easy they are on the streets. It's not surprising in this part of town, but they should ramp it up a bit, stay in line with fucking inflation at least.

Another mob of them are hanging on the next corner, ready to pounce, so I cross away from them before I do something I shouldn't. My dick isn't meant for pussy that's tainted. It only goes in high-end cunt with a clean bill of health and a mouth that stays shut after the event. It's best that way. Safer to my business and my family. No connections. No distractions. No chance of death in the middle of it, apart from that one bitch who was after blood for the bullet hole in her father's skull. Shame, she was attractive for a whore, enjoyable to fuck with.

My phone rings in my pocket.

"Shifty says the girl's booked for eight-thirty," Jonathan says, his tone quivering around the jaw I punched this morning. Cause—effect. He didn't pick seven when the dice rolled on his desk. "She knows what it's about." Fucking right she does. A hundred K is a substantial about of gambling debt for one girl. It's beyond comprehension how Shifty let her rack it up in the first place.

"She a whore?" It's the only reason I can see for Shifty allowing it. The idiot's always been partial to a hooker with the ability to wrap him around her fingers. It's a trait I've let slide 'til now.

"I'm not sure, Mr Cane. I believe she's been running the debt up for some time. Clearing some, before getting deeper in. It's been the least of my concerns lately."

I end the call and carry on along the streets back towards the Regal, one foot in front of the other as I run numbers around my mind and draw in some of the decaying air. It feels good to be back on this ground. My hands hardly touch it anymore. They're too busy at a computer, running Cane through accounts and systems rather than hitmen and murder. We've still got them. It's necessary to have that backing, but I no longer participate in that part of the game. I employ people like Shifty for that instead. And I fucking pay them well—well enough that a hundred grand should not have been racked up. Not that I give a fuck about the amount. It's nothing to me; it's the principle that counts. This is how it starts. Little backhanders, people forgetting to pay and getting away with it. Lies, manipulations, women taking control with their pretty batting lashes and their deviant little grins. Trouble starts like that. The control gets lost under the mess of who owes what to whom. It's why I'm here. A damned reminder that Quinn Cane doesn't miss a damn thing and he doesn't tolerate inaccuracies and fuck ups. My boys don't fail me. If they do, they die.

"Mr Cane, Sir," the doorman says as I walk up, holding his hand out to wave me through into the building. "Nice to see you back again. Have a good stay."

Good is an exaggeration. Good would have meant Hannover sorting all these problems prior to my arrival—before I even got on the plane would have been better. I nod at the faceless man nonetheless and travel through the apartment building towards the elevator, hitting the button for the eighth-floor restaurant. The Cane apartment is two floors above that, somewhere I'll be heading the moment I've dealt with this bitch.

The doors open and Shaun greets me, his face only remembered because of the whores he organises when I'm here. High-end. Professional. They come out of West London somewhere. Perfected and polished. All with a clean medical record, so I fuck into them bare.

"Your table's waiting, Mr Cane."

Of course it is. Everything is always waiting for me. Colbort wasn't when I arrived at his home, though. He hid at first when he saw the Cane number plate turn into his family's home. I watched the curtains twitch and smiled. Then he came out with my fucking casino keys in his hand. He begged for ten minutes as I stood in front of his house, my brain considering torching it, and then he pleaded for his family's lives as he signed paperwork. It amused me. Still does.

"Shaun, a woman's coming. She'll ask for Jonathan. Have her sent through when she arrives."

"Yes, Mr Cane."

I walk on towards the table, now entertaining myself with the look on Mitch's face as he came into Hannover's office and saw me waiting for him. Four threats were all that was needed. One on his wife, one on his son, one on his daughter, and one on his entire fucking portfolio. He folded on that one, knees buckling to the fucking floor as he grovelled, the thought of money more attention-grabbing than his family. I could have fucking shot him for that insult alone, still might if the mood takes me, but at least he's focused on getting my dirty money clean again rather than making Hannover's life difficult.

"Sir," the waitress says as I arrive.

I don't answer her as she takes my coat and gloves, nor am I interested in the lips she presents. I just take my seat and stare out at the London skyline, trying to remember the last time I was here while my fingers roll my dice. A year? Two? I don't know. I've not been needed for a while, but I do remember the reason. I killed three men that night. Three of London's finest gangland wisdom makers. They were dense enough to deny us access to a particular deal. It was one Father needed to complete for a debt we owed. I was flown here within three hours of the phone call.

No one has denied Cane a thing in England since that night.

The small room only houses six tables. It's the place I always eat when I'm here, as do the few other wealthy residents in this building. The main restaurant is behind the shutters, kept for the less well-endowed to discuss their meagre lives. We don't mix with the masses. Why should we? We're nothing like them. We expect higher standards. Perfection. There are no half measures. No try. They do, and they do it exceptionally or lose their jobs, if not a limb with the mood I'm in tonight.

"Boss." Shifty arrives.

I look over my shoulder, watching as his thirty-something bulk wades through the tables, just avoiding knocking two of them over.

"Tell me about my money, Shifty."

"Ah shit, boss." I turn back towards the skyline, tightening my loose smile into a sneer. I know what's coming now. Fucking distractions. He's been fucking the woman. Shame, I like Shifty. "She's special, you know?" No, I don't.

Nothing is special enough for that sort of cash, especially when it's not your money to give away.

"You're fucking with my money, Shifty."

"Nah, boss, you'll get it tonight. We've got plans."

A waiter arrives as I'm thinking, my usual bottle of Lauquen Artes Water on his tray and a tall glass beside it. He pours, the glug of the liquid reminding me of Hannover's gurgling throat this afternoon as I squeezed the breath out of it. Perhaps Shifty needs a reminder, too.

"What do you think of debts, Shifty?" He doesn't answer as I reach for some nuts the waiter sets down and flick one into the air, catching it with my mouth. "They need paying, right?"

"Boss she's coming with it. She is." *Is she hell?* Whores that rack up a hundred grand don't have a hundred grand to pay back, let alone the interest I've now added. I toss another nut and let the ivory dice spin in my fingers some more, wondering how best to play the night and waiting for him to come into my eyeline again. He does, his bulk slowly edging round to block my view. "She won't let me down, boss." I snort at him, interested in what he thinks his little bitch will do to repay her debt. "She won't." He looks offended, a show of affront glancing his brow.

"Why?"

"What?"

"Why do you think she won't let you down?" He looks as shifty as his fucking name suggests for a second or two, his feet hitching back and forth.

"We wanna get married."

The cubes of ivory in my palm crush together, frustration making them grind into each other. I take a sip of my water then toss another nut into the air to give my teeth something to do. My boys don't get married unless I say it's alright. Marriage causes problems, certainly a marriage based on a foundation of fucking lies. It makes them weak and reachable, which means I become the same through their flaws.

"When she turns up, without my money, you're going to fuck her in front of me." He blanches as I stare past him out to the skyline and keep spinning my cubes. "The entertainment while I eat can help me decide."

"Decide what?"

I twist the seat to aim myself back at him, taking another sip as I watch the crease in his brow turn to a scowl of annoyance. "Whether you put a bullet in her after."

"Boss?"

"That, or we can roll these dice now. Have her pick a number when she gets here." I flick one of them at him and watch his hands grab wildly at it before it lands, presumably hoping to delay fate. I just chuckle in response, smiling at his cacophony. That's why marriage isn't a beneficial concept to my world. It confuses, makes decisions harder than they need to be. "Your choice, Shifty."

That's it. He knows the score. He's been inside Cane business long enough, and approaching this topic wasn't best served with a debt looming to cloud my judgement on fucking renditions of love. Shame of it is, I probably would have let him. He's been good up until now. Dependable, no nonsense. I would have assumed he'd pick a useful whore to bed down with, though. One who would have been loyal to our world. He's as good a sidearm as I've had before. Unfortunately for him, he's picked a cunt, one who's coming without my money in her bag.

He paces about as I hear the waiter place my entrée on the

table behind me, the smell of lemon sole diminishing the taste of nuts. So I turn and grab a napkin, indifferent to his turmoil. Whatever the fuck he chooses is fine by me. I've already legalised my casino today, and cleaned up my laundering racket. One hundred K has become marginally irrelevant, other than the principle that needs shoving down throats. Maybe I'll fuck her first, work it out of myself that way, presuming she's clean. He's always had good taste.

CHAPTER SIX

Emily

Friday drags.

Jenny displays either nerves or excitement all morning, and it's a distraction. I want to get through the day and get to the date part.

Over the week I've built this up into something much bigger than it will likely be. It's just a date. A first date that could lead nowhere and be hideous. That is the only thing keeping my rational feet on the ground. I can't stop the whimsical fantasies from fluttering about in my mind if I let them, though.

"Don't forget, dress up. Don't wear something that hides you. And introduce yourself as Jenny." She hands me a cup of tea half an hour before I get to escape home and get ready.

"I won't. Don't worry. I don't see the problem, anyway."

"Trust me."

"And where will you be? I mean it—if the guy's gross or a loser, I'm bailing. I don't care if he writes you a snotty review on your dating app. If the guy you're seeing tonight is so great, you might not need to go back to blind dates."

"Let's not get too hasty, Emily." Although I don't miss the secret smile that twitches at her lips. "So, what are you wearing?"

"I'm not sure if you've seen it. It's a beige, lace—"

"Beige? What's sexy about beige?"

"Okay, taupe or cream. But it's a pretty dress. Lace with coloured flowers decorating it."

"And the neckline?"

"It's a sweetheart line." Jenny raises her brows, impressed that I haven't described it as a turtleneck.

"Okay. Text me when you're there. And thank you." She looks me in the eyes and delivers the thanks with such sincerity I wonder what's gotten into her.

"You're acting funny. It's just a date."

"Yeah, I know. You don't mind if I skip out now to get ready?" Jenny smiles and twists her hands in front of her.

"Sure. I'll be following behind."

I close down the studio, put the cups in the sink and lock up. It's already dark out, but the forecasted rain hasn't begun to fall yet. I make it home in plenty of time and have to resist rushing to my room to get ready.

I haven't felt this restless energy in months. None of the previous dates I've been on have sparked this reaction and some of them I'd already met a time or two. What is it about this blind date that has me in a flutter?

I finally relent and go to my room to get ready. I wash my hair under the scorching hot water of the shower, and while the conditioner does its thing, I wonder if I should go the full nine-yards. There's no way I'll be sleeping with anyone on a first date, so I don't know why the thought even creeps into my head, but it has. My bikini line takes a few more minutes than I expect to tidy, but when I step out of the shower, I feel silky, smooth, and sexy. I've buffed and scrubbed, and now I can feel the invisible confidence it gives me, just feeling good in my own skin.

I pull open my underwear drawer and rummage at the bottom to find one of the few sexy sets I own.

The black, cream, and gold filigree pattern is gorgeous. Luckily, the material of the dress is thick enough that wearing a black bra underneath won't show. I holster my boobs and then ease into the dress.

I dry my hair and attempt to straighten out my waves. It will do.

It's truly a pretty dress, and I can't help but turn and flick the skirt out a bit. I ignore my hammering heart and swallow down my excitement, turning back to my reflection in the mirror. My mismatched eyes always confuse me when it comes to makeup, so I stick with neutrals. A lick of mascara and a sweep of blush is the extent of my skills. No smoky eyes or liquid eyeliner for me.

My jewellery box sits on the dresser and I open the lid. The charm bracelet my grandmother gave me sparkles at me and I pick it out of the protective confines. I think better of it, though, and put it back. I'd be devastated if I lost it. I'd rather keep it safe than risk it.

I take the tube into town and will grab a taxi to the hotel. I wrap a fine, grey scarf around my neck in an attempt to keep the cold out. By the time I exit the tube, the heavens have opened. I dash down the street and thrust my arm out, hoping for a black cab. It only takes a minute before one pulls over and I jump inside, but the rain is relentless. I dash the droplets from my face. "The Regal, please."

It isn't a long journey and certainly doesn't offer enough time to dry off.

I pay the cab and manage to make it inside the hotel without drowning in the rain. I try to shake a few droplets from my hair, but my attempt to straighten it is completely pointless now. I can practically feel my hair frizzing out of place. My heart beat has cranked up in pace, and I can't escape the empty feeling in the pit of my stomach at walking in here looking like a drowned rat. I prefer to assume my damp palms are a result of the rain rather than my nerves.

"Good evening, welcome to The Regal. Do you have a reservation?" The maître d' does a good job of ignoring my state of dress.

"Table for Jonathan Hannover?" I smile and pretend that a small piece of me isn't dying inside. I don't miss his arched brow when I tell him who I'm here to meet.

"Certainly."

As he leads me through the immaculately dressed tables, I banish the dashingly good looking man that has featured in my daydreams from my mind, and replace him with a more modest guess at who will be waiting for me. *If we ever arrive.*

I'm led to the back of the restaurant, to a screened off section. It's private, or seemingly so, with only a handful of tables. My eyes drift closed for a moment before I open them to look at the guy I'm meeting.

The air is stolen from my lungs as my eyes cast over him. He's casually sitting at the table fiddling with something in his hand. He's not looking towards me. He's concentrating on the plate of food in front of him. My face flushes with embarrassment. Did I get the time wrong? I stand there, taking the time to absorb the man. Movement catches my attention and I turn to see another man standing to the side of the table. My eyes dart between the two. Jonathan still hasn't acknowledged my presence, but his *friend* has.

"Mr Cane." The waiter eases me towards my chair. Cane?

I thought I was meeting Jonathan Hannover? Although, I can't really complain as I'm here under Jenny's name. Jonathan, or Mr Cane, finally looks up. He doesn't stand to greet me, nor does his face reveal any exterior sign that he's even registered my presence. His firm jawline and brown hair frame his handsome face. Cool, blue eyes that remind me of a frozen lake stare at me as if in challenge.

He moves his gaze from me to his friend and back again. His disinterest hits me in the chest, and it takes me a moment to compose myself. As first dates go, even blind ones, this isn't going in the right direction.

"I'm Jenny," I blurt. The words sound false, but I go with it.

Jonathan's lack of reaction unnerves me, not to mention bringing a friend along and starting without me. My anxiety spirals. I was prepared for a geek, a toad or a slime ball. This handsome man is a fantasy I didn't put any stock in, and I wish I had. Despite the confusion and hurt that are radiating from my chest.

I tuck myself behind the table and attempt to act unfazed, as my hands try to tame my messy hair behind my ears, but it's no use. I must look a wreck. My carefully straightened, glossy hair, is now a mop. My fidgeting is uncontrollable and is only spurred on by Jonathan's totally cool exterior. He turns to face his friend and I see an expression pass over his friend's face. He looks shocked, but I don't know why. I dare to move my eyes back to Jonathan, and there's a spark—a flint—behind them, but only for a second. My eyes travel down his chest, and I can't help but catalogue his wide shoulders, hidden behind his crisp, midnight blue suit. The bright white shirt creates a sexy contrast. *He looks far too good.*

I look around the pristine dining room. Soft mood lighting creates a sensual atmosphere, and gleaming glasses twinkle on the handful of tables. Still, Jonathan hasn't said a word.

"Would you excuse me?" I don't wait for an answer and slip back out of the restaurant towards the ladies. I barge in, pushing the heavy black wooden door open. I stop in front of the letterbox shaped mirror. My earlier fear is realised when I see the state I'm in. My silky blond hair now looks more like messy bed-hair. I go over to the hand dryer and position it to help give my hair a blast of hot air. I scrunch it, adding volume to the natural wave and, without the water, it doesn't look so bad.

I re-apply a sweep of gloss to my lips and pinch my cheeks to put some colour back into them. I use the hand dryer to dry off my skirt and smooth it back down. My jacket is a lost cause, so I remove it, hoping to leave it in the cloakroom to dry. I stare at my reflection, satisfied that I can at least go out there and hold my head up. His attitude so far is shocking. Who doesn't introduce themselves or even say hello when their date arrives? Or starts without them?

If I weren't so attracted to him, I would march back out into the rain. But I am interested, and feel a little stubborn. If he doesn't want a date, he should have just cancelled. I'm here now, and I can't deny I want to hear his voice. I take a couple of deep breaths and exit the ladies, stopping the closest waitress.

"Can I leave this in the cloakroom please?" She smiles before taking my damp jacket. With a sliver of confidence restored, I go and face the gorgeous Jonathan once again.

I pull on all of my inner courage to muster a genuine smile as I return to the table. "Sorry about that." I ease back into my seat. His penetrative glance is now riveted on me and it sends a shiver down my spine. I reach for the glass of water that is now waiting for me.

Jonathan's stare doesn't drop, but it's hard to keep our eyes locked. The longer I do, the more uncomfortable I grow. My pulse quickens, but not in a sexy way. In a dangerous one. Like his stare has triggered a dormant fight or flight response and everything is screaming for me to flee. *The sensible part of me is telling me that as well.*

He's done nothing apart from sit and look at me, but I've had more of a reaction to him than anyone else in my past. The idea that you can have an instant reaction to someone is stupid, or so I thought, until tonight. With all the other crap around this date, I should be out the door. And I'm about ready to give in to my rational brain. All of my muscles tense, ready to stand and leave.

"Your name isn't Jenny, is it?"

I flush with embarrassment for the second time tonight, my cheeks heating as he calls me out. I knew pretending to be Jenny wouldn't work.

"No. My name is Emily."

"At least you're honest." He leans back in the chair and stares coldly for a moment, making my embarrassment level triple, and then, for the first time, he smiles at me. I would never have described a smile as dangerous before. It's a social expression reflecting pleasure or happiness. Yet Jonathan's smile has my heart stampeding in my chest, and my stomach quivering. "Later, we're going to find out why you really came here tonight, Emily."

I swallow past the nerves and offer a less than confident smile in return.

"But for now you should know my name is Quinn. Please, sit." He waves his hand at the chair.

"Quinn? I'm sorry, I'm a little confused. I thought I was meeting Jonathan Hannover."

"And I thought I'd be meeting Jenny. Seems like we're even." He closes his knife and fork and sits back in his chair. "Jonathan works for me."

I reach for my water as if I can hide behind it. The man lingering behind Quinn moves closer and whispers something I can't make out. Quinn just shakes his head ever so slightly.

I place my bag on the table and fight the urge to check in with Jenny. *What the hell has she gotten herself into?* I keep my hands in my lap and look over to Quinn. He's looking at me, his eyebrows drawn together.

"Perhaps we should call it a night. I can see you're not here for a blind date. Excuse me."

"Sit down." The order makes me jump a little, but he smiles again. "You're right, Emily. You're not what I was expecting, but you're here. Let's at least salvage something of the night." He looks at his friend with what I can only describe as a wicked sneer. "I've already ordered. Pick something for yourself. I'll have the kitchen add it to mine." He nods to his friend who moves to retrieve a menu from a neighbouring table. My hand shakes as I take it from him, not sure whether to stay or not.

"No, really, I think it's probably better if I leave you to it."

"Sit," he snaps, cutting me off before I finish my sentence. I gawp at his gravelled tone, still stunned at the first order, then shoot my eyes round to look at the other man again as my backside hits the chair. "Don't mind Shifty. He's got a soft spot for women, don't you, Shifty? A weakness." Shifty offers me a tight smile, or an attempt at a smile, before he hauls himself back to where he's been lurking.

"Is he staying here?" I whisper as I run my eyes over the menu, still unsure if I should be here or not as my stomach knots, but not from hunger.

"Yes. Anything, take your pick?" I hadn't noticed, but the waiter who showed me to the table has returned to clear Quinn's plate.

"Um, sure. Everything. But I'll go for the lamb, please." Quinn looks to the waiter, which quickens his pace.

"Yes, Sir." He scurries away.

I hear the vibration in my bag from my phone. I glance at it, but Quinn slowly shakes his head. What would I tell Jenny, anyway?

"So, Emily. As you're on a date, I expect you're hoping for conversation. I'm sure there are a number of polite topics we could start with."

"Yes. But I find it hard to believe you don't know how to act on a date." The desire to flee is only growing stronger. Good looks and a heavenly voice only go so far.

"I don't date, Emily. You're lucky I'm feeling indulgent tonight. It's not one of my usual traits."

"So what are your usual traits?"

He chuckles. "I don't think we know one another well enough for that type of conversation." He leans back and stares. "Tell me what you do for a living?"

"I'm a photographer. Portraits, mainly. I have my own studio in Pimlico. What about you?"

"Friends, family?"

"Yes, my best friend Jenny works for me at the studio. My parents live in Oxford." This suddenly feels like an interrogation, not a few friendly getting to know you questions.

"Ah, Jenny? So you took her place because she's your friend?"

"Yes," I say, straightening my back and sitting taller in my seat.

"Honest and loyal. Good characteristics to have." He picks up his water and sips.

The waiter appears and places a sumptuous plate in front of me, before delivering the same to Quinn.

"And a bottle of the Krug Grande Cuvee, Shaun. Two glasses."

"Very good, Sir."

"Champagne? I thought you didn't know anything about dates?"

"It's a drink I like. Nothing to do with dates." His cold eyes slip to my chest for a moment before meeting my eyes again.

"I haven't met many men who enjoy champagne."

"You haven't met men with any taste, then."

I don't know how to respond. There haven't been many guys in my past, and I'm starting to wonder just what this man is all about. He lifts an eyebrow and gives me a stunning smile that turns my insides upside down before starting his meal.

The champagne is delivered and poured. Quinn sips and nods his approval to Shaun who then pours my glass. "To honesty and loyalty." Quinn's toast might be a little awkward, but we clink, and I take my first taste of liquid bubbles.

The food is delicious, tender, and full of flavour. The champagne is the best I've tasted, and Quinn is devastatingly handsome. He's charming for the rest of the meal. If it wasn't for the strange vibe from Shifty and the embarrassing and awkward start, on paper, the date is going brilliantly.

"You still haven't told me much about yourself. What do you do, Quinn?"

He clears his throat and runs his napkin over his mouth, taking his time to answer. "Today, I gained a casino."

"Oh, wow. Are you in the entertainment industry?" I don't miss the weird grin Shifty makes out of the corner of my eye.

"Not exactly entertainment, depending on your viewpoint." He stares for a minute, then returns to his food. "I work across several sectors. Business is all just numbers to me. Profit and loss."

"You built the business yourself? I know how hard it was for me just to buy my small property for the studio."

"I took over the family business. Built on what was already there. It's more than it was, less than it will become."

"Impressive." He sounds so sure of himself. He radiates a confidence that is far more than just inflated ego.

"Hard work pays dividends. The rewards are just bigger for me than most." Quinn's eyes capture all my attention as he speaks. All this talk of business and success makes my mind wander back to the fantasies I conjured before the date. The romantic part of me wants to let my imagination spark, but there are too many questions I need to ask.

Quinn's attention is pulled from me by his phone. He frowns at the screen before standing and walking out of the restaurant. Despite my annoyance, it does give me a fine view of him walking away. He's a hazard to my weak heart.

"You're Jenny's friend?" the man lurking in the shadows asks.

"Yes, why? Do you know her?"

"You could say that." His jaw is rigid, tight with tension, and the relaxed air that I'd finally reached disappears.

Before I can dwell further on the evening, or what Shifty has said, a hum of sensation rushes over my body.

"Please excuse me. I had to take that call." Quinn's warm breath caresses my neck as he whispers in my ear, his deep-toned voice sending shivers fleeing over my body. His hand gently squeezes my shoulder as he passes, going back to take his seat.

I watch, enthralled by this gorgeous creature, and all thoughts dissolve in my mind. His cool blue eyes roam my body and my cheeks flush in response.

The connection between us, thick with anticipation, is interrupted by a cough from Shifty. It breaks the trance I was falling into and my mind snaps back to the present and what we were talking about. *Jenny.*

I look over at Quinn, desperate to know more about him. "Why was Jenny coming to meet you?" I wish my voice sounded stronger. "She doesn't do anything that I can see would make you work acquaintances."

"We had some terms to discuss. Shifty will speak with her later. It doesn't matter now." He glances to his friend and they exchange a silent conversation. "I'd rather focus on what's happening here, Emily." My eyes drop and I reach for my flute. The intensity of his stare is disarming. I drain my third glass of champagne. The effervescent bubbles are starting to loosen my nerves and the tension that's clung to me since walking in here.

A waitress clears our plates, and I can't help noticing how her eyes remain glued to Quinn like she's waiting for him to notice her. She's pretty. Long, glossy blond hair, barely a size eight. Her over-glossed lips are in a perfect sexy pout waiting to smile. But Quinn pays her no attention. He tops up my glass for the fourth time and gives me the warmest of smiles. It sends my stomach into a storm, and I can't help but feel triumphant over the young waitress. It urges me on and my earlier question has slipped away.

I lean forward and rest my forearms on the table. "Would you mind if I looked at the dessert menu?" I look up at him through my lashes. All my inhibitions have abandoned me.

"Take your pick."

"You won't indulge?"

"My idea of dessert isn't something I order off a menu." He doesn't hide the appreciative once-over he gives me. "At least, not here."

Flirting. I am flirting with a sexy man, and he's flirting back. It is the best high in the world. Added to the champagne, I can't stop the smile from lighting up my face. I bite my bottom lip and take the menu that has miraculously appeared at the side of the table.

I'd forgotten Shifty is still in our company.

I read over the words, but I don't take anything in. I've got half an eye still on Quinn. My pulse skips up a beat, and I press my thighs together as I run his words back over in my mind.

Innuendo is one thing. Following through is something very different. He might be teasing me, no real intention to see me again after the check is paid. The thought makes me sad because despite the strange and intimidating circumstances, I like this man. He's mysterious and sexy and unlike anyone I've ever met before, let alone shared a date with.

I block the questions and try to focus my eyes on the

dessert choices.

"I think we're done with the date part," he says suddenly. My eyes lift, uneasy. "Indulgence doesn't belong at this table any longer."

Quinn stands, drops his napkin on the table and seizes my hand in his. I gasp at the contact, still unsure, but he leads me out through a back entrance of the restaurant, my feet struggling to keep up.

"Shifty, bring her belongings and leave them on the foyer table. I'll be in touch."

He pulls me forward and I all but fall into him as he turns to a bank of elevators.

"Where are we going?"

"We're going to be honest with each other."

CHAPTER SEVEN

Quinn

I keep tugging her hand as we step out into the foyer in front of my apartment, interested in the hesitation that lingers in it. I've not had someone hesitate behind me in a long time, not that I've held a hand for a long time either, but the nerves are endearing for some reason.

"A hotel room?" She giggles her question.

"My apartment."

"Oh." She sounds impressed, which makes me chuckle as I swipe my door card. She's cute. Sweet natured. The term halts my chuckle, turning it to a confused musing as we continue inside. "Wow, look at that view." Fuck the view. There's only one view I'm interested in.

She's over to the windows before I have a chance to stop her, her feet tripping over the rug as she goes. Her heels aren't even high. "It's so vivid, magical even. I could take photos for hours up here. Look at the lighting from the buildings."

All nerves seem to disappear as she stares out my window and gazes over London. It's nothing compared to the fine sight of her standing against it, especially now her tension's evaporated. She's beautiful in this guise, annoyingly. More so than the nerves and twitches of earlier. Lean figure. Great assets. Contours that make me want to look at them, draw them even. And those eyes. They smile at the corners constantly. One blue, one green. Two sides of the same coin. They're intriguing to me, reminding me of my dice as they roll the air. A fuck like Jenny would have been preferable for the type of entertainment I was thinking of, easier to fuck into and then get rid of. This girl isn't going to be like that. She'll be clingy, needy. She'll expect something that isn't going to happen. It's the type of thing I don't need, or want.

I walk up to her, still admiring the view that has fuck all to do with London, and pull my jacket off.

"You do this often?" I ask, knowing the answer before she speaks.

"What?"

"Follow men up to their rooms?" She giggles, her face looking coy as she glances at me.

"God, no. I think I must be drunk. Either that or—"

Her breath catches as I run a finger across the back of her neck and turn her towards me, air filtering out again as she rights her feet.

"You nervous, Emily?"

"Yes." I smile at that, unsure of the last woman who was nervous of me. High-end cunt doesn't get nervous of anything. It gets paid; that's all it cares about. But this pretty thing? She's real. Lips quivering as I watch them. Teeth nibbling over them as she trembles in my fingers.

"I like that you are." She frowns, her eyes darting to my chest to avoid my gaze. The confusion is as charming as her nature, for some reason causing my interest to deepen rather than dissipate like it should. "You've never been fucked by a real man, have you?" Her eyes fly up again, shock written through them at my words. Missy's never had someone fuck her, or fuck with her, by the look of it. I smirk at the horror etched on her features, her arms wrapping around herself regardless of my hold on her. "Scared Emily?" She takes a minute to look at me, then shakes her head.

"I wouldn't be here if you scared me." Stupid girl. "Maybe that's the champagne talking, though."

I move in again, knocking her arms from around her waist and drawing her into me.

The first press of my lips against hers spirals into something it fucking shouldn't. It's gentle and tender, her mouth quivering under mine. It doesn't feel usual to me. It feels intimate, like I should give a fuck about what I'm doing. I back off instantly, removing my lips from hers and travelling them along her neck instead. That's enough for my dick to wake up, reminding itself of what I brought her here for. Fucking is what I'm after. A fuck to relieve this tension. That's all. And it keeps going from there. Breathy little moans from her as I make my hold fiercer. Occasional gasps as I let myself get on with the plan and begin pushing her against the window. She smells like sex and sin, the sound of her groans making me want to get deeper and wait for her screams to come.

"Quinn." She breathes my name, causing me to half falter on her neck. It vibrates inside me like a fucking memory of a sound I haven't heard before. I grab her thigh and hitch her leg up, hoping to rid myself of the sensation, but she says it again as she grabs hold of my hair.

My mouth is straight back to hers before she has a chance to say it any more. This isn't what she thinks it is. This is fucking, and I start that process again before I think any more about it. I push her harder, grasping out at limbs and eventually hauling her towards the bedroom rather than fucking her where she stands like I would a whore.

Clothes tear as she starts getting rowdy, surprising me as she grips on and begins devouring my mouth. My shirt goes first as we tangle past the rooms, her dress will be next as I throw her towards the bed. She giggles again and turns, her body looking too damn perfect in the room. Fucking giggles. She's drunk, or dirtier than I thought. Either way I'm fucking her in the next ten minutes.

"You a dirty one?" She looks away from me, reaching behind herself to unzip her dress. But she looks at me over her shoulder and gives me a sexy smile. "You're drunk."

"I know what I'm doing, Quinn." No she doesn't. She hasn't got a fucking clue what she's doing. Not that I care.

I smirk as I stare at her, watching her peel the dress down her body. It's fucking divine. Everything about her is. It should be for a hundred K, too. She's going to work every penny of that off tonight, and if she doesn't, she might work it off another night as well.

"Touch yourself." She blanches for a second, her fingers hovering around the dress before she gets it fully off. I keep smiling and pull at my tie, all the time enjoying the way she flusters around each move. "Make yourself come, dirty girl." She gasps, seemingly shocked at my crudeness. I just keep undressing, doing nothing to pull back the remark.

"I… I don't do that," she stutters, all brazenness disappearing.

"You do now." I walk over, discarding my pants and sitting on the bed. "Get the dress off and put those dirty little fingers between your thighs."

She gapes, still with no movement other than eyes that roam my whole frame. Good, let her look. Let her get a real long look at what's about to get inside her. Nothing about this is soft. There's nothing nice here, regardless of the gentlemanly appearance I gave her tonight. Nothing gentle or tender. It's hard and fast. Calculated and cold. I don't love. I fuck. That kiss, whatever the fuck it was, wasn't real.

"I've got no time for hesitation. Do what you're told."

She does, slowly. Her hands release the dress and it slides down her body. She fidgets as she stands, and then lies back on the bed, taking the command with little argument. It pleases me more than I'd like to admit. She keeps up with those breathy little moans as her hands travel along her body, making my dick scream for pussy it's not getting yet.

She's a natural at dirty. Her fingers have a reality about them, hesitant in their crawl across her skin. It's a raw corruption. Real. It makes my dick throb for the filth I could get from her. Pretty little girl turned dirty whore, just for me. Not the pay check they'll get at the end.

"Inside you," I say, as she hovers around the edges of her pussy, fingers dipping in the top of her panties. "Make yourself squirm for me, dirty girl." She hovers still, unsure maybe. The uncertainty drives me mad, enough so that I snatch at her legs, scraping the fabric down her legs so I can see more clearly. "Now." She gasps as she scrambles away a little, eyes wild at my tone, and kicks out at my hands on her. Screw that. She's not stopping now. I've got a dick like iron that needs pussy, and a woman who's going to do something about that.

I'm over her before she knows what's happened, my hands pinning hers to the bed and my weight settling between her thighs.

"You teasing me, Emily?" She shakes her head rapidly, air puffing from her mouth again as my body pushes into hers.

"Too dirty for you?" She squeals like a fucking mouse, eyes flicking between mine and the door. I rub my dick against her and watch them snap back to me, a moan erupting with her next breath. "I think you're dirtier than you want to admit." I gaze at those lips of hers. They're quivering again, her eyes haunting me with memories I don't have. And my mouth wants to be on hers again. It wants kissing and fucking combined, my dick already engaging the decision before my mind's caught up. She gasps and closes her eyes as I slip inside an inch, her heat making me moan out in torment for more.

I gaze at her as she tips her head back, more moans and groans coming as I inch in further to prolong my own escape.

It's like a different planet here. No crime. No whores. Just me and her, fucking like real people do.

"Quinn," she says, her wrists flexing against my hands. "Please."

I drop my head away and aim for the lace bra encasing her full breasts. They're as divine as the rest of her, ripe and lush, their flesh bouncing over the top of the fabric as her chest heaves in and out. It makes me grab at one, perversely feeling the need to squeeze it harshly and mould it around in my hold like I do whores. She yelps and bucks into me, her pussy trying to drag me further inside as she keeps pushing and writhing around.

"Tell me you're a dirty little whore." Another yelp comes as I bite through the fabric, teeth bearing down on the pert nipple that screams for escape. I'm ravenous for them, enough so that I scrape at the material, yanking it away from her skin and pushing it up to expose her to me.

No words come from her as I lave my way around

her breasts, though, just more moans and groans, her body undulating beneath mine. "Tell me, Emily." Still nothing but her innocent gasps and yelps of a carnal lust she knows nothing of. I slap out at one of her breasts, watching the way it bounces and shudders. It makes her shove down onto me, her pussy heating my dick that's fit to burst. I back out again, lessening her grind. "You want it harder, you talk to me. I want to hear that dirty mouth of yours."

"Please, Quinn," she gasps, her hands reaching for my hair. I knock them away, one of them forced onto the sheets again as I rear up over her and lever an inch in and out. A small slide in, the tip ready to shoot come inside her like a gun unloading.

"Please. I can't…" My fingers slide down, tracing her curves before finding that clit and rubbing at it. She's like a canon in my hands, ready to explode at my command. Trembling, quivering. Lips opening and closing as I find my way around her. It's a fucking epiphany or some shit. It's vibrant and alive. My little whore, one who's bucking and grinding down, filthy little moans as she forges her pussy towards me. I sneer at the whole fucking thing, annoyed with my interest in it as I watch her move and surge in my hold. "Please, Quinn."

The last sound of my name on her lips makes me flip her over and shove her head into the pillows, my hand hooking under her chin to pull her face back up again.

"You want me in that pussy, you beg me for it." She gasps again as her ass rises to me, her head sinking into my hand like it's meant to be there. "Come on dirty girl, beg me for it."

I slap at her ass, the sound of it drowned out by the immediate scream that leaves her lips. Still no fucking words, though. It maddens me, making me become rougher to get want I want. I like a dirty talker. I like the filth that springs from their mouths in the heat of the moment, and I definitely want it from this clean living little devil. "I want that pretty little accent to beg like a whore, Emily."

"Please," springs from her mouth again, as I pull her up to me and lick along the side of her face. Fuck please. I want her talking about cock and pussy. I want her moaning around my dick, letting out breathy little gasps as I fuck it down her throat. "Oh, God." She stalls in my grasp as I slap at that ass again, delivering four more to wake her dirty little mouth up.

"Tell me you want me to fuck you, dirty girl." She squirms, tears springing from her eyes as I pull her upright and sink my fingers inside her. The feel of her on my hands makes me yank on her pussy, another finger pushing in to widen her hole. "You desperate?"

"Oh, God, Quinn, I can't..." She fucking can.

I slip my fingers out of her, spreading the wet hole and leaving her vacant of anything. She pants and moans in my hold as my teeth and lips lave her neck, teasing her into saying something other than please.

"Tell me and I'll fuck you." Nothing but broken gasps and wretched sobs. They harden my dick, making it damn painful not to be inside her. I stretch her hole again, gently tracing the edges of it, teasing until she's got nothing but tears and breath left to fight with. She's so fucking soft in my fingers, like petals that know nothing of carnage. "Two words, dirty girl." I push my dick against the hole, levering it up and down, slicking it through her juices. "Two words and you get it, Emily." She pants and presents her ass again, her head trying to lower to the sheets. Dirty girl wants fucking in the ass, too.

She might even get it if she begs enough.

"Please, Quinn. Fu…"

I chuckle as the word sticks in her throat, still swiping through her and groaning out my impatience. And it fucking slips in of its own will, my hand barely restraining the need to follow my own plan as I yank myself away.

"More, dirty girl. Say it." She squirms and moves around, knees hitching on the bed and ass rising up and falling down.

"Fuck," she mumbles. The sound of it coming from her mouth has me ready to shoot my load over her back. It rings the air with obscenity and connotations of fucking truth. Pleases and fucks. That's what I want from this little mouth. I push in a little, stopping the need to come instantly.

"Again," I snarl out, grasping hold of her hair and pushing it down to the mattress.

"Please." Fucking pleases. I shunt her pretty little mouth further into the bed, ready to beat her 'til the right words leave it. "Fu… fuck me, please." It flusters out of her lips, her head mangling in the sheets as she braces her hands out. She gets a small drive inwards for that, making me grate my teeth to hold the come channelling its way through me.

"Again, dirty girl." I slap at her ass, then knead it with my hand. She bucks and grinds, making me grab tighter and force her to still to stop the erratic show of need. "Move again and I'll drive this dick down your throat instead." That stops her dead in her tracks. Her gasps stop. Breathy moans stop. All fucking noise stops. And her body halts immediately, perfectly balanced in my hands at the thought of sucking dick. It makes me smile. Presumably guileless little girls don't deep throat often. She will for me. "Say it again. Louder."

"Fuck me." It comes quietly and quickly, as does the drive

of my dick straight into the depths of her pussy. Fuck. The room spins as I hit the end of her, my fingers grabbing tighter to her hips for balance. I close my eyes and let the sensation wash over me, pulling my dick out and propelling it straight back in again.

"Jesus Christ," she mumbles from beneath me.

"Again, Emily," I growl, leaning over her and starting to fuck into her steadily. "You want harder, you keep talking." She grunts as I forge back in, the slick feel of her around me making it hard to hold off. And that sweet voice sounds so good full of fucks and moans. It sounds like sin and evil nights, all fucked up with innocence screaming my name.

"Fuck me, please."

Her hand reaches back, her nails trying to grab at my ass and shove me further in. My dirty fucking girl. I give her harder, letting myself fuck with little care for the yelps and groans coming on each drive inward. She wants hard, she gets hard. Dirty little girl can have as hard as she wants. I toss her body forward, pushing her flat against the mattress and spread her legs wider.

"Fuck me… Fuck me… Yes, God, yes… Quinn!" She keeps talking like that and she can get it all night long.

The room blurs in my madness to get deeper into her. It's a whirlwind of sweat and carnage, the sounds of sex splitting the quiet in the room. And it falls so easily from her mouth the harder I drive into her.

"Yes! Fuck, oh God, oh God… Don't stop!"

Screams and shouts for more fall freely, nails digging in as I haul ass around and move us to the next fucked up position I think of. I'll degrade every inch of her if I have to. I want all the sin she's got, every ounce of filth. One fucking night of me being real and alive, not just a man who unloads for release.

I feel her clench as she grabs onto my neck, her orgasm beginning to pulse around my dick. It spurs the last bit of myself I was hanging on to, making my dick explode and pull me into her. Her mouth is on mine the second it happens, tongue driving in, lips mashing against mine as if she's fucked like this her entire life. And I damn well kiss her back, too. I snatch and grab at flesh, pulling it into me and letting my cock throb inside her pussy, all the time kissing those sweet lips like they're a lifeline of some sort. It pisses me off. The whole damn thing pisses me off, especially the little mewls she gives me as she starts calming down on my dick, the occasional pulse reminding me where the hell I am.

Fuck.

My lips rip away from hers, incensed by my own reaction to them. She whimpers and gives in completely at that, her body just buckling in my hands as her head lolls back. I just stare and sneer at her closed eyes, my breath as laboured as hers. I should drop her. I should drop her and tell her to get the hell out of my apartment.

I don't.

"You're fucking beautiful," I mutter, tracing the lines of her face.

I don't know why I said that. She is, though. There's something about her that makes her more beautiful than anything I've ever set eyes on before. I just wait and stare. I wait for those eyes to open and let me see them again, barely managing to contain my dick's throb for more fucking. I don't fuck a damn thing twice. I move on to something else that keeps me occupied.

"Quinn," she says, her head rising back up, lips breathing the name as if she's never felt it on them before. She's right, she hasn't, but she's going to. She's going to say it for a while longer yet. We'll keep fucking all night, maybe more if I feel like it.

She's going to fucking scream it for me until I get my money's worth.

CHAPTER EIGHT

Emily

"Where… What…?" My mouth feels furry, like I've been drinking heavily and not had enough water. I lift my head and try to move, but I feel funny. I'm… sitting. I test my limbs, but my arms won't move. Panic clears through my foggy head, and I jerk my arms, still unable to move them. I can't tell where I am or what's going on. My heart pounds, flooding my body with adrenaline.

"You're awake."

"Quinn? What… what's going on?" I can't see him in the darkness, only hear his smooth voice.

"Debts are going on, dirty girl. Jenny wasn't prepared to pay up. She obviously thought you would. One hundred grand is a larger debt than one night of fucking."

His words bring back memories of last night and what I let him do to me. God, I can still feel him between my thighs. I'm tender from his treatment of me.

"A hundred thousand pounds?" I focus on the alarms sounding in my head and shove my memories away. My heart beats wildly in my chest as my mind plays catch up. How could Jenny owe that much? "I don't understand. Jenny asked me for money. I loaned her five thousand pounds. She said she needed it for her flat."

All my senses start waking up, but I still can't make out anything in the gloom. I shift my body and find I can widen my knees and move my legs, but my wrists and elbows are restrained.

"Innocence lost, huh? Your friend," he says, disdain in his voice, "has screwed me over for a hundred thousand pounds. Spent it all on drugs and gambling. Shifty's little weakness has caused you some problems."

"Jenny doesn't have that kind of money, and neither do I." Panic heats my body as I start to realise just what a mess I've walked into.

"No. But that doesn't mean I won't get what's owed. We started last night. You spread those legs willingly enough, gave up that pussy without any real hesitation. You couldn't get enough, could you?"

His finger runs down the side of my face, and I flinch at the contact. I didn't hear him cross the room or notice his voice growing closer.

"The next time I come in you, I won't be so gentle." His hot breath tickles my cheek, and I feel the sting of tears as I grit my teeth together. "No one can hear you scream in here, dirty girl." I hold my breath and try to keep all the fear and panic locked inside, ignoring the crude remarks. I listen for Quinn, but I don't hear or feel him again until the sound of the door slams shut.

I wait.

I wait and hold it in, refusing to give in to the utter hysteria clawing up from the pit of my stomach and invading every single cell in my body.

A small blub slips past my lips, and it echoes around me. One soon turns to two, and the next thing I hear is my inconsolable howl into the darkness. I scream and shout as hot tears stream down my face.

It's over as soon as it began. The rush of anger gives way to fear, and I quieten quickly. My blubbers turn to hums as I try to cling to some comfort. I pull my legs up to my chest and move to wrap my arms around them, but I can't. My arms are held fast. My legs drop back to the floor in defeat.

How can anyone do this? Kidnapping isn't something that happens in my world. I take photographs of families and babies. I can't be mixed up in some revenge plot to collect on an unsettled debt. Quinn sounded like some kind of monster. I tick over the information he gave me. It turns my stomach, souring any memory I have of him.

But his touch is still on my skin. I can feel his fingers digging into my hips as he held me to him. He took me so completely, forced me to let go. I've never felt so alive or free. Sex has never been like that before—raw and passionate and desperate. Quinn gave that to me. He unlocked something within me that I'd never dreamed of, something so completely satisfying that my body is struggling to adjust to the situation I'm in now.

The hot tears coat my cheeks and I hate that I can't brush them away. I need to get a grip and try to see things for what they really are. Quinn isn't what he made out. After he fucked me senseless, he was gentle with me. He was insatiable. With my inhibitions destroyed, he set about taking his time over my body.

His hot mouth worked at my breasts until he was hard again. He bit and sucked at my nipples until I thought I'd come from that alone. He knew what he was doing. We were having fun, or so I thought. He fucked me again. Draped my legs over his forearms while he hammered into me. And I got off on watching his toned body dominate me, taking me like no one else has. His fingers played me so well I didn't even realise I was doing everything he asked until I'd done it.

I saw the danger. That split decision to stay at the table or flee. I should have listened to my intuition.

The inky darkness plays tricks on my mind. No matter how many times I blink, the black doesn't clear. My vision hasn't returned. Not even a pinprick of illumination as I close and open my eyes in an attempt to focus on something. Anything.

My stomach aches, and a tight gripe sends a spasm of emptiness through me. I feel hollow. And my mind wants to add to this nightmare by replaying last night over and over. I can still feel him. His touch, his tongue, his lips. They're seared into my skin, my body accepting the contact and committing it to memory, easy to recall.

Except I don't want to now. I don't want the memories of us. I don't want to feel the breathless lust that stirred in me. For the first time in my life, I felt utterly desired. Worshipped. But it was fake. False.

How can any of it be more than a lure as I'm now sitting alone in a black room? I close my eyes, seeking comfort from the simple act. But there is no comfort. Quinn's face, his charming smile haunts my vision. That dangerous smile that set off some internal warning that I gave no heed to.

Instinct has developed over thousands of years, honing us to threat, yet I ignored it because of a pretty face and orgasms.

Shame douses me, chilling me to the core. It gnaws at my gut, adding to the hunger pangs. My bladder starts to swell, adding to my discomfort. The pressure bears down, making my stomach feel impossibly bloated, ready to pop.

I ignore it. I ignore it all. I block my mind and picture my song sheets in front of me. I see the complex assortment of notes on the page and try to remember the sounds they make.

But the noise I hear doesn't match the notes in my mind. It's the mystery song that has been playing through my head since last week. I squeeze my eyes shut and hum the notes—stringing them together as if I have to finish the composition myself. My voice grows stronger, and notes merge into words as I fill the emptiness with song.

"Will you let me see the dawn? Will you let me see the sea? I can see your light. Won't you let me be?" The words echo around the room as I repeat the lines.

Minutes pass, I assume minutes, before the words dry up and the tune dies. My head drops forward, suddenly feeling too heavy to hold upright. My cheeks are damp from tears I didn't realise I'd cried. I sniff. It's undignified, but in this situation, it doesn't matter. My tongue sweeps out to moisten my lips, but it sticks to them they're so dry. They feel cracked and chapped, and it highlights the thirst now scratching my throat. My stomach floods with pain as I shift on the chair. It awakens the throbbing from my bladder. I press my thighs together in a vain attempt to stifle the need to go to the bathroom.

What's Jenny doing right now? Is she worried about me? Will she have even given me a passing thought? Looking back, it's so obvious. She knew she was sending me into the lion's den. She knew she couldn't go to that meeting, and my heart splits a little more as I wrap my mind around her betrayal.

Nausea rolls in my stomach knowing she sent me in her place. I feel sick, and saliva pools in my mouth. I lock my teeth together fighting against the inevitable, but I can't. My stomach convulses, and I lean to the side of the chair as I vomit. The acid burns my dry throat, and I spit, trying to rid my mouth of the vile taste. I can feel the strings of spittle still clinging to my lips. I puff and blow and spit before I give in and lick my lips. The tang is bitter.

What I'd give for a glass of water.

I banish the thought from my mind, as if Quinn might hear and test how far I'll go for a sip to quench my thirst and cleanse my dirty mouth. Thinking his name brings the images back. The vision of his handsome face and his smile haunts me as I catalogue everything I let him do to me. My stomach rolls again, but I swallow and let my head fall back to stare at the ceiling. I can't make out any of the details but pretend I can see ceiling tiles or poor artexing. Anything to take my mind off my body and the situation I'm in.

I can't work out the time. I feel tired. Bone dead tired. But I have no reference for day or night. All I can tell is that my bladder is ready to burst and I don't think Quinn's going to simply open the door and let me go home.

I cross my legs and squeeze my thighs. The pressure in my stomach is astonishing. At least the need to go to the bathroom is something to think about other than my stupid behaviour. I must have dozed off at some point. My neck feels funny like I've rested in the wrong position for too long. I twist my wrists in their binds, but they haven't miraculously come loose. The rope still bites into my skin and rubs it raw if I move too much.

"Quinn!" I scream into the pitch blackness. "Quinn!" I

listen, but there's no answer. No movement. I'm so desperate to go to the bathroom I'd rather face him than be left alone down here.

Light floods into the room and I have to squint to focus on what it is. A large television screen flickers to life in front of me, casting the room in a dull gloom. The shock is enough for me to forget the concentration I need to hold my bladder. Heat seeps out from where I sit. The humiliating sound of liquid dribbling off the chair and onto the floor fills the room.

I choke on a sob as I realise what I've done, but can't stop it. For the first time in what feels like hours, I can relax. The acrid smell of urine wafts around me, and I'm disgusted with myself. I'm suddenly back in primary school where the toilets always smelt of wee. If I could crawl up into a ball and hide, I would. How could I have done this? I sob quietly with a mixture of shame and relief. At least the pressure has dissipated from my bladder, and I feel like I can breathe again.

The respite is only temporary. The screen that shocked me now comes to life, a dark image on the camera. Black and white. A woman, in a similar position to me. I turn my head and look around the room to see if this is some sick video feed of me. There's not enough light to see into the corners of the room, but the woman on the screen hasn't moved.

I stare at the screen and watch two other figures enter. Both prowl around the woman as if they're summing her up. I flush in panic as I realise that this isn't something I'm going to want to watch.

One of the men stops in front of her and begins to undo his trousers. The other man stands behind the woman and forces her head down to take what the first man is offering. The volume on the tape picks up, and I can hear her protests, her body lashing out as best she can as she's forced to comply.

I turn away, trying to look at anything but the screen and the deeds I'm being subjected to. Is this what my fate will be? My eyes flick back to the screen as the man's dirty groans of pleasure begin to sound out of the speakers. He's getting off on what he's doing to her, the other man offering encouragement and support.

Two more men enter the frame and immediately untie the girl. She thrashes around as she's handled to her feet. One of the men, the biggest, grabs her and slams her up against a wall at the far side of the screen. He rips her clothes from her. Screams and pleas ring out loudly from the woman.

He's going to rape her. But all I can think about is how forcefully the man's handling her. It's how Quinn handled me. It's part of the reason I lost my fucking mind to lust and forgot my rational sense. The control. The force. I got off on it.

My eyes blur as I watch the woman being jerked about by the man. Her cries for him to stop are ignored, and I can see him forcing himself on her.

I begin to cry. I didn't think I had any tears left, but seeing this play out is sick. How I feel about it is sick. I fidget and try to position myself away from it. The tune I've been humming comes to my mind, and I grab hold of it in my mind and sing it as loudly as I can, competing with the screams and laughter that play out in front of me.

I want to close my eyes. I want to shut off the world I've found myself in and pretend this is just a nightmare. That I'll wake up and I'll be in Quinn's bed in his hotel and he'll be as charming as he was during dinner and when I slept with him.

It's a ridiculous fantasy. The humming from my voice dies down and makes way for more gasps and groans from the footage. The woman is now on her knees being taken from behind and being held by two others, with the last man forcing his dick into her mouth. It's vile. But I can't turn my head. I can't look away before my eyes sneak back to the screen.

I want it to stop, but it plays on. The woman is continually violated. She's passed around the men like a piece of meat. The fight has left her limbs. She no longer struggles, like a part of her has accepted her fate. The men don't give up and fuck her again and again, taking turns, and sometimes raping her together.

I bow my head and cry, imagining the fear and disgust the woman must be going through until the noises quieten. My notes build in my chest, and I force them out, drowning out the last pleas. The light from the screen highlights the vomit and urine on the floor around my chair, and despair engulfs me.

CHAPTER NINE

Quinn

Chicago

My hand turns the volume up in my bedroom as I towel off my hair and stare at my screen. She's there for me to see, my dirty little girl, still letting her tears and sobs come as she tries not to watch the fucking around her. She feels it, though. I can tell by the way she twitches in the chair and keeps flicking her gaze anywhere but the entertainment I've provided for her.

It's been on loop for a while now, past debts being paid. That woman begged and pleaded for her life as her husband watched on. Others over the years have done what our world does best—they paid the debt quietly. Took it for their family's lives. My own mother knows that feeling well enough, two weeks paying off my father's debts.

Never again will we be in that situation.

I drop the towel and head through the room, trying to wake myself up. I got an hour or two of sleep as we travelled here. I was too busy watching Emily to care for more, some inherent fascination I haven't quite come to terms with yet keeping me wired. She's had a straight ten hours from England to here, helped by the drugs to keep her under.

I snort, remembering her face as she woke up, finally understanding what the hell she'd gotten herself into. Some friend Jenny is. Jenny should be smothered in her sleep for such deceit. Although, it's made me consider if she might be useful to my business. Deviance like that deserves a medal in some respects. Clever, if not disloyal.

"Quinn?" I turn out of the bedroom at the sound of Josh's voice downstairs, instantly muting the sound of past debts, and head downstairs towards him. Not that I care if he hears. He is a Cane after all and not dense to our fucked up sensibilities, but I do care if he knows Emily's five feet beneath us. "You back?" He knows I am or he wouldn't have dared walk in here.

"Yeah," I reply, tucking my towel around my waist, and trying to work out why I'm keeping her here a secret. No one knows about her. Only Shifty, and he only knows because he carried her onto the plane before we took off.

"Where you been?" I stare at him as I cross through the stark, white lounge, picking up my phone from the glass coffee table as I go. He looks like shit, as if he's had a hard night on the booze and fucking anything that moves.

"Why is that relevant to you?"

"Wondered." I narrow my gaze and glance at the crumpled Armani he's trying to wear, considering what he's about to ask me for. Little brother only ever comes to me when he's fucked something up.

"What have you done, Josh?"

"Nothing." He follows me as I raise my brow and head for the kitchen. "It's just that I thought we could hang out, you know, brothers?" I scowl and turn back to the counter, swiping my watch and dice on the way. Brothers? We couldn't be further from each other if we tried. I've made it that way to keep him away from things he doesn't need to know.

"I haven't got time, Josh," I reply, walking back towards the stairs to get dressed. No time or inclination. I've got a dirty girl to play with and business to attend to. The last thing I want is to babysit and attempt to play happy families. We're not. We're Cane blood. Nothing is happy here other than that fact. My only commitment to him is making sure he stays alive and safe.

That's all.

"You want something to do? Go see Mother. Keep her contented. Or Father."

The last of my words are muttered beneath my breath, irritation lacing my tone as I think of the lie Josh believes is true. Fucking happy families. He thinks the sun shines out of our father's backside, that he cares for Mother and us. He doesn't. He cares about this business I run, the money it makes, and the name attached to it.

"I'm fucking bored, Quinn. I want some responsibility. I'm a Cane, too."

I snort as my feet take the stairs back up, then glare across my shoulder as he begins following me. He stops immediately, a frown etching his face. He knows better than to come into my home and treat it like his own. He's got his own place to go roaming around.

"Go home, Josh. Sleep it off."

"I deserve a fucking place in this business," he snaps, stamping his feet like a damned toddler. I swing back to him, my feet coming back down at pace.

"To do what?" He goes pale and takes a step away, remembering the last time he raised his voice to me. That didn't end well for his face. "Come on, Josh. What? What can you do?"

"Nate's involved," he mutters petulantly. I glare at the comeback. Of course Nathan is. Nathan counts numbers as well as I do. He's the accountant, running the entirety of this business's money once it's been laundered and is useable to us. He keeps us clean in the eyes of the Feds and any other fucker who dares look into us. The few I can't buy off, anyway. This fuck up couldn't count to twenty if his life depended on it. I stare, unsure how to handle the situation in front of me. Maybe it is about time he did something. Maybe it would reel him back in from his extravagance. Fuck knows. "I just feel like I'm on the outside all the time, Quinn." There's a weakness in his voice that softens whatever irritation was beginning to build in me.

"You are, Josh. It's safe there. Mother would want that." I shake my head at him and move to go back up the stairs.

"Fuck safe. I'm not a baby." I keep walking up the stairs, more interested in getting back to my dirty girl than the hissy fit that's about to erupt from his mouth. "I'm a man, Quinn. Let me prove it." The thought makes me snort again and roll my dice, wondering if the dick needs a dose of fate delivering. "I can do Cane business, Quinn. I can."

"Close the door on your way out, Josh. I'm busy."

The slamming door doesn't go unnoticed, but I'm too engrossed in Emily again to care. I lean back into my chair and rub my scar, slowly raising the volume on the screen. Groaning and fucking assaults the airways again, lifting my mood to one of amusement rather than family responsibilities. Damned child. Even my dirty little girl's got more about her than he has.

She still sits down there, apparently dried up of tears and sobs now. And she's humming that fucking tune again. It's constant, like a noise interfering with my mind. It nearly drowns out the grunts and high pitched wailing of fucking, bringing tranquillity over what should be a cruelty chamber.

It pisses me off, and the roll of my dice slows as I think of my next move with her. I don't even know why I brought her here. Pay off the debt? That other whore owes me money, not this girl. I could have had my fun and let her go after the one night. Found Jenny instead. I didn't want to. I wanted more time with her. Unfortunately for her, I know fuck all about dating. I know pain and how to amuse myself with it. High-end cunt usually does the job nicely, but one night with something real and I stuck that needle in her neck myself, ready to fly her here without any other thought on the matter. She just didn't wake up after she fell asleep in my arms. I got dressed, got her dressed, and then called Shifty to make the arrangements.

I didn't see her again until we were on the plane.

I frown at the image of her arms bound to the chair, then continue down her skin and see a pool of piss at her bound feet, vomit to the left of them. The vision makes me sneer at my own interest in it, some perverse part of me enjoying her embarrassment, the other uncomfortable with it.

Finally, dressing myself, I go to her, crossing through my pristine lounge and heading to the back stairs to the gym. The doors slam as I enter, my hand helping the movement so she knows I'm coming for her. The thought amuses me. Perhaps it's the pitiful little whimpers that fall from her mouth, or maybe it's the way she smiles and giggles, like some fresh new thing that should be broken in.

I cross the expansive room full of weights and gym equipment, bypassing the corridor to the pool, and head through the back passage to the room I deem appropriate for something that needs reminding what Cane is all about. Not many have been here. Only one other than her. I never have anyone in this house who isn't useful to me, friends and family excluded. This place is personal to me. It's somewhere I bring only the closest to me, or an enemy I can't put anywhere else for fear of someone helping them escape.

Sobs are the first thing I hear as I approach her door. Sobs and then that fucking tune again. I stop and listen to it coming back at me, the melancholy causing a shiver to ride through me. It has some significance to me, something that bites into a part of me that my mother manages to pull out. It's annoying, riling me into thoughts of weakness and fault.

It's not something I intend to deal with, and the hard shove of the door, signalling my pissed intent, only proves my point. She gasps as I step in, her eyes immediately flying from mine to the ground beneath her.

"You've made a mess, Emily," I say, wandering closer.

She shivers and shudders, her body trying to coil away from me. Tough. There's no getting away from me. Not until I'm ready to release the debt I'm owed. The money's gone, spent. I might as well get some more merit for its worth. I'll fuck around with her for a while, watch as she breaks apart on me and get my satisfaction that way.

"I'm sorry," she mumbles, the words drowned by a choke.
"What for?"
"The mess." It's so pitiful from her lips, like the sobs I know so well from those other women who took their families' debts and paid them off. "I'll… I'll clean it up if you let me."

I arch a brow at the state of her, watching as she twists about again. "Please, untie me." She looks back at me from under her lashes. "Please, Quinn. I want to go home. I don't know what you want from me, but I don't have the money Jenny owes."

"Yes, you do. I want my money's worth, Emily."

"I haven't got that much," she says, wide eyed. "I told you that already."

I flick my dice in the air, weighing up my options as I sweep the outskirts of the room and watch her body shake. It's a beautiful representation of innocence in my home, something that makes me aroused. Nothing is innocent here. Nothing has been for so long. And this one really is.

She's pure.

Untouched by my world and its insidious charms. It's a shame I barely give a fuck. Maybe if I did I might imagine something more civilized than I am doing.

"What will you do to pay me off?" I ask, circling toward her and throwing my dice. She shakes her head, another sniff of tears coming. "No answer to give?" There's nothing quick enough for my liking. I snatch the back of the chair to get us away from the mess she's made, yanking it across the floor to back her up into a corner. "How do you like the show?" I peer into her wide eyes, watching as the colours brighten through the glistening. "The fucking around you? Has it turned my dirty girl on?" Her head shoots down and away from me, lips mumbling something I can't hear. So I grab her chin and force her to look up to the screens again. "Tell me you liked watching them touch her."

Nothing comes back at me as she shakes in my hold, eyes staring at the screen and watching three men fuck into Cane property. She's so fucking pretty like this—wide eyed, her body quivering and quaking for me. Some part of me might even admire her innocence as she tries not to look, which makes me back off and throw my dice again.

"Pick a number." Her eyes come back to me, but only briefly before they fall back to the floor. I spin the dice again, throwing and releasing them into the air to give her the idea, before catching them again. "You've got from two to twelve. Choose."

"I don't understand what this is, Quinn. Who is that, and why are they ra…" She stumbles around words, unused to getting real grit through her teeth. "Touching her?"

"Raping. Is that the word you want? They're claiming a debt, dirty girl. It's a business transaction in my world. Nothing more." Her eyes widen further, full comprehension of my world sinking in. "Choose a fucking number. Hope it matches the one on the dice when they land."

The dice fly from me, the cubes twisting in the air, my eyes still trained on the panic in her eyes as she watches them go.

"Ten," she splutters out. I follow her eyes as she glances down at them by her feet. Ten's a good number, but even without looking at the cubes I can tell it's not the number on my dice.

"Shame. Let's see how dirty we can get you."

She baulks away from me as I lean in, her whole body trying to get away from what's coming. I don't even know yet, but I can't stop the need to get inside her again, filthy or not. I want that pussy wrapped around me. I want that dirty little mouth screaming my name as if it's the last one she'll ever say.

The chair scrapes as I turn it and claw at the binds around her to get her ass available to me, but the stench of vomit wafts over my nostrils. It stops me, suddenly disgusted with its foul aroma.

"Please, Quinn," she whimpers, her whole body trying to fold into itself. "I don't... I don't want this." The fuck she doesn't. She's my dirty little girl. She'll fuck on top of that vomit if I make her do it, her knees sinking into the vile liquid. "Quinn, please. Let me clean up first."

Clean.

I back away, frowning and scooping my dice from the floor then look at the two fives facing me. I chuckle slightly, wondering how fate made them change to her number as I grabbed them. Clean. Perhaps she does deserve a chance at clean.

"Looks like fate's given you a chance." Something about the thought makes me feel warmer, calmer even. Still, it doesn't stop me wanting to taste her pretty lips, see if the stench still radiates on the innocent like it does every other whore. She looks over her shoulder at me, meek eyes filled with half released tears, and smiles quietly. It's enough to draw me back to her and I grab her chin, reminding her that nothing is going to be negotiated beyond my control. "Half a damn chance, anyway."

That's all it is. Half a fucking chance at decency because of her purity in this immoral world I've brought her into. Maybe when she's clean, and after she's proven her dirty little mouth can pay some more of that debt off, I'll let her out of here. Allow fate's intervention to tell me what the fuck I'm doing with her, or why I brought her here at all.

CHAPTER TEN

Emily

I turn my face away from Quinn, but it doesn't stop him. He squeezes my jaw and forces me to look at him. My gaze locks with his. I'm nervous around this man. I'm frightened, caught between panic and dread. But my body warms to his harsh handling, even after closing me in a dark room for god knows how long.

He searches my eyes as if he's looking for something. I try to keep a poker face, but I'm useless at shielding my emotions or feelings. I'm an open book, and I'm confident that a man like Quinn can read me, even in the dark.

He crowds me and takes a harsh kiss. It's rough and punishing, and I do everything in my power not to respond to him.

"You taste disgusting. You're not worth one hundred grand like this," he sneers.

At this point, I'd agree. I've been in this room, sitting in my own pee for hours, the dry taste of sick still lingering in my mouth.

He stands behind me, and his fingers work at the ties that keep me in place. I plant my feet firmly on the ground so that I can run as soon as I'm able. His hands rest on my shoulders as he moves from one side to the other. My heart hammers in my chest, waking my body up as I see my chance.

The room is only lit by the screens, but it's enough for me to make out the shape of a door across the way from me. Quinn's hands move down, and I feel the slackening of the tie. I push my weight onto my legs and press off hard from the ground, ready to run. A sharp pain flares across my scalp instantly, stopping me in my tracks.

"You move when I say you move." My hands reach up to my head, trying to relieve the pressure, but he's grabbed a handful of my hair roughly. "Don't make me regret my decision, Emily. Or I'll choose some other way to get my money's worth."

He drags me backwards, and I stumble on my shaky legs. He manoeuvres me through the room to another door which he opens and pushes me into. Bright lights blind me momentarily, as I blink to adjust to the harshness. We're in a small shower room.

Quinn still has hold of me by my hair, and his other hand starts to yank at the zip of my dress. He tugs it down and pushes it from my shoulders. I want to fight with him, keep a semblance of my modesty. But I don't.

"Peel your own underwear off."

With shaking hands, I slip the wet knickers off and add them to my dress.

"Clean yourself up." His command is harsh, but it's an act that I'm desperate for. I feel dirty and vile. Perhaps some hot water and soap will make the prospects of surviving this situation better.

He lets my hair go, and I chance a glimpse at him over my shoulder. He's leaning back against the door, blocking my escape, and watching me like a hawk. My feet edge closer to the shower, and I reach in to turn the water on. My arms cross over my boobs in a vain attempt to conceal some of myself from him. I know that after last night my body won't come as a surprise to him, but this Quinn, this kidnapping monster, is a new person to me. I've not been intimate with him, and I want to keep myself as far from him as possible.

I step under the stream of water. As it falls over my skin, I can't describe the relief it brings. I open my mouth and drink the warm water, rinsing my mouth and quenching my painful thirst.

My eyes close and the water takes the fear and trepidation away. Under the spray I can pretend that the outside doesn't exist. I can pretend that I'm not trapped against my will. I move about and try to clean the rest of my body, still mortified that I wet myself in that chair.

"You're clean enough for what I've got planned. You'll be fucking dirty again by the end of it."

Quinn's voice shatters my illusion of peace. He leans in past my body and shuts off the water. My scalp flares again as he grabs me and hauls me out.

"Oww! You could ask," I mumble, wishing I felt strong enough to stand up to him.

"I don't ask. I take."

He shoves me out of the bathroom and back into the room where the rape scenes have been on a loop. He pushes me forward, and I fall, crashing to my knees. I take the moment of freedom to sprint for the door in front of me. My body slams into the wood and I grab for the handle, rattling it in desperation. It doesn't open.

I put my back to the door and watch him across the room.

"Did I not explain things clearly to you? You owe me. You'll pay me however I fucking choose." I shake my head, my body temperature plummeting with the water cooling on my skin. He stalks across to me and I look around the small space for somewhere to run to. "You move one step, and Shifty can have my seconds. Do you want that? To be treated like the girl on the video? I know you liked it."

"No!" I protest, my voice shaking from the chill.

"Don't lie to me." His voice quietens. He's only a few feet in front of me, his eyes glinting with the same danger I ignored last night. "Now when I touch your cunt, it won't smell of piss. I'll get just you and those dirty thoughts you're fighting with."

I shake my head vigorously. Perhaps he'll give up? I know it's a stupid thought. Silently, he moves until we're nose to nose. I hold my breath, but he snatches it as he plunders my lips. He's forceful and punishing, and it's everything I loved last night and want to hate now. An unyielding door is all I'm met with in my attempt to shrink away. I press myself against it as much as possible, but I can't escape.

His calloused hand grabs my boob, palming and squeezing. I shove his chest and twist my body away, but I have little effect on Quinn. And even worse, my body responds. Flutters of nerves heat through my body. I turn my head, desperate to break the sick connection.

"Mmm. Better." He grabs my neck and marches me into the middle of the space. I drag my feet, protesting in any small way I can. The video still plays, and he turns me around so I can see one of the screens. "Kneel down."

My arms cross over my torso, shielding myself again. It's as if I'm a small child, not a confident woman who went out on a date yesterday. I feel insignificant. Vulnerable.

"Kneel," he growls, and the shock sends me to the floor. *I will not cry. I will not cry.*

I sit back on my heels and lean forward, bracing my hands on the floor. My eyes drop and watch the light from the screen dance before me. I dig my fingers into the floor, willing my trembling lips to stop. The tops of Quinn's shoes come into my vision.

"Time for me to drive this dick down your throat." He chuckles a little at my gasp, my eyes widening. "See how good that dirty mouth really is."

His trousers drop to the floor revealing his sculpted thighs. His cock is already hard, jutting out towards me. Last night I was nervous, but I felt sexy and desired. It was an ultimate fantasy I was happy to get swept away in. This is a nightmare people watch on screen. But I'm trapped and I honestly don't know what he'll do next.

I scoot backwards, but Quinn snatches my hair, dragging me towards him again like a bad dog. He pulls me up so I'm level with his crotch.

"Open up, dirty girl." He shoves the tip of his cock against my mouth and I try to baulk away again. He doesn't let me. His hold becomes fiercer, making me panic and part my lips. The salty tang makes my mouth water as I stretch my jaw wider to accommodate him. My stomach rolls but I fight against it.

Quinn's hand grips my hair tightly, keeping me still. I feel the pressure as he forces more of his cock into my mouth. It's suffocating and my throat starts to protest, getting tighter, restricting my breath. Saliva pools and leaks at the seal between our flesh and I screw my eyes shut, blocking out as much of the experience as I can.

"You're going to take all of me. Right down that innocent

throat of yours." He thrusts into my mouth, both hands now holding my head to his crotch. I can feel him at the back of my throat, and my body starts to gag at the intrusion. It's stifling. My eyes water, leaking down my face as saliva dribbles from my chin.

Quinn makes a few moans as he withdraws and shoves back in, a few strokes before holding his cock in my mouth for what feels like minutes. I grab onto his thighs for support, and my nails dig into his flesh.

"You enjoying being my dirty plaything?" His voice is low and seductive, and just like yesterday it affects me. I *like* that he's enjoying himself.

Panic stirs, and I thrash in his hold. I try to move my head, but his grip stops me. The burn in my jaw spreads to my cheeks, but I block it.

My body starts to shake, but it only causes the grunts from Quinn to get louder.

"Open your eyes, dirty girl."

I do as I'm told and look up at him with watery eyes and a disgusting face.

He bites his lip and tilts his head back as he thrusts in hard, choking me as he hits my tonsils. He looks down at me again, and our eyes lock.

His hold loosens, and he pulls his cock from my mouth, only to pump jets of come all over my chest and face. The warm fluid coats my cheek, some of it falling to my breasts and running down my cleavage.

He grabs my hand and hauls me up, spinning me around so my back is against his front. His fingers wrap around my neck with enough pressure to stop me from moving.

"I'll bet the whole hundred grand you owe me that your

pussy is dripping for me," his voice whispers in my ear. His arm wraps around me and I try to knock him away, but he just seizes my wrist. "Behave yourself. You're my property to fuck with until I say you're done."

"Will you let me go if I'm not wet?" I have to ask. I know that my body responds on some dark level I'm ashamed about, but perhaps if I know there's a way out I can fool myself. He laughs.

"You think it fucking matters if you're wet or not?" He pulls me tighter and lets go of my wrist. My heart pounds in my chest as if it's just as desperate to escape as I am. "Let's see how many fingers I can get inside your snug cunt, dirty girl." He cups my sex with his hand, and I'm blasted with the memory of last night and my false bravado thanks to one too many glasses of champagne.

I feel his rough touch, and to my horror, it's good. He pushes his finger inside of me, and it takes all the strength I have left not to moan in pleasure. He digs inside of me, pulls out and then adds another finger.

"Shall I make you come like this? With my fingers?" Another finger gets pushed in, making me gasp. "Or can I get you to spread your legs further for me and beg?"

"Please… Stop. I don't want this. You're a monster."

"A monster who can do this?" He curls his fingers inside of me, and I gasp again with pleasure. All of my muscles relax, and I feel myself sink into Quinn.

He repeats the move, and I feel utterly under his control. His puppet.

"My dirty girl likes it rough. I already knew that from last night. You feel this?" He presses his cock into the small of my back. "I'm going to take this ass and take your cunt as many times as I want. And you'll get off on it."

"No." I shake my head frantically, caught between wanting him to stop and yet yearning for him to carry on. It's sick. "I don't want any of this. You can't force me." Fear mixes with the odd cocktail of desire and sin already confusing my brain.

Just to spite me, he rubs at that magical spot inside of me with the pad of his fingers, and my body convulses in his hold, betraying every word I've just said.

"You're already mine. My plaything. And such a pretty one. How much do you think you're worth? A thousand? Ten thousand? I've paid for high-class cunt. You're not in that league so far."

My blood turns cold at his insults. How am I going to stay in this room until one hundred grand is paid off? Panic chokes me and I twist and shove his arm out of the way. This time he lets me put distance between us. My body misses the contact straight away, rubbing salt in my already open and bleeding wounds.

He lifts his fingers to his mouth and sucks them clean, embarrassing me further by how crazy I must be to be turned on by him. Shame gnaws at my insides, but I ignore it. Feeling sorry for myself isn't going to get me out of this place. Nor will it stop Quinn from further proving his point.

I bolt to the corner furthest away from him and curl up against the wall. My tears silently track down my face. I bury my head in my knees while I try to gather some strength.

The room's deathly quiet for a moment, so quiet that my pounding heart eases off for a few beats. I look up, but Quinn hasn't moved.

"Why?" I plead. "You could have kept me in your

apartment. I'd likely have done all sorts of things with you willingly. Why take me here? Why treat me like this?" I force my voice to fill the room, but it's frail and weak.

"I've told you. You owe me a debt and Canes always collect debts. I chose this way."

He really is a sick bastard. He had me completely fooled. Innocent little Emily, happy to have a date. Falls into bed with a stranger because for once she wants to have a good time and not think about the consequences.

"Do you enjoy this? Seeing me like this? You said you've had high-class girls before."

"I'm not going to fork out on girls when I have perfectly good cunt right under my roof." He walks a step forward, still sucking his fingers clean. "Whenever I want, however I want. Remember that."

"I won't." I pull my knees tightly against my chest, shielding myself from him.

"Careful, Emily."

"No, I can't. I won't sleep with you." He chuckles.

"Who said anything about sleep? You're not here for sleep."

"Please, Quinn. No." The tears are back and I don't even try to hide them.

"Stand up." I hadn't even heard him cross towards me. "Don't make me repeat myself."

I stand, using the walls to support my body. My legs feel like limp noodles, and my head throbs from the stress.

"Don't tell me no. It's a waste of your breath. Accept it. There's no way out."

"You can't force me. I'll … fight you. You'll have to fight me."

He's on me in a second. He's so fast I don't even react. I'm wrapped in his arms, my face plastered up against the wall.

"Understand this. It's my fucking rules here. If I choose to strap your ass to a table and fuck you 'til you're nearly dead, I will." He licks the side of my face and gives me room to breathe again. "You should think about how you act towards me. Squirm or not, fight or not, I will get my damn money's worth. If you think I give one fuck how you respond to that threat, you're wrong. Battle me as much as you want."

His footsteps fade, and I hear the sound of the door opening.

"Quinn, wait. Don't leave me in here again. Please?"

He doesn't respond and shuts the door. I don't even have the energy to follow after him. At least I'm not tied down. I push off the wall and wobble towards the bathroom.

Pink cheeks, blood shot eyes, and milky white come dried over my chest. I look horrific. I turn the shower back on and take the small pleasure it brings. I clean myself off, washing my chest and between my thighs, trying to forget the ache that's still there. I scrub with my hands in place of a washcloth and drink the water from the spray.

Maybe if I stay under the water for long enough, it will wash the guilt in my stomach away, too. Or the shame. A host of emotions I've only loosely been familiar with now plague my existence. All because I met a cute guy and thought I could have some fun.

Quinn called me his dirty girl. Well, that's exactly how I feel. Dirty and used. I should be distraught. But instead, my body enjoys his rough handling, his naughty mouth. God, I'm messed up. At least my tears have dried up.

I finally turn off the shower and look around the bathroom for a towel. I find one hanging on the back of the door and swaddle myself in it as best as I can. But it smells of him. It reminds me of him and falling asleep in his arms, feeling on cloud fucking nine. *How stupid.*

The tune that has kept me sane pushes out those memories and I start to sing.

I leave the light on in the bathroom and go back into my 'holding room'. Thankfully, the video has stopped and in its place is a grey flickering screen. White noise. It's peaceful, in a warped way. At least compared to what I was subjected to before. A swell of sorrow interrupts my song, and I go back to humming the tune instead. I curl up across the room from my new view and wait.

My eyes jump open and I suck in a deep breath, as if I'm suffocating. I blink and make out the confines of the room. The memories smash into my mind as I come awake.

I'm shivering, wrapped in a damp towel. My limbs are heavy and cold to the bone. I need to get out of here. My stomach groans, the knotted hunger pains now difficult to ignore.

I climb to my feet and make it to the bathroom. I use the facilities and search for another towel. Anything to provide a sliver of comfort. I open the door and let the light wash out into my murky prison. My eyes land on the door across the room. It was locked last night, or whenever Quinn was last in here, but I can't just sit in here and wait for him to turn up again. I've got to try something.

My heart beat rockets to life as I slowly cross the room, looking for cameras and reaching for the door. Quinn's watching in some sick video feed, isn't he? He told me he knew I enjoyed watching, so he must have seen me before. I don't care. I've got to get out of here.

I lock my hands around the handle and take a breath, pushing down on it. The door creaks open.

CHAPTER ELEVEN

Quinn

Staring up at the main house, I wait for Nathan to arrive. He crosses the paths through the grounds with his head low, some representation of the fact that he hates this life. He knows everything, just like I do, but it pains him more. That's why he's the accountant. He counts the numbers, moves the money, keeps us as clean as we can be, and then spends the rewards from that manoeuvring. If I need him for anything else, which is rare, he'll do as he's asked, but he's never quite hardened up like a Cane should. Never quite able to give less care than average people do. He's loyal—loyal to his family, loyal to me—but he despises everything we stand for. Constant damned challenges at me, little digs into my thickened skin. Thank fuck he's at least learnt to be as hard as stone with his glasslike stare, our family resemblance only highlighting that to enemies who dare to forget their obligations.

Perhaps he should get some fucking dice of his own, ease the burden that way as I do.

"Quinn," he says, the crisp lines of his grey suit as sharp as his jaw. "How's Father?"

"Breathing."

He snorts and then frowns, turning back to gaze at the main house with me.

"You ever gonna get married? That monstrosity will need new blood once he goes."

Not a fucking chance.

"You know as well as I do what would happen to another Cane wife, Nate. There's always a debt somewhere that needs paying."

He sighs and turns around, his briefcase highlighting the business meeting we're about to have as he heads into my house.

"Didn't know you cared enough to worry about that," he mutters, opening his laptop and resting it on the dining table. I don't. Never have. I can't damn well afford to and neither can he. I just stare in response, no answer to his taunt. If he had to deal with what I do daily, he wouldn't care either. He shakes his head at me and sighs again, sprawling paperwork across the table. "On that topic, Mother looks like shit. Has someone upped her meds yet?"

"You know what happens when we do that. It's not worth it, Nate. She needs some sort of life." He shakes his head again and goes back to his paperwork, sliding himself onto the seat and booting the spreadsheets up. "You want her comatose permanently?" I look over his shoulder, watching the numbers pop up on the screen, and search them for deviations against my own spreadsheets.

"You know I don't. She just…" He pushes the chair back, another huff coming from his mouth. "Fuck, Quinn. She's not even on this planet most of the time."

She was when six of the Mortoni family had their fun with her.

I lean in closer to the screen, wondering why October looks lighter than it should.

"It's not a planet she likes very much, Nate. Leave her where she is. It's nicer there most of the time." I barely entertain the conversation. "Where's the two mil gone from the Russian account?"

The door clicks behind us and makes me spin toward it, wondering who the fuck it is. Nate's head turns just as quickly, his hand reaching inside his suit for the Beretta he always carries.

Josh ambles in, his dishevelled appearance instantly pissing me off. It makes Nate withdraw his hand and clear the paperwork, ready to stow it if I give him the nod. There's nothing here to worry about.

"Josh, we're busy. Go play somewhere else," I snap, irritated at the thought of him seeing her and starting his mouth running. Nate I can cope with; Josh I can't.

"Father said you were having a meeting, told me to come join in." Did he? Interfering old bastard. I snarl at the thought, turning back and closing the laptop lid.

"I told you, Josh. No." I swing back to face him fully, my feet finding their way to the door to show him out of it. "No meetings. No job for you. Go fuck around with something else."

Nate snorts and pulls out a pack of cigarettes, the click of his lighter showing his contempt for little brother.

"Yeah, Joshy. Go smash another car up like a good little boy."

"Fuck you, Nate," Josh booms, his body growing to its full height and proving he's not quite the little brother Nate thinks he is. I shove him backwards, ready to stop the family spat before it begins. I've got no time for it, and no desire to have this dick in my house while Emily could walk up at any second. I don't even know why I left the door open for her, or why I put clean clothes on the floor for her to find, but I'm fucked if the first vision she gets of partial freedom is going to involve Josh and his mouth.

"Leave, Josh, before I make you." He frowns at me, his body rumbling with aggravation. It makes me glower at him, ready to beat him back into place if he wants that retaliation. "You wanna do this with me?" Still he frowns, flicking his eyes between me and Nate. It's enough for me to shove him again, reminding him who has control here.

It's not my fucking father, that's for damn sure.

He continues glowering until I see him give up. His head drops a little, his feet backing away a few steps towards the door. Whether it's out of respect or the fact that there are two of us here to fight against, I don't care. He'll do as he's fucking told. I can keep him safe and alive that way, protect him.

A noise echoes at me from across the room, making me spin on my heel and look down through the space. She's standing there by the bottom of the lounge, the oversized blue tracksuit drowning her small form as she cowers and grabs at the stair rail. I scowl in response, wondering what the hell to do with Josh in the vicinity. And then there's a split second when I see a spark of tenacity threaten. It rises in her whole frame, making me question what the fuck she thinks she's about to do with three men in her path. Her eyes shift from mine towards the door behind me, a half step forward joining the thought.

Josh is suddenly by my side, his body pushing past me slightly, and I watch her body slump in defeat as she realises her fate. Good. She'd be fucking dense to try running here.

"Who's this?" Nate asks, a puff of smoke clouding the space around him.

"Yeah, who *is* this?" Josh asks, too, charm pouring from his lips as he walks in her direction. "New plaything?"

I watch Josh going to her, her frame edging away towards the wall as he goes, and roll my dice in annoyance. Nate stands up and comes to my side.

"Debt," I reply, backing towards the dining table and lifting the lid on the laptop.

"Where from?" Nate asks, turning to face me. I don't look at him. It's fuck all to do with either of them.

"It's personal." I flick through the numbers again, ignoring her and trying to find the missing two million. "The money, Nate. Where is it?"

"Switched to Geneva, through Columbia."

She squeals suddenly, making me look over my shoulder at what's happening. Josh is attempting to cajole her to the seating, all the time defending himself as she bats him away. Why the hell he's behaving so gentlemanly is beyond me. He takes women as quickly as the rest of us do, no thought for their comfort.

Eventually, she gets partly dragged to the seating, him smiling the entire time in the hope that he can get in her pussy if I let him.

I won't, not this time.

"Quinn?" My name trembles from her lips as she curls her body up into the white couch. I don't answer. I'm not here to make her feel comforted. She probably thinks the three of us are going to enjoy her for a while. And while that's not fucking happening for anyone but me, I like the sense of fear she's emitting. It arouses me, her innocence mingling with my lacking morals. She's pretty in this guise, small and weak, and fucking distracting me from the task at hand—money.

The door knocks sometime later, Maria coming in with trays of food for our lunch and breaking my quiet stare at Emily. She walks straight through to the main table, no speaking as she goes like a good servant. She's been here long enough to know how to serve me. Quietly. Like a fucking mouse who's never seen.

"You had enough?" Nate asks, his fingers putting paperwork into folders as I keep looking though more documents.

"Yeah." I flick my eyes back to Emily to see her still curled up as she fiddles with the bottom of her hoodie and tries to avoid Josh's eyes. He's been interrogating her about where she's from, who she is. She's looked like a deer caught in the cross-hairs for most of it. Every time she lets her shoulders relax, he takes another shot at her. Luckily for her, she's kept her mouth shut for most of it, the occasional look at me for guidance on what she should say. She's had nothing in response to help. "For now—we'll do it again next week."

It's been interesting watching her deny him everything he usually gets so easily. Amusing even. I expected her to be squealing and trying to back away from him, trying to run again maybe, but she's been quiet and subservient after the initial look of terror. Whether that's through intelligence or fear I don't know, but it's shown that she's learnt her place here.

I close the laptop and wander over to the table, grabbing a bread roll and tearing some off.

"You want some food, dirty girl?" I ask, pulling out a chair. Her eyes fly to mine, her fingers instantly stopping fiddling at the hem of her top. Nate is silent as he comes to the table.

"Dirty girl? That's not nice, brother," Josh says. "Her name's Emily."

I smirk at him then look back at her, amused at his manouvering around her. He's always been good at that, at least. If there's one man on this planet who can get a woman to spread her legs through charm alone, it's Josh.

She nods, her body hitching itself to stand. I throw some of the roll at her before she gets a chance to move. I didn't say she could eat at the table with us. She'll stay there. Pick at whatever offering I give her.

"Quinn," Nathan says, contempt heavy in his tone. Fuck him and his sensibilities. I arch a brow, shutting his mouth before he opens it any more. He knows better, and what does he think this is? Marriage plans?

Dick.

We eat after that, Josh eventually leaving her side to join us and dive into Maria's home cooked meals. They're the only ones any of us ever get. It's normally elite restaurants, delivering precise plates of no fucking food at all. It reminds me of our youth as we eat and talk, the atmosphere becoming more comfortable than it has for a while between us all.

"Seriously, though, what are you doing about Mother?" Nate asks.

"What the fuck do you want me to do, Nathan?"

"I don't know, but she's not right, Quinn. There's insane and then there's…" I glower at him, cutting the conversation dead and flicking my eyes to Emily. He looks at her as if he's forgotten she's here. Josh hasn't; he's spent the entire time gazing at her and smiling. A predator waiting for his moment.

Well, he won't fucking get it with her.

"Just leave it, Nate." I turn in my chair, focusing myself on her fidgeting as she cowers into the seat looking small and appealing. It stirs my dick. "It's time for you two to leave," I say, getting up and grabbing at a plate. "I've got things to do." Like fucking into this debt that needs paying back.

I start layering some meat onto the plate, another half eaten bread roll joining it.

"What about something to do then, Quinn?" Josh asks, his chair scraping my polished floors.

I sigh and look back at him, wondering where the hell I can place him. Nate gets up, too. It makes me look between the two of them, noting the family resemblance and smiling at it. Tall, broad, dark hair, blue eyes. One cut sharply, the other softer in his look but no less threatening because of it. I don't know if it's the family reminiscing, or the fact that dirty girl is screwing with my mind, but Josh is right. Regardless of me not wanting him anywhere near us, he is a part of this, and if something should happen to either Nate or myself, what then?

"I'll think about it, Josh. Find something." He looks like the cat that got the fucking cream, his smile widening into the same one he gives my father as he begins to leave the table. "As long as you both get the fuck out of my house now."

Nathan raises his brow at me as he picks up his bags, tossing his napkin down.

"You sure?" he asks. No, I'm not sure, but something has to change.

It's a constant question from Josh's mouth lately, and while it might piss me off, it's also something that needs dealing with. He's not a child anymore, and this business is getting deeper and thicker into criminality with each passing year. He wants to be part of it, he can be. I just need to work out where. Find something safe for him to do. Safe isn't a concept we've lived in these past ten years. It could be a damn sight safer, though, if the right fucking players took over in the right places.

The closing door behind them signals the beginning of something more interesting, especially for my dick. I walk over to Emily, a plate of food in my hand and a glass of wine in the other.

"Get up," I snap, already thinking about the feel of her pussy around me. Her throat might have been good, but it's nothing compared to what's between her thighs.

She moves as quietly as she has been sitting, gently placing her feet onto the floor and fiddling with her outfit again. I look her over, enjoying the way she tucks her hair behind her ears, attempting some kind of perfection in this fucked up world she's in.

"You clean?" I fucking hope she is, not that I give too much of a damn if she is or not for what I've got planned. She wrings her fingers and nods.

"Yes. Uh, thank you for the clothes." She needn't thank me. I just don't want the stench of vomit invading my nostrils again while I fuck her. "And for letting me out of…" She fumbles around the rest of the words, muttering them. Maybe she said dungeon. I don't know, or care.

"Come upstairs," I call back to her. Nothing happens as I get to the bottom of them, and I turn back, catching her as she spins her head back from the door to me. "Try running, Emily. Give that shit a go." I keep walking away, climbing the stairs and looking down at her. "You're in my estate on the outskirts of Chicago. Guards patrol the grounds, three of them with dogs. All of them armed." She stares at me, shock all over her flawless fucking face. "Didn't realise?"

She shakes her head.

"Well, you are. It's a long way home, Emily. That's if you can get past my men first."

She frowns at that, and eventually I hear her feet moving to follow.

"Were those men your family?" she asks, barely any volume in her voice, as I turn into a bedroom.

I place the food and drink down on the mahogany table by the chair and walk towards the windows, closing the curtains.

"That's not relevant to you."

The swish of the dark blue fabric instantly blackens the room. So I walk to the lamps and switch them on one by one, uninterested in anything but what this dirty girl can do for me in the next hour before I have to leave.

"You can stay in here while you're with me," I say, wandering back to the chair and getting my dice out of my pocket. She doesn't say anything as I sit. No thank you or appreciation. She's probably right not to. Nothing is going to be nice about her stay, other than orgasms if I can be bothered to ensure she gets some. "Take the clothes off, dirty girl." She hovers just in front of the doorway, barely moving short of the twisting hands in her grip. "You can do this the easy way or the hard way, Emily. But you should know from last night that the hard way hurts far more." I stare at her over my shoulder, the roll of my dice easing around my hand. "You might even pick the right number if you're lucky, get a chance at what you want."

Her feet move after that, eyes narrowed as that option presents itself, and her fingers slowly reach for the hem of her top.

    Clever girl.

CHAPTER TWELVE

Emily

What I want is to get out of here. Although, now I know I'm in America, I'm not even sure how I'll get back home. *How did he even do that?*

My fingers stall as I raise the hem of the sweatshirt. It drowns my frame, keeping me hidden and safe. It's been the only shred of comfort since this all started. That and the few morsels of bread that I've been allowed. I've kept half an eye on the plate of food Quinn brought up with him. My hunger dominates my body. That and the fear of what will come next.

I force my attention back to Quinn, who's looking at me expectantly, his hand rolling those dice as if they hold all the answers in the world. My arms cross over my stomach and pull the top over my head. I'm naked under the top and trousers. Quinn might have been kind enough to leave them for me, but he didn't go so far as to make me comfortable.

My boobs bounce free, and I drop the sweatshirt on the floor.

"All of your clothes. I won't ask again."

I wiggle my hips, and the loose-fitting bottoms crumple in a heap at my feet before I step out of them and wait for my next command.

It doesn't come. Quinn sits and looks me up and down

like one might survey an object before buying. I suppose in his mind, all I am is an object. A possession for him to use as he sees fit. One that owes him one hundred thousand pounds.

My eyes flick around the room. Plush carpet supports my feet, immaculate décor, the biggest bed I've ever seen. It's a far cry from the room I was in for my last *experience* with Quinn. It was easy to see him for the vile monster he is in the dark. Here, I can see his strong jaw and handsome face. It's like the first night all over again. Except for the wining and dining.

"I'm ready for you to work some of that debt off now, dirty girl."

My legs turn to mush, freezing me on the spot.

"What… what do you want me to do?" I know it's a stupid question.

"Spread your pretty legs like you did on Friday and show me how much that pussy's worth."

I drop my eyes down to my hands, twisting them together as I stand motionless. Emotion clogs my throat at the thought of having sex with him again. I don't want this. I don't want any of this. "The dice… you said I could…"

"Don't get ahead of yourself." He storms across the room and smacks me across the cheek. The pain flares across my face and shocks me into awareness.

Quinn's lips smash into mine, and his body crowds me back against the wall. His hands roam my curves before pinning my arms above my head. The material of his suit rubs against my nipples, sending sparks of awareness through my system.

"I warned you, Emily. The easy way or the hard way. I'll enjoy both." He spins me around and shoves me against the wall as he did downstairs, kicking my legs wider and pulling my arm up behind my back.

His finger trails down my spine, so softly it betrays the rest of his actions. My body tenses as he follows lower and lower until his finger is resting at the crease of my bum.

"I'm going to enjoy taking your ass." He smacks my bum with three quick swats, distracting my mind from his words.

I brace for another volley, but his lips trail across my shoulders and up to my ear. Each kiss lessens the pain and discomfort I'm suffering and turns it into a form of pleasure, a whimper bubbling from the back of my throat.

His arm reaches around, and he rubs my nipple between his thumb and forefinger. I want to hate his treatment. I want to feel repulsed by him. But I don't. And it's that knowledge that turns my stomach more than the position I'm in.

Quinn's fingers move to my core, eagerly thrusting inside of me.

"Wet for me already?"

I keep quiet, thinking of anything but what his fingers are doing to me. It's a replay of downstairs. His talented fingers play me like a puppet.

"You'll cry out for me this time, Emily. When your cunt squeezes my cock, I want to hear you."

I bite my lip in defiance, but it doesn't stop him. He releases my arm, and I feel him loosening his belt and trousers. He pushes his hard cock between my spread legs and then forces my arms to brace against the wall.

He grunts as he forces himself inside of me, his cock stretching me, filling me completely. It knocks the air from my lungs, and I jolt forward. He's not holding me close to him. Instead, his fingers grip my hips as he draws up and thrusts back. His movements are jerky and harsh, but that doesn't make it any less pleasurable. I feel myself growing softer for him, enjoying the feel of his cock inside of me. It's humiliating how I respond to him. I never had sex like this in the past. Rough and urgent. The question of consent doesn't bother Quinn, and more alarmingly, I don't seem to have the trouble with it I wish I did.

"A few fucks in and you're dribbling pussy juice all over my cock," Quinn pants, but doesn't still his punishing rhythm.

Heat rises in my body, spreading through my limbs as his cock continues to impale me. It's brutal and raw, and I like it. I gasp, trying to gain control over myself and the climax building in my body.

He shifts his stance, hitting deeper inside of me, and I can't stop the gasp that echoes in the room.

"You want more, dirty girl?"

It's like I set Quinn a challenge. He fucks me so hard I'm sure I'll have bruises on my hips, but I can feel how easily he slips inside of me, how wet I am at his treatment of me. All my muscles begin to contract, and my toes curl into the carpet as a sheen of sweat breaks over my skin. Arching my back, I let my body take over and hear a moan of pleasure from Quinn. He moves one of his hands and plants it on the centre of my back, forcing me forward even more and changing the angle again.

"Move your legs wider," he commands, and I shuffle my feet out.

He returns his hand to give himself more traction and fucks me until my body quivers on the verge of orgasm.

His panting breath, my racing heart, the throb of my clit all conspire against me until that blissful moment when everything explodes and pure pleasure washes over me. "Yes,

yes… please…. more."

Quinn obliges my cries. My body rules my mind and lets the bliss wash over me. I register that Quinn has stopped pumping into me as my mind switches back on, leaving me groggy and lightheaded.

I'm picked up and tossed toward the bed where I crumple into a sated mass of limbs.

"I've not had my fill. Show me your wet cunt." His words make me feel degraded, but compel me to move. My knees tumble outward, giving him a truly pornographic view of me.

Quinn's eyes burn into my skin. First my boobs, and then travelling down to the apex of my legs, now spread open for anything he may want to do. He strips his expensive suit from his handsome frame before crawling onto the bed to claim me again. My legs are hoisted around his waist and he shoves his cock into me again.

My body relaxes completely from Quinn's thorough treatment of me, and I put up no fight. What's the point? He can have me; I'm resigned to the inevitability of it all.

He slams his cock inside of me over and over, and I curse my body, warming to him once again.

"Your cunt is desperate for my cock, dirty girl."

I block his words and close my eyes to his too appealing body. He fooled me once, and that's how I got into this mess. But it doesn't stop the buzz taking over my body, the slow and sensual build from Quinn's movements hitting me in all the right places. He grinds and swivels his hips, igniting all the nerves in my clit. I dig my hands into the silk sheets to stop me grabbing for him.

"Go on, Emily. Let yourself go," he grunts, tension and strain in his voice.

I try to block it out, pushing the feelings back down and riding them out, but they build stronger and stronger, like a tsunami ready to drown me.

My eyes open to look at Quinn. Both of us, gazes hooded with lust and desire, lock onto each other.

"Fuck...Yes!" His roar signals his release and I watch in awe at the ropes of muscle tensing down his neck as he tilts his head back. The sight, together with what he's doing to my body, tip me over into oblivion for the second time. Stars dance in front of my eyes as they drift shut again, and I let my body calm.

***

My eyes flutter open. The room is quiet, and it takes me a few moments to remember where I am. I'm comfortable and... warm. Fine, silk sheets encase me in the softest bed I've ever been in. Part of me wants to roll over and go back to sleep, but I know that's an impossibility. My stomach lets out an embarrassing growl and reminds me that I've not eaten for what feels like days.

I sit up and look around the room. The lights are on, but Quinn is nowhere in sight. The deep breath releases from my lungs, a sigh of relief, and I go to move from the bed. My body aches, tired and used from all the *fucking*. I used to think the word was so crude. That's all changed now. After everything that Quinn's done to me over the last few days, sex will never be the same again. I'm not sure I could even protest and claim rape. Two minutes with his fingers on me and I turn to putty in his hands. His wicked, cruel and devastatingly delicious hands.

My stomach takes another roll and nausea from what I've done bursts through me. A buzzing starts in my gut and grows louder and louder. *What have I done?* Dizziness swamps me, and my heart pounds. Tears threaten, but I don't want to cry anymore. My head falls back to the pillow, and I look across the room.

The plate with a few slices of meat and bread sits on the table across from me, a glass of wine at the side of it. I dive out of bed, my legs giving out and landing me on my knees. I don't care. I crawl the last few feet and pull the plate down into my lap. My fingers grab the bread and stuff it into my mouth.

My taste buds go mad over such a simple morsel. I gorge on the small selection until there isn't a scrap of food left on the plate. The minutes tick past as the food settles in my stomach and I take in the room around me, listening to anything from the other side of the door.

The pounding from my heart is the only noise I can hear.

There are no ambient noises from downstairs. Of course, Quinn threw his brothers out before ordering me up here. Josh and Nathan. Their resemblance screamed family, and I didn't need Quinn to tell me they were all related. Two other versions of Quinn. Josh radiated danger and this time my body screamed at me to listen. I felt his eyes stalking me, like he viewed me as little more than a toy. His other brother, Nate, seemed less intimidating, almost kind.

With the food now sitting heavy in my stomach, I push myself off the floor and go towards the door. It worked for me once. Perhaps he left it open again. I twist the ornate handle, but it just jangles. The door doesn't unlock. I rest my head against it and try to tap down on the panic that spikes. Positivity eludes me. *At least this room isn't a dark box like yesterday.*

I explore the bathroom and freshen up before pulling on the sweatshirt and tracksuit bottoms. I curl up in one of the small sofas by one of the windows. It's dusk out, and I can't see anything but some trees from the window.

Am I really in America? My eyes start to water and emotion chokes me. If it's true, I've got no way of leaving—no passport, no documents of any kind. Nothing. Fear chills me, and defeat settles on me like a cold blanket.

My life, my business and my world are thousands of miles away, and nobody even knows where I am, or what I did on Friday. Apart from Jenny. But given it was her who set this up, I have to question whether she was ever my friend in the first place.

I think back to what Quinn said to me in that room. How much *do* I think I'm worth? How long will he keep me if I have to pay off one hundred thousand pounds? He doesn't need to prove to me how serious he is. The bruises on my hips tell me, along with the shame in my heart at how I let this happen.

The song I've clung to ever since this all started trickles into my mind, the notes appearing one by one. They build in my head until I can hum along and be lifted away to a place that has some hope.

* * *

I'm back in the chair. My arms are free but there's something wrapped around my ankle. I can't move. I can't escape.

I kick out my leg and try to shake my shackle free as my mind wakes up from my dream.

"Careful. Or I'll change my mind about letting you have free reign up here." Quinn's voice startles me and I pull my foot out of his grasp.

I sit up and look around the room again, wishing I could get over the startled fear that douses me every time I wake up.

"Time to start being of worth to me. Go and clean yourself up and put this on." He rests a dress bag on the bed next to me.

"What is it?" I ask, knowing that it's got to be some sort of outfit. My eyes run over Quinn and note the crisp tux he has on.

"It's what I want you in for tonight."

"Where are we going?"

"Fewer questions, more moving. Shower. You look like a cheap whore."

The words of retaliation are on the end of my tongue, but I don't have the nerve to speak them. "Hurry up." He glowers, and I can't help but scuttle into the bathroom.

I step inside the room-sized shower enclosure and set the waterfall head running. Steam cloaks the room in a matter of minutes, and I happily hide under the spray.

A glass ledge at one end of the shower holds a range of products, and I set about soaping and lathering. I haven't had a proper wash in days, and the feel of soap over my body is heavenly.

I emerge from the bathroom wrapped in several towels, covering as much of my body as possible. Quinn is sitting in one of the chairs on the far side of the room, running his dice through his hands.

"Your outfit is on the bed. I'd hurry if I were you." He watches me with amusement shining from his eyes.

"I need to dry my hair."

"You have a towel."

I look at him with a stunned expression. My hair will look like a rat's nest unless I blow-dry it. "If you want to go out, I suggest I blow dry it." My sudden nerve to talk back pleases me.

There's a knock at the door, but Quinn is on his feet before I can flinch, moving toward the sound. He brings back a bag and hands it to me.

"You'll need these. No hairdryer. The only thing you'll blow is me. Now get your ass dressed and ready to go out." He rips the towel from around my chest and runs his gaze over my naked body.

I hide in the bathroom with my bag of… toiletries. A hairbrush, moisturiser, makeup and perfume. All brand new. And a toothbrush and toothpaste. I can't help but smile at that simple luxury.

The brush works the tangles free before I towel dry my hair, repeating several times to get it as dry as possible. I fluff it and run my fingers through the locks before giving up. The makeup is all smoky eyes and red lips. Despite trying as hard as I can not to look like a cheap hooker, I do. Right now, that's how I feel. Mascara and some rouge for my lips are as far as I go.

It's clear Quinn has some plan for tonight. And somewhere in my brain, I've decided to try to do as Quinn says or wants. He may be holding me prisoner, but he's also my only way of escaping this.

I wrap a towel around my torso again before heading out. My feet try to move with purpose and without fear, but his eyes follow me as I head towards the bed. My fingers unzip the garment bag and I'm assaulted by a glittering black dress.

The fabric slides free from it's confines as I hold it up. A deep, plunging neckline, together with spaghetti straps and an even lower back has my heart stammering.

"I can't wear this." The words are out of my mouth before I can think.

"You will."

"I can't. It won't fit," I protest.

"Emily, you'll wear it, and that's final."

"Underwear?" I ask, looking over at him. He just smiles and shakes his head.

The towel slips as I perch on the bed, attempting to climb into this gaudy creation. It hugs my hips as I pull it up, covering as much of my boobs as I can. The tiny straps feel like they could ping free at any moment, releasing my chest for all to see. I stand and pull the zip to the side, fastening myself in.

It's a perfect fit. The hem is cut on the bias and falls below my knee to my ankle on one side, rising to my mid-thigh on the other. The problem, though, is the dress barely covers my nipples. All I can see is cleavage, adding to my hooker look.

I fidget and try to pull the dress around to cover more of me.

"Turn around and show me."

My head drops and I squeeze my eyes shut. Resigned, I shift to show Quinn.

"Very nice, dirty girl. You'll do nicely."

"Quinn, please, I can't wear this."

"Why not?"

"Because…" I gesture with my hands at my chest.

Quinn stands and walks towards me. My eyes flick

between his and try to read what he'll do. He places a finger at the hollow of my neck and draws a line down over the flesh of my chest to the edge of the dress. "You look just how I want you to. Now…" He takes his dice from his pocket. "Shall we see if your ass is as tight as your cunt?"

I step away, fear infusing my blood. I shake my head but get nowhere as I back into the bed.

"You can't run away. You're mine to take as I want. Now, give me a number."

"Seven," I shout. He rolls the dice, but I don't wait to see my fate. I scramble over the bed and try to escape to the bathroom and lock myself in.

"Looks like I'll only get to fuck your pussy now." He beats me to the door and spins me around, slamming me into the wood. He wraps his hand around my throat, and with his other hand, releases his fly and his hard cock.

"You look much more the part like this, dirty girl."

He hitches my dress and shoves his dick against my tender flesh. I try to fight, but as soon as he's inside of me, he uses both his hands to subdue me.

He's rougher and more ferocious than ever. He pulls me against him and lifts me, shoving me against the door and using my weight to benefit him. Each thrust of his hips pushes me up the door, and as much as I don't want to, my legs creep around his waist to keep me in position.

His eyes are fixed on my chest, watching them bounce and jiggle with each move of his hips. I look down, and it's an erotic sight. I've never been taken with as much intent as Quinn has shown me. Conflicted emotions twist and turn in my mind, as he carries on, groaning and driving in. I don't want this. I shouldn't want to be treated this way. Yet, just like before, my body relaxes and warms to Quinn. I'm tender and feel used from earlier, but that doesn't make this any less pleasurable. My back scrapes the door, causing pain, but my fingers grip onto him for more. It feels closer than I could imagine for some reason.

"I can't get enough of fucking your cunt," he grunts, gritting his teeth, his orgasm taking over before he stills, leaving me hanging.

He releases me, letting me slide down the door to my feet as he tucks himself away and turns from me.

I'm left feeling empty and... unsatisfied. The feeling confuses me further as I watch him move. His come now trickling down my inner thigh, I sneak into the bathroom to clean myself up.

"Emily!" he shouts.

"What?"

"We're leaving. Now."

"I need shoes and something to wear over this."

"Shoes are here." He hands me a pair of black patent leather heels that look like skyscrapers. I've never worn more than a modest heel, and these look like they could do permanent damage. I slip my feet into them and immediately feel like I'm falling forward.

"That's all you're getting."

"I can't walk in these."

"Tough. It's what I want." He storms off out the door, and I'm left stumbling behind him. I catch my reflection in a mirror as I follow him downstairs. I might as well be naked for all this dress covers.

Humiliated and cheap. He's just fucked me for his pleasure and is now parading me in front of whomever. Anger ignites somewhere deep within me. Everything is out of my control. All my choices have been taken from me and I'm now little more than a puppet to amuse Quinn. The thought is horribly sobering.

CHAPTER THIRTEEN

Quinn

The bright lights of Chicago invade the car as we pull up, highlighting her ample cleavage and plunging neckline. I smirk, amused by her discomfort and humiliation, and then exit the car to walk over to Rody by the door. He nods his head at me, crossing his arms over his chest as I weave through the crowd queueing to get in.

"The Russians are already here," he says, "playing your tables like God gave them every right to screw us over." I chuckle at that and smooth over my tux, already knowing they will. I don't care. We make more money out of their gun running than they could ever win back from me, regardless of me handing some over to them tonight for previous runs.

Emily looks fucking ridiculous as she suddenly clambers out of the car, struggling to balance in her heels and grabbing the driver's hand for support.

"What's this?" Rody asks.

It's none of his business is what it is.

"Date."

He laughs and glances over her frame, appreciating curves he's got no right to even look at.

"Unusual for you." I'm not sure if he means the date aspect, or why I even said the word, but to have said she was a debt would have been absurd. No one takes a debt out of the four walls they're kept inside, let alone brings them to a casino. She trips over the kerb, awkwardly trying to tidy her black-sequined dress after her mistake. "She gonna keep doing that all night?"

Probably.

I frown at him as he laughs and opens the glass and gold door, inexplicably interested in her inept actions for some reason. It might just be that she fucks without care once the right mood is forced upon her, or the fact that she's nothing like anyone I've been with before.

Fuck knows.

Marco Mortoni comes into view as we walk in, his sharp demeanour owning the ten feet around him. Much as I might fucking hate it, he's good at what he does, and we've spent enough time dealing with each other now to understand our dynamics. Regardless of the past.

"Quinn," he says, nodding at me as I pull Emily into my side.

"Marco. Trying to win some of your money back?"

He laughs and walks with us, unconcerned with the wealth we continue to move between families.

"I want to talk with you."

Does he? I keep walking towards my private section, annoyed with his presence in what I'm considering downtime.

"Times are changing." I stop and look across at him, tucking Emily behind me for some fucking reason. I know they are, have done since I took over, but this is the first time Marco's mentioned it with any seriousness.

"And?"

"Mortoni's changing with it."

He looks nervous for a half second, eyes flicking around the room. *Is it fuck.* We might have discussed it before, card games and drunken talk, but the words coming from him now haven't got any damn strength.

I chuckle at him, amused that he thinks he's got any sort of power. The only way anything will organise itself into a new order is if someone knocks off the father, Joe Mortoni. By the look of him now, that killer is unlikely to be Marco, and few else would dare.

"Yeah, call me when that happens."

"I'm calling you now." I stare for a few minutes, trying to work out what the fuck he's telling me as Emily fidgets behind me. He looks around again, acknowledging the crowds. "Somewhere else?"

I shake my head, needing a stronger version of this fucker to come at me if we're going to have this conversation sober.

"Not tonight," I reply. Tonight I've got other business to deal with. Marco isn't part of it. "You know what needs to happen, Marco. That's not Cane business."

I turn and start walking, pushing Emily in the direction we're heading and dismissing the conversation. It's not something I'm discussing until we're all ready.

He's not yet.

"You need a drink to calm those nerves, dirty girl?" I eventually ask, leading her through to the lavish rooms towards the main casino.

She doesn't answer; she just tries to squash her cleavage back into position and flicks her eyes around the space. I yank her over to a corner and slap her hands away from them, exasperated with her constant jiggling and fidgeting.

"Leave yourself the fuck alone," I snarl, grasping her by

the arm and leading us around the corner to my private bar. She immediately blanches in my hand, feet tumbling over themselves again. "What the hell is wrong with you?"

"If you could just give me five minutes to compose myself. This dress is obscene and makes me look like a cheap whore, Quinn." My brows rise at the sudden venom in her voice, ready to slap her little mouth shut for it. "I'm sorry, is there a bathroom somewhere that I can—"

"You've had the entire damned journey here to prepare yourself. Behave." She gawps, eyes wide and near glaring. "You're about to meet the Russian mafia, Emily. Get yourself together or I promise you'll not like the fucking result."

I shove her onto a plush velvet seat and let go, furious with her for reasons I can't put my finger on. She aggravates me with her constant fidgeting and flustering. I'm not used to it. High-end pussy doesn't fidget. It blows and goes, the only care based on whether it did well or not. This constant twitching from her puts me on edge, regardless of my interest in it.

"Why Russian?" she asks. What?

I grab the drinks the waitress has already poured for me and then wander back over to where I left her.

"What?"

"Russian? Why not Italian, or American? And are you Mafia?"

My brows rise further, perplexed at this mouse who has suddenly dared turn into a tiger. Perhaps it's the expensive dress I've made her squeeze into.

"None of what you've asked is relevant."

I stare past her, looking through the glass wall to view the clientele for the evening. They're all the same as they usually are. Wealth resides here. Wealth and criminality. The entirety of Chicago's premium, dressed for a night of gambling and alcohol. It's the place they come to unwind or do business. I've made it that way, elevating it to more than it was before I took over. The feds know. They stalk these corners, too, an occasional try at my tables, hoping to win big and at least get some Cane money from my hands. They've got nothing else on me. Never will as long as Nate does his job properly.

"Can't you at least tell me why we're here?" No. She'll deal with whatever I throw at her tonight so I can indulge in her reaction to it.

The thought makes me flick my eyes to her cleavage again, then walk over to the window to look at the crowd by the blackjack table. Three of the Russians are at it, two of them laughing and moving their chips around.

"Regent?" she asks. I look back at her to see her fiddling with a chip she's picked up, tracing the lines of the name across the middle of it. "That's a British word. Why is an American casino called that?"

"I'm British," I reply, for some reason remembering that fact more and more since her voice has been infiltrating my ears.

"You don't sound it." Too many years living here to sound anything but American. "And what's that got to do with… Oh, you own this, too? One of your interests?"

I nod and keep staring at her fingers, wondering why she's even here. I shouldn't have brought her. None of this is what I should be doing with her. She should be at home in the basement, doing nothing but getting on all fours as and when I choose.

"You ever played a table?" I ask.

She looks up at me as I walk around in front of her, startled and still trying to organise her dress.

"No, seems that's Jenny's misfortune, not mine."

I smile at that, glad that her friend did have the stupidity to gamble herself into a debt too large to repay. It's what brought my dirty girl to me.

"Everything in life's a gamble, Emily." I offer her my hand, telling her to get up. She does, quickly, still managing to trip over nothing. "You should learn to play the odds better than you do, and trust instincts you clearly don't have yet." She frowns at me, fingers snatched away from the hold I was about to give her. "You wouldn't be here if you'd listened to your gut, would you?"

"She was my friend," she mutters.

"No, she wasn't."

She pulls in a breath, searching for a retaliation. There isn't one for her to find. Her *friend* is nothing but a falsehood. Someone who took her innocence and civility and screwed it over. Those guts of hers need hardening up so she realises life is not about flowers and graciousness. Life is fucked. You either own it, or you get screwed by it.

"You want a chance at winning that debt away from your ass?" Her eyes widen, hands finally stilling against her side.

I flick one of my dice in the air then catch it, wondering what the fuck I'm doing.

"You play a table well enough for me, and you can take your chance at freedom."

"But why would you do that?"

"Entertainment." I point out through the window. "I want to see how well that mind of yours can manoeuvre around the Russians, who are currently taking more money than I care for."

"But... I don't know how to play. I don't even know what game that is."

"Blackjack."

"What?"

I turn from her, a smile on my face as I leave the room. She follows, scrambling behind. "Quinn, wait. I can't. I don't know how."

I start reciting the rules to her as we keep moving, the words coming as quickly as they always do. I've played for so long I don't think about them anymore. It was my release when I was younger, my way of forgetting about the things Father made me do.

Now I don't give a fuck.

"A soft hand is one with at least one ace, which might still count as one or eleven points," I continue, rounding past the slots and nodding at Nate as I go. She hurries again, trying to hear my explanation over a ruckus of noise at the craps tables. "And if you get a pair, or any two ten-point cards, then you can double your bet and separate the cards into two individual hands. Split, understand?" There's a gasp from her at one point, making me swing back to see her cowering away from a man who's reached for her. I snarl at him, causing him to back off instantly and hold his hands up.

Fucking right.

Nate smirks over his shoulder, waving me off and turning back to his whore. I look at her for a minute, overdone makeup signaling her availability to any who will pay well enough, then signal the two standing behind her to follow me. They start across the floor towards me without thought, long legs gliding with perfection in every stride.

"Could you recap on surrendering?" Emily asks, coming into my eye-line, a look of determination written over her soft features. I snort, acknowledging the word for more than she means from her innocent little mouth, and then carry on weaving through the din of sound.

"You, or the Russians, forfeit half the wager, keeping the other half, and you don't play out the hand." Whore one catches up with me, her smile as false as the fingernails she latches onto me with. Emily blanches at the sight of her, a frown descending as I keep going and watch the Russians cheer at their achievement in screwing Cane. "But that option is only usable on the initial two cards in my casinos."

Whore two arrives then and gets in front of Emily, her full figure and white dress blocking her view of me. I don't care. It will be amusing to see how much tenacity she's got in obtaining her freedom. Dirty girl is about to ride out her chances, and she's getting no help from me other than the explanation I've just given.

She gently pushes through the crowd until she's in front of me again, eyes flicking between me and the table we've arrived at. The Russians cheer again, one of them finally noticing I'm here and acknowledging me with a tip of his lips.

"So, just get twenty-one, right?" Whore one laughs at her, making her blush.

"Oh, she's cute," whore two cuts in.

"The object of blackjack is not to get twenty-one, it's to beat the dealer," I eventually reply, smirking at how cute my dirty little slut is becoming. She frowns at me again, and I point at a seat a woman's just vacated. "Beat the dealer, Emily. Try your luck."

"New player," the dealer calls as Emily slides onto the

stool.

She looks at the table, barely able to touch it. Her fingers waver, and then begin fiddling with her dress again nervously. Drey Parker, the dealer, looks at me.

"One hundred," I say, smiling at the thought.

He turns to his runner, whispering the number, and twenty chips each worth five grand land in front of her before she's organised her dress. She picks one up, seeing its value, and flings her eyes back to look at me, surprise etched into every part of her face.

I nod, nothing else. This is her chance at beating this world she's stumbled into. She wins me more or she loses the lot and we carry on until I think she's worked another hundred grand off her debt.

The whores close in as I call for more drinks, ordering some strong liquor for the Russians to throw them off their game. They smile in reply and then laugh, too caught up in their own self appreciation to notice the four whores I've ordered over to help them forget how to bet.

* * *

Six hands down and Emily's beginning to lose any chance she ever had. It's fucking comical as she flusters, chips tumbling from her hands as if she's terrified of every toss. I'm not losing a damn thing. It's going back into my bank anyway, but the way she looks so lost makes my dick harden with every shuffle of the deck.

Whore one reaches for it, her fingers playing with the damn thing as she moves in front and begins rubbing her ass on me. I push her out of the way, more interested in watching my dirty girl throw her chances away than fucking bought pussy, and watch Anton slide across to her. He whispers something in her ear, showing her full view of his cards. Emily notices, nods at him, and suddenly straightens her backbone. I narrow my stare, some element of jealousy pissing me off. It's enough for me to knock whore two's hands from my shoulder and walk over to Emily.

"I'm losing," she whispers as I approach.

"You are."

It's all I've got to give her. I'm not helping her. I've got no interest in her gaining any amount of freedom from me. I'm only here because Anton's too close for fucking comfort. And it doesn't stop the fucker from invading my space again to lean into her ear. She smiles at something, another nod and then glances back at me.

"They don't like you very much," she says.

"Nobody likes me very much, dirty girl."

I stand there watching fail after fail, another ten thousand disappearing with every hand that gets drawn, her face falling further with each loss. It makes me smile wider with each one, my mind wandering through ideas of how to amuse myself with her once we're home. Maybe I won't even wait. I'll fuck her in the back room. Have some of these Russians get involved so I can watch. Give Russian roulette an entirely different meaning.

I snort, and run my hands across her shoulders, pinching them.

"Another chance gone, Emily," I say with a chuckle.

She sighs in my grip and lays out another five K chip, waiting for the next card to come.

"You're enjoying this, aren't you?"

My lips have tasted her shoulder before I've stopped myself, my fingers travelling towards her neck and tipping her chin back to me as I stand again. Enjoying it? Enjoying would denote something of relevance. She isn't, other than my money. Or she shouldn't be.

"You're an entertainment, dirty girl. Nothing more. I told you."

I flick her chin away and take a step back. She's only got twenty thousand left. It'll be over soon and I can get on with whatever I'm going to do with her. I bank left, nodding at Anton and pointing towards the back room. We're not here tonight purely for entertainment. I've got business to discuss. Like each other or not, we run money through the same countries, and I owe Anton half the last run.

"She's a peach, Cane," he says, folding his hand and pushing off the stool. "I should take her back to Russia with me, trade the old hag for her purity."

I raise a brow at his weathered features grinning and then watch her push the entire amount she has left into the table, frustration shoving the chips forwards.

"Not your usual fuck." No. Nothing is usual about my dirty girl, and I don't want this fucker anywhere near her.

"You want your money, Anton? I suggest we go to the back room."

"All business again? Do Canes ever have enjoyment these days?" No, not when there's serious money involved, especially mine. "When your father was here, we would drink vodka long into the night, fuck whores 'til they begged for mercy." I glance back at Emily, watching her fidget with her hair as her body leans forward, hoping for decent cards. She doesn't get them delivered. She loses. Game over. Her one chance gone.

"Your peach could be pleasing for the night?" I snarl and look her over, the hunch of disappointment in her shoulders written in neon fucking signs across them. "She could pay that money off without you having to hand it over to me. We all win. Yes?"

She hangs her head, elbows braced on the wood and fingers massaging her temple, the dress clinging to all the right fucking places. Another debt she pays for. Win-win. What would it matter? They take her as the debt owed rather than my money.

The thought makes me sneer, unsure if I'm enjoying the prospect, and fight my instincts back down to my guts.

"No fucking her. She's worth more than that to me."

Anton chuckles and slaps my back, the others crowding round him as he calls at them to leave their game. Emily still doesn't move. There's only the slightest shake of her shoulders showing tears I can't see. Fucking tears aren't helping her now. She just lost the only chance she had.

I nod my head at her, telling Anton he's got a deal. The resulting speed of his henchman's stride is immediate. One of her arms is grabbed, the force making her yelp in surprise and turn back to me for aid. She's not getting any. This is the world she's in now. She'll suck these three off and then we can leave when they've had their time with her.

She stumbles from the stool, the clientele around her barely noticing the chaos of her movements. They're still too busy concentrating on cards to give a fuck about her welfare, hoping to screw the house out of some of our wealth. Nothing screws this house anymore.

I turn and start walking away, following the Russians as

they drive through the crowds. Nate gets in my way, his eyes boring into mine with questions he shouldn't fucking ask. Why he thinks she's anything special to me I don't know, but he does. He's been shoving that thought into my mind since he saw her first-time round.

"You coming?" I ask, offering him some of her mouth too if he wants it. He shakes his head and steps aside, still frowning at me. He won't frown when he gets his cut of the money she's about to save us.

She's dragged after that, feet tumbling again as she goes, her head constantly looking back at me. She's scared. I know how she feels. I remember the first time I held a gun, first time I saw what my father had made us all become.

Tough. This is the real world. Shit ain't nice sometimes when you fall into the wrong part of it.

"Quinn?" she says, lips trembling around my name as they lead her through the masses.

Rody arrives in my eye-line with the bag of money in his hands, followed by another one of my men, his hands opening the doors we're all heading for. I shake my head at him as he offers it to me then watch as the other Russian grabs her arm and hauls her inside.

"No one comes in, Rody."

He closes the door behind me, the lock of it as ominous for her as anything she's ever heard. It makes me fold my hands into my pockets and wait for whatever's coming next, a smile lingering at every perverted thought I'm trying to hold at bay.

She's pushed into the middle of the room by both of the henchmen, Anton heading over to the drinks tray in the corner and pouring shots of vodka. None of them are for her. They're for us. We're celebrating another victory in screwing over the feds with our type of business.

I snort as she scrabbles around the floor, ass shuffling to try to reach a safe corner. Fuck all is safe in here. The only hope she's got is that I don't get aroused watching her suck three cocks and decide to join in. That shit won't end well for her.

"Quinn?" she pleads again, fear etched into the question, her eyes trying to lock onto mine. It causes me to study her mismatched eyes for a moment too long, making me frown at the intent in the room.

I turn away from her voice, aggravated by her ability to weaken me. Quinn isn't here. The slight part of me she manages to reach on occasion just sold her mouth for Cane money. She'll suck and take whatever these boys want, paying some of her friend's debt off as she does.

Anton comes over as the other two move towards her again, his hand offering me a shot glass.

"I'll enjoy this one, Cane."

I bet he fucking will.

I smile and take the glass, downing it and grabbing the bottle from his hand as I move to a chair.

"You've got thirty minutes, Anton. Get on with it."

He fucking chuckles again and gulps down his own drink, one hand already reaching for his belt as I sit and watch her cowering in the corner.

"I don't understand…" The rest of her sentence is halted as one of them gets his dick out and moves closer to her. Her eyes widen, heels digging at the carpet to push her further into the corner.

"Wait," Anton snaps. "The boss wants his turn first."

My hand pours a shot and tips it down my throat quickly, resentment idling in my guts. It intrigues me enough to pour another as Anton's steps get closer. The sound of them pisses me off, making me think of my mother in that fucking room all those years ago for some reason.

I snarl at myself, irritated with whatever underlying issue is getting in the way of business.

"Pretty kitten," he says, reaching for her neck and pulling her towards him.

She fights, her body trying to edge away from the hold he's got on her, nails flaring out at his face. It's stimulating to watch, stirring me up and making me question why I'm letting them at her. She's my dirty little girl. Not theirs. I could be fucking her myself, enjoying that mouth of hers.

One of the others laughs as she struggles against Anton. Their jeering and taunts piss me off as much as Anton's steps, but still I watch, another shot sinking down my throat. Business is business.

"Quinn, please," she begs, her dress riding up her thighs with her continued struggle against him. I watch him brace her back to the wall again, his dick getting closer to her mouth, and then see her snap her teeth at it before it gets there. The slap that lands on her face sends her flying to the floor.

"Bitch," he snarls, his body hauling her back up before she's got a chance to breathe from the impact. She's turned like a rag doll in his hands, like she's given up.

I sneer at her lack of battle, reminding myself of my mother's fight at me when I visit her. That's what real women do. They don't give up after one harsh command. They fight and show their venom regardless of circumstance. She might as well be nothing more than one of my whores with this show of weakness.

I check my watch, seeing the minutes tick by without one of them managing to get their dick in her mouth yet.

"Nineteen minutes, Anton," I call out as I open a button on my jacket and rest back into the seat. That's what she's got left to deal with. This might be a deal, but it's a deal I control. If she's got any intelligence about her she'll make those nineteen minutes as difficult for them as possible.

She glares at me, trapped by his hands, some element of that passion I know she's got returning. I tip my watch at her, tapping the surface of it with a smile and watch her whole body gain some rigidity at the thought.

Anton doesn't waste any more time. He tugs her into the middle of the room, little care for the fight that's beginning to come from her once more. I spin my dice, watching determination starting to inch into her features as she kicks the heels from her feet. Seventeen minutes now. I'm willing her to use them wisely. I don't know why. Perhaps it's this fucking feeling in my guts telling me something's not right here.

I catch the other two out of the corner of my eye, both stroking their dicks and getting themselves ready for my dirty girl's throat. It makes the dice slow in my palm, the tension in my fingers deliberately crushing them quietly.

"Fuck you!" she shouts, her body giving everything she's got to get away from Anton's dick pressing at her face. The other two grunt. I know why. It's the same reason my own dick's hardening beneath these expensive pants.

Fight.

We all want it. Some show of power against us. Whores yield. Real women show their disgust. They might do as they're told, but they don't do it willingly. They prove their guile.

And she's turning more vicious with every passing second. Hair flying around, nails wildly scratching at anything she can get to, another shove from Anton only seeming to heighten her instincts to battle him off again.

Russian cursing comes from his mouth, another grab at her before she counters, shocking him enough to get a chance to run. Her bare feet launch her across the room, scrambling away from his hold. She's fucking beautiful like this. Wild and untamed, the civil world leaving her as she battles for her life in the middle of this carnage she's been forced into.

"Fuck you all."

She pants out as he grabs her more harshly and pins her against the wall, more Russian pouring from his mouth. She fights again, her shoulders twisting and turning to get him off her, but it doesn't work this time. He shoves her down to the floor with such force she yells out in pain, all the time steering his dick at her again. She splutters around his cock as it's forced into her mouth. The smirk I thought would come doesn't.

I check my watch again. Eight minutes. It's eight fucking minutes I'm not giving them anymore. That one yell of pain stirred an emotion in me I didn't know I had for any woman other than my mother. Protection.

"Let her go," I snarl, feet lifting me to stand. All eyes turn to me, including hers above the dick that's pushed down her throat. Nobody moves, but Anton does eventually remove his dick from her mouth. Wise fucking choice. "Rody," I shout. He walks in, the sound of the door opening making her look towards it. I snatch the black bag from him, tossing it into the middle of the room. They want a fight about this they can fucking have one with me. I'll play all night if they want. Either that or they can zip their dicks up and take their money. "Take her home, Rody."

Anton moves a step, one set of fingers still latched onto her hair in a show of possession, the other reaching inside his jacket. "Be careful with whatever fucking thought you're having, Anton," I snap. "You sure you wanna play with me?" Rody moves closer to her, his own hand hovering around the long coat he's wearing.

I spin my dice and watch them all, unconcerned about bullets being fired in here. Nothing will happen. We all make too much money off each other for a woman to get in the way of it, regardless of how fucking edible she is.

He stares at my hand for a full minute. I feel the seconds going past, my dice spinning as they do. One turn in my palm, another, the pressure becoming less with each rotation now I know she's not sucking anyone's dick but mine.

"Have the bitch," he eventually spits, throwing her head to the floor. She scrambles back to her shoes, cornering herself again. Rody moves in tentatively and grabs her, his hands pulling her upright and moving her out of the way. I watch her go, my eyes glancing at her ripped dress as Rody pulls his coat from his shoulders and wraps it around her. "Your father was more obliging with his debts, Quinn."

I'm not my fucking father.

CHAPTER FOURTEEN

Emily

My body won't stop shaking. I sit in the passenger seat with Rody next to me, making me feel even more uncomfortable. He looks out of place, like he doesn't know what to do. At least his coat covers me.

A wave of shudders tremble through my body and I sink further back into the seat, making myself as small as possible. Tonight was a complete nightmare. I thought what Quinn had already put me through was bad enough. Serves me right for assuming the worst was behind me.

The chance he gave me might have been fleeting, but I held onto it as a sign of hope. Hope that there may be a way out of this disaster other than paying with my body. Quinn shattered that small beacon of light. His disregard for me hurt, and that was a pain I don't need to process on top of everything else.

It's clear he doesn't give a damn about the money he is owed, otherwise why would he give me more to lose? I am a possession for him to use as he sees fit. Hand me off to someone else for fun. My stomach twists and my mouth fills with saliva. I can still taste Anton in my mouth. I shudder again and close my eyes. Tears leak through my lashes, staining my cheeks.

Rody doesn't speak or move for the entire journey home. I noticed his eyes on me earlier, though. I pull his coat up to my neck, covering every square inch of me I can. I want to pretend that I'm not in this situation. Red hot anger bubbles in my stomach. It mixes with the feeling of repulsion that's been with me ever since Anton laid a hand on me. Disgust creeps through my mind and slithers into my bloodstream, making me feel as dirty as the whore they all took me for earlier.

The journey back is smooth and quiet, a small mercy from the trauma of the night, and I can feel part of my body giving up, succumbing to the need to shut down and recuperate. There was a part of me that was intrigued when we were on the way to the casino earlier. I've never been to America, and I couldn't help but peek out the window at the lights and silhouettes of buildings as we travelled. Now, I want to barricade myself in 'my room' and never leave.

The car pulls to a halt, and I barge open the door, tripping over the end of my dress as I exit the car.

"Here." Rody offers his hand to help me, but I just ignore him and clamber to my feet. My heels sink into the gravelled driveway, but I find my balance and march to the front door. I can't help but notice the house as I approach.

It's elegant and modern, all large windows and clean lines. I push the distraction away and grab the door handle. It's locked. "Arghhh!" I scream, the frustration pouring out of me. I've come up against door after door that are locked, and I've had enough.

Two men in dark uniforms round the corner of the house at my outburst.

"All's clear, guys. False alarm." Rody dismisses them. Quinn's security really do patrol the property. Rody punches some numbers into a keypad to the side of the door and then puts a keycard into the door to open it.

I kick my stupid heels off and fling them into the lounge before I storm through the kitchen and up the stairs. My door isn't locked, and my fist slams the door as loud as possible before I let out a wailing scream and collapse in a heap on the floor.

The emotions from this evening vent, but it's not enough. I rip the dress from my skin and run for the shower. Hysteria creeps in as I scrub every part of my body. The spray immerses me until my fingers have pruned and I'm numb. I take the toothbrush from the counter and brush my teeth until my gums bleed, spitting blood into the white sink.

My breathing begins to still, the adrenalin from my outburst diminished. I crawl into bed and wrap myself in the sheets.

If I could take a pill to block my thoughts, I'd happily down it right now. My mind is determined to play over the evening's events. The scandalous dress Quinn made me wear, the chance at freedom that wasn't even a real chance, and finally, the Russians.

And to top everything off is my confusion over how I reacted to Anton, versus my reactions to Quinn.

I fought Anton, kicking out and resisting him as much as I could. I wouldn't have given in to them, no matter how tired or how much pain I was in. That wasn't the same as when Quinn came into the room. Sure, I protested. I didn't want to do anything he told me, but there was something at the back of my mind that allowed me to give in to him. His behaviour warps my mind. First, he romances me, then kidnaps me, then offers me up to pay his debt.

My eyes squeeze closed and more tears stain my cheeks. I curl up on myself, fighting the chill that comes with the realisation that I've allowed Quinn to treat me like a whore, but no one else.

I long to be home, in my house, in my own bed where monsters and gangsters don't exist. I want to go back to my business, capture smiling families and happy couples and not have nightmares about dark spaces or men who take without asking.

He'll be back soon. Maybe then I'll kick and scream and fight with all my strength, and he'll give up. I dry my eyes on the pillow, unashamed of the salt and snot now on his expensive sheets. Deep breaths. That's what I need, but the few classes of yoga I took years ago don't help my quest to find some semblance of calm. My breathing starts to speed up, and the hysteria I've been balancing on the edge of threatens to pull me under again.

My minds pulls the page of sheet music from my concert, and I murmur the first few bars. The notes get stronger and louder, and it immediately calms me. My lungs fill with air, and I sing the complicated Bernstein piece.

Time blurs along with the notes from my mind. The tune becomes a hum, or my own strange kind of lullaby. My eyes drift closed and sleep whispers at the corners of my brain.

The click of the door breaks my concentration, and I silence my voice. I lay as still as possible, listening for the footfalls of Quinn. A sudden bolt of panic runs through me that it might not be him. How would I know if he's even home? The panic simmers in my chest as I strain to hear anything, but all there is is silence. The faint smell of Quinn's fresh aftershave reaches me as I regulate my frantic breaths. It is him. Relief and dread wash over me as I admit to myself that I'm glad it's him over Rody or some other man he wants to pay his debt to.

I wait. For his voice, for his hand snatching me out of bed. Nothing. It's unnerving.

And then the edge of the bed dips. My heart pounds and every muscle in my body tenses, ready to fight. All I can hear is my pumping heart beating loud and steady in my chest.

Warm infuses through my skin as Quinn slides up against me. I push off, ready to run, but his arm clamps around me like an iron girder.

"Shhh," is all he says.

His body is warm and offers comfort. I'm like a block of ice, unable to move. He doesn't shift his arm or try to move me. He simply lets me be, warm and…protected in his grasp.

Exhaustion hits me, and where my eyes were sore and tired, they are now heavy, like they've been holding up the whole world. They drift shut, despite the situation, and darkness claims me.

***

The morning comes far too soon, forcing me to consciousness. I immediately scramble up in bed and look around the room. I'm alone. Everything is where I left it last night. My dress is discarded on the floor between the bed and the bathroom. No sign of Quinn.

My heart rate levels out and I ease back into the warmth of the covers. My stomach gives a loud grumble, and reminds me that I've not eaten properly for days.

I head to the bathroom before looking for something

to wear that covers some skin. Hanging on the side of the wardrobe is a cream coloured jumper. On the chair next to it, a neatly folded pair of black leggings. An interesting choice, given the last outfit I was asked to wear. Still no damn underwear.

I put my new clothes on and go to face the door. I refuse to get my hopes up because if it is open, it will give me a new dilemma. My hand encompasses the handle and eases it down. The latch clicks and the door jolts open.

Before I move a muscle, I listen. Is this a trap? Is Quinn waiting for me to try to escape? All I hear is muffled talking, and it sounds like it's coming from downstairs. I swing the door wide and find the top of the stairs empty. The smell of something sweet, and possibly toast, invades my nose and focuses my mind. I creep down the stairs and wait at the bottom, gathering the courage needed to face whoever is in the kitchen. I can hear Quinn's voice now, that low rumble he has that turned me to mush the first time we met. There are two other voices, and I guess that his brothers are back.

With my head held high, I turn into the kitchen and take sure but small steps into view.

"Em, how nice of you to join us. Come over. I saved you a seat." Josh beckons me over to the table and the empty seat next to him. Quinn's eyes flash daggers at his brother, a glare accompanying them. "What? There's plenty of food. Besides, we don't want her wasting away. Needs to keep her energy up. Otherwise there's no fun." Josh smiles at me, a full-blown Hollywood smile. On anyone else, it would be a stunning smile. A handsome man who could bed any woman he chooses. But there's something behind his eyes. A darker, murkier side of him. It's the same reaction I had to him at the first meeting. I wanted to shrink away from him and all of his questions last time we met. The charm he flashed wasn't enough to calm my destroyed nerves.

Instead of taking a seat next to him, I walk around the table and sit as far away from all of them as possible.

The other brother, Nate, chuckles as he gulps from his mug of coffee. Quinn isn't sitting down. He's lurking around the kitchen, constantly moving. I keep my eyes focused on him, wondering if he's going to punish me for daring to move from my room.

An assortment of delicious breakfast treats fills the table. A stack of waffles in the middle has me reaching for one before I consider asking permission. I bite the sticky treat, letting the sugary goodness dissolve in my mouth. It's all I can do not to moan around the mouthful.

I devour the waffle and take another before I reach for the jug of orange juice and pour myself a glass. The conversation between the brothers has stopped, all three of them now showing me all their attention. If I weren't starving, I'd be worried, but I block out their gazes and continue eating.

"Our girl has an appetite." Josh leans back and runs his eyes over me.

"She's not *our* girl. She's mine," Quinn spits, scowling at Josh, but he doesn't shift from the kitchen.

"Ignore them. I'm sure you've not had a lot of food," Nate whispers towards me, encouraging me to keep eating. His lips twitch into a sort of smile.

Quinn hovers, glowering at Josh and seeming to ignore me. I carry on eating, happy to have something tasty in my stomach.

"This is why you're not in my business, Josh. Your lack of

awareness proves that you have no place getting involved."

"It's not your fucking business, Quinn. My name is Cane, too."

Quinn snorts, his feet moving toward Josh. "When you start acting like a Cane, I'll treat you like one."

"What, like you? You're such a fucking role model."

"Guys…" Nate starts, but a swift look from Quinn soon stops the rest of his sentence. All their eyes then shift to me as if I'm interfering with some family debate.

"Em doesn't mind a little banter. She's not here to pay attention. She's here to get fucked. Pay off her debt." Josh stands up, throwing his chair back as the words leave his mouth. I freeze, my body now on red alert.

"Josh, watch it." Nate looks disgusted at him.

"Hey, Josh." He turns to look at Quinn, not seeing the hard-right punch squarely aimed at his jaw before it's too late. I gasp, surprised at the action. "I told you," Quinn growls. "My debt. Fuck all to do with you." He grabs Josh by his collar and drags him out through the kitchen.

He comes back a moment later without his brother.

"Eat your food, Emily," he admonishes me. "Nate, I want to review the figures we have after the Russian job. I want them watertight."

Quinn and Nate start some small talk about business, the altercation with Josh forgotten about. All money and accounts. I don't track it all, but it's clear that Quinn's business dealings aren't all above board. Nate keeps half an eye on me throughout. He offers me tea, and his presence begins to settle me.

Quinn doesn't say anything else to me. He just frowns and scowls, all the time looking ready to punch someone else. He keeps clenching his right hand, the knuckles a little red from hitting Josh.

"You might want to put some ice on that," I offer.

He looks at me with a puzzled expression. Our eyes fix on each other, and for a moment I see the man who I first met, everything else slipping away. I'm caught between wanting to go back to Friday night and re-live it all over again—the carefree excitement, the danger, the sheer daring of sleeping with someone on a first date and wanting it again—and wishing I never met Quinn.

"Ice is in the freezer." Quinn gestures to the appliance in the corner and looks at me expectantly.

I look at Nate, who just does his little non-smile thing, then go to the kitchen and take a cloth hanging on the cooker to lay it out ready for ice. The fridge freezer is ginormous. How Quinn has enough food to fill it is beyond me. I tug open the door and cool air blasts me. It turns out his freezer has little but ice, vodka and a few pizzas. I take the bag of ice and shake a few cubes free.

"Here." I take the seat next to Quinn and place the makeshift ice pack on his hand. He looks at me, staring deep into my eyes as the coolness seeps into his damaged hand. I press my hand on top, making sure it doesn't slip. In that moment, I want to ease his pain. It's an absurd thought. I should be gouging his eyes out, not wanting to help him. But a calmness descends, easing the tension that's been rife between us. His eyes study me, as if he's taking mental notes of every freckle, every blemish on my face. The intensity of his eyes reminds me of our first date. They held such secrets then. Such promise of what could be to come.

He smiles for the briefest of moments, and I'm stunned,

like I was on our date, at how handsome he is. "Thank you," he says, his hand covering mine.

"You're welcome." I let go of the ice, my fingers slipping from under his, and retreat to the seat next to Nate. Quinn's brows pull down into a scowl, transforming him into the man who's terrorised me for the last…how long is it? "What day is it?"

"What day? Thursday."

My eyes widen, and I pick at the waffle left on my plate. How has it nearly been a week? I look around the room, panic blooming in my chest. Someone will be missing me, won't they? I can't just vanish for a week.

"You need some more clothes."

"Excuse me?"

"Do you want to wear leggings and a jumper every day?" Quinn counters as he stands, keeping the ice wrap on his hand.

"No. Clothes would be good. And underwear."

"Don't push it, Emily."

"Give her a break, Quinn."

"Not your business, Nate. In fact, we're done. Email me the figures, and I'll review them. We can look at the casino accounts tomorrow. I want a full analysis of wastage against the other operating models."

"You got it."

Nate stands and shoves his phone into his pocket. "Don't forget to stand up for yourself. Chin up," he whispers before leaving.

I wait for Quinn to say something, anything to give me a read on his mood. It seems off. Or at least it's off compared to what I've seen of him. "Do you want me for—"

"Shhh. Don't speak," he scolds. I pull my knees up to my

chest and wrap my arms around them. Quinn's mood swings are impossible to follow. It adds to the confusion pickling my brain. I yo-yo from being scared, interested, turned on, repulsed, ashamed, and back to attracted to Quinn, in the space of a minute.

"I'm going to check on something."

"Okay," I whisper, unsure if I should stay where I am, see this as an opportunity, or be disappointed he's leaving.

"I'll be back, and then we might go out."

"Out?" Fear sobers my mind as I recount the last time Quinn wanted me to leave the property. Out implies something I won't like, something that makes me nervous. I'd rather stay here than have that happen again.

"Just us this time. Don't go anywhere, Emily. I'll know if you try something."

CHAPTER FIFTEEN

Quinn

Fresh, cold air hits me as I walk for the main house, bringing my brain back from the fog she's induced. I glare at the structure, for some reason annoyed with its possessive hold on me. I shouldn't be, but something about Emily's fingers under mine makes these grounds feel as insidious and underhanded as they really are.

Nothing here is owned from real achievement, not like she does with her little business. We took it. My father did. He took this place as a repayment, just like I still take what is owed to us now. We have always taken. We scheme and coerce, forcing debts to be honoured in whatever way I now see fit. It's still as it has always been, but now, walking across this path to get to the only woman I should give a fuck about, it feels uncomfortable.

It started last night when I found her crying in her fitful sleep, tears proving a test I've never felt before. They looked so pretty on her as she lay in that bed. They had a grace about them that doesn't belong here. They weren't tears of fear or recrimination for a stupidity that brought her here; they were from confusion. And rather than that fact, amuse me and make me play with her again, it distracted me. Enough so that I laid down beside her for a while and let her drift deeper into sleep.

An hour of dealing with Russian tantrums and two

fucking guns aimed at me should have been enough to wind me into a frenzy. It should have left me desperate to fuck deep into her and rid myself of the angst. It didn't. It made me feel something other than hatred, and that unusual sensation sent me straight to my bar for clarity.

None came.

The gravel crunches underfoot as I join the main drive and look up at my mother's room. She's up there, one hand stroking the curtain she's tidying. She doesn't see me. No eye contact. No acknowledgement for her boy. She just keeps fucking about with the material in her other world. I snort, wondering if Emily feels like she's in another world. She is, one she doesn't belong in. That fact was proved by my reaction to the Russians last night. The same reaction that just made me hit my own brother for daring to open his mouth in front of her, let alone being so familiar with her name by shortening it.

"Mr Cane?" I look to the right, noting Maria as she scurries to my side, alarm all over her face. "Your brother took your car." I raise a brow at her then look behind me at the drive to see both mine and Nate's cars gone, Josh's still sitting there. "We tried to stop him but he—"

I wave her off and move towards the house again, a slight huff at the thought of him trashing my car coming from my lips. I don't care. Perhaps I should, would have a week ago, but not now. Now I'm too busy trying to understand this feeling inside me, find some order in it. Some part of me might even admire his little attempt at retribution if I bother thinking about it. It shows more backbone than I give him credit for. He is our father's son after all.

I stride through the hall, heading for the only comfort I've ever known. She won't be there for any real sense of sanity, but she's more genuine in some respects than any of the world around me. She's the last honest, decent thing that lives here. It's inevitable that the one time I need her guidance she'll be elsewhere, but for once I'm hoping for some lucidity to come from her mouth.

The stairs take seconds, and before I've fully thought the words through I knock briefly and enter her room, the lock snapping back into place the moment I close the door.

She spins, venomous eyes raking over my frame, her hand reaching for a vase to her left.

"Mother?"

Her whole body softens, eyes suddenly becoming those of the woman who used to sing me to sleep.

"Quinn, baby. Look at you." Her fingers leave the vase then, returning to her side as she walks forward a few paces. "Still so handsome. When did you grow up to be so big?" I smile back, watching as she finds that elegance she's always possessed. "Quinn looks sad," she says, the trail of her long red evening gown dragging the carpet. "What's the matter? Tell mummy. I'm going out soon. You need a lullaby before bed?"

"No, Mother."

"And you're not even in your pyjamas yet. Your father will be grumpy." I couldn't give one fuck how grumpy my father is, or has ever been. Still, this mood is useable.

She moves off to the side, reaching for her shawl and a bag. I stare for a while, a smile on my face as she prepares for one of her imaginary nights out.

"Where to tonight, Mother?"

"The ballet," she muses, her feet swaying from side to

side. "You know how I love the ballet. We're flying to New York. Maria will look after the three of you for a few days." She wanders over to the long mirror, her fingers setting her diamond drop earrings in place as she gazes at her outfit. "It's our anniversary. Your father always treats me to special dates when it's an important night." I sneer at the thought, remembering those other nights when he fucked the entirety of Chicago for fun. "Dates keep the romance alive, Quinn. Without romance there's nothing to fight for. It all becomes pointless if the fun goes out of a relationship." She drapes her gold shawl, straightening the matching diamond necklace beneath it. "You'll understand one day when you're old enough to fall in love." She smiles at her finished effort and pats her hair, pushing the curls into place softly. "Love, Quinn," she says, her head spinning back to me, "Is the only thing worth fighting for."

I stare with little appreciation for whatever world she's currently in. Love has been irrelevant to me for so long I can't remember the feeling in any way.

"How did you know with Father?" She frowns at me, her eyes glazing slightly as she tries to understand my question. "That it was love, Mother."

"Oh, silly boy." She walks over and takes my hand, leading me to her bedroom. "You want to sleep in our bed tonight?" I shake my head, but she keeps pulling me to the four-poster until she sits on the comforter and pats the bed next to her. "You just know, Quinn. Love changes what you thought you knew. It's not like the love for Mummy and Daddy." She strokes my head, her nails scratching slightly as she tugs me down to her chest. "It's a beautiful feeling. You'll give everything for it one day. You change when the right one comes along."

There's quiet for a few minutes, nothing but the sound of her room and our breaths. It makes me remember a time when I wasn't so hardened. Playful fights with two younger brothers. The smell of pancakes in the kitchen, both of those thoughts based in the English countryside where we used to live before this became our life.

The sudden ripping sensation that rakes at my scalp makes me grit my teeth, fists clenching before they do damage to the woman causing the pain. She turns me away from her, nails digging into the flesh on my neck as she yanks at me and then kicks out, screams breaking the quiet of a few seconds ago. My head lolls back, a sigh coming from me as I let myself take the brunt of her anger. She kicks again, her heel making contact with my shin, and then her weight's gone. I look up, searching the room for her and find her at the other side of it, a book in her hand ready to attack me with it.

"You're after more, aren't you?" she spits, a scowl marring the reposed elegance of minutes ago, shawl hanging from her shoulder. She reaches for another book, one in each hand. "You've done enough, taken enough. My family's fucking debt is paid."

My eyes drop to the carpet. Debt paid.

Because of love.

"Mother?"

"Get the fuck out. Why can't you leave me alone now? Why? I want to go home."

"Please, Mother, calm down."

"Fuck you and your family. You've had your fun. Let me go home to my boys." The thought sickens me, my eyes trying to stay on the carpet rather than acknowledge her body for what it became. She stares, wild eyed, her chin still held high as she prepares for more men. "My family owes you nothing anymore."

I take a step backward at that, and then another, my hands up in the air in some offering of contrition. She glares, books still poised and ready to launch at me.

"It's alright, Mother. I'm leaving."

She spits, the phlegm dribbling from her chin as she braves a step towards me and throws one of the books. I dodge it, wondering if I should or not. Perhaps a good attack at me would do her good, get the angst out, and calm her down. And then as quickly as the venom came, she looks like a lost soul again, her eyes beginning to temper and return to a calmer self.

"Quinn?" I stop, lowering my hands back into my pockets. "Why are you here? You should be in bed, young man." She flicks her gaze to the book in her hand and smiles. "Did you bring this? Such a loving boy. You've always been like your father. Let's read it, shall we?" She wanders to the bed, straightening her shawl again. "Quickly, come on. He'll be here soon to pick me up. We're going to the ballet." My feet back away slowly, a sneer etched onto my mouth as I watch her settle on the bed, until I turn and head for the door.

I'm nothing like my father.

The lock clicks behind me and I look along the landing, following the lines of the walls that lead to his room. I could go and show him how much I'm not like him, finish the fucker. The gun under this suit gives as few fucks for his existence as I do. There are no qualms here, barely any sense of loyalty to him anymore. There are only four members of this family as far as I'm concerned. His relevance to my thoughts has become nothing but bitter memories of a man who dropped his guard so badly that my mother, his wife, had to pay the price.

My gaze drops to the balcony and stairs, the lavish decoration highlighting the money this family has achieved with its constant corruption and dishonesty.

It tips my lips, a true smile coming with the thought of how solid we now are, because of me. Nothing can touch us. No enemies I haven't got covered. No threat. No need for any retribution or repayment of debts.

I pull in a breath and listen to the sudden scream and thud of flesh against wood behind me, my mother's body trying to break through the wood encasing her insanity. Nothing will do that to us again. There's nothing coming for me that I'm not ten steps ahead of. I'm in control of everything that my father couldn't govern. I was within a year of taking over. We're safe now. Contained. Able to breathe a little more calmly than we did back then.

Firm strides lead me away from him, narrowed eyes finally leaving the landing as I reach the bottom steps and head for the entrance hall. I pass Maria as I go and nod her upstairs to my mother. Not that she needs to be told. She's always there, protecting her from self harm.

For now, though, regardless of the state I've left her in, it's time to leave this godforsaken heap and live my life for a while. Try to understand this sentiment Emily brings out of me. Use it maybe. It's confusing to me, bringing a sense of discord to what is normally so simplistic. Numbers and death. Charts and money. And yet, with her around, I'm slowly feeling trapped in unclear territory, as if the feds are on my ass for something they've got over my head. They haven't got anything on me. They've got nothing on any of us, but that's the feeling that's tainting the clear air I walk out into.

I stare at Josh's car, considering why Emily affects me in ways she shouldn't. She's just another woman. Just another pussy to delve into. But the way she held that ice on my hand, the way my own hand touched hers was fuck all to do with pussy. That's emotion and interest in something that does not belong in my world.

Minutes pass and I find myself pressing the Lamborghini's lock, the door rising upwards in front of my eyes. I don't know what I'm doing, but Mother said romance was important, that I'd know love when it hit me.

Maybe that's what this is. It's not fucking wanted. She should stay locked in that house, be sent back to England even. Women like Emily don't belong here, irrespective of my need for those innocent eyes to connect with mine.

The engine revs, the purr of it reminding me of youth and unencumbered thoughts before I became head of this enterprise. I stare at the main house then flick my gaze down the drive towards mine. I can smell her in there, even from here, see her as she wanders aimlessly. Confused and alone. It makes me spin the wheel, purposely focused on getting the fuck out of here for a while, and hit the accelerator so hard gravels flies out behind me. I snort, amused at my childish actions. Fuck. Where the fuck am I going? I'm Quinn Cane for fuck's sake. And what? This woman is controlling how I act? Screw that.

I floor the damn car back in her direction, both irritated and elated at the thought of taking her with me. I don't know where to. Who gives a fuck? We'll just go on one of those dates Mother talks so fondly of. She can take some fucking photos or some shit. *Smile.*

The brakes slam on and the car rakes the gravel up again, the slide of the back wheels landing me precisely where I aimed for. I'm out and barging through the front door before I've thought rationally about anything.

"Emily?" I shout, not seeing her anywhere. She rounds a corner in front of me, the cream jumper and leggings making her appear cute for a reason I choose not to think about. "We're going out."

She stops, her eyes widening as I march over to her and grab her by the arm, dragging her back out and towards the car.

"Out? But I haven't got any shoes on. I'm barely dressed, Quinn." I couldn't give one fuck about shoes. We'll get some while we're out.

I shove her towards the car then round to the other side to get in myself. I'll take her somewhere to get some shoes, and a coat. Whatever the fuck she needs, we'll get later.

There's silence as the car screams out of the drive, more dust flying into the air. It's the most irrational behaviour I've ever given in to. It makes me feel like I'm seventeen again, a smile tipping the corner of my mouth as we head out onto the freeway and I rev the damn thing faster.

She doesn't speak. There's nothing but the occasional gasp, her fingers clinging on to the seat as if we're about to crash any second. We might. For once I don't give a fuck. I'm out of control, barely giving any thought to my priorities as we speed faster towards Chicago.

"Where are we going?" she eventually braves, one hand now clinging to the seat-belt.

"Out."

It's all I've got. I don't know where, and the skyline coming into view doesn't help me offer her any clarity. Boots and a coat first, then we'll walk the riverwalk. Grab a coffee. Talk, maybe. She must be going mad holed up in my house permanently and it'll do me good to get some fresh air away from the grounds. That's it as far as I'm concerned. No plans. No procedures. No looking over my shoulder and negotiating the next move, concerned for the fate of my family. We'll just be alive for the day, see where that shit takes us.

We pull up outside a boutique on Oak Street, and I barely offer her time to breathe before getting her out and marching her inside. A startled woman looks her over, her manicured appearance disgusted with what I'm presenting.

"Boots, coat, scarf and hat," I snap, not caring for a conversation about Emily's unkempt appearance. She's got more about her than this bitch could ever offer.

She raises a brow at me and wanders off, seemingly irritated with my invasion into her sanctuary of calm, but returns with a selection of upper class garments. Emily's eyes brighten, but she's nervous, unsure. I can tell by the way she's fucking fiddling with her sweater. I nod at her, giving her the confirmation she needs to take a closer look at the sophisticated clothes on offer. She reaches for the cream coat, taking it from the bitch's hands. Fine. I throw my card at the woman, amused as she tries to catch it.

"Get dressed, Emily," I say, still watching the uptight bitch frown at Emily. Fuck her.

When the debacle has righted itself and I've had fuck knows how much money taken from me, I turn to see Emily staring out of the shop window. It's a picture in itself. One I would have drawn myself years ago. High collar, a blue scarf wrapped around her neck, a slouched beanie at an angle, and heeled boots that make me lick my lips and imagine no clothing at all.

"You ready?" I ask, coming up behind her.

She turns, a warm smile coming from her as she nods out the window.

"It's huge out there. Chicago, I mean." I smirk at her, wondering where the hell she thought she was. Everything here is huge. "I've never been to America. I don't know what I thought, but it's real. It was dark last time we came in. I couldn't see the scale of everything." I open the door, my hand waving her through as I snatch at a pair of leather gloves on the counter beside me.

"Sir, you can't…"

"Sue me," I mutter back, more interested in the ass that's walking back to the car as I slam the door and quicken to catch up. "No, we're walking from here," I say, grabbing her and turning her in the other direction. She flinches in my hold, a confused look marring her smile of moments ago.

"You don't have to grab me all the time. I'll follow you, Quinn." I ease my fingers, suddenly realising their constant grip on her. "It's not like I can go anywhere without you, is it?" I chuckle at that and look along the street, still wondering what the fuck I'm doing here. "So, where are we going?" I don't know, but I want her next to me as we go there.

I start walking, winding my way through the crowds of shoppers, and turn my head to look back at her. She's staring upwards, her body bumping into everything she's not looking at. It makes me growl and reach back for her hand, pulling her closer to me as I head to the coffee shop in the square.

"The light," she says. "Look at it, Quinn. It's amazing.

The glass reflects it beautifully."

I don't look. I keep hauling her ass through the people, occasionally frowning at someone who barges into her because she's still not looking where she's damn well going.

"Emily," I snap, watching her feet tripping over themselves for the tenth time. She gasps, the sudden realisation that she's lost her balance catching up with her, loose arm flailing. I snatch her to me, levering her from the pavement before she hits it fully. "Jesus, woman. Your mother never teach you to walk?"

She pants in my hold, her lips inches from mine as I stare into those different coloured eyes of hers.

"Not … not in these heels," she says, the words fluttering softly from her lips. I look at them, barely restraining the need to kiss them and forget Anton's cock buried inside them. They're my lips now. Nothing else is going anywhere near them. Not one other thing but me and my body will touch those dirty, beautiful, full, soft lips again. My tongue licks my own, remembering the gagging sound she makes when I'm balls-deep in her mouth, the way she whimpers as I tighten my hands on her, then moans my name. "You can let go now," she says quietly.

The sound of her brings me back to the present. I shake my head, amused at my mind wanderings, and then search the area.

She's sitting on a bench within seconds, pressed onto it by my hands.

"Don't run, Emily. I'm warning you. Chicago's not nice to pretty things who don't know what they're doing." She frowns for a second then nods, but she's got that look of tenacity that comes every now and then, the same one that came when she fought the Russians off. "I'm serious, Em. You sit here and wait for me. I'll be back in a minute or two. You run and I'll find you. The result won't be nice."

She smiles. I don't know why, but her second nod gives me more assurance that she's understood me. I back off, all the time watching her as she watches me, until I finally trust her not to run and turn into the crowds. She'd be stupid to try it anyway. Where can she go? She's got no money, no hope other than what I offer her.

The only way she's ever getting home is if I release her, and, at the moment, that's not happening any time soon.

CHAPTER SIXTEEN

Emily

I watch as Quinn mingles between passers-by and gets lost in the crowd. I could do it. Run. Or at least try to escape. He wouldn't be able to find me quick enough to stop me reaching the police. Or would he?

He's been all over the place the last couple of days. I don't even know how to start understanding his behaviour or his mood. I snuggle further into my coat, the soft material of the scarf cutting down the chill. One minute I'm a possession for him to use and disregard as he pleases, then next he's comforting me. Although, whether comfort was Quinn's intention, I'm not sure.

My head feels scrambled. There's a connection between us, an almost invisible line that pulls us together. My body wants one thing, but my sanity implores me to see sense and understand that this will never end well.

My eyes gaze at the tall buildings lining the river. It's more beautiful than I thought Chicago would be. The sun is bright, and the blue sky could be that of a summer day, rather than the start of winter.

I stand up, a sudden rush of courage telling me I need to try everything in my power to escape, but it's fleeting. What can I do? What options do I have? No passport, no money or credit cards. Will anyone believe me? Or will they think I entered the country illegally and lock me in a cell for the next however long?

My knees bend and I sit back down. Maybe staying with Quinn for a few more days is the right decision. I can talk to him, make him see that taking me home is the right thing to do.

"Here." A cup of steaming coffee is thrust into my hands.

"Thank you." I clutch it and wait for Quinn to sit.

"I also got you this." He pulls a box out of a bag. A box with a picture of a Canon EOS 5D on the front. My lips spread across my face and a jolt of joy warms me from the inside out.

"Quinn, this is…" I'm not sure what to say, that edge of confusion chipping away at my initial excitement. What does this mean? More money on my debt.

"It's something to keep you occupied. You've been held up at home too long. Take some photos."

"It's very generous considering I'm working off a debt to you. Can't I give the gifts back and take it from my total?" I know it's unkind not to be grateful, but I don't think those rules apply when talking to your kidnapper.

A scowl crosses his face, and I regret my words. I should be thankful that Quinn was looking to try to ease my comfort.

"It's a gift, not a fucking negotiation."

I nod and fumble with the box, trying to open it with my gloves on. Quinn snatches it away and opens it, pulling out the camera.

"Wait, won't it need charging?"

"It's covered." He doesn't do anything else but hand me the camera. I flick the on button and see it's already set up.

"Thank you. I didn't mean to be ungrateful. But it's very confusing. One minute you're giving me to someone else, the next you're giving me gifts."

Another set of frown lines rivet his forehead.

"Come on. We're going to walk." He stands and shoves the bag and box into a nearby bin.

I put the camera strap over my head and pick up my cup of coffee. If I look around and force my mind to cooperate, I could be on another date.

"I'm glad you didn't run. I wouldn't have liked having to track you down."

"Okay."

"Take pictures. Do what you'd normally do. Entertain me."

I sip my coffee and hand him the cup to hold before I line up a couple of shots. It's awkward, like he's assessing me for something, but this is the first taste of normality in the longest week of my life. I can't give it up.

Ten minutes later, I'm in my element. Quinn doesn't hurry me or move me along. He just stands and watches as I do something I love. And that love infuses every cell of my body, building a small wall against anything else that can happen to me here. Quinn wants me to have this. He can't be the monster he's making out if he then gives me something that offers me such joy. It also proves he was listening on our original date, and not just planning to terrorise me.

I turn around and try to take a photo of Quinn, but he gives me a look that would stop anyone in their tracks. I walk the few feet back to him and take my lukewarm coffee rather than pushing the issue.

"Can we find somewhere to sit down? My feet aren't going to last in these heels."

"You should get used to walking in heels. I like you in

them."

The flush on my cheeks is unexpected. After everything he's done to my body, a simple compliment makes me blush. "Here." I gesture to another bench dotted along the edge of the river. I don't wait and go and sit.

"Are you close to your brothers, and please don't keep looking at me like I've said something horrendous? I'm trying to make conversation. Whatever this is we're doing, it was your plan." I'm pleased that my voice shows no sign of intimidation.

"Fine. Yes, I guess we are close. To a degree. Nate yes, as he works for me, but Josh, less so."

"Nate seems… nice."

"Nice? What the hell makes you think he's nice?" He chuckles and looks bemused. "There's nothing nice about any of us."

"Well, he didn't like you calling me dirty girl, and he wanted me to eat. So..."

"And that's enough, is it?" He shakes his head and stares away for a few moments, looking into the distance. "You *like* me calling you dirty girl. That's all that should matter." He leans back to me, mouth hovering around my ear. "Gets you wet for more of me inside you." He snorts at my frown, then turns away, back to the view. "Nate might be the more decent of the two of us, but it doesn't stop him having his fun with his whores, Emily. Make no mistake. He's the same breed as I am."

"And what about Josh?"

"Josh is little more than a spoilt child with a big bank balance."

"But he's different than you two. He makes me feel

uncomfortable in a way that you and Nate don't."

"Well, at least some of your senses are working." He holds out his hand for me, and I take it. "Come on." My hand settles in his grasp, and an odd feeling of security washes through me. I know how dangerous Quinn must be. If he wanted something truly terrible to happen to me, he would have done that already. He wouldn't be here with me now. It's the shred of comfort that keeps my sanity in check.

"Were you always like this?"

"Define this? This tall, this handsome, this charming?" He offers me a genuine smile, and I'm reminded of how attractive he is, his flawless face, except for that small scar on his chin. His smile blinded all of my senses once. It does it again, making me giggle at his playfulness.

"No, that must be in your genes. I mean a gangster. Is that what they call you? I'm not sure, but from what I've seen that's what I'd call you."

"I told you, I'm a businessman."

"Yes, but your business doesn't seem to be all that legal."

"Owning casinos isn't against the law."

"Yes, but you introduced me to the Russian Mafia. I'm pretty sure working with them is. You kidnapped me, for god's sake."

He squeezes my hand at that remark, a shot of pain racing up my arm.

"Keep your voice down. I am not a gangster. We're not in the 1940s."

"How did you get your scar?"

"What's with all the damn questions?"

"Conversation," I reply, waiting for a response from him. He scowls and looks out at the river, refusing to answer.

"Okay. I'm sorry."

I can't help the pang of disappointment. If I know Quinn, maybe I can rationalise some of his behaviour. Understand why I react to him in the way that I do.

We continue down the path for a little longer, my hand still in his. The ache in the balls of my feet starts to throb and the enjoyment of the outing fades.

"The scar was the start of it. My introduction into Cane life," he suddenly says. My brows shoot up, wondering why he's changed his mind.

"What do you mean?"

"It's evidence of my first kill. He came at me from behind."

"Who?"

"The man my father sent me to finish." He chuckles at my wide eyes. "We don't live in the world you do, Emily. Haven't done for a long time."

"You let your father push you around then?" He scowls again, huffing at the question and leading us over to the rails overlooking the river.

"Not pushed around." He leans over the rail, looking out across the expanse of water. "It was expected of me, Em. It became my job." I gaze at him, wondering what that life must have been like. "If it wasn't me, it would have fallen to Nate or Josh."

"So you did it to protect them from this life?" He doesn't answer that. He sighs. "So they didn't have to do what you do?"

My eyes scan his face as I wait for an answer, desperate for him to show me more of him. As if drawn like a magnet, my fingers come up to trace the line of his jaw and his scar.

Such a little mark, but I now know the significance of it. His stubble scratches on the pad of my thumb as I rub against it.

"What are you doing?" he asks, snatching my hand away and grabbing my wrist.

"Trying to get to know you. You're hard to understand, Quinn, and I need to try and figure this all out."

"There's nothing to work out. You're here for my amusement. That's all."

Every time he says something like that, it crushes the bubble of hope I've been building.

"If that's true, what's the point of all this?" I hold up the camera with my free arm. "Huh? You gave me something that has given me happiness. You've spent thousands of pounds on me even though I'm supposed to be paying you back. Help me understand, Quinn."

"Dollars."

"Excuse me?"

"Dollars. I spent dollars." He lets my arm go and looks back out over the river.

Frustration burns through me, extinguishing the joy from a few moments ago.

"You are a constant contradiction, you know that? You threaten and intimidate, but then your actions betray you. I can feel this between us." I gesture between us, hoping to make my point clear. "It's not in my imagination. You know it isn't. And I think you're taking your anger at that out on me."

He pushes off the rail, but I don't get an answer.

"Come on, Quinn. I'm just trying to understand." Still no response as I try to keep up with his lengthening strides. He stops abruptly, swinging his gaze back to me.

I won't let this go. It's the first real glimpse of the man I met on our date and that's who I need more of. That's how I'll survive this.

"Why did you hit your brother?" My fingers wrap around his right hand. "I think you protect people that you care about. You may not see it, but I'd like to believe that. That deep down you want more for the people you care for than what you have."

"You think I'm protecting you?" He tilts his head, studying me.

"In your own way, yes." I smile, knowing I've managed to make him think for a moment. "It doesn't have to stop at protection. You can build a happier life, away from what your father pushed you into."

"I'm a Cane, Emily. There's nothing else but that."

"Your name is important to you, isn't it?"

"I've built an empire around it. It means something. It's more than just a name, Emily." He's quiet for a moment, and I realise I've pushed too far. "I think we're done for today. You'll fall off those heels soon. Come."

And just like that, we're heading back to the car.

Quinn broods all the way home. Or at least it's my interpretation of brooding. He doesn't look my way, doesn't engage in conversation and keeps a death grip on the steering wheel. Of course, I'm happy about the last part. This car is a death trap in his hands.

We head up the gravel driveway to his house and he's out of the car and helping me before I can even attempt to pull myself out of the low seats.

"Is that yours as well?" I nod towards the mansion that stands proudly overlooking the grounds below.

"Everything in the Cane name is mine."

"Who lives there? Your brothers?"

"Enough with the questions, Emily."

"I'm just trying to understand you. You do all of this… stuff to me, and I want to see more of the man I first met on our date."

"Johnathon."

"Excuse me?"

"You had a date with Jonathan."

"No, I saw you. You weren't pretending. Otherwise, I'd have never gone to your apartment."

"Believe what you like, Emily. Now, get your ass inside. My patience is about worn out."

He stands in the driveway, waiting for me to obey like a good girl. Well, tough. Not today. He's given me an inch, and I want my mile. I wander up towards the bigger house, intrigued as to who lives inside all those windows.

A flick of movement catches my eye, and I stare up at the third floor. The curtains move again, and my feet are taking me closer before I can stop myself.

"Emily!" Quinn shouts, his patience gone.

I ignore him, wanting to get a closer look at who's in the room. Does he have a wife? A mistress? My body runs cold at that thought. Not just because of his behaviour, but because I don't want him to belong to anyone.

A woman comes into view, and my heart thunders in my chest. I need to see her. I need to find out who could love Quinn. I grab the camera that's still swinging around my neck and twist the lens to focus on the window. An older woman, dressed in a cream nightgown looks out. She's frail, or at least looks unkept. Her hair is a tangled mess, running down in a messy plait to the side of her head.

"Put the camera away, Emily." Quinn's beside me.

"Who is she?"

"None of your business."

"Your mother?" It couldn't be his wife. She is much too old for him. The relief is painful to take.

I accompany him back to his house with no further upset.

He doesn't say a word. No explanation or clarification.

We go inside, and I drop into the nearest chair, but jump at the clatter of metal hitting the glass table in front of me. A matte grey gun sits looking at me, the barrel facing away. Fear slices through me at the thought of what Quinn will do. Perhaps I pushed him too hard and now he's fed up with me.

"W…why do you have that?" I ask.

"I'm always carrying, Emily. Don't go anywhere without protection." His words remind me that no matter what I try to believe, Quinn lives in a world so far removed from mine he might as well be on another planet. "Have you ever held a gun before? Or even seen one?" I shake my head vigorously, drawing myself away from the weapon. "Well, maybe it's time I introduce you to my other slice of heaven." He stands and grabs the gun from the coffee table before grabbing the lapel of my coat and dragging me to my feet.

"Quinn, I don't want to. Stop. It's fine. I don't want…"

"You do what I want, and right now, I want to show you how to use my gun." He circles around me and reaches for my hand, pressing the cool metal against my palm and encasing my hand around it. "There you are. Now, hold it properly. Let's get your other hand to help." He pushes my left hand and moves the palm to cup the base of my hand, raising my arms so I'm aiming the gun. "There." My hands shake as I take the weight of the gun. Quinn's lips are at my ear, his breath tickling my neck. "This is a big gun. A forty-five calibre. It's killed a lot of people." He whispers the words as if caressing my skin with them. My hands begin to tremble as I hold it, the weight pulling my arms down. "Keep your arms up and locked out, Em. How will you shoot someone if you can't aim?"

"I'm not going to shoot anyone, Quinn."

"It's easy. All you have to do is squeeze the trigger. Wrap your forefinger around that little lever and pull."

"No, it's not that easy to kill someone. You're talking about firing a gun. There's a difference." I can't fight off the thought of a bullet ripping through someone's flesh as the end of the gun waves unsteadily out in front of me. My body starts to shake, terrified of what Quinn may make me do next.

"Of course, before you pull the trigger, you have to slide the safety off. This gun is too big for your hands, but I can pop that little switch easily." His hand comes up around mine and presses a little switch on the side of the gun.

"Is it loaded?" It's a stupid question to ask. Of course he'd have it loaded.

"Yes, we'll get to loading the clip later." He drops my arms and steps around me. "What do you think?"

"About what?"

"The gun. How does it feel in your hands?" He steps further away from me out of my direct aim, a smile playing at the edge of his lips.

"It's cold. And heavier than I thought."

"Uh huh."

"Quinn?" He's looking at me standing in the middle of his front room holding his gun. He looks… pleased.

"Don't drop it. Not yet." He walks towards me, this time in my line of vision. I have the gun. It's loaded, but at no point

191

do I think of it as a way to escape. All I can focus on is the damage it could do. How dangerous this is, yet Quinn carries it with him everywhere he goes.

"Now, I'm protecting you." His smile broadens as he steps right up to my side. The closer he gets, the less my body trembles, the weight of the gun growing lighter with every step.

"I don't need a gun."

"You're in my world, dirty girl. We all need a gun." He takes a deep inhale as one hand encompasses mine holding the gun, relieving me of its burden. "I like the way fear smells on you. Almost as good as when you're wet for me."

He bites at my throat, stunning me, before he moves to wrap his arms around me. He pushes his crotch against my leg and I can feel how hard he is. The sound of the gun hitting the glass table makes me flinch as he pushes me back onto the sofa.

"You didn't shoot me, Emily. You didn't run. Even with my gun."

His words sink into my psyche as his hands cover me. They roam my body, removing layer upon layer until I'm laid bare for him.

He's right. I register that this wasn't just his warped way of protecting me. It was a test, and in Quinn's eyes, I passed.

CHAPTER SEVENTEEN

Quinn

My father's office smelt as old as he does when I worked in it this morning. It smelt of decay and rot, just like he does. No matter how many times the servants clean it or layer it with fragrance, it always harks back to what he did to our family. Too much booze and the opinion that he was above the rest of the mobs. He played the wrong damned hand that day. He sat in a game of cards with Joe Mortoni, putting his trust in lowlife scum to do his job, and drank his way to celebrations rather than staying on top of the deal going down. The sequence of events unfolded before he had time to do anything about it, Joe not giving a damn. He got a prize either way.

A damn game of cards.

The thought causes a snort of indignance as I stare the fucker in front of me down, waiting for his explanation of why my own shipment through Columbia has been delayed. One thing this Cane doesn't do is avoid the ground beneath my feet, or forget where the money's made.

Spanish pours out of his mouth, his body erupting with hand gestures and tired excuses. I roll my dice, watching him look at his sidekick, too annoyed to give a damn whether he's related to families I should care a fuck for or not. This happened once before, early on when we started dealing with him. Traceability leads back to half my coke being off-loaded in Bolivia, so this dick can syphon off a few hundred grand. Two weeks later, and it's all back to me ready for distribution. The fact that the dick's made his money by deceiving me, not mentioned. I let it slide the last time, not bothered by the money as long as I got my own, but now it's over a month late and it's having an impact on Columbia's distribution rate, which in turn makes me look like a fucking fool who can't manage his business.

That shit's not happening.

The sidekick looks fidgety as he stands there and hovers his hand around his jacket pocket, ready to draw a fucking weapon should the need arise. That pisses me off more than the continued lies falling from Rohas Denago's mouth.

"You understand?" Rohas says, taking a step towards my desk. "It's on its way."

I roll my dice again, waiting for some fucking truth and sneering at his deceit. I'd probably calm this fucking storm rising inside if he'd been honest, find a way to end this business dealing sensibly, but coming here and lying to me, the whole damn time having a threatening gun under a coat to save his lying ass, is not the best way to approach this situation. "Quinn?"

Still I say nothing as the dice grind in my palm, telling him everything he should already know. I'm pissed, aggravated by the issue, and don't want this dick screwing up my business any longer. I should have killed him the last time, had him fucking drowned on the way over, but professionalism took over. It's not something I give one fuck for this time.

"From what I can work out, you owe me around four

hundred grand, Rohas. I want it."

He looks shocked, hands flying up into the air to defend himself, the other dick taking a step forward towards Rohas' back. I smile at that, watching the way his hand slips under that jacket, ready to protect at all costs. At least they're a loyal pair of deceitful fucks. "You give me my money, get the shipment to my client in two days, and you get to walk out of my office alive, Rohas." My office. The one I came to after I couldn't damn well deal with the stench of my father's inability any longer. The memory from this morning was enough to remind me about staying on top of everything, which is why this meeting was called. I'd rather have gone back to Emily and fucked the morning away, but this has become untenable, and no one fucks a Cane over any more.

I press the buzzer under my desk, calling Rody as arranged, and lever the gun from its holster beside it. He walks in within seconds, followed by two more of my men, and shuts the door, guns already aimed at the backs of Rohas and sidekick. I chuckle and look at the faces of dicks one and two, swinging my laptop screen towards them and entering codes so he can transfer my money back to me.

"You fucking inbreed. You think this is a game you can play with me?" I growl out, pulling up my gun and laying it on the desk beside the screen.

Games. It's all fucking games and deviations for these kinds of players. Always has been. Who gets the most money, who launders it quickest, who accumulates their wealth fastest to track their ranking up the chain. It's fuckers like this who caused my mother's rape, caused her turmoil to this day. My father's shipment got hijacked on the way to Puerto Rico by these types, then got lost through the masses as he got high on whores and missed it all happening behind his back. It was Joe's money he fucked with, though. Cane and Mortoni worked together on the biggest deal they could manage for the first time. Cane connections, Mortoni money.

My father and his damned ego fucked the whole deal up.

I stand and round the desk, dragging my fingers over the wood, still able to feel the blood that lingers in its mahogany from others who thought fucking with me would be useful to their ascension up the ranks.

Rohas looks green, an insipid colour rising through his body as he realises his little fucking lie has been processed and dealt with long before this meeting started.

"I've not got the money," he says, watching me get in front of his face and trying to back away. He slams straight into dick two, who has a gun pressed to the back of his head.

"That's unfortunate," I reply, rolling my sleeves up and waiting for more from his mouth. Nothing comes out of it as I stare, wondering what to do with him. I should have Rody kill them both, have it done quickly and cleanly, but it's pissed me off enough to want to get my own hands dirty. The whole scenario smacks of old school revelations and the kinds of things my father accepted, ignored. Look where that shit got Cane.

It's not happening again.

I've grabbed the fucker before his mouth finds something to say, pushing him over to the window and causing the blinds to ricochet about the surface. He struggles, his hands pushing at my chest in an attempt to get away while his body twists in my hold, grunting and wailing. I just squeeze tighter with my hand, feeling the sinews of his neck beneath my grip and constricting it further. The thrill rushes back into memory, riling me up and boiling blood I've kept at bay. There isn't any getting away from this room for him. None. No one fucks with me, and this insidious world he plays, the one I counter with every move to keep us safe, needs to remember that. Have it fucking spelt out in blood if need be.

He sputters and coughs out incoherent words as I grab tighter at his damned throat, watching the life drain from his features, eyes wide and hands clawing at my shoulders. I sneer at his attempt and stare into blackening pupils, noting the dilation and enjoying the final thought of death. It's been a while since I've seen it by my own hands, felt it in them. Bullets always nullify the impression it leaves on my skin, making it feel like a cleaner affair, but this happening in my fingers now is cold, merciless, regardless of the warmth beneath them. It's what Quinn Cane was a few years ago when Father told me where to go and what to do. A killer's symphony is what he called me. His boy the killer. He was proud of me for it.

I snarl at the thought and glare at Rohas' weakening frame, annoyed with his lack of fight. Fucking inbreed is right. He should have had the cunt behind me pull the damn trigger, waged war on Cane that way, but he didn't have the balls to dare, did he? Thought he could lie his damn way out and screw with my family, threaten it, and so now here he is, dying with no fucking chance of avoiding it.

"Shouldn't have fucked with me," I grind out, letting my fingers tighten further and feeling his hands drop from my shoulders. The blackening pupils dilate further, the small snatch of brown almost disappearing as I hear the final wheeze of breath and hold him against the shuttered window. "Shouldn't have let the suit fool you."

Silence then, only the sound of his body falling to the ground as I let him go and sneer down at it. Killer. It's the vicious part of me I've tried to leave behind, reducing its need to unnecessary in my business lately. It reminds me too much of the stench of Father on my skin, taunting me with my inability to kill that cunt, too, and lowers our class to old school disciplines that should be left to rot with him.

Not today, apparently.

I roll my sleeves back down and turn to look at sidekick. His head's lowered as he looks at Rohas' lifeless body, a shaking hand still hovering around his fucking jacket. He should give that shit a go, see how far it gets him with my current mood.

"You know where my shipment is?" I ask, giving him a chance at life.

He nods repeatedly, his eyes slowly coming up to mine. Good.

I turn back to look at Rohas' body, nudging his face with my shoe, waiting for something to affect me. Nothing does. No guilt. No remorse as I gaze over the corpse. My hands reach for my dice, slowly rolling them around in my palm. There's nothing coming back at me from the floor but the occasional spasm of early death, the twitch coming from muscles giving in. My own body remains still, not one fucking tremor to show a conscience. That's long fucking gone, left behind so I could protect my family and all that comes with that obligation. It's what this skin and flesh were trained to do, what they have to do. No emotion other than what's necessary. Just keep the power strong, the enemies weak.

The only emotion I seem to feel comes from my dirty girl, and that's becoming less to do with fucking than it should be.

River walks. Dates.

"Rody, go pick her up. Tell her to wear something nice."

I turn back to the four of them, wondering if I should kill the sidekick, too, but the shipment is in his damned hands, waiting to get to my channels. "And get this dick to Nate. Have him handle the negotiations before I kill him." Rody smiles at me, nothing to do with the order. It's to do with Emily and the thought that maybe a Cane could be happy with one woman. He's a dick, too. If he thinks any of us deserves one ounce of fucking happiness, he's wrong.

I snort at him and nod my head at the other two, turning for my desk. "You pair can get rid of this stench from my office."

I don't hear anything else after that. I'm too busy getting my shipment back in order to give a damn what happens to Raphael Denago's son. The boys will work it safely enough. They always do. Raphael will call me in the next few days and ask me about the shipment and where Rohas is. I'll tell him he's six feet under, and then explain how much money his son has been skimming off our business dealings, followed by how much the rest of his fucking family stands to lose if there's any comeback. That should end the damn conversation before it starts.

Honour amongst thieves.

***

An hour later and I've called Rody, sending him towards a downtown bar with my date. The thought makes me chuckle as I rev the car and head out onto the freeway, ready for a drink and something to wipe my mind of the night. It's not how it should be. This isn't what I intended when I brought her here, but it's happening without my consent. She's burrowing in somehow, making me question shit I had no intention of questioning. I don't even know why, or how. She's just there, somehow asking me to think about her rather than the hour or two more of work I should be doing. I've spent an hour achieving nothing but thinking about getting my dick inside her, wiping away what my hands did earlier. I didn't even know I needed it wiping off me 'til she started smiling in my head and talking of new lives out there for my kind. It's fucked up.

But then so is my life.

The lights dull as I head to the other side of town. Macy's Cavern is on the outskirts. An old colleague, Marcus Tannery, bought it three years ago after leaving his old life behind. He cleaned himself up, became legit, and now he spends his time entertaining us to the standards we require. Everything is on tap—girls, booze, drugs—as long as we've got the cash to pay for it. I have. Not that I need anything other than her legs wrapped around me and a little pain to bring on that whimper that comes from her lips. Fuck, that's nice. She mewls the sound, lets it come from her as if she's scared she'll break, perhaps not giving a fuck if she does or not. A little more backbone, some toughening up, and she'd fit right in around here, be something worth the thought I'm giving her. She could become some kind of permanent fixture in my life, someone to have around and get into whenever I feel like it. Enjoy.

The hell am I thinking?

My dice are rolling in my palm by the time I pull up to the building. I don't know why. There are no decisions to make, no problems to solve. Nothing I can't work out a logical route for, but still they grind as I get out and pass the keys to the doorman.

Several guests nod at me as I enter. We're all the same clientele. Always are. Gangsters, as Emily would call us. Fucking gangsters. Makes us sound like my father would have liked to have been known. Shame he wasn't quick or clever enough to hold that accolade in his day. Probably did for a while, I suppose. But then he let the booze take over, let his ego be stroked too high so he missed the ground beneath him being raked up and over.

Nothing was ever more important than ego with him, still isn't. He never cared for his wife or children. Never gave a damn for any of us. Still doesn't to this day. It's what caused his own failure, the fucking sentiment that nearly broke Cane. If you don't do it to protect what you care for, what's the damn point? That's how I keep us strong now. I think of my obligations first, who I need to keep safe. Fuck whatever dirt I have to claw through to make it happen. People die every day whether I kill them or not. That dick just wanted the top-level wealth without the graft, barely able to stand the thought of messing his suit up to get the job done. Never could get his hands fucking dirty.

Good job he left that shit to me. At least he learnt one thing from his mistake.

He taught me well.

Pulling at my cufflinks, I head through the hallways looking over the women and not feeling a damn thing for any of them. My dick's aimed solely at the innocent eyes that should be waiting for me somewhere in here. She's nowhere to be seen as I enter the main bar area and look around. There are too many bodies to see clearly so I weave through them, searching, only to come up with fuck all again. I look to the bar and see the regular barman sipping his scotch with a few other guys and lifting his chin at me. He points through to the other small bar, a smirk on his face as he toasts me and wanders off, shaking his head.

The air clears as I enter the room, the smoke from behind filtering out. I gaze around through the new thinner crowd, this time able to see each and every frame on show. Still I can't see her. I flick my head back to the main room, becoming irritated with my dick's weep for entertainment, then hear a sultry giggle coming from the bar. It makes me spin back instantly, hearing the same tones in it that I heard from her on our river walk. And there she is, partially hidden behind Marcus who is hovering around her. My feet are storming across the space before I've thought, ready to beat the shit out of anyone who would dare go near her, especially Marcus.

"You hoping to fuck her?" It's the first thing I ask him from a foot behind his damn back. He turns on me, eyes level with my chin, and slowly looks up. "'Cause I'm thinking you'll have to get through me first." He chuckles and takes a step to the side.

"She was worth a shot, Quinn." He's right, she is. Still, fucker can back right off with his charm and attributes. I stare at him and close the space to her, ownership pouring from every part of my frame. That's what she is—owned. Mine.

He chuckles again and tips his glass of amber at me, winking over at Emily. "You know where to find me." A fucking growl leaves my throat at the thought, enough so that I barely contain the fist that wants to lash out.

"Thank you for keeping me company, Marcus," she says.

"You've been a real help." Help? The fuck does that mean? I turn to look at her, wondering how Marcus could have been of any help other than giving her information. "Oh, don't look at me like that. He bought me a drink and filled me in on some… things." My brow rises at the shortness in her tone as I watch her clamber down from the stool. "I quite like them actually," she says, tripping over her heels and crashing into my chest. "What are these again?"

"Bellinis," Marcus says. "Big ones." I lift her back onto the seat, putting her down with a thud and listening to her light burst of giggles.

"Oh, how very Prince Charming of you." The fuck?

"How many?" I ask either of them.

"Two, so far," he replies, her own mouth too busy gulping down more of the damn stuff. He chuckles and watches her with a smile, shaking his head at something. "Where'd you find her?" he asks. None of his damn business. "I'd say she's a keeper, Quinn." The fuck would he know?

I tighten my hold on her, feeling her ass slipping off the chair again. "Doesn't matter. You pair have a good night. Enjoy yourself."

Enjoy myself? I stare at him again. My dick agrees with the thought, but something about her carefree laughter, or about the fact that she's drunk, makes me more interested in sobering her up.

"What are those dice all about anyway?" she asks out of nowhere. "I mean, what grown man plays with dice all the time?" The fuck was that? I let go of her instantly, watching as she slides from the stool and lands vaguely on her feet.

"Coffee, Marcus. Large," I snarl out, grabbing her by the arm and leading her over towards the couches. "And two of the specials. Fast." Marcus nods at me and turns away.

She snatches her arm away. "Do you always get everything you want?" she huffs, her body brushing past me and heading for the sofa. "Well, I want more bloody Bellinis. That's what I want." I watch her for a while, wondering how the hell she thinks having more booze is going to help her situation. She's too fucking cute, feet still tripping over themselves, her ass swinging to the beat of the music as she reaches for whatever bottle she can find behind the bar. I should fuck her across it, wipe the sass out of her mouth. "In fact, maybe you should have some, too, lighten that attitude up a bit." I snort, amused at her analysis of me. She's probably right. I could use a few drinks after today. I'd like nothing more than to get blind drunk. Drunk enough that the world spins for a few days and I can forget everything, remember what it was like when I didn't have to protect everything. "I could ask how your day's been, pretend this, whatever it is, is real."

She pours something into glasses, adding a cherry she's found, then pours something else in and pushes one across the bar at me. "So, dice? Let's try a conversation, shall we?" I narrow my eyes at the idea of explaining anything to her. "Or if you need something a little easier to start, how's your day been, dear?" She beams at me.

Angsty is how it's been. And for some reason, the one thing I need to make that sensation fuck off is sitting right in front of me, her mouth sassing me as she tilts her body towards mine. I smile. She's the reason for a lot of things and despite everything, I've enjoyed every fucking word she's delivered in this mood.

"You need to sit down and eat some food," I say, turning

away from her and heading towards the dining tables. "Maybe then you can have some conversation." She laughs behind me, a sudden eruption of more sultry giggles making me smile and pull out a chair for her. "Ass, sit."

"Masterful," she says, still giggling as she sways her way over.

She'll get a lot more than fucking masterful if she carries on much longer.

CHAPTER EIGHTEEN

Emily

He smiles at me, that mega-watt beautiful smile that had me on the first date.

I have no idea why he summoned me here, but I'm done with sitting in the corner and waiting for Quinn to decide what we're going to do, or allowing his mood to dictate my life. Rody dropped me off at a bar and put me in the hands of a man who was happy to supply me with alcohol. It seems that was the perfect situation to get under Quinn's skin.

I stifle another chuckle as I think of his face when he found me at the bar with Marcus. The romantic side of me, the one that has blasted to the forefront of my brain with every sip of Bellini, is enjoying the respite and indulging in this version of a date. Although I can see that Quinn is less than impressed.

"So, how was your day?" I prompt, serious about making this an actual date.

"Complicated."

"Complicated good, or complicated bad?"

"A little of both. More of the good, perhaps." He shows me that smile again, and I struggle to stop my stomach flipping over at how good he looks. And the more he smiles, the better. The man I first met is showing his face more and more frequently.

"Here you are." A woman delivers two large mugs of

coffee to the table and doesn't hide the sexy grin she offers to Quinn. I shake my head at her lame attempt to win his attention, not that he appears to look.

"If you don't want to talk about your day, how about you explain those dice?"

A frown creases his brow. The more he resists telling me, the more I want to know. As if it's a secret puzzle piece to Quinn that will help unlock another part of him.

"What do you want to know?"

He's stalling, but I'm not going to let that stop me. I pick up the bucket of black coffee and take a small sip, hoping my willingness to play along will encourage his loose tongue. The thought of loose tongues has me smiling before I've thought. I cough, trying to organise my inappropriate mind fog. "Why do you have them? What do they mean to you?"

He pulls them from his pocket, as if needing to check that they're still there.

"Two steaks, with red wine and shallots." Marcus interrupts us. I'd love to be annoyed at the intrusion just as I'm getting somewhere, but I can't. I'm starving.

"Thank you, Marcus." I give him a warm smile of thanks, but it seems as though my being friendly to any member of the opposite sex annoys Quinn. As I look at him, he's staring daggers at Marcus, the v between his eyes deeper than ever. "You can stop looking like that. I was being polite. Marcus has been nothing more than a gentleman, which is more than I can say for you most of the time." His sudden smirk is disarmingly sexy, killing any element of bite I had in my comment.

"If I'd known alcohol was the key to bringing you out of your shell, I would have plied you with the stuff earlier."

I sink my fork into the succulent steak and begin to cut,

shaking my head. "Well, it worked for you the first time, didn't it?" I counter, before taking a mouthful.

"If you're not careful, that's exactly what will happen here. Gentleman be damned."

"Not until I get to the bottom of those dice." He halts his knife and fork for a beat before continuing. "I mean it, Quinn. You've opened up to me before. Is this so hard to do?"

"No, you're the only fucking person I've talked to about any of this shit. It's strange, considering talking to someone. It isn't something I do."

"There's nothing strange about it. You just open your mouth and let the words fall free. You might feel better afterwards?" He looks confused, the meat hovering around his mouth before he bites into it and leans back in his chair.

"Why would you say that?"

"Because I think you carry a burden around with you. Like a type of armour against the world you work in. I want to know more about the man beneath it." I move my hand to cover his, and for a split second, he lets me. Our eyes meet and lock together. A chaos of thoughts and feelings mix in our eyes as we stare at each other, and I long for him to give me another little piece of him. "You don't have to carry it alone."

The last sentence causes a shift from our moment, his hand pulling away from mine before I can keep it there.

"Whatever burden you think I might carry is nothing to do with you," he mutters, looking back to his food.

The silence continues for a while as we eat, making the air uncomfortable, and I hate the feeling. It makes me edgy again, fearful of what's coming next. He was coming back to me, that man I first met, and now he's gone and I don't know how to reach him when he closes down on me like this.

My eating becomes more of a nibble, and I try to meet his eyes occasionally. He barely responds, certainly not with conversation, but eventually a smile begins to creep across his features. It's small, boyish even, making me smile in reply as I slice through my steak.

"You keep coming for me, don't you?" I raise my bowed head, looking at him from beneath my lashes. "Ballsy, I'll give you that."

"I'm just trying to understand you," I reply, looking back at my vegetables and smirking at some kind of near breakthrough.

"Why?"

"Because we're—" His knife and fork clatter to the plate suddenly, almost making me jump out of my skin. He smirks.

"I prefer jumpy. It suits you."

I smile at that, for some reason happy with the thought as I close my own cutlery and lean back on the chair.

"I'd say you enjoy both, Quinn."

He pulls in a long breath and stares, his eyes never flickering away from me. They're the type of eyes that would have made me look away before. I still might sometimes, but not at this moment. We need this. *I* need this. I need it to make sense of the feelings forming in my heart and what I'm starting to think of as us.

"Sometimes it wasn't easy," he says.

"What?"

He chuckles, his smile widening. "You ever done anything wrong?"

I frown a little, not understanding the question.

"No, I don't suppose you have, have you? Never hurt someone. Never had a run-in with the law. Never had to beat a man to get information out of him. Torture him."

My eyes glance around, worried someone can hear him. He snorts, dismissing my concerns as irrelevant. "You think you're not surrounded by men who've done worse?" I shake my head, suddenly understanding what he's saying as I glance again at the people around us. "None of us are born this way, Emily. We're made. Formed."

I nod and blow out a breath, waiting for more and trying to hold my head up regardless of the topic. Any snippet of information, good or bad, is a way of getting inside his head. It's about him opening up and letting me in.

"It wasn't easy at first. Some things were harder to do. The dice helped me choose. Still do."

"So the numbers…"

"Not the numbers, the fall of fate."

"You're saying that you…" I stall my mouth, barely able to get the words about murder and torture out. "That you do what you do based on a pair of dice because you can't make a decision on right and wrong?" He snarls and drops his eyes, shaking his head.

"Right or wrong for whom, Emily?"

"For humanity."

He smiles at me so broadly my insides flutter, hardly able to contain my infatuation with his handsome features.

"And there are those innocent eyes again. Cute."

The condescension in his tone makes me glare, unable to stop his comment making me feel belittled in this room. It's not like I grew up in this like he did. I don't know how it all works, or why. It's all horrific as far as I can tell.

"Calm your ass down," he says, still smiling at me. "I'm just saying that my sense of humanity is my family alone, nothing more. Threatening them, or me, is like taking a chance with fate, Emily." He gets the pair of dice out of his pocket again and lays them in the middle of the table, a pair of sixes upwards. "I guess it all became like gambling to me. Serious threats are easy to deal with at the table. Someone pulls a gun, you pull one back and defend yourself, but the minor ones, the ones you have to make decisions about, guard against future threats based on? They're harder to determine."

I don't understand, but then I'm no gambler. A point proved by my useless attempt in his casino. I frown and cross my arms, annoyed with my own naive view on the topic.

"Sometimes, I just had to let fate decide the right route forward. Give me a steer through my own indecision." He shrugs his shoulders. "You want an answer, there it is."

"That's it?"

"That's it."

"You run what you do, and you do what you do, based on fate?"

"Not all the time," he says, getting up. I follow his movements, willing the conversation to continue, while hoping he doesn't give more than I can take. "If you'd been in my office two hours ago you'd understand that. I'm going to get another drink. Wait here."

He walks across to the bar. The woman who delivered our coffee is only too happy to serve him immediately. She's all fake boobs and inch-thick makeup. From here, it looks like she applied it with a trowel.

I stand and march over to join him. If he's getting another drink, I want one, too.

"Hey, so, what are you ordering?" After the conversation we just had, I need to change the subject and move it to safer territory.

Quinn looks at me, his eyes drawing together at my question. "A shot. You've had enough already."

"Really? Since when did you get to decide what and how much I get to drink?" I lean against the bar and wait for his answer.

"Be careful, Emily."

"Oh, come on, Quinn. You brought me to a bar. I can have a drink."

The woman behind the bar comes back with a glass filled with clear liquid and places it in front of Quinn. The look she gives me leaves no room for misinterpretation. Her nose scrunches up as she looks down at me.

"I'll take that, thank you." I swipe the glass before Quinn gets a chance to grab it and raise it to my lips, tipping my head back and downing the liquid. The alcohol burns down my throat, and my eyes start to water. I swallow down the choke that threatens to burst from my mouth.

My heart pounds in my chest as I turn to look at Quinn, the heat from the shot now burning through my body and filling me with confidence that I've never known. I tilt my head at Quinn and wait for his response, my stomach turning with nerves at what he might think of my bold move.

"Out." Quinn turns to the woman. "Everyone out of the bar. Now."

"I'm sorry, Sir, I'm not—"

"Don't even finish that sentence. You will, and you'll fucking do it now. Go get Marcus." He stares her down, and she backs away, a quiver to her lip.

Not even a minute goes by as I stare into his eyes, some inner confidence spurring me on, before Marcus arrives at the side of him.

"Quinn?" he asks, a smile on his face as he turns to me.

"I want everyone out, and the bar secure in two minutes."

Marcus nods and parts the crowds easily, somehow managing to begin clearing the room with little more than a few whispered words in people's ears. Heels clatter and a few male voices grumble, their baritone echoing back to me as they leave, but before I know it I'm staring into a room alone with Quinn.

I back up against the bar as Quinn turns his predatory eyes to mine. The Dutch courage from the alcohol evaporates in an instant.

"What's the matter, Em? You look a little nervous." He lifts his brow, a playfulness about him while still being his usual dangerously alluring self.

"No. You've just proved that, like always, you get what you want."

"And right now, I want you."

My eyes flash around the room. "We're… in a bar."

"I don't fucking care. I wanted your ass before I even got here. All your sass has made my dick even harder."

I flush at his words, but inside I'm gleaming. It was a risk to act the way I have tonight—letting my guard down—but it seems we both benefit if we just act like two normal people who met under regular circumstances.

"I want to fuck you wearing only those boots."

I look down at the boots he bought me that are a death trap to wear. He's serious, though. He stands in front of me, and his fingers work to loosen his clothes. First his jacket, then his tie. Each layer is removed with precision and purpose.

After everything we've been through, there's no hope of

being able to pretend that I'm not affected by him. The intent in his eyes is crystal clear. His voice has dropped to that sexy baritone that dances across my skin.

I'm helpless to divert my eyes, and I keep them riveted to his slow striptease. He's undone the buttons of his shirt revealing a glimpse of his chiselled chest. He's a devastatingly handsome man who's turned me into a crazed woman. My life was simple and solid before I met Quinn Cane. Now it's anything but.

"Your turn, Em. And don't pretend not to be turned on by me. I can see it in those eyes."

I don't flinch and summon my courage to do as I'm asked. I have less to remove than Quinn, and set about unzipping the pretty lace top and sliding the skirt over my hips.

"If you want the boots on, I can't take off my tights." I go for playful to mask my self-consciousness. I'm standing with my boobs on display, wearing barely a thing in a bar.

"A simple scrap of material won't stop me getting at your cunt." He walks to me, fists the material over my thigh and tears it. The tights disintegrate in his hands as he pulls the material from my skin. "Better. Now you look as dirty as I know you are."

He seizes me, melding our lips together as his warm body presses against mine. His hands lock us together, but I don't feel the need to run or fight. I sink into the growing anticipation of his touch, the inevitability is something I can't deny.

Quinn cradles my head, controlling the depth of our kiss. He sets the pace, leading me down a lust-fuelled path that I want to explore. My eagerness surprises me. He's made me more comfortable in my skin, forcing me to accept my body for what it is. I may not be model perfect, but what I have has captured Quinn.

He can't keep his hands from my breasts, and he rubs his palm over my nipple, sending pulses to my clit.

"Never hide these from me," he pants.

I nod, still in awe of my reaction to his handling.

His lips move south, travelling down my throat and along my collarbone. It tickles, and I can't hide the little giggle that escapes. I give in to Quinn and let him have me. It's the first date all over again. He takes command of me in a way that no one ever has, and it's just what my body has craved all these years. He's made me feel sexy and wanton, amongst other emotions.

"Feel how hard my dick is for you." He moves my hand down between our bodies and I wrap my fingers around him through his trousers. "For you, Emily." He groans, and his satisfaction spurs me on to be bolder. My fingers reach for his zip so I can grip him tighter, and he reacts in kind, biting down on my nipple, sending spasms of pleasure through my body.

"You like me rough, don't you? Like me talking dirty?" His hands grip tighter, firing me up into a frenzy of need for him. "Fuck, I can't get enough of your pussy. Bend over the bar. I'm not waiting for this."

He releases me, and I angle myself, leaning against the bar, my bum in the air."

"Those boots look fucking delicious. But that ass. Em, it's mine. I'm going to take you, and soon. You'll be begging for me." My mind races, but he focuses my thoughts by running a finger through my wetness. I close my eyes, wishing I could keep hold of this feeling. My pulse quickens, and my skin flushes.

He slides his palms up and down my spine, warming my body further. It's as if his touch calms a part of my psyche that he already owns. The palms press firmly into my flesh, and I moan in pleasure.

"You gonna shout for me? Take this dick and moan out my name?" I nod, knowing I will as he pushes my legs apart. They stretch wider, wanting to give him all the access he needs. Like this, open for him to use, the boots don't bother me but enhance how naughty I feel. That and his dirty mouth and I'm ready to beg for anything.

He doesn't hold back. The jangle of his belt reaches my ears before I feel the material of his trousers against my skin. His cock slides between my lips, plunging home before I'm ready. I wince at the intrusion, but his rhythm doesn't let me draw breath. My body relaxes as his hands travel over the curves of my hips, anchoring me to him. Each jolt rocks me forward.

It builds a delicious pleasure inside my gut, and I long for it to burst free.

Suddenly, Quinn withdraws, confusing me as to his change of heart. But before I can protest, he's pulling me to a nearby sofa and dragging me on top of his lap. He grabs my hip, pushing me into position and then lowers me down on his shaft, filling me completely.

"Now I can watch those innocent eyes as you come all over my cock." He smiles before lifting my boob to his mouth. He sucks the nipple, making my pussy contract. My hips flex forward, grinding down on him. My clit screams for attention, and on shaky legs, I raise up a few inches and slam back down ensuring I give attention to all my hotspots.

"That's my dirty girl." Quinn lounges back, giving me

free access to his chiselled stomach. I rest my hands on his shoulders and begin to move with more confidence.

Heat races through my body, the tightening of my muscles not far behind. Before Quinn, I didn't know an orgasm could be so devastating. I rock faster and faster, chasing the bliss I know will come.

He holds my hips as my body's movements grow wilder, keeping us together. Our eyes find one another and lock me in place. Every slide of passion registers in our eyes, displaying the true emotion behind the act as we chase the climax we both now crave.

"Yes, oh, God... Quinn."

"Fuck me. Keep fucking me, Em."

"Yes... oh..." My mouth gasps for air as my nerves explode, my climax ripping my body apart.

"Jesus, woman," he snarls, pulling my mouth to his.

I can't breathe, and our tongues duel as we both flood each other with orgasms. It's furious and desperate, our bodies churning against each other, sweat dripping from our skin as we chase our sensations, until eventually it's still and quiet again, calm.

I'm aware of Quinn, but can't keep my body upright. I collapse onto his chest with a satisfaction I've only just learned about seeping through my heart.

We don't move right away. I expect to be dismissed the moment Quinn has used me, but tonight feels... different. Like something has morphed, closer to that first night. I don't feel like his dirty debt. Used, yes. But there's something there that wasn't before. Our invisible connection tying us closer maybe.

Of course, I must be suffering from some kind of mental breakdown. I've done things with Quinn no one in their sane mind would. How could I introduce him to my parents knowing he kept me in a basement for days tied to a chair and forced me to watch a gang rape?

He runs his mouth along the side of my neck, intensifying the sense of closeness and making me yearn for something that's not real.

"You're humming."

"Am I? Sorry."

"Don't be. I like it," he muses. It breaks the moment, though, and I climb off of him, embarrassed that I have no control over myself. "I think we should get dressed."

Emotion constricts my throat as I busy myself with finding the garments I happily removed for Quinn.

He doesn't respond but watches me as I walk to the bar, naked apart from the boots. His eyes are on me the entire time, the gentle hum from my senses telling me he's still watching.

I pull the top back on, covering myself, and slip the skirt back over my hips. He stands and sets about doing his shirt up and I hand him his tie. He grabs my hand and pulls me into his chest. I burrow my head against him, suddenly overwhelmed from this evening. His arms reach around and hold me close as I feel the gentle press of his lips against my head.

Each day he grows more and more confusing than the last. I don't recognise myself anymore. How can I with how I behave with him?

Do I prefer the softer side of him? The one I can justify my behaviour for. Or would I rather he be the monster I first saw, so I can claim my actions were in self-defence. A survival need. I shouldn't even be here. I should still be trying to get away, running from this whole thing, and yet I'm here enjoying all this.

Once more, tears threaten my eyes. Is it right that I have feelings for Quinn? Are they true feelings, or a figment of my warped mind?

"Time to take you home, Em."

His deep dark voice is now a comfort. He kisses my head one final time and winds his fingers between mine before moving to fetch his jacket.

He doesn't let go of my hand as we make our way down to the car, and I cling to the meaning I hope is behind his small gesture.

CHAPTER NINETEEN

Quinn

I've fucked her everyday for the last week. Most days, multiple times. My dick can't get enough. She's mellowed around me, like a part of her has accepted her fate, and she's just as eager for me to treat her as my dirty girl as I am to prove she is. I've allowed her in the grounds, but I've not taken her out again. It was too much of a risk to my own rationality, and no smile or good mood from her will convince me otherwise.

I stare at her moving around the lounge area, a cup of tea in her hand, part of me uncomfortable with the vision and wanting to tear the clothes from her back. She's intruding. Everything about her intrudes on what I was a week or so ago. She's changed something about me, made me see life differently. I smile more. Laugh more. I feel the need to talk with her more each day. Not about anything in particular, not like it was at first. Now it's conversation about the inane. She's lulled me somewhere with her giggling and pouting lips, causing a lift of my own that seems reserved for her alone.

It started on the river walk, as I gazed at her taking photos, and it's carried on since then. I tried to stop it with the gun show, rein in this feeling, but I can't. I needed her after I killed Rohas. I needed inside her to wipe it away, clean it somehow. Just her. Day after day the same feelings creep through my bones, reminding me of my youth in those English fields. They're the same fields I should send her home to before she slips through the cracks into an underworld she's not meant for. Women like her are too precious for this world. They're naïve to its shortcomings, regardless of that fight she put up against the Russians. It only seems to be the constancy of business that hardens me again each day, phone calls reminding me of my obligations. Nate tells me of my next run of money, pulling me back to it. Spreadsheets become fuller each time I add another debt repayment to them. If she only knew the entirety of the business she wouldn't look at me with those soft, hopeful eyes.

She'd run.

I frown as she puts her tea down and picks up a glass ornament, holding it to the light to watch the colours bounce off its form. They cascade from its sharp edges, rainbows filtering over the wooden floor and warming the stark white atmosphere. She smiles at the illumination, watching the dancing circles cross the ground beautifully. It's the same damn reason I bought the fucking thing.

"Careful," I mutter softly. "That's worth more than your debt to me." Her eyes widen, fingers grabbing more ferociously to the piece. "Wouldn't want to double your time here, Em." It's a fucking façade. The debt. I've spent more on her with the Russians and her clothes than she owed in the first place.

She scowls at that and moves to lower it back to the table, delicate fingers gently placing it where it came from.

"It would look better in the far window," she says, pointing through the length of the room." The sun would draw better light through it." I raise a brow at her, remembering the position I had it in when I first got it home.

"You rearranging me?"

"Hardly." She drops her hand. "It was just a suggestion."

"How about you come suck my dick. That's a better suggestion." Her lips curl upwards, my dirty little girl shining through her smile alone. I loosen my belt, ready to have her mouth around me for a second time today. "How about we hear that gag that comes so sweetly from your throat?" She picks up her tea and sips it, eyes looking over the top of the cup at me.

"How about you let me make a phone call to my mum, let her know I'm alive?" What the fuck was that? I stare, oddly aroused at the fact she's coming back at me with something. "I call her every two weeks, Quinn. She'll worry if I don't, come looking for me."

"We're not negotiating, Em."

"How about we do?"

"What?"

"How about you let me make a call, perhaps send a few emails, and then you can do whatever you want to me for the rest of the day."

"How about I do that anyway, not giving one fuck for what you want."

She giggles. It fucking infuriates me. Not because she's not taking me seriously; she knows all too well what happens when she questions me, but because I like it. I like it enough that my own mouth smiles back at her as I get my dick out.

"Yes, that's an option, but what about me seeing a little more of that man who took me to the river walk. The one who talks to me." My eyes narrow at her, my fingers slowly pulling on my dick.

"Take the clothes off and I'll think about it."

She takes another sip of the tea, still not removing her eyes from me.

"You promise?"

The fuck have promises got to do with anything?

I laugh, trying to remember the last time someone asked me to promise something. Fucking promises are for pre-pubescent ten-year-olds who still crawl to mother when they cry.

"I haven't promised a fucking thing for fifteen years, Em." She frowns, a slight huff coming from her lips as she takes another sip. "The only thing I'll promise is that if you don't get your clothes off and your lips around this dick, your ass will be the next thing it gets driven into."

That seems to stop the petulant behaviour.

She pulls her top off, revealing her sumptuous figure, before biting her lip and moving her ass over to me, breasts swinging at me as she moves. They make me want this dick between them, watching as it pushes back and forth between the soft, full flesh. She kneels in front of me, one hand placed on each knee ready for whatever I want her to do.

"Lie back on the floor," I say, pushing her slightly. She does. No argument. No fight like she used to try for. She's as pliable in my hands now as I want her to be. And that dirty smile comes back, too, as she makes herself comfortable. It's small, barely visible to anyone else, but I know it. Her breath quickens, legs parting before I've told her to part them.

I shake my head at her, closing them back up and crawl up her body, licking her pussy as I go. She moans immediately, filling me with a pride I've never cared for before her. I never gave a fuck about any pussy before her, but I do now. I stare down at her body, watching the way she arches her back up to me to touch her. It pleases me more than I understand, some element of emotion swelling along with my dick, and it takes no time for me to push her breasts together and forge my dick through them.

She looks shocked at first, her mouth an open hole of expectancy, waiting for me to drive it inside her, but I don't. I want to watch my come explode on her neck, over her mouth. I want to mark her in that way, make her wipe it into her skin and wear it for the rest of the day.

I push her breasts firmer together, watching my dick as it plunges through them, the tip of it engorged as it aims and tips her chin each time.

"Fuck," I growl out as I see her hands move to cover mine.

"You like that?" she asks quietly, her chin tipping down as she reaches her tongue out.

I've never seen a sexier fucking thing in my life than her lying here on my floor, every part of her ready for me to use, her hands pressing against her tits. I lean upwards, letting her take the weight of them and driving my dick through them time and time again. She groans, her tongue managing to swipe saliva across me with every quick ram through I make.

She squirms beneath me, her pussy calling for my hand as she pants around my dick. I reach back, still fascinated by the sight of her, my dick getting closer and closer to her with every slide.

"Please, Quinn," she pants out, her mouth managing to touch the end of me this time. She widens her legs and squirms again, the feel of her wet pussy suddenly thrust into my hand. "Please." I smile. Dirty girl's well and truly fucking desperate for it now. I swipe my hand through her, rubbing the slickness to her ass. She stops for a second, realising what I'm doing.

"You're about to earn that phone call you want, dirty girl," I snarl, my finger foraging into her. She tenses instantly, her head tipping away from my dick as I change our position a little. "Lift your ass to me." She doesn't. She shakes her head and tries to move away from me. That infuriates me for all the wrong fucking reasons.

I'm off her and flipping her body onto all fours before she gets a chance to make another move.

"What happens when you say no, Emily?" Her whole body stops fighting me, ass still high in the air and ready whether she wants it or not. "That's right. You know it's a damn sight easier on you when you don't fight me, don't you?" I look down at her cheek resting on the floor, watching as she gasps breaths in and waits for my hand to go where no one's been before. "Fingers or my dick?" There's no movement other than her panted breaths and quivering lips. Good. She'll take whatever the fuck I feel like giving her. That's currently my dick given her struggle against me.

I slide my hand through her pussy again, letting the action lead to her ass and rubbing the juices into it. My thumb pushes against the wall of tense muscle, my fingers kneading into her cunt to relax her. She writhes slightly, enough for me to slap at her cheek and make her still again.

"It'll hurt more if you fight, dirty girl. Relax."

She whimpers as I push again, sending my dick into a frenzy at the sound. Fuck, she makes such innocent noises. They're mine. My whimpers. My mewls. My groans and moans coming from her lips. It makes me sink a finger into her mouth, letting her suck at it to take her mind off my continued pressing at her ass. She goes mad, her tongue swirling, lips sucking at it like it's a fucking popsicle, and I force through the barrier of her ass before she has a chance to think.

She gasps instantly, a cough following, so I ream at the fucking thing, stretching it and making her howl out.

"Quinn?" she pants, her ass moving slightly in my hand.

"That's it, move yourself on it." She does, small shifts back and forth, getting herself used to the sensation as my fingers still work her pussy until she starts moaning again. "There you go," I say, dragging my mouth across her back and watching her ass begin to eat my thumb, swallowing it down to the knuckle. "Good little dirty girl." She moans again, her shoulders rising to get a better position and purchase on the wood. "You ready for my dick now?" She gasps as I withdraw the thumb and immediately replace it with two fingers instead. "You need stretching more?" I hover a third, shifting my frame around behind her and drawing my tongue through her wet lips.

She pushes back at me, widening her legs and mewling with each move back onto me. My tongue digs in deeper, swiping the length of her and rolling up to her ass.

"Quinn."

My name groans from her lips, fucking emotion pushing it into my ears and making me hungry for more. It's enough to take my hand to her breast again, rubbing at the nipple and teasing more sounds from her. My fingers slip from her ass as my body rises, dick ready to dive into her innocent hole that belongs solely to me. And I lean over her, pulling my hand from her nipple back up to her hair. I snatch her head back to me, flinging her torso upwards so I can bite into her neck and feel the tension she's holding onto.

"You ready for me, dirty girl?" Her gasp makes me smile, tongue roaming over the spot I've bitten down on. "You gonna give me that sweet ass?" She shudders as I swipe my dick over it, coating myself in the juices I've put there. "You're gonna feel me for weeks here." I push my dick between her flesh, letting my hand hold her throat up to me. "You're gonna remember everything about the first time I took something no one else has." I ease at it harder, my thumb levering the tip inside and forcing the hole wide again. She yelps, a small cry of frustration coming from her as I keep shunting into her and she moves away. "You will let me all the way in, dirty girl. Push back at me." She doesn't. She just quivers and wavers in my hand, unsure of what she should be doing or why she's doing it. I couldn't give a fuck how she feels. This ass is mine now, as is the rest of her.

I tug her back again, forging my dick in harder to break that last resistance, and then groan myself as my length finally sinks inside her.

Still she remains silent, nothing but breathing and her body sending shockwaves along my dick. She squeezes slightly, as her ass adjusts to me, then whimpers against the force of my hand on her neck. The sound makes me release her and lean back to watch my dick slowly slide back out of her.

"Tell me you like it, dirty girl."

I ease back in, slowly building a rhythm and waiting for her back to arch up to me. It does within seconds, an unconscious cry coming from her as she starts to feel the sensations building. My fingers roll between her legs again, flicking her clit to help her let go and feel the tension that's building between us.

"Quinn, please." It's the first time she's asked for it, and the shunt of my dick straight back into her has her lowering to the floor, ass higher than before and ready to take more of me.

I pull out again, leaning back over her and biting into her spine, my own ass beginning to power in as I search her pussy for everything I own. Fingers drive in, the feel of my dick in her ass making me crazy as I massage myself and her.

"You're so fucking good for me," comes from my lips, the strain in my balls near to making me explode. She mewls at that, and reaches her hand back, desperate fingers grabbing at flesh so she can hold onto something. I give her my hand, letting her take the fingers and mangle them into her own.

"Oh, god, please, Quinn." Another shunt, hard drives coming from me as I grunt at her offering, come beginning to channel its way through me as the friction keeps building. "I need... Oh god, I need…" I damn well know what she needs. It's the same thing I do.

"Tell me," I bark at her, hauling her ass closer to me as I do, and wrapping my hand around her to press on her clit. "You fucking scream it for me, dirty girl."

"I want to… Fuck. Oh god, I'm coming." She gasps again. "Oh fuck."

The sound of those words coming from innocent lips drives me insane, the need to come inside her powering my ass harder towards her and forging my dick deeper.

"Again, Em."

"Oh god, Quinn. I'm coming. I'm coming. Keep fucking me… Please, fuck me."

The come explodes from my balls, blinding me as I grab hold of her and lessen the intense drives. It shudders through my spine, ecstasy roaring through my cock as my lips bite into her back. She groans, her body shivering and halting its manic drive back at me.

All movement stops. It's just me and my dirty little girl, both of us groaning and grunting, the fucking air as soiled as I'm making her. I shove in again, luxuriating in the feel of come spilling inside her, and still shaking from the pressure of her tight ass gripping my dick.

There's quiet then, nothing else as my lips rest on her back and I look at her shaking form. Sweat glistens on her skin, making me smile and rock into her again. It's my fucking skin now. Not hers anymore. I've taken her cunt, taken her mouth, taken her ass, and I've taken her innocence fully with all those holes.

I lick across the sweat, tasting the salt, and slowly rock my hips again. She moans quietly, soft sounds coming as she breathes my name again. I scowl at the way it eases from her, knowing she shouldn't be calling it so sweetly but damned if I'm going to stop her saying it. And her fucking fingers beginning to soften their grip on mine pisses me off. Enough so that I can't stop squeezing tighter to remind her who now controls everything. She'll let go when I'm ready for her to relax, stop clinging to me when I say she can.

The emotion is something that makes me frown at my own thoughts, still rooting myself inside her ass and wondering why she means anything to me at all. She's not like the other whores. She's embedded herself here somehow. Her smile, the way she manages to force me to soften for her without doing anything. It's constant. Irritating. It's like I lose my mind when she's around me. Change, to accommodate what she wants. Fucking phone calls? Not a hope. It's all maddening.

I release her fingers, sliding my dick out of her and tucking it back in my pants. What the fuck is going on? I shake my head at myself, watching her body crawl into a ball and try to hide in the wooden floor.

"Go clean yourself up," I order, noting the come that leaks out of her.

The sight of it makes me smile regardless of my irritation with her. It makes me smile so much I turn before she sees it and head to the kitchen. It's not fucking right. This smiling, this need to converse with her—fucking chitchat about irrelevant topics. It's not me. None of this is what it should be. I should go put her back in that downstairs room again and bolt the door. Make her pay the rest of her friend's debt and send her home. I snort, still amused at my own ability to cling on to the thought this has anything to do with a fucking debt anymore. There is no debt. There hasn't ever been a fucking debt for her to pay. I played it for my own benefit, used it to have more time in her cunt.

I snarl at myself and grab a bottle of whisky, barely managing to pour it into a glass rather than glug it from the bottle.

"Quinn?" she says behind me, expectancy labouring her tone.

That fucking name. The way she breathes it. Fuck.

I tip the glass up to my mouth, downing the liquid in one gulp, leaning against the countertop to stare at the cabinets.

"I said go, Emily." It comes from my lips softer than my intentions suggest, my eyes focused on the glassware in my vision rather than the thing I want to turn and look at. "Clean up."

"You could come with me?" she whispers.

My hand picks up the bottle again, pouring another shot and considering just ending this. She's right. She has a life away from this, one I'm holding her from for no reason other than selfish purposes. The thought of her going has me gulping down another shot, ire mixing with the confusion I'm trying not to acknowledge.

"Why would I do that?" I mutter, unable to stop the turn of my feet to look back at her. She stands there, hair wild from me grasping it, sweat still glowing on her skin, highlighting colours that wake my dick straight back up. "You're the one with come spilling from your ass, dirty girl." She frowns a little, her hands starting to twist themselves around each other.

"I just thought that maybe..."

"What? That I gave a fuck?" I snort again, drawing my eyes over her flawless body and raising the bottle to my mouth. "I don't, Emily." I damn well shouldn't. "The only thing I give a fuck about is you being clean for the next time I put something inside you." Her whole body slumps, her eyes immediately dropping from mine as her head nods. Good. She shouldn't be getting any ideas about love or romance. There's none here for her, no matter what my mother talks about or what my own emotions are playing at. Fuck love. "Go back to your room. Scrub that cunt and ass clean like a good girl before I have to force you to do it."

She looks like she's about to burst into tears, bottom lip quivering as she goes without any more stupidity coming from her mouth. I sip from the bottle again, letting the heat burn through me as I watch her climb the stairs. There's nothing here for her but a version of a man I've become. No love. No honour. No Quinn in softened tones. One date or not, this fucking alternate existence between us that has developed or not, we are nothing more than a debt repayment. That's all this Cane has to give. It's all I can give her. And that fucking time is coming to it's end. It has to before I lose my mind completely.

CHAPTER TWENTY

Emily

My body aches. I feel sore all over, and the tears that bubbled up downstairs now flow unchecked down my face. I am a stupid girl, clinging to some ghost of an idea that Quinn could care for anyone other than himself.

My movement is awkward as I hobble towards the bathroom. My tender flesh is burning from his use of me. He's been threatening anal sex since I first got here. I didn't expect to enjoy it, or how painful it would be after.

The sick feeling that invaded my stomach when I woke up in the chair in the basement has returned. The cold and sickening feeling that I am trapped, despite some lame gestures from Quinn to prove otherwise. He is in total control of me and my future, and I can't see anything but hurt and pain.

The glimpses he's shown me of Quinn as a man, Quinn as a protective brother, must just be a ploy to gain my compliance, because every time I push him and see a crack in that toughened exterior, he reverts to the monster in the dark. I will only be a debt to him. A toy. His dirty girl to use and abuse.

A sob escapes, echoing in the bathroom. I hide in the shower, letting the water wash away the evidence of him still cooling on my legs. As I look down, pink water runs down the drain. I'm bleeding. He's made me bleed.

I give up washing and just lean against the cool tiles. The water pummels my back, and I focus on the steady rhythm of the water beating down. It pulls me into a daze, my mind growing numb, unable to concentrate on thoughts or questions. I give myself this time to switch off.

My body starts to shiver, and I notice the water has run cold. I turn it off and warm up with a bath towel. I perch on the edge of the toilet seat, but I'm too tender to sit comfortably. The stab of pain brings back the evening's events and why I shut myself off.

I am a naive and stupid girl who deserves to have her sanity checked. Why, after everything that Quinn has put me through, do I continue to look for the good? It's too much this time. And it's not because he sodomised me. It's his disgust at me afterwards, that I'd dare to show some way for us to connect. It wasn't on his terms, and so he can't process, or won't accept it, and shuts down.

I have to stop thinking in some sick Stockholm syndrome world. I only have feelings for Quinn because he's the first man to... The sentence dries on my tongue before the words are spoken. I don't know *why* I have feelings for this man. But I do know they are there, rooted inside of me, bending me to their will whenever he's around. Making me see the man he *could* be. For every flutter or glimmer of hope I have, there is a tidal wave of shame and repulsion that follows.

I wrap myself up and go back out to the bed, gingerly sliding between the covers. My bum still hurts, so I choose my side to lie on and curl up in a small ball.

My mind plays over the last few weeks and it becomes

starkly clear. I can't stay here. I can't be complicit in letting this carry on. Escaping or calling for help is what has to happen. Quinn won't let me go, and he won't tell me when the debt has been paid. I'm pretty sure that his mind has shifted where that's concerned. I can't pinpoint when exactly. Perhaps when he stopped whatever the Russians wanted to do with me, but regardless, he's not letting me go anytime soon.

The big house. That will be my first stop. Reach the house and find a phone. Call for help. See if there's anyone who can help. The woman in the window, perhaps? Or the housekeeper, Maria.

All the opportunities and possibilities start to unfold in my mind. If I don't at least try, I'll never be able to look myself in the mirror. I need to do this to build some of my own sanity back, to piece together something that I lost the first time I let Quinn take me despite the circumstances. The Emily who was excited to go on a date with a stranger is a long way from the woman I feel I am now. It's such a short amount of time, I know that, but my perception of time has slipped. The days tend to merge into one another here.

My plan dries the tears from my face and infuses me with new purpose. I slip from the bed, put some leggings and a jumper on, and pull my hair into a messy bun. I check my face in the mirror and decide that it doesn't matter if I look a wreck. I am one. And it's by Quinn's hand.

I force myself to put on a brave smile and ease the door open and listen. Voices rise from the kitchen and I go to investigate. I peek around the corner and see Josh slumped over the table. Quinn lords over him, his face a picture of contempt.

"The Mortonis? Of all the fucking people to play with,

you chose them?"

"I'm sorry, Quinn. I just wanted to prove to you that I had a place at the table. You wouldn't listen. I thought I could show you."

"And now you need my help." He spits the words, clearly furious, a deathly silence following after. "Again."

"I'm sorry." Josh sounds desperate. Gone is the full-of-himself character I met the last time he visited.

I decide to make my presence known and step from my semi-concealed spot. Quinn straightens the moment I come into view. His eyes are trained on me as I walk through the kitchen, past where Josh is sitting, and pull out a mug from one of the cabinets.

"Can we help you?" Quinn asks.

"Emily, I'm glad you're here." Josh's words sound desperate. I turn to face him and am shocked at his appearance. He's barely recognisable. His previously clean veneer has disappeared. Messed up hair, a black eye and cut lip. His white dress shirt is dirty, with only half the buttons meeting in the right places. Blood splashes the collar. He's a wreck, and that's before I've even looked him in the eyes.

He sports a few days of beard growth, adding to the rough look. His eyes look to meet mine, and I see them filled with something familiar. Fear.

"I owe you an apology, Emily. I wasn't particularly pleasant to you when we met last. I understand you're a guest of Quinn's."

"Okay, thank you."

"Well, I'm sorry. You won't have to deal with me being around any longer." His apology is so sincere, and I can't help but feel sorry him, whatever mess he's in. Right now, I don't need any further confusion to add to my muddled mind. I nod at him to show my acknowledgement.

"She won't see any more of you, period," Quinn growls. He looks at me, seemingly bubbling with fury still. "Em, go, so Josh and I can talk." I don't answer Quinn, but continue to make my tea, taking my time. "Emily. Leave." Still, I ignore him.

The water splutters out of the machine into my mug, drenching the tea-bag. I walk to the fridge and retrieve the milk. "Emily, I don't know what the hell you're playing at, but get the fuck out of here before I make you."

He can rant and rave all he likes. I'm not going to answer him. I won't be frightened anymore. He can't touch me, and if he does, there's nothing left for him to do that he's not already done.

I brew my tea and then waltz out of the kitchen to the lounge where I curl up on the sofa as delicately as possible. I sip the tea and try to feel the outward appearance of calm I'm portraying. Of course, it's easier said than done. I feel like I'm walking on eggshells and I'm certainly winding Quinn up, but my decision is made. I can't live like this anymore. I have to fight for me, no matter how sick it makes me feel inside.

His tailored trousers walk into my eyesight. I look up and see him looking furious, brows knotted together and his eyes piercing me as they always do.

"Don't push me, dirty girl. You won't like the outcome."

I stare into his rage-filled eyes, looking for a trace of the man that forces my heart into a flutter. "I'm not moving, Quinn. I won't be summoned and dismissed on your whim anymore. I thought you'd come to see that over the last week. I thought we got past this?" The small part of me that had convinced myself things were different is clinging on to our past experiences.

He pauses and considers my words for a moment. Perhaps they're penetrating through his exterior, but I think he's more taken aback by my sudden show of strength.

"You're mine to do with as I please. Freedom is at my fucking discretion." His voice is low and menacing. "Get your ass out of this goddamn room."

"Go and yell at your brother somewhere else, Quinn." I turn my head and take another mouthful of tea.

His arm swings in an arc so fast I only see a blur, but I do hear the smash as my mug is flung across the room, shattering against the wooden floor. All of my hope splinters, along with the mug now lying in a hundred sharp pieces on the floor.

"You'll do as you're damn well told, Emily." I stand up, willing my own temper and glare in response to his actions.

"Go and play with another one of your skank whores, Quinn. I'm not doing this anymore. You can throw me back in that cell for all I care. I'm fucking done."

I don't let him return my anger and march back up to my room. If only I could lock it behind me. Adrenaline pumps through my veins, filling me with a determination I've not felt before.

Quinn's treatment over the last few weeks has toughened me, making me grow stronger without even realising it. I would never have spoken to him like that in the past.

I take a few deep breaths, focusing on my composure. I can't risk staying here any longer. If his little outburst has taught me anything it's that Quinn will only show me a part of himself that he's comfortable with. He'll always defer back to his normal.

Tonight, or at some point in the early evening, I need to leave. That's if he doesn't lock me in the room again.

I walk to the wardrobe and open the door. A handful of items now hang from the rail. The cream coat he bought me before walking the path of the river, a few different jumpers, the stupid cocktail dress. The clothes are an accurate reflection of the changing moods of Quinn Cane. I pull the coat from the hanger and set it on the foot of the bed. I'll need it. Plus a small part of me wants to take it as a reminder that not everything in Quinn is bad. He has the capacity for kindness, chivalry even. I've seen it, felt it; it's just been stolen by the world he's been forced to live in.

I don't bother changing and slip under the covers in the clothes I'm in. I close my eyes but know it will be hard to get any sleep. But still, I try.

At some point in the evening, I must have dozed off. My eyes fly open, but I remain still. The creek of the door must have woken me. My heart jump-starts in my chest and threatens to give me away. The edge of the bed dips and I feel Quinn slide on top of the covers next to me. I remain frozen still, pretending to be asleep.

"Em?" he slurs. It's obvious he's been drinking. He stinks of whiskey. He edges closer to me, seeking... something. "Shouldn't have got mad."

Pinpricks of tears threaten so I screw my eyes shut, blocking out his attempt at an apology. I don't want to hear it. It's too late. I'm leaving. I just need to be patient.

His arm snakes around my waist, pulling me back to him. I tense, hoping he's not going to try to wake me up, but he doesn't. His breathing starts to even out, and I take tiny breaths, anything to ensure he's not disturbed.

Hours pass. The clock on the dresser is visible from the shaft of moonlight falling through the drapes.

Two, three, four in the morning arrives. I can't wait any longer. My window will close, and I'll be trapped. I might have toughened up, but I know Quinn's broken me before. How can I fight him, knowing what I've already done? Knowing how I feel?

I edge my leg to the side of the bed, pull my body out of his grasp, and pause, making sure he doesn't stir. My heart beats so loudly I can feel it through every muscle in my body. I make it out of bed and stand, looking back at him sprawled out, his arm now reaching for an empty space.

The boots he bought for me are next to the wardrobe. If I have to run, I won't be fast, but I'll have to try. There's no other option. Of course, he might find me at the bottom of the stairs with a broken neck from tripping in these things. I slip my feet inside the stupid boots and wrap the coat around me.

Quinn doesn't move a muscle. The creek of the door is the only barrier. I hold the handle and press down as softly as possible. Inch by inch it opens until I can slip through the gap.

My heart wants me to turn back. If I go through with this, I might escape, I might get part of my life back, but I might also have to press charges. Talk about my experience to a courtroom of people. Explain how I took presents, let him have me. The camera is sitting on the side table, capturing the day when everything felt… different. Emotion I have no right feeling wells inside my chest.

I turn and creep down the stairs. There's a quiet to the house that doesn't exist during the day. It's utterly still. Eerie.

My steps turn purposeful. I don't have time for regrets or what-ifs. I aim for the front door without any more hesitation and walk through it, quickly orientating myself to head for the house up the drive. Three little beeps stop me from moving forward. They repeat, and I suddenly realise how foolish I've been. Of course, Quinn would alarm his house. My legs pump, and I begin running as fast as I can just as the alarm splits the quiet.

I don't look back. I concentrate on putting one foot in front of the other and keep going. The gravel driveway leads right to the other house. It takes longer in the heels than I'd hoped, but I'm halfway before I hear him bellow out into the night.

"Emily!"

I stumble but pick myself up. Fear drives me hard. My original plan to reach the house and call for help evaporates. I won't have time. I need to run and hide or find someone to call for help for me.

I reach the steps of the house but can hear Quinn's feet pounding on the dirt behind me. "You won't escape, Emily. Stop running."

"Never."

My legs burn from the sudden exertion, but I ignore it and run past the steps that lead to my possible freedom, detouring to the side of the house. I don't make it.

Strong arms wrap around my waist and pull me to the ground. I brace with my hands, but land hard, knocking the wind out of me. He twists me around and tries to straddle me. I kick out and thrash, my body wriggling and rocking my hips. His hands reach for my wrists, but I slap them out of the way, swinging for him as hard as I can.

"Stop it, Emily."

"No."

"Calm the fuck, down" he says, pushing me back towards the gravel.

"Fuck you. I won't let you do this anymore," I spit out, furious that I didn't make it away from him.

"You're mine."

"No, I'm not. I'm Emily Brooks." I keep my legs and arms moving, landing kicks and punches against his body.

"Stop fighting me."

"Never," I grit out, digging my nails into his cheek and scoring them down his skin.

"Fuck." He sits back up, letting go of my upper body, and I dig my elbows into the ground to try to pull away from him. I get out from under him, but his hand wraps around my ankle and drags me back.

"I told you. You're mine!"

"Not anymore," I spit at him and start screaming at the top of my lungs.

He wrestles me to standing and puts me in a chokehold, dragging me back down the drive. Tears burn on my cheeks, the fight that was so vital a moment ago dissolving in his arms. I go limp in his hold, in hopes of making it as hard as possible for him to move me.

Quinn wins, though. The entry to his house is patrolled by men dressed in black, all waiting for him. He nods and then tosses me back inside his house. My moment of bravery may now cost me far more than I've already lost. He locks the door behind him and stands over me, still lying on the floor.

"You'll fucking pay for that." I spin onto all fours and glare up at him.

"Do your worst. But understand this. I will fight. I will never stop fighting, or trying to escape you." My teeth grind together with conviction.

He stares for so long I don't know what on earth he's going to do. I hold my postion, continuing to glare at him to prove my point. Not anymore. I'm not doing whatever this is anymore. Evenutally a sigh leaves him.

"What number, Em?" he says, a snarl forming around his mouth.

"Sorry?"

"Give me a fucking number to play with."

"Seven." I'm fed up with his games.

He takes his ever-present dice from his pocket and chucks them in the air. My heart beats frantically with the possibility that they might land in my favour. They scatter as they hit the floor, bouncing and tumbling, and my eyes search in desperation for what they show.

He steps around me, moving towards them and blocking my view, and a small chuckle follows.

"Seems like fate's given you a choice," he says, his hand scooping them up and then putting them in front of me to see. I stare at them, looking at the three and four. "Seven it is. Stay or go, Em. What will it be?" Quinn's rage has vanished from his voice. There's a sorrow, a finality that has replaced it. "But understand that if you go, that's it. You stick to your decision."

I know why he's checking with me. He knows how I feel, or at least must have some idea. He must feel it between us, too.

"Go. I want to go home."

He stares, if only for the briefest of seconds, but it feels like hours.

"Fine," he eventually says as he walks toward the other room, pulling his phone from his pocket. I hear him on the phone, a few words that I don't track, and then he's back in front of me. "Rody will be here for you in an hour."

He turns and doesn't give me another look, his footsteps echoing away along the hall and finally out of earshot. I pull myself from the floor and sit on the sofa, confused and scared. I should be over the moon with relief. But all that's sinking in is that I'll never see Quinn again.

Cold invades my skin, sinking through to my bones. A tiredness washes over me and I fight against the need to close my eyes.

I sit in the front room staring out the window and watch the sky turn from pitch black to grey, the sun threatening at the edge of the world.

"Time to go." Rody walks into the room and beckons for me to follow him.

"Where's Quinn?"

"That's none of your business. Come on, you have a plane to catch."

Disappointment chokes out any sense of ease that I'm finally out of this mess. Maybe I thought he'd see me one last time. Come and say goodbye.

I stand and follow Rody.

"Here." He passes me my clutch bag from my first date. My phone and keys are still inside. The phone's dead. Useless. But at least I have it back.

The ride to the airport is silent. Rody keeps his eyes straight ahead, and I'm amazed that I was concerned to be in the same car as him only a handful of days ago. It's like I'm not even seeing the world through the same eyes anymore. Something about him, all this, seems honest now.

Rody escorts me to a small jet plane, positioned in an

airport hanger. It's not one of the big airports and I don't seem to need the passport I haven't got. I don't care, anymore. I just follow. My feet climb the steps and I take a seat in the opulent leather chairs spaced out in the cabin. Rody joins me, sitting opposite.

"You're coming, too? I ask. He nods, nothing else.

A few crew join the aircraft. A pretty lady wearing a flight attendant's uniform brings me a bottle of water. I muster a small smile but curl up into a ball and tip the seat back. I just want to close my eyes and wake up at home, pretend that this was all just a nightmare.

***

Rody parks outside of my house and looks back expectantly. I take a minute to get out of the car, but don't say anything as I slam the door and head to the pavement. The car pulls away, and I'm left looking at my home. It's the afternoon. The street is quiet, but I feel like it must be the middle of the night.

Finally I'm home, and I take my keys from my purse and push open the door, smiling at the familiar sound of squeaking. It's cold, the heating barely on as I'm usually out during the week and I only turn it up when I'm at home. I push open the door to the front room and a gasp of air rushes into my lungs.

My eyes scan the room, but I don't find the familiar comfort from home. Anything electronic, my cameras and some of the furniture is gone. The small sofa remains, but anything of any value is missing. Magazines, papers and other material litter the floor. I barge out and check on the bedroom. The same. Drawers opened, the wardrobe empty. The small wooden box I keep some of my jewellery in is emptied on the bed. The silver charm bracelet my Grandmother gave me as a child is missing, so is anything real. A few glass bead necklaces remain.

Hysteria bubbles up and tears that I've become so familiar with streak down my cheeks. The only other person to have a key to my place is Jenny. It seems she wasn't content with setting me up with a gangster to take her place; she needed to steal from me as well. I look for where the phone was, but even that's gone. I shove my phone charger into my mobile and wait for it to have enough power to phone my parents.

My heart drops to my stomach when I think about the studio. I didn't consider Jenny would rob me. If she's done this, I fear for the business.

An inner steel, developed over the last few weeks takes over and I force the waterworks to stop. I pull a change of clothes from the dresser and chuck what I'm wearing into the bathtub. They're covered in dirt and blood from my fight with Quinn. The cream coat I wanted to keep for some silly sentimental reason is ruined.

I take my purse and keys and make my way on the familiar journey to the studio. My head pounds, I don't even know what day it is. My eyes are scratchy, and I keep them riveted to the floor, embarrassed that people will see me in such a state.

I rush from the tube station and around the corner until I can see the studio that I invested so much of my life building.

There's a *closed until further notice* sign in the window, which sends my heart sinking to my stomach. I open the door and look around. The computers are gone, but everything else is there. A pile of unopened letters litter the doormat. A letter on my desk, in what I recognise as Cheryl's handwriting, catches my eye. I tear it open and scan the words.

Sorry that you're struggling personally. Jenny explained the situation. I have to find a new studio. Take care. Cheryl. A cheque for her last session accompanies the note.

I thought that I'd lived through my nightmares these last few weeks. It turns out that other fears can hurt just as much as physical pain.

I've lost everything. I have no business, no savings, and my belongings have been taken. The enormity of the events hits me, crushing my spirit until I collapse onto the sofa.

CHAPTER TWENTY-ONE

Quinn

My fingers roll the dice, unsure what to do for the best. Josh has fucked up. He's still grovelling as I gaze at him in the corner of my downtown office, the black eye lessening with each day that passes. Of all the gambles to get involved in, Joe Mortoni's family gathering was not one he should have been anywhere near. Drunk or not.

I've spent three days trying to alleviate the tension between our two families, offering thousands to cover the debt, but Joe wants the casino Josh offered as collateral. My fucking casino. Or Josh's life. Neither of which is fucking happening.

If only I could roll these cubes of ivory for family.

"You need to get out of my sight for a while," I drawl, barely containing the rage that continues to thunder inside my chest. "Go hole your ass up in the old family home. No one knows it's there." Josh stands, a sneer developing to cover the grovelling of a few minutes ago. He opens his mouth at the same time as my dice spin in the air. It's enough of a threat for him to sit the fuck back down.

I catch them, grinding them as I stare.

"I don't understand why Joe's being so serious. I was drunk. I didn't know what the fuck I was saying. He should never have—"

"What? Taken you seriously?" I stand at that, looking him over like the pain in my ass that he is. "You think Joe wouldn't take a shot at having Cane goods if he had a chance?" I wander over to him, just holding back the need to blacken the other eye. "The fuck were you thinking? You offered my property on a game of cards, Josh. Mine." The last of it roars from me, my hand fisting the dice and wondering if I should just throw the fucking things anyway, family be damned. Perhaps fate will deliver an answer for this screw up.

"I just wanted to prove—"

"That you're a waste of space." I finish the sentence for him, annoyed that he's even fucking speaking. Three fucking days that cunt's been on my back, asking when I'll have the keys for him. It's three days I've counted the loss of money we'll make because of a damn card game that should never have taken place. "How many times have I covered your ass now?"

I back away before I do something stupid, like strangle the shit.

"Calm down, Quinn. Just let Joe have it. We'll cover it with next years launder." I spin on Nate, scowling at his level approach. My patience is about done here. I've no intention of giving Joe anything. I shouldn't have to, regardless of the honour in debt.

My dice crush again, reminding me that I'm in control of our future, not Josh. I need him gone, safe from my anger if nothing else. Nate smiles, knowing exactly what's pissing me off more than anything to do with Josh's screw up.

That fact pisses me off further.

I snarl at him and round back to my desk, shouting for

Rody as I sign some papers. He comes in, a stern expression on his face as he glances at Josh.

"Get this dick out of my sight and on a plane to the old family home."

This time Josh doesn't protest. He stays silent, giving me a chance to think about how the hell I outmanoeuvre Joe. Maybe if I just raise the amount they'll fuck off, until then, I don't want Josh anywhere near harm.

"Come on, son," Rody says, a softening in his tone as he opens the door and waves Josh to him. *Son*—the term irritates me, but not as much as the fact that Rody was the last person to see Emily.

I scowl at him, too, and scrawl another paper, too wound up to ask the fucking question I want to. She's the real reason I'm confused. I can't concentrate. Everything is overblown and exaggerated. This thing with Joe should be easy, manageable. In fact, I should be enjoying it and playing the fucking game like I always do. I'm not.

"And don't fucking come back until I call for you, Josh. I'm warning you." His feet stop midway across my office, the hesitation proving his disdain for my thoughts. I look up at him, my last thread of patience drilling into his eyes. "You get back on a plane before you're told and I swear, Cane or not, I'll pull the fucking trigger myself."

He nods slowly, capitulation apparent, but his eyes tell me a different story. They always do. They did when we were young, and they still fucking do now.

Deceitful, entitled little shit.

"Quinn?" Nate says, his body rising in the other corner, nerves in his tone. I stand immediately, scattering papers from my desk and slamming my fist on the top of it. Josh stumbles back, sucking in breath and all but tripping over the rug.

"This all fucking ends now. Do you understand, Josh?" Nothing happens. No movement. No nod from either of them. I walk around the other side again, ready to rip his useless tongue out of his skull, but Nate moves closer. I halt and sneer at his brotherly show of affection, unsure if Josh deserves that from either of us anymore. "This is your last fucking chance, Josh. Get out before I regret that thought." He does, his body backing along the wall until it slides through the open doorway and Rody follows him through it.

A long sigh comes from me as I stare at the opening, my body trying to calm down. What a fucking mess. Gambling my casino away on a drunken flip of a card? He doesn't deserve anything Cane. If he wasn't one he'd be dead by now, my own hands throttling the life out of him.

"You could just call her," Nate says.

I turn and grab my phone, tucking it into my pocket as I slam the laptop closed and head from the room. Call her my ass. She's nothing to me. I told her the dice landed on seven, even though they didn't, and gave her a choice. Perhaps I hoped she'd choose to stay. She didn't. She chose to fucking leave me. Her call.

He catches up with me, his stride falling into step with mine as I turn through the back doors and out onto the road.

"What are you going to do?" he asks as we wander on past my car.

"Walk." He keeps walking with me, pulling his coat higher as we weave the crowds and aim forward. Christ knows where to. I just need to walk, get some of this energy out. "Then go see Joe personally. See if I can smooth this fucking thing over before he sends his dogs in." Nate doesn't speak as I keep forging on. He's clever like that. Gives me space to think. Unlike Josh who just keeps pushing me.

"I meant about Emily."

I stop, my body hovering around the pavement like a fourteen-year-old who got his dick touched.

"What?"

"Emily."

I stare at him, fucking annoyed at his self-righteous attitude and longing to beat the ever-loving crap out of something.

"She's gone, Nate. Debt paid." As it should be. Fucked with and released. "Finished."

"Is she fuck. Look at yourself," he snaps, his hand waving over my suit. "The Quinn I know wouldn't have been concerned about old Joe stripping a casino. He would have thrown it at him and then won it back the next week. The fuck's going on with you?" I glower at him and walk on again, hitching my dick back into place and refusing to enter a conversation about her. There's nothing to talk about. She's gone. That's all there is to say. "And what the hell are we walking for?"

I don't know. I just need to walk.

By the time I look up from my walking I realise Nate isn't with me anymore. I tuned him out after fifteen minutes of continued attempts at talking to me about Emily, and kept my head focused on how to organise Josh instead. Nothing has clarified itself.

I need a fucking drink.

Three turns around city blocks and I walk into Candy's whore house, not sure why I'm here. Perhaps I need to fuck something. Something dirty. Something that'll remind me of the filthy high-end whores I fuck, not the innocent eyes I can't stop imagining.

My own eyes draw around the interior, checking out the clientele who frequent these joints nowadays. It's the same as it's always been. Scum.

"Well, well, well. Cane. What you doin' here? You lowering yourself to walking the whore's boards?" Hardly.

I sneer at Tony as he walks over to me, his hand already fisting the inside of his jacket for a gun. Fuck knows why. Just because I don't come in here doesn't mean I don't pay him money on occasion.

"Put it away, Tony. It's as much use as your dick." He cools his grip on it, relaxing his hand back down and turning us both into a waiting area.

"What can I do for ya?"

"Drink."

One of the girls comes waltzing in almost instantly, a bottle of scotch in her fingers and a glass in the other set. I look her over, watching the way she oozes everything a good whore should. Perfect figure. Lean body. High tits, and legs that go all the way up. She's a stunner alright. Hair perfected in a chignon, and glistening lips that beg to have something rammed inside them.

I'm not the slightest bit fucking interested.

It pisses me off further than I already was.

I snatch the drink she pours and down it, holding it up for her to fill again. Then down another one, hoping my dick remembers what the hell it should be thinking of. It doesn't, so I take the damn bottle, throw a wad of dollars at Tony, and leave.

I end up walking circles around Chicago, no clear route

for anything, until I eventually arrive back at the car. The last of the liquor sinks down my neck and I toss the bottle towards the trash, aiming my keys for the car. I'm going to see Joe. Sort this mess out. Who the fuck does he think he is? He should have known Josh was drunk. He did know Josh was drunk. Fucking wasted I should think. Honour amongst debt? I choke on the thoughts as I pull the door open then slam my fist onto the steering wheel. It's no way to do business. He'll have a fucking chance at me rolling my dice before he gets a fucking thing from Cane wealth. I don't care who his family is, or how much he took from us before. He's not fucking taking it again.

The car screeches onto the highway, my foot flat on the accelerator as the engine roars and revs the roads. It's all a blur. I can barely see the lights, let alone think of stopping for them. Sirens blare somewhere, making me pump the gas for more power. There's nothing left, causing me to slam the brakes on, heave the wheel, and rocket the fucking thing down into dirty back lanes. It gives me time to think some more, analyse shit without the continued scream of sirens. I don't give a fuck who tries to catch me. I've got everyone in my pocket. If they managed I'd smile and flick them off, more cash tossed out at them. No one says no to Cane. No one can touch me. No one scares me. And no one fucks with me.

Apart from the old cunt I'm heading to.

And her.

I slide my gun out, laying it in my lap as I slow down into the groves. More prosperity passes me by, the huge houses reminiscent of those of movie stars and their happy families. I sneer at it all. Nothing is happy around here. We've forgotten happy. Left it behind us so we don't have to remember what it was like. If some of us ever even knew what it was.

Her song comes into my head as I gaze at Joe Mortoni's gates, the lilt of it at odds with the carnage that could be coming. It might be melancholy in some ways, might even be sad, but it's full of light, and breezy, too, its summer days in this winter gloom descending. Light for my dark.

I lean out of the window to press the buzzer to the house, but the gates swing open without a hitch, my numberplate already recognised as I drove up to them. Such is this computerized life we live. No men with guns stand here now arming the gateway. Not like they did when I first entered this world. No, they'll be waiting up there for me, their weapons unclipped and ready for use should I try anything. They're right to be concerned, the mood I'm in, who the fuck knows what's about to happen?

My tongue rolls over my teeth as I drive the incline, watching the house come into view. Four men wait, two of them talking into ear pieces. I snort, wishing Josh was here to earn his keep for ten minutes. Perhaps he should see this sometime, understand this gritty side of business that I've tried to pull us all from. It might help him understand why I keep him out of it. Why, even after his fuck ups, I still want him safe and out of this fucking life I hover over.

Marco wanders out, his tailored suit framing him and his eyes trained on my arm like a goddamn pit bull. I'm not surprised. He knows as well as I do how these situations can play out, especially given our conversations over the last few years.

I slide my slice of heaven back in it's holster and get out, hands slow to move as I aim for sober and walk towards him.

"Quinn," he says.

It's not a greeting like our last meeting at the casino, more a fucking warning. It's one I pay no heed to as I keep going past him to get to Joe. Marco doesn't pull enough damn ropes yet, irrespective of him suggesting he did. He won't until his father ends up like mine, unable to leave his room for lack of oxygen. Or dead. It's a damn shame because this whole fucking situation wouldn't have happened if he was in control.

He falls into step with me as I stare around, our bodies turning in unison through the house, suits depicting the image of decency. We're not, not as much as we portray. We're fucking lingering, that's what we are. Neither in nor out of this damned world we were forced into. Guns still ready should they be necessary and yet no real desire from either of us to use them anymore.

A chuckle comes from me as I see the card table and remember the last game here a year or so ago.

"You ever get any better at poker, Marco?" I won a half a million that night. And two nights with his girlfriend. She was hot. Sucked dick like a pro.

"Fuck you, Cane."

Obviously not.

"Ah, Quinton Junior." My hackles shiver in repulsion, fingers gripping my dice for fear I might shoot the old man before he gets another chance at talking. "That gun holstered?" I nod, scanning his face and barely pushing away the thought of him holding Mother down. "Brought my keys?"

"No."

He leans back in his plush chair, slowly lifting his crystal glass of liquor and sipping it just as Marco moves behind him. Joe smiles as I keep watching, noting another guy that's come in from a side room.

"Won it fair and square, Quinton. Your father was more honourable with his debts." I crick my neck, remembering the look of my mother only a few days ago, her hands holding the book out in defence.

"Josh was drunk, Joe."

"You should learn to control him better." I sneer at that and move to the seat opposite him, unbuttoning my jacket. "Like I do my boys." He chuckles and pours me a drink.

I flick my gaze to Marco, knowing damn well the crap he's had to go through to be controlled. It's the same heavy-handed guidance I took from my own father for years.

I take the drink offered, brushing my trousers off, and glance over my shoulder at the other guy who's moving in my peripheral. It makes me smile, blood rushing through my veins at the potential of this gun doing damage to this fucking family.

"You and I both know my casino wasn't his to gamble with." I look into the fire, rolling my shoulder to ease the tension building there. "It wasn't a fair game, Joe."

"Everything's a fair game, Quinton. Your family knows that as well as mine." My brow lifts, annoyance rising at the thought but acknowledging that fact.

For some reason, Emily's fiery little eyes come back at me from the flames, her sweet tune humming out notes that don't belong in this room. Fair game. He's right. It's all fair game. Just like it was when I took what I wanted from her.

The tune keeps coming, amusing me as my fingers roll the dice and I look back at Joe. Fair game. Just like these fuckers standing here now. I never have asked Marco if he was there when this old cunt fucked my mother, if he had a go himself. He would have only been thirteen at the time. Old enough to get his dick up.

"You fuck her?" I ask, lifting my eyes from Joe and up to Marco hovering behind. He frowns and tilts his head, confusion written all over his face. "My mother? Did you get your dick inside her?" He looks at Joe, no intention of answering me.

"Quinton, that's a long time ago," Joe says, clacking the crystal against his teeth as he takes another drink. The fuck it is. It happened yesterday as far as she's concerned, and it happens every damn time I visit her.

I stand up, rounding the furniture to get in front of Marco's face. I know Joe did. Know his brothers did, too, and his cousins, but this ass? This one pisses me off the most. Years the two of us have played cards, gambled our nights away in some pretence of working together, but the fury still lies underneath my skin. It waits like a fucking storm, ready to destroy the thing that ruined my mother's life and hinders progression away from this old school shit we both deal with.

I stare at him, snarling at his lack of answer and wishing he had the fucking balls to get on with changing this family. We both know what needs to happen here so business can move the fuck on. Both know that a trigger needs to be pulled, signalling the demise of some more archaic tradition. He's just not brave enough to do what needs doing.

I am.

"You fucking enjoy it, huh?" He just looks at me, still waiting for Joe to approve his answer. That thought alone makes me smile wider, knowing that he's not allowed to answer for himself. Standing here with a gun in his coat, waiting for papa to tell him what to do with it? He should grow the fuck up. Do what needs doing rather than fucking around with the half thought. "Still daddy's little kid, huh?" He glowers at me, his frame moving a step towards me. I laugh, hearing the safety being released on the gun from the other cunt in the room.

"Quinton. This isn't revenge. She paid your family's debt. That's all it was." I snap a mocking glare at Joe, as he finishes his self-righteous speech, then flick my gaze back to Marco. "Stow whatever thought you're having, son." Stow it?

I laugh again, fever fuelling my blood to where it needs to be. This fucking thought's been rattling my head for years. It's time all this old school debt handling was removed from our lives so we can move the fuck on with real business. We've done it their way for too long. Years of doing as all the old men say. Not anymore.

The room goes quiet apart from a crackling fire, and I continue staring at Marco, waiting for him to man up or leave so I can organise the next generation of Mortonis for him. It's gone on long enough. Some fucking sham of honour making us do shit to women that has no damn room in our world any longer. My dirty girl's proved that to me. That and the memories my mother shows me every fucking time I enter her room.

"You done with this shit?" I ask, eyes still levelled at Marco and waiting for him to answer me.

He frowns, then nods once, reaching for his gun. I don't look at him any longer. I smile instead and put some fucking trust in the hope he'll counter the gun that's covering my back. Either fucking way, it's time for the old man to die. Time for all this shit to be buried. If he can't do what needs doing, I will.

I stare past him out the window, feet backing me away

to get in front of Joe again, and remembering Emily's words about protecting the people I care for, wanting more. She spoke so softly about it, creating some image of smiles and love that's never been a part of my life. It was as distracting as she was, still is.

"It doesn't have to stop at protection. You can build a happier life, away from what your father pushed you in to."

"You raped my mother, Joe."

The words mumble out of me, still thinking about whatever the fuck those words meant from my Emily. He smiles, not caring about my anger and powered into not giving a fuck by these two dicks he thinks protect him.

"It's the way it's always been, Quinton. Honour amongst thieves."

"Fuck you."

He frowns a little, his fingers tightening around his glass and then putting it down on the side table as if he's about to stand. "Sit the fuck down old man."

"You'll respect the debt, Quinton."

Marco backs away, his fingers hovering around the gun beneath his pristine suit. I snarl at both of them, not giving a damn who lives or dies in this room.

I pull my gun, aiming at Joe's chest before he's got a chance to move. Marco draws his as quick, the barrel levelled straight at my head. I smirk at Joe's shocked face, amused at the triangle of weapons and wondering who's gonna pull first. Whatever happens, this cunt is dying now. He's dying because of my mother. He's dying because of what my father turned me into. And he's dying because I'm not fucking living like this anymore.

He stands and moves into me, some senile thought

imagining he can still tell me what to do, as his chest hits the barrel.

"Quinton, you're drunk. I've known you long enough to see when booze is taking over your level head," he says, his hand reaching for the end of my gun as a mocking jeer settles over his face. "Put the gun down before something happens." Condescending fucker. I stare, my hand as still as it's ever been regardless of the liquor still swimming through my blood. "Your father wouldn't have been so stupid."

I'm not my father.

My finger pulls the trigger, a hole splitting Joe's chest open the moment I do, blood splattering back at me. Another shot rings through my ears. I brace, ready for the bullet to drive into me, unsure if we're all going to fucking die, and swing to Marco. He sneers and walks past me, gun aimed over my shoulder at the dick behind.

I nod at him as he walks over to the other guy, another shot being fired straight into the head of his crumpled body, and I smile as I turn back to Joe. Done. Finished.

Blood pours, his eyes still widening after the event. I watch his half-slumped body begin dying and pick up his drink to down it as I lower my eyes to look into his face. It's twisted about, the handsome old smile gone from his lips as he realises what's happening. Children have fucking grown up, that's what's happened. We've taken over, removing old debts as we do.

"You played the wrong family this time, Joe," I say, reaching for the decanter and pouring another drink as he gurgles a breath. I chuckle, amused at the look of shock that still lingers around his eyes. "Should have looked closer to home, old man."

Marco arrives at my side, his long legs standing above his father's decaying body. I watch another of the few founding fathers exit this world they created, disgusted with the blood that bubbles from his mouth.

"I was young, Quinn," Marco says. I glare into Joe's eyes, watching as they begin fading away. "I did as I was told back then." I narrow my stare and push the anger away, letting it go to places I'll not have to deal with again. "It's done now."

I nod, not at him, but at the sentiment of what he's saying. Nothing like the old times will continue now. We've organised a new generation, one that can pride itself on modernisation.

The past is gone.

Two sets of shoes come running into the room, and we both spin, guns pointing at the threat. The guards look confused, their barrels flicking between me and Marco, until Marco holds his hands up and glares at the pair of them.

"This piece of shit needs disposing of," he snarls, walking in front of me. "You work for me now." I smirk behind him, holstering my slice of heaven and wondering where the fuck we all go from here. Home is where I'm going.

Home to organise the beginning of a new future.

CHAPTER TWENTY-TWO

Emily

I sit and stare out at my garden. It's the only part of my house that Jenny didn't touch and the only place that gives me any comfort. It's like I'm a stranger looking in on my own life the rest of the time.

Mum and Dad were pleased to hear from me. Jenny had told them we'd gone on an unexpected holiday. They didn't think to worry as it had only been a few weeks. Of course, I played along. I couldn't bring myself to admit what had happened. I didn't go to the police. There was no one else to tell.

When I charged my phone, I was saddened to see so few messages. A handful of texts, mainly about choir rehearsal, but that's all. Quinn could have kept me for another month and I don't think anyone would have noticed. I hadn't realised my life had grown so insular. I've worked so hard on my business that friendships have slipped through my fingers. And now, I'm left wondering if Quinn was the wake-up call I needed.

That thought sours my already grey mood. I can't shake the feeling that I miss him. A nagging at the back of my mind, like I've forgotten about something but can't remember what. It's the most ridiculous feeling in the world and I wish I could forge forward without this strange doubt lingering.

I've emptied the rest of my savings replacing my camera

and computer for the studio. It will take some time to build up what I can offer clients again, but I've worked from nothing before. The camera was the vital purchase. I can't be a photographer without one. Credit cards are there for emergencies and this counted as one.

My wardrobe was only missing the dresses I hoarded and never wore regularly. Of course, Jenny didn't take any of the everyday wear. Why would she? Everything else I can make do without. Nothing keeps my attention or can stop my mind from replaying the last few weeks.

It turns out I came back on a Friday. I've been gone three weeks. It seems like the longest time of my life. So much has happened and I'm still processing it. I can't sleep. I can't relax in my own home. I don't feel safe, which is ironic considering where I've been. My mind keeps playing tricks on me. If I thought I was going insane for behaving the way I did with Quinn then I'm positive I need to see someone now. I've grown paranoid about the house and studio, checking and re-checking the door to make sure it's locked when I come in, and repeating the precaution throughout the evening as well. The same goes for the studio.

And I don't want to admit or face the real problem.

I've spent time in the studio, first trying to ensure all my bills are paid, but then going through my old account files for my past client list. With the new computer set up I can start to build again, using the small mailing list programme I have to get back in touch with them.

I've missed five bookings over the weeks. My inbox is filled with messages, and I have some refunds to process. It makes me feel incompetent. I worked so hard and now I have to start over, and no one can know the reason behind it. That's my secret now and mine alone. Every day I have to wake up and crawl through the shame and regret that drench me before I can look to the future. But every day it's harder, and my mind blurs the details, making me question everything I've locked away in the shadows of my mind.

***

The weather has turned. The rain lashes down as I run from the tube to the studio. A puddle forms around where I stand in the doorway for too long feeling lost. Jenny's desk is empty now. I've moved it to the side and placed a beautiful vase filled with cut flowers on it. I turn on my computer and hang my coat up in the back room before switching the kettle on.

I hear the chime of the bell and pop my head out to see who's come in.

"Mrs Banks." My heart sinks. I left her a message on her answering phone to apologise. The deadline for her album has just passed, and I have nothing to give her. Jenny even took my hard drives. "Mrs Banks, I'm so sorry."

"I'd just like to say how disappointed I am. I came to you and trusted you to help mark my anniversary. I don't know what personal problems you have, but I thought you were a professional." She storms into the studio, bristling with anger.

"I am. I just—"

"You had plenty of opportunities to inform me that you needed more time. But I heard nothing from you. The studio was closed when I came for my appointment, and now we won't have anything for my husband."

"I'm sorry. If there was anything I could have—"

"I'd like my photos."

"Mrs Banks, please." I gesture to the sofa, but she straightens her stance. "I'm afraid that… Well, it's just, I was robbed and all my equipment and computers were stolen. I won't be able to give you the photos back."

The door jangles again, and I glance out the corner of my eye to see who it is. My blood runs cold as I recognise the man. He shouldn't be here. He *can't* be here.

"Emily, I don't want to sound harsh, but you've had weeks to get in touch with me about this. You sat here and promised me that I'd have a wonderful gift. Perhaps if you were married for as long as I have been, you'd better understand. I trusted you, and now I have nothing to show for it."

"Mrs Banks, again, I can't apologise enough." I plead with her to understand, but how can she if all I'm telling her is a half-truth. My eyes flick between her and my unwanted visitor, who's still lingering in the corner near Jenny's desk.

"I'll expect to see the money I paid you returned to my account."

"Of course. I've already made arrangements. It should be cleared in the next day or so."

She nods and turns to leave.

"Goodbye," I call after her.

"She got her knickers in a twist." Shifty pushes off the wall and comes further into the studio.

"What are you doing here?" I stand, facing a man I hoped I wouldn't have to see again.

"I've been stopping by, seeing if Jenny's still around." His eyes dart around the space, living up to his name.

"Jenny?" I question, not sure I believe that.

"Yeah."

"Shifty, she's gone. She set me up, stole my money and anything else she could get her hands on, and has gone."

"Right." He nods, looking around the room and shoving his hands deep into his pockets.

"How did you meet her, anyway?"

"At a club. Then saw her again at a game."

"A gambling game?"

"Yeah." He nods.

"You allowed her to run up debt?"

"She was always good for the money."

"Well, not this time," I mumble.

Realising how Shifty being here isn't a concern, I go and finish making my cup of tea.

"So you don't know where she's gone?"

I finish brewing my tea and go and sit at my desk. "No, Shifty. She didn't leave a note after tossing my house and stealing whatever I had of any value. If she's got any sense, she'll never come back. After what she's done… well." I wish I could verbalise how gutted I feel. Jenny's betrayal is harder to take than anything else. What happened to her for her to hate me enough to send me to Quinn, knowing it would never end well?

"Alright."

I take a sip of tea and hear the bell, signalling Shifty's departure. I let out a slight breath and resist going to the door to lock it. I'm at work. The shop needs to be open. I can't close it just because I feel uncomfortable, certainly not after the money I've had to pay out to replace everything. But Shifty's visit has brought everything to the surface. The date, my impulsive reaction to Quinn, the kidnapping, his back and forth behaviour. I swipe the stack of magazines from the coffee table, scattering them across the floor.

My cheeks are damp before I realise I'm crying again. A storm of confusion and shame cloud my mind and pull me deeper into despair. For every step I take in claiming my life back, I fall back three. I cling to the memory of my hands tied to the chair in the dark room. The fear and anguish I felt reminds me that I should be glad to be free. But when I remember, my mind doesn't block out the pleasure that Quinn always managed to give me, or the way my heart began to beat for him.

Am I strong enough to put the pieces of my life back together when, if I'm honest with myself, I left a part of my heart with Quinn?

By 4:30 p.m. I'm ready to leave. I turn off all the lights, lock the camera and laptop away in a small safe I've purchased and hid in the back storeroom, and grab my coat.

I rummage through my bag to find the keys and look up, straight at a shadowy figure in the doorway. He looks familiar, and I can't help the jolt my heart gives as my mind jumps to some romantic notion that Quinn's come back for me.

"Quinn?" My hopeful plea is pathetic.

"No. Close, though."

"Josh?"

"Thought I'd pay you a visit." He steps from the doorway, closing it behind him and sending a riot of panic through my system.

"What… why? How did you know where… where I work?"

"Relax, Em. I'm not here to hurt you." His smile looks wicked in the dark, and I wish I could turn the lights on. "I had a visit from Shifty, that's all."

"Shifty? Why would he come and see you?"

"Because he thought you could use a hand." He rests his hand on the door, blocking my exit. "Now, if we're going to have this conversation, why don't we grab a cup of coffee?" Josh might have apologised the last time I saw him, but do I want to strike up a friendship with him? A bubble of hope that he's come to talk to me about Quinn fills my chest. What would I do if he wasn't here? Go home to an empty house and drive myself half crazy? We'd be in a public place. What can he do to me in a café full of people?

I nod and pull my coat tightly around my body, as if it can offer another layer of protection to my heart. Seeing Josh brings all of my memories flooding back. He opens the door and allows me to exit. I lock the studio and only manage to check it once before he steers me along the pavement.

"I told you to relax, Em. Shifty mentioned you're struggling a bit, that's all."

"I'm fine."

"The shop looks far from fine. So do you." I try to brush off his comment, but it hurts to hear it from Josh.

We walk to the closest coffee shop, and he seats me at a table in the window. It's surprisingly quiet, though. Not what I wanted.

He doesn't ask me anything, just goes to the counter and then returns with two mugs of steaming coffee.

"Big brother might not be around any longer, but that shouldn't mean you can't benefit from the Cane family. Shifty said your business is suffering."

"I'm fine." My protest sounds lame, and I'm distracted by Josh's mention of Quinn.

"You're stubborn."

"Maybe. But my business doesn't involve you. Quinn said I wouldn't have anything to do with him again." I'm caught between wanting to be here and wishing Josh would leave all the questions.

"I'm not Quinn, although, perhaps you wish I were?"

"He kidnapped me for three weeks." My defence is an obvious one and I know Josh will see through it.

"And he sent me here so I can be out of the way and no longer be a burden. He has his flaws."

"Pretty big flaws."

"But we both love him anyway."

"I don't love Quinn. He's a bastard." I hug my coffee cup with my hands, not wanting Josh to see the lie.

"I don't think that's how you really feel, is it?" He leans back, smiling. "I know what he's like, Em. He screws around with whores for fun. He's never had a… pet like you before. Someone he wants to fuck on a regular basis. You must have something he wants."

My eyes flash around the coffee shop, praying that nobody is within earshot.

"Suddenly ashamed, are we?"

I can't help the blush that flares over my cheeks at his words.

"Maybe it's your innocence that Quinn liked, or those mismatched eyes of yours." He leans in closer and I have to fight my reaction to pull away.

"What do you want, Josh? I told you I don't need help, and I've listened to enough."

"Quinn ruined your business."

"No, he didn't." I shake my head furiously.

"If Quinn isn't prepared to look out for you, I am. He shouldn't have just dumped you back here. He might get away with it with me, but not with you."

His sudden sympathy throws me. I watch his eyes, searching for any sign he's playing me. It's so hard not to see Quinn in his features. He looks just like him. A smaller, leaner version, but so similar.

"What did you do to make Quinn send you to England?" I ask, wanting to shift the focus to him, and find out why he's been sent here.

"I lost a bet to a man our family doesn't like very much."

"Can't you just pay it? I don't think Quinn is struggling financially."

"I bet his casino. I owe the casino that he recently acquired."

"A casino? How can you even do that when gambling?"

"You'd be surprised what you can win or lose at the right game."

"What's Quinn going to do?" The question's out before I can stop it, and I hate that I'm so desperate to hear the answer.

"I don't know. But I'm here, so it's not my problem to solve. He'll find some way to settle the debt. He always does." His voice trails off, as if he knows the hurt that comes with his comment. I was a debt, used as a settlement in place of Jenny or her money. I don't say anything else and concentrate on my coffee. My mind races with thoughts of Quinn and his business dealings. Is there any hope that his business could be the right side of legal one day?

"You didn't talk much when we first met back in Chicago. Was that because Quinn told you to stay quiet?" Josh breaks our silence.

"He didn't tell me anything. I didn't even know you'd be in the house when I walked up the stairs." A shiver runs down my spine as I remember those first few steps outside of the room. How petrified I was that I'd find myself in a worse scenario.

"You must have done something truly terrible to make him send you away. I'm surprised he did. He needs company. He takes too much on, paranoid that the Cane name will lose power or some shit if he doesn't handle everything himself."

"You sound a little bitter, Josh."

"No more than you are. Besides, I still think I'm right. You want to see him again. Or something's changed. You wouldn't be sitting having coffee with me if it hadn't."

"Maybe I think you're all bluff and no bite? Besides, you can't be any worse than your brother." I regret the words immediately. Josh's previously calm frame turns to stone, his eyes darkening as I inwardly panic. And then it's gone, in the blink of an eye, and I have to wonder if I imagined it. His lips tilt into a funny half smile.

"Come to dinner with me." He phrases it as a statement and not a question.

"Dinner? I'm not sure that's a good idea." My choices were limited when he barred my exit from the studio. Voluntarily having dinner would be another alarming decision on my part, and sure evidence that I need to see a shrink. I need to look at moving on with my life and not grasping at threads that will keep me connected to Quinn.

"Because you want to know more about Quinn, and I have the answers. You can even see where we grew up."

"What do you mean?"

"I'm staying at our old home. The one we had when we

were truly only children. Before we went to Chicago and things started to turn for the worse."

"I'm not sure Quinn would want me to see where he grew up." The temptation to ask more is right on the end of my tongue, but I know I'd be stupid to do this.

"Fine. Your call. But here's my number. I want you to call me if you have any problems, okay? That's all." He pushes a card across the table to me. I pick it up and stuff it into my pocket.

"I don't understand. Why are you being so nice to me?"

"It's obvious that you mean something to Quinn. Family means something to us. He's treated you no better than garbage. I want to make that right. It's only dinner. I can try to explain a little about Quinn and what he's like."

It's a carrot that's hard to resist. But my flight reflex is in full working mode, despite my dubious state of mind, I know not to put myself in a vulnerable position again.

"That's very kind of you, but I'd really like to put all of this behind me and move on." I stand and button my coat, suddenly desperate to be away from Josh before I change my mind and agree to his offer.

"Don't be a stranger, Em. It would be such a shame." I don't look back, but hear… something in his voice as I push open the door and into the cold night.

The strange encounter plays on my mind all the way home. I finger the card, turning it over and over in front of me, undecided as to what to do. I can't simply forget everything that's happened. As much as I might like that, it's unrealistic to me. Finding out more about Quinn is a lure so appealing that I am considering calling Josh back. He seemed pleasant, kind even. A complete contrast to who I first met. But can I trust him?

My phone chimes and breaks my trance.

In case you want to get in touch with the Cane that you do care for. Josh

I read the text message and the accompanying contact for Quinn.

How did you get my number?

You are Emily Brooks, owner of Studio B? Your number isn't hard to track down.

Why?

Call it an act of good faith. Dinner, tomorrow night. 7pm. I'll text you the address.

CHAPTER TWENTY-THREE

Quinn

Nate closes the files down one by one, his fingers working as efficiently as they always do. I gaze at him working, thumb rubbing my scar at the thought of modernising the business, and then look up through the windows towards the main house. No more reliance on old rules or traditions. No more need to bow to the will of other families. There are only three major players left from the old world now that Joe's dead. In the states at least. Other countries have their own generations to deal with. Here, we are now moving forward in a new vision. Marco, like me, is aligned in our vision. He's allowed me to do what needs doing, no comeback on our family for my actions in his presence. Whether it was because of my inward need for revenge or not isn't relevant, only that it's now done.

There are only the other families to pull on board going forward, all three of whom will succumb to their business needs when they see the Canes and Mortonis aligning tighter.

Threatening them with power.

"How's Marco handling the death?" Nate asks, standing and walking over to the bar.

I stare at my view of the main house, unconcerned about Marco and wondering when the time will come for my father to be taken the same way. He deserves as much as Joe got, more so given the past and his inability to protect his own family. No one ever touched a Mortoni woman, only the girlfriend I had on the flip of the deck, and she wasn't a real wife.

"Funeral's next week. We're both invited to go and grieve the old man's departure," I eventually reply. He smirks and holds up a glass to me, toasting the air between us.

"Should be interesting. He's obviously grief stricken." Hardly, he just needs us there to make our world believe he killed his father himself as we've agreed.

I gaze at the house still, trying to pull together thoughts that have been with me for three days. A new generation of Cane business. New strategy. New protocols. A new direction. Perhaps a life like Emily leads is simpler. Less threat to life. Less countering and manoeuvring. Less looking over our shoulders, worried where the next menace will come from.

"How legal are we overall?" I ask, tipping my eyes to him. He chuckles and closes the laptop, gulping back a shot and offering me one. I shake my head.

"You just killed Joe Mortoni, Quinn. I'd say we're not legal at all."

I wave him off, standing with a small smile and pocketing my hands as I walk closer to the window. My dice rattle in my pocket, making me grip them and remember her telling me she wanted to go back home. I pull them out and grind them round to a four and a three. Seven. That's the number she blurted out. Fate fell well for her, offered her a chance at freedom again. Freedom from me and this world I've been born into.

"What could we do to run smarter, Nate?"

"We do run smart."

"Cleaner then." He frowns at me, gripping his drink

softly and looking at me across the kitchen space, eyes full of interest. I snort at him, amused by his need to become a decent human being. Not that he's ever been far from that anyway.

"You know that as well as I do. We close down. Run the money 'til it dries, siphoning it through offshore accounts, then clean it back up through whatever we can buy legitimately."

He rounds the island unit, coming to the window to stand beside me.

"How long would it take?" I ask, trying to translate the multiple accounts in my head as I keep staring at the view.

"A year, two maybe. I've got an exit strategy already mapped out. Did it a year or so ago."

I turn to him, admiring his acumen and nodding at the thought. Two years to clean up and back out.

"You could lose what needs losing to make us untouchable?" I ask. He laughs and pulls at his cufflinks to roll his sleeves up. "I'm serious, Nate. All out."

"We're already untouchable, but I could make us more viable to the tax system. Make our reality as clean as a British whistle alongside our appearance, if that's what you're asking for." That's exactly what I'm asking for. I nod at him again and turn back for the view, dice beginning to roll comfortably round my palm. "Although, you'll be bored, Quinn. We'll be nothing but a money-making machine with less ability to coerce profit." He wanders away, making me swing around with him and follow him through to the main lounge. "You were born for what you do. It's in your eyes all the time. Has been since you came home that night."

I sigh and sit in one of the chairs, remembering that night and wondering what would have happened if I hadn't killed for the first time. He smiles and runs his hands through his hair, probably as uncomfortable with the thought now as he was when he cleaned my scar up all those years ago.

"You enjoy it, Quinn. Always have as far as I can tell. You're a cold bastard. You get your fucking kicks out of this life."

Enjoy. Interesting word for the life I've lived so far.

I don't enjoy a damn thing.

"No, Nate, I just needed the world to think I did. You, too."

He scowls at me, a confused expression settling and expectancy written all over his face, then walks straight back out of the room. I sit, staring at the doorway and listening to glasses clinking as he comes back in.

"Talk," he says, the tone he normally reserves for Josh in his voice. "'Cause that just confused the shit out of the last ten years of my fucking life, Quinn." He fills me a glass and lands it roughly on the glass table in front of me next to my dice, the frown as deep as it gets. I chuckle, enjoying his snarl of irritation. He looks all Cane. Exactly what I've made him become whether he liked it or not.

"You think I had a choice?" I reach for the glass and lean back to look at him again, brow raised for an answer he can't damn well give me. I didn't have any fucking choice. "It was me or you. Me that did as I was told, or you that would have had to do all those things I've done. The same ones you sneer down your fucking nose at me for." He stares for a second or two longer and then drops his eyes. He's fucking right to. He wouldn't have lasted doing what I've done. Never could have handled it. The blood. The fights. The fucking death and threats. He would have lost his grip on all this, weakened us.

"I chose me, Nate."

Quiet descends as he thinks about that. Typical Nate, thinking his way through a problem and trying to document his way out of it. Count the numbers, find a solution. Only this time there isn't one. There never was. Big brother stepped up to the plate to keep him safe. Keep both of them safe. Just like my mother asked me to.

I'm damn tired of it.

"You've never said."

"Why should I? The business needed to run. It's been running. Fucking improving."

That's all there is to say. What the fuck talking is going to achieve I don't know. He knows me better than anyone, and that's barely enough for him to understand half of what goes on in this head of mine. It's a place he doesn't want to be. Shouldn't be either. Hell, it's a place I haven't wanted to be sometimes.

I drink some more, sipping at the dry scotch, and stare back through the lounge in the direction of the main house. Fucking loyalty.

"This is Emily, isn't it?"

"What?"

"All this." He waves a hand at me, a slight smile forming as he moves to a chair. "This emotion. It's not you. You fell for her."

The thought makes me imagine her naked, four feet from where he's currently standing, my dick in her ass and her whimpers calling my name. I smile at the image, still able to feel her skin in my grasp.

"How much did she owe you?"

"Nothing."

She owed me nothing. And yet she gave me everything.

The sound of that song comes into my mind, eyes blankly locking onto the spot I'm thinking about. It's been with me since she left, along with the feeling that something has been lost by her going. I sip my drink again, trying to work through the sensations she's left me with. I feel empty, as if her presence in this house made it more alive, made me more alive. The corners of my mouth tip again, a memory of her coming down the stairs more enamouring than I gave it credit for at the time. It makes me twist over my shoulder, following her ghostly form down them, for once not tripping over her feet. She was so much bolder by the end of our time, even daring to try running from me. She spat and kicked like the best of them.

My dirty girl.

"Then why was she here?" he asks.

"I stole something I wanted. Nothing more than that."

It's something I still want.

I reach for my dice again, scooping them from the table and leisurely rolling them around. Perhaps fate should tell me what to do about her. She's in here with me. In this room. In this house. Hell, she was even there when I pulled the trigger on Joe, her sweet melody coming from the flames I stared into. No woman has ever stayed with me like that. That's what Mother talked about. Love.

"There wasn't a debt to be paid?" he asks, surprise in his voice.

"Not by her." He shakes his head and turns away, dismissing me and heading out of the room, disgust evident in his stride.

"That's fucked up, brother, even for you," he calls back,

his frame disappearing out of my view.

The main door slams, signally his irritation. I sigh and digest the words. Even for me. It's true. She never owed me that money. Never should have been taken away from her life, but I took her anyway. I behaved like my father would have, no care for morality or civility. I just took, and then I carried on taking just like Cane always does.

A frown creases my brow, disgusted with myself about the whole fucking thing, irrespective of my enjoyment of it. It pulls visions forward of my mother and her life, the madness in her mind borne of people like me taking what we want. The thought causes concern to creep in, making me snort at the sensation. I should find out if she's alright, if she's managing her way out of the fucked-up hell I put her in. I haven't even asked Rody if she got home safely. I didn't need to. He nodded when I saw him, telling me he'd done his job. That was enough for me at the time.

It's not now.

I swipe out my phone, searching for her number, then remember I haven't got it. What a fucked-up world this is. I steal her, play with her, treat her like dirt and then don't even have the fucking foresight to have her number in my phone? I growl at myself and stand up, glaring at the door to the basement as I pass it by and remember locking her up down there. I'm a fucking animal. I've been moulded by a generation that inflicts cruelty to negotiate terms. Nate's right. It's all fucked up. I've behaved just like my father to someone who deserved nothing but respect.

Not anymore.

The dice roll, the throw of them at my kitchen counter coming without any real thought from me.

"Nine," I mumble, watching them spin and bounce the surface. One lands on five, the topple of the second unsure whether it should land on four or not. I've scooped them up before it gets a chance to land fully. It's close enough for me.

I snatch the keys off the table and straighten my tie, some pretence of the decency she deserves making me concerned for how I appear. It's strange, making me chuckle at myself and remember her fingers tracing my scar. There was such a softness in them as she frowned and gazed, her mind asking questions she shouldn't have had to hear the answers to.

I head out of the house towards my car, part holding myself off doing so, and yet unable to stop my feet driving towards an airport I shouldn't head for. Women like her don't belong here with us. They should be exactly where she was before me. Forging her way forward in life. Appreciated in her community for qualities that this world I'm in bypasses as inconsequential.

"Where are you going?"

Nate's voice makes me spin back to face the house. He's sitting in the formal garden area, drink still in his hand as he glares at the main house and then tips his head to me.

"Out."

"Where?"

"I need to…"

I need to what? I don't know myself, but I do know I need to do something. I need to talk to her, or see her. I need to know I haven't fucked her over like Joe Mortoni and his family did my mother. My chest aches for something I don't know what to do with.

Nate sips his drink and waits for an answer, no help on the matter as a smile starts to spread.

"You're in love, brother."

I scowl and turn for my car again, not interested in discussing whether I am or not. This isn't about love. This is about apologising for something that should never have happened. Making sure my fucked-up sensibilities didn't just screw over someone's life and destroy it. It's about modernizing and changing our future, something I started with the bullet in Joe's dead body. Something she started when she breathed my damned name and it finally meant something to me other than business.

"Don't bring her back, Quinn. She's not meant for this."

The car door slams and I spin the wheel to get me away from his words, foot flat to the floor as I power out of the drive. Not fucking meant for this? He's damn right she's not, but that's not stopping me wanting her in my grip again.

I phone for the plane as I travel towards Chicago, ordering it ready in the next thirty minutes. It won't be. There's no fucking way they'll be able to turn it around in that time. I'll have to pace the hanger, hungry for something I can't get to quick enough. I don't even know why it's so fucking important to me, but it is. It's like a nagging I can't get out of my skull. A lingering imprint of a past I want rid of somehow.

By the time I arrive an hour later, traffic hindering my route, the plane's already waiting for me and ready to go. I chuckle and grab at my dice as I climb the steps, releasing and catching them, amused by fate stopping my need to pace. These damn cubes I hold have guided so much of my life. All the decisions I couldn't make. All the times I faltered. They've served me well, showing the world a monster who couldn't care less for the decisions they made.

"Good Evening, Sir," the stewardess says.

I nod and carry on through to my seat, indifferent to her conversation. I'm not here for servants or small talk. I'm not here for things that answer me with what I want to hear, their sycophantic voices belying their truths. I'm here because I am, for once in my life, in need of someone who counters me. Someone who offers the possibility of this new future I'm creating, breathes life into it with me. It's consuming enough to make me reach for my phone and turn it off, needing time to process my own emotions without interference from others. Cane can be damned for a while.

The thought resonates as I stare out onto the runway, engines already powering up to get me to her. The sound of them inches my gut closer to the realisation that Nate was right, irrespective of my dismissal. I am in love, but with no right to be. I have fallen for someone so far from my world I don't know how to pull her into it, or even if I should. What do I have to offer an emotion like love? Lies, deceit. Manipulation and avoidance. A world still steeped in death and destruction? Nothing will change for a few years. Maybe a tilt of the axis for a while, but we are still Cane until we become legitimate. We still have a business to run, deals to complete, most of which will still have repercussions should the deal go bad. This gun will be lodged in my jacket for some time yet.

My fingers rub at my chin, feeling the hard ridge of the scar and imagining her under a blade like that. She'd never even held a gun before I forced one into her hands. But with me, as part of Cane? She will need to know how it feels to have life threatened, be ready for it. She will need to understand that every day of her life because no matter the changes I make, and no matter the life I try to forge, there will always be someone waiting in the background for us. It'll keep coming forever regardless of how well Nate or I count the numbers down.

The wheels take off, and the ground of Chicago disappears into the distance beneath my feet. I just keep staring and think about what the fuck I'm doing up here, still confused about the correct angle to use when I get to her. Maybe I'll make these cubes spin again when I see her, let fate make that last decision.

CHAPTER TWENTY-FOUR

Emily

The number programmed into my phone burns my mind with possibilities. My thoughts clog with what ifs and maybes, all redundant because the sugar coating I give them is nothing like the truth. The truth is raw and dirty and shameful. In my head, I call Quinn and he admits to missing me as much as I miss him. He admits to the reason why he took me, and he comes back to London, and we start again, the same connection pulling us together, the same chemistry that exploded between us.

But that's all in my head. The reality and my own fantasies blur more and more with each day. And Josh is to blame. He planted seeds of doubt and hope with his words, and I haven't been able to forget them.

I should be getting out of bed and heading to the studio, but I can't face it today. And I still have to decide if I should meet Josh. Yesterday morning that would have been an easy question to answer, but now I feel divided. He's been kind. He didn't need to check in on me, but then again, why would I trust him?

I've never been one to mope around feeling sorry for myself, but that's what I'm reduced to. I feel lost, like I don't know what direction I'm travelling in anymore or if I'm even the same person I was.

Hours roll on, and I can't focus. I'm trapped by wanting something I know I can't have. I want the Quinn who existed in mere glimpses, showing me that he's there under all the harshness, threats and steel he's built around him. Just enough for me to latch on to and drive myself crazy. I imagine him as a child. Innocent and carefree playing with his brothers. Before he got that scar and sunk himself into the underbelly of society that he now calls business.

I pick up my phone and with a rush of adrenaline, fire a message to Quinn.

I miss you. Emily

Tears catch in my throat as I force them not to fall from my lashes. I shouldn't miss him. How can I miss what he did to me? Anger and frustration replace the adrenaline, and give me a moment to think clearly. I head for the shower to freshen up. I can't do anything sitting wrapped in my dressing gown.

The hot water brings a comfort I immediately recognise, and I let it suffuse around me. I need to get some air. Some perspective. Maybe I should visit Mum and Dad. Keep my mind off of the last month. But I'll have to re-schedule the few appointments I've managed to get booked.

I opt for something far easier to try and conquer my mood—taking photos. It always lightens my spirit and turns my attention back to the good that's in the world. I push aside the pang in my chest at leaving the camera and the shots I took in Chicago. It might have only been for a few minutes, but that day was special.

I dress in warm clothes and wrap up with a scarf and hat. The studio camera is locked safely at work, so I grab my old

35mm from my room, more like an antique now, and head out. The Nikon was one of the first cameras I owned, and luckily Jenny didn't find it in the box under the bed. I haven't used it in years, and it might not even work, but I need to give it a go.

The light isn't special, and the day is classically grey and cloudy, but I feel more like me than I have in days. My cheeks have pinked up, and I have life back in my blood.

My phone stays quiet in my pocket while I'm out. I'm not sure if I want Quinn to return my silly text or not, but I refuse to be disappointed if he doesn't. He gave me a choice, and I took it. This is of my making, and although I might not understand everything that happened over the last few weeks, I need to accept it and move on. Coming to terms with my ordeal and the resulting emotions is a priority, and I decide to seek out a counsellor next week.

No sooner have I hung my coat and scarf in the hall than the doorbell rings. I keep the safety chain on before opening it.

Josh smiles at me warmly, as if he's expected. "Hello, Em. I hadn't heard from you, so decided to save you the trouble of finding your way to mine. I have a car." He points to a black Mercedes parked a few spaces down the street.

"Josh, I wasn't expecting you. I've just got in, actually, and wanted to text you to apologise that I won't be able to—"

"It's not anything special, Em. Come on. I know you want the company. I'll wait here for you." He crosses his arms and smiles again.

"Okay, just let me get my things." The door's still on the safety, so I shut it and dart into the front room. The thought of going to Quinn's old home lights me up inside. The lure is too fierce, and Josh has been nothing but courteous since I arrived home. It might not be wise for my mental health to maintain a link to a relationship I'm pining for, but right now, I don't care.

I grab my phone and fire a quick message to Quinn.

Josh gave me your number, in case you were wondering. He's taking me to dinner at your old house. It will be nice to get to see where you grew up. I meant what I said before. Emily

I grab my bag and take my coat off the hook before venturing out.

"Great. Shall we head out? It's about an hour's drive to the old place."

"Are you sure? I don't want you to go to any trouble."

"No trouble. It's all ready. Besides, I don't want you to miss out on seeing more of the Cane family history." He opens the passenger door and waits for me to get in. He rounds the car and climbs in, starts the engine and pulls away.

The journey through town is slow due to traffic, but when we clear the city, we make better time. There's still something that doesn't sit right regarding Josh, but I tap down on my overreaction until there's something more concrete. Right now, I need to be calm. Plus, I'll be able to find out more about Quinn.

"When did you move from London?"

"When we were kids. Quinn must have been ten or so. Dad's business was expanding. He needed to be in the states, or so the story goes."

"And you kept the property all these years?"

"We had an old family friend, a caretaker if you will, who

looked after the place. Neither Dad nor Quinn liked to get rid of anything that was Cane property. Something to do with their God complex, perhaps."

Josh may jest, but I know he doesn't mean his words to be taken lightly. From what I've seen, Quinn does play God over Josh's life, and rather than share things with his brother; he pushes him to the side.

The roads get narrower, and trees and fields replace the houses. It's certainly out of the way. Josh turns into a long drive and heads up to a handsome house. It's nothing as grand or impressive as the mansion back in Chicago, but a large detached property with plenty of privacy.

"Here we are." Josh parks up and heads towards the door. He holds it open as I step over the threshold. "Let me take your coat."

The entrance is dark, and there are few lights on inside. A single light bulb hangs from the pendant in the hallway, showing up dust specs in the air. All it needs is a chill and the abandoned house stereotype would be complete. The hallway is open, with high ceilings and parquet flooring throughout. A sweeping staircase sits to the right, with spindle banisters, and a dark-red carpet runner up the centre. Doors are ajar on either side of the entrance, but Josh leads me towards the back and into what turns out to be the kitchen and dining area.

Vibrant aromas of tomato and garlic assault my senses and remind me of eating with my parents. A homey feel replaces the eerie sense I got in the hallway.

"I hope spaghetti is alright for you? I had Rebecca start things off. I think I'm capable of boiling the pasta."

"Sounds lovely. Who's Rebecca?" I ask, wondering who this might be.

"She's the wife of Nigel, the caretaker. They live on the next road and look after the place."

"I'd love to have a look around." I peer back out into the hall, trying to imagine Quinn and his brothers playing as children.

"How about a drink first. Wine?"

"Um, sure." My smile is hesitant. I'm not a big drinker and the last thing I want is to get too tipsy.

The oval table at one end of the kitchen is set for two, but it's the photos hanging on the wall that entice me. Three grainy colour photos of boys of varying ages playing in fields hang in plain frames. It's clear who Quinn is without even trying to identify him. He stands taller than his brothers, the centre of all three photos, and he's smiling, carefree and happy as any child should be.

My heart aches for him as I think what his life could have been if his family had been different—away from the gangsters and shady business dealings that seem to rule his life now.

"Wine." Josh hands me a glass of red and I watch him take a large mouthful, and his eyes flash down to my glass expectantly. I bring it to my lips and take a tiny sip. "Sit. I can show you the place after we eat." Josh pulls out a chair for me, and I ease myself down.

"So. What were you all like growing up?"

"Oh, the usual. Out getting into mischief." His answer is vague and disappointing. I want details like favourite toys or games. What Quinn's hobbies were.

Josh busies himself in the kitchen, stirring the pan and watching over the pasta. My eyes roam around, and I can't shake the anxiety that's swept over me. Josh has been nothing but polite, but he also makes the hairs on the back of my neck pay attention, and not in a good way. I sip my wine and practice my patience.

He returns in a few moments with two steaming bowls of spaghetti. "Here. Bon appétit."

"Thank you, it smells delicious." I haven't eaten much all day and am starting to feel light headed. The wine wouldn't have had time to hit my system yet, and surely a couple of sips wouldn't have affected me like this. I put the wine down and wait for Josh to start before sinking my fork into the noodles of saucy pasta.

We eat for a short while in silence. I'm happy to enjoy the food rather than make polite conversation. The draw of coming here to find out more about Quinn has lessened with the anxiety that has started to simmer in my blood.

"Have some more wine." Josh tops up my barely touched glass and I take another sip. The pasta is delicious and the first proper food I've eaten in a few days.

"I can't remember much of this home. We left when I was so young. Of course, Nate and Quinn don't talk about the past. It's one of those topics that we all know to keep clear of."

"That's a shame. I got the impression you were all close?" My attention grows and I try to encourage Josh to keep talking.

"Oh, we're close. But there are things that we just don't discuss. We share most things. Quinn is generous when it comes to the perks of the business."

"He pays you? I didn't realise you had a job with Quinn. I thought that's what you were arguing about?"

"I have money. Quinn sees to most of my expenses. Cars, booze, drugs, anything I want, it's mine. Girls."

My fork stills at his mention of women. I force my hand to keep moving the food towards my mouth, open, close and chew. The last thing I want is for Josh to see he's rattled me so easily.

"More wine?"

"None for me. I'm not a big drinker." My glass is nearly overflowing so I take another small sip.

"Shame." Josh tops up his glass.

Despite the food, my head still feels light, and my eyes suddenly feel like I've been awake for a week. I blink, focussing and fidgeting in my chair to shake myself awake.

"It's unusual for Quinn to have a girl at the house for more than one night. Even more unusual for him to keep her to himself." Josh's lips curve into a sleazy smile, and the anxiety that I had kept under control is let loose and pumping around my body, adding to my groggy head.

"How did he fuck you? Did he tie you up and force you? I'd have liked to watch that."

"You know, I think I'm done here." I stand, but only just manage to stay upright. My head swims as I stagger along the hallway, dizzy and confused, grabbing my coat as I pass. I slam my hand down on the door handle and smack right into the wooden frame. It's locked. My anxiety explodes into full blown fear as I realise I'm trapped here with Josh.

"Em, why the rush to leave? We were just getting acquainted. Isn't this how Quinn did it? Wine and dine you before fucking you?" I dump my coat and flee up the stairs, taking two at a time, my muscles draining of energy before I've even reached the top. "Oh, you've just made this so much more fun!" Josh shouts, and I can hear the edge of crazy in his voice.

I turn left at the top of the stairs and into the second door on the left. A bedroom. I close the door as softly as I can and look around the dark room before rushing to the window. There's a slanted roof below which leads into the back garden, so I quickly work to throw the window open before crawling under the double bed.

I take a few deep breaths and force my heart to return to a reasonable beat. The cold breeze sweeps through, chilling my skin and sending goose bumps over my arms.

The room is quiet. The only sound is my breathing, deafening my ears in the confined space. I hold my breath and try to listen to any noise coming from outside. I didn't have time to look around to see how big the upstairs is. Four bedrooms maybe? I close my eyes and pray Josh picks another one to look in first, and that he believes I'd try to escape out of the window.

Minutes pass. At least, it feels like minutes. Still nothing. The room grows colder as the air continues to whistle in, the smell of the damp evening freshening the musty scent in the room.

"Emily... Emily... come out, come out wherever you are."

The door opens, and I squeeze my eyes shut tightly, not wanting to see him come in. I hold my breath, but this time it burns in my chest making my lungs bleed with pain. The not knowing where he is gnaws at my stomach and I give in, opening my eyes. I can see the tips of his shoes walk around the bed and stop to the left in front of the open window.

"Huh, well, perhaps that's what Quinn saw in her. Feisty little thing. You can't run, Emily. Quinn might not want to share you, but he's not here now!" He bellows the last part out of the window, and I thank heavens he took the decoy. My mind races with what my next move will be. I left my bag in the hallway with my coat. I've no phone or way of letting anyone know where I am. Déjà vu haunts me.

"Nice try, Em, but I don't take you for the adventurous type." Josh drops down next to me, reaching his arm under the bed and swiping at me.

"Arghh." I roll away, kicking at him as I crawl out the other side. Josh scrambles over the bed and reaches for me. He grabs my hair, but I lash out and smack him in the face before I reach for the door and rush out. The top of the stairs comes into view, but I feel him grab my ankle at the same time. It sends me off balance, and I stumble forward. With nothing to catch me, I land on my hands and fall down the stairs, tumbling down and landing hard on my side at the bottom.

It takes me a minute to right myself. Pain flares through my shoulder and head as I try to stand. Steady footsteps force me upwards, but I slump back to my hands and knees and crawl into the room closest to me, hoping there's another door or way out. My head pounds against my skull and my vision skips in and out as I make it further inside the room.

"Is this what big brother had to do? Fight you into submission? Not his usual style. High-class hookers are what he usually favours. And although you have tits to fucking die for, I'm not seeing anything else. Do you have a magic pussy? Is that it? Do you fuck like a dirty whore?"

I block out his words and pull myself along the dusty carpet on my forearms. I've survived this before; I can survive it again. But as I think the words, I know I won't. Quinn and I were… different. I'd already fallen for his charms before the nightmare began. I gave myself to him, even though the shame may eat me alive, it was my choice. This isn't. And I'll fight it every second, just like I did the Russians. Whether I'll find my way out of this is another question entirely.

Josh's hands push against my back, forcing me into the carpet. He twists my arm, wrenching my shoulder, and another shock of pain radiates through me. I struggle, whipping my good arm around to make contact with his face and turning onto my back, but I'm as much use as a wet rag. I barely hit him.

He straddles my hips, his weight forcing me to still. "That's better." He pins my arms out to the side and brings his face close to mine. "I've enjoyed our little game, but understand this. I'll take what I want from you, and it won't be anything like dear ol' brother. He gave you up. That means you're fair game now and I intend to have some fun."

"Please, Josh. Don't do this. I don't want this."

"Shhh, but I think you do. I think this is what you want." He traps my wrists in one hand and sets about tearing at the button to my trousers.

I thrash my hips and my arms, trying to shove Josh's weight from me, but it doesn't work. He shoves his hand inside my knickers and gropes at me. He's rough and harsh and he tears at my delicate flesh, forcing his way inside of me.

Tears track down my face as I cry. "Stop it, please… Don't. Don't do this," I scream. Bile rolls in my stomach as he continues to dig his fingers inside.

No, no, this can't be happening.

I feel weak and feeble. When Quinn and I fought, I found the strength I needed and that's what I need now.

He loosens his grip on my wrists and plants his palm on my shoulder as he leans into me. His other hand goes for his buckle, the sound of his belt loosening showing he intends to carry out every last word he's said.

Pressure builds in my shoulder as he leans into it. The pain flares as his strength overwhelms me, my breath catching in my throat as I try to process what's happening.

"You're my fucking bitch now." His sneer lights up his face as pain burns through my body. "I'm going to shove my cock in each of your holes and you're going to take it."

"No… no… Josh, please," I sob, before giving one last surge of strength to dislodge him and escape. He removes his fingers, but only so he can smack me around the face. The heat fires across my cheek and throbs, dulling the ache from the rest of my body.

At least his hands have left me now, but then I see why. He flicks out a blade that gleams even in the dim light. My heart races and the fear that floods me threatens to take over. I look at Josh and try to see something of his brother in him. I'd do anything to be back with Quinn right now. I shouldn't have asked to come home. I should have stayed and forced more from Quinn.

"Stop it, Josh. No. No! You're hurting me… Josh!" My panic infects my muscles and I thrash under him.

"Now, keep still, or I might cut you." He grins, the white of his teeth shining in the darkness and making him look as mad as he's acting. He runs a knife against my blouse, cutting the buttons free. He then digs the tip of the blade into my cami top and pulls down. The tearing noise fades into the background as I feel the hard edge pinch against my skin. It bites, and heat follows the line of the blade.

"Well, fuck. I made a little scratch."

I turn away from him and squeeze my eyes shut. My body

is in agony, screaming for relief.

"No, I want you to watch, bitch." He pushes the blade into my cheek, forcing my eyes to open up. The blade feels wet, and I can smell the tang of metal. He pulls the knife against my skin and again, it bites before heat replaces the cold metal. I try not to cry, but the searing pain across my cheek is too much. My mind flashes images of what must be a ghastly cut on my face and I pray I'm overreacting. Somewhere inside of me I know Quinn would never have done this to me. I might not have realised that right away, but on that day by the river, we both trusted each other.

I hold onto that memory. The first time there was anything concrete between us, something real for him. Being with him has given me an inner strength I need to use now. I take a few deep breaths and try to remain conscious, but my mind swims in and out of clarity.

"Quinn always shared the whores he fucked. It was a Cane perk. He'd arrange for us all to fuck them. Pass the skirt around. We'd all get high and drunk and fuck all night. I knew it was different with you the minute he hit me. After everything I've done to prove myself, that's how he repays me. Well, I'll show him."

"H-he won't like this, Josh. He'll be mad at you." I stammer the words together, hoping to give him pause.

"He doesn't give a crap about me. Never has. All I've ever wanted is to work beside him and Nate as their brother, help run the business that is my name. But oh no. Quinn won't let me near his precious empire." Josh leans in closer, studying the incision on my face. "He pushed me away, Em. Tossed me aside again and again, when all I wanted was for him to be proud of me. That's all I wanted. Is that too much for me to ask?"

I shake my head as best I can, trying to placate him.

"Well, it's too late now. He thinks he can shove me out the way, then he can pay the consequences."

Josh starts eyeing up my body and my skin ripples with disgust. The fabric of my clothes hangs loosely at my side, my body open to him. I don't want him to cut me any more, I need to kick my brain into gear and work out a way to escape.

"You have really pretty skin. It looks so tender." He makes another pass with the knife, pressing in hard enough to pierce the skin and drawing a snake-like pattern down my chest to my stomach. The sting from the cut throbs. My whole chest feels like it's covered in cuts. Josh leans in, watching his handiwork as he traces the lines again and again. The tip of the blade runs over the flesh of my boob, close to the nipple. His weight shifts and gives me a fraction of room.

My right arm is still outstretched, and I force it to feel for anything I can use as a weapon. There's a fireplace next to us. My fingers edge inch by inch, searching until I feel something hard and cool. I wrap my fist around it and swing.

An ear-piercing clatter startles us both before I arc my arm and hit him with the metal object in my hand. A loud thud signals my strike and I feel Josh's body go limp and stumble away from me a little. I don't leave it to chance and clobber him again.

He slumps to the side, and I push him further from me. He sprawls out on the carpet, his legs and body resting near the entrance to the room. I slide myself back on the carpet until I hit another wall. I clutch the metal fire poker in my hand and bring my knees up to my chest. I cower in on myself, but right now I don't have the capacity for bravery.

Tears track down my face and cause the cut to sting even more as the salt mixes into the wound. I want to wrap myself up, but I'm afraid to look at what Josh has done. The slight tickle of liquid seeping down my skin tells me I'm still bleeding, but I can't look. Looking will mean I have to acknowledge what he's done. My bleary eyes lock onto the doorway where Josh's body lies motionless.

The gentle tick-tock of a clock comes into focus and I concentrate on the sound. Terror rules my body, but the regular sound stops me from going into panic. My mind shuts down to my fear response and I'm only just hanging on to reality. The pain I felt a few moments ago is fading to a dull ache as I focus on nothing else but Josh's body. I need to be ready. I can't let him touch me again. I can't let anyone touch me again.

CHAPTER TWENTY-FIVE

Quinn

I blast the horn, blaring my voice out of the window to get the British traffic to move out the fucking way. He's making her dinner? Dick. And I know exactly why he's taking her to our family home, because it's quiet. It's the same place I'm trying to get to as this damn traffic pushes me backwards. I only need to get through this fucking town and I'll be on back roads. I snarl at a woman who turns to look at my constantly hammering horn, and eventually round the wheel and turn the car onto the pavement, frustration fuelling the move.

A shocked onlooker scrambles out of my way as I ride the kerb, feet rushing to get away from my accelerator pushing hard.

What the fuck Josh is up to is anyone's guess, but it's just the sort of thing he'd do. He probably just wants a cut of big brother's prime fucking meat. Pissed at me for not letting him have a go at her ass, and equally pissed at me for sending him back here so I didn't beat the shit out of him.

Open road finally comes into my vision, small lanes funnelling into narrower ones, English countryside overhanging the edges. I round each one at speed, focusing on my destination and hauling the Jaguar into tight corners only to flatten my foot again once I'm out of it. Fucking dick. He deserves a beating for this, let alone all the rest of the shit he's caused this family over the years.

I thought I'd got it organised in my head. Thought the plane journey's silence here had given me time to think and understand what I was going to say to her if I found her in a state, but then I turned my phone on again.

I'd woken, showered, got into some clean clothes, and then found the car once we landed. It took thirty seconds to read two texts from an unknown number, and the moment I realized they were from her, I floored the car.

She misses me.

The first part of this journey was spent trying to work out what the fuck that means. How does someone like her miss someone like me? But by the time I let whatever the fuck Josh is up to get into my mind, I lost care about what it means, only that it was fact and she needed me.

Loose chippings are kicked off the tyres, their crunch tightening my vision along the black petering-out roads. I've driven them before, but never at such speed. It makes the car rebound roughly as I swerve the banked sides, metal hitting something as I do. Until, finally, the half mile drive comes into view.

I brake hard and veer off, cornering into it as if something's on my tail with a barrel aimed at my head. There are no limits to what I could find. I've cleaned up all sorts of shit for my brother over the years. Sex, drugs. Whores near dead after his play parties. A couple of deaths, some show of his useless fucking power to the rest of our world.

He has no power. I do.

The thoughts increase my fury at his devious behaviour, making what was annoyance at his insidious game turn into full on rage. It's so like him to do this sort of shit. Wind big brother up. Get some attention. Have something that's not his just because he's a spoilt little boy who never fucking grew up. Perhaps I should have worked him harder, been harsher with him. Taught him some better manners at least, because this woman is not his to have. She's mine.

The house is only half lit up as I approach, the outside lights showing the garden's country charm, but there's only one or two lights on inside. I slow, watching for movement, and let the car quietly creep the final few turns onto the courtyard. The main lounge is dim. One bedroom the same, a low glow coming from behind drawn curtains. Bile rises at the images that circulate my head. They're fucking in there. He's turned the charm on, smiled his sweetest fucking smile and managed to get his dick inside something that isn't his to get into. The thought of his fingers anywhere near her repulses me, fuelling hatred that I didn't know I had for him. Family or not, this is the last fucking straw.

I get out and walk the pathway, trying to contain the need to let fate have its way with the little cunt. I told him I'd pull the trigger myself. I just might if the first thing I find is his bare ass smirking at me.

My key quietly lodges in the lock, unable to twist regardless of my pressure on it. He's dead bolted it. It makes me stall and check the edges, looking for how easy it would be to kick down and surprise him.

"Josh," I call out. "Open the fucking door." No sound comes back, even after a minute of waiting. "Emily?"

Still nothing.

"Josh, you've got ten fucking seconds to get your ass down here before I break this damn door down." It's loud enough for the next fucking village to hear, but still there's no response.

Dread begins to crawl through me, some latent memory of his behaviour when he's done shit he won't own up to. Without thought, my foot kicks at the door, not enough power to do anything to it. I grab hold of the sides, increasing my strength, and crash at it again and again until it flies open, hinges rattling as it slams against the hall wall.

It's quiet inside. No movement. No sound. I glare up the stairs at the dim light shining down, building myself up to the fucking climb that's going to lead me to them, and then take a step forward. My footsteps clack the parquet floor, sounding my arrival more than the slam of the door. I'm pissed. Aggravated with him for fucking her and annoyed with my feelings about that. I'm fucking jealous. Jealous and bitter. I can feel it biting in with every footfall, acknowledging this love I'm only just admitting.

A noise to the left catches my attention. I twist my head, listening for more. A slight murmur of something, something I can't quite hear. I walk towards it slowly, checking the stairs behind again and then turning back in the direction of the noise. It's coming from the lounge, but the moment my hand reaches the handle, it stops.

I push to widen the door, but it nudges against something, so I push harder and notice a man's foot. I shove it fully, opening it, and find Josh slumped in the corner of the room, his hand on the back of his head. I pull my gun, instantly backing up to him and glaring around the room for threat. It's as silent as it was when I first entered.

"Emily?" There's no response. I turn and haul Josh up against the wall, still searching the room for her. She's nowhere to be seen. "What happened, Josh?" I ask, lifting his hand to inspect a large gash. "Who's here?" He doesn't answer, so I rest him back and stand to look for Em again. "Emily, where are you?"

Four steps across the lounge to the fireplace, gun aimed at any dark shadow, and I find her. She's huddled in the corner, her knees up to her chest and a twisted look on her face. She just stares back into the room. I scowl at her, noticing a grate poker at her side. It lies two feet from her outstretched arm, her fingers still open as if she's dropped it there.

I crouch in front of her slowly, getting in her eye-line, and frown at the slash on her face.

"Did you do this to him?" She doesn't acknowledge me at all. No sign of life as she keeps gazing straight through me. "Emily?" Makeup tracks her cheeks enough for me to see the fear she's dealt with. Her face is frozen in her last moments, just like Mother's does sometimes. It's etched with terror, tears imprinting the bloodied streaks that fell. "It's Quinn, Em. You're safe."

Josh groans behind me, a muttered rally of words coming from him. I spin to look back, suddenly noting the blood on his right hand. "What happened here?" I ask again. I look back and forth between them. There's still no movement from Emily, but Josh begins pulling himself to his feet. I narrow my eyes at him, disgusted with the thoughts currently circulating my head. The only reason I can see for her attacking him, if that's what happened, is rape.

"Did she do this to you?" I ask, the gravel in my voice barely containing my fury. He scowls and touches the cut on his head again, bringing it to his eyes to see the blood. "Josh?"

"Bitch said no," he slurs.

Any element of containment is gone the second he admits it. I stand and storm over to him, drawing the fucking gun up again just for the satisfaction of shoving it into his mouth.

"I should damn well put you down," I spit, sick and tired of him. "I've taught you better than this. She's never been yours to touch. I warned you, Josh. You're just fuck up after fuck up."

He laughs and glares in return, his hand reaching for my gun and trying to knock it out of the way before I pull the trigger. I grip tighter and shove it at him, my other hand grabbing at his skull and jostling him back to the floor where he damn well belongs. The whole fucking situation disgusts me.

"I learnt from the best," he growls, his cheek grating the floor. I glower at the words, ready to pull the trigger if he means I taught him this. I've done nothing but protect him my entire life. Screw up after screw up, juvenile behaviour gone wrong.

"The fuck does that mean?" I ask, pushing his head one more time and then backing off. "I never fucking taught you to rape women." My gun smacks him hard on his cheek, blood flying from his lip as I pull it away. "You're your own fucking fault, Josh. I'm done shielding your ass." He spits onto the floor and coughs, another fucking laugh following it. "This damn well sickens me."

Emily whimpers and then hums behind, causing me to turn and look at her. It's like a damned siren's song calling me back to her, notes drifting quietly from her lips. I step to her, ready to pick her up and get us both away from this cunt. Family or not. This is over now. I'm done with whatever the fuck he's become. He's got no place in the family after this.

Still there's no movement from her as I gaze at her fragility. She's like a fucking ghost sitting there, skin as white as the vest top draping her frame.

Suddenly, my body goes from beneath me, the weight of Josh crashing into me sending me flying into the coffee table. I struggle against him, hands grabbing for anything I can get hold of, my gun falling from my fingers. The table collapses, splinters of it puncturing my skin as I heave wildly at him and wrestle my way out.

"The fuck you doing?" I shout, forcing him away from me with another shunt. He flicks out a blade, and backs towards Emily. I spin to her, ready to kill this dick if he goes anywhere near her again. Still she hums her tune, her eyes blank as he sneers at me.

"This is all your fault, Quinn," he states, malice coming from him as he gets in my way and blocks me from her. I frown and then scowl at him, one step forward. "Stay there," he snaps, holding the blade up and slicing it through the air. "You should watch this. You'll be proud of me. You made me this way, brother."

I halt, wondering what the fuck he's talking about, and glance at the gun behind him. He smiles like the dick he is, wielding his blade and backing another pace towards her.

"You're not fucking touching her, Josh."

He comes at me like a madman, hand manipulating the knife in my direction as I try to move, but it's too late for me to duck. I brace my arms out in surprise, hoping to keep him far enough away for the steel not to stab me, but he's so quick that we both go storming towards the far wall until I grunt from its impact on my back. He pushes away from me and tracks the floor back to her.

"My turn first this time, big brother," he whispers. "I'll show you I'm worth this fucking name. Fuck her right." Something inside me snaps. Worth this name? He's not worth a fucking thing anymore, certainly not Emily.

I run at him before he has another chance to breathe, one hand reaching for the blade as I slam him towards the fireplace. The air shunts out of him, back colliding with the wood as I turn into him and hold the blade away from us. He grapples over my back, fist punching into my ribs, enough to make me wheeze and roll forward. We both fall, legs kicking as I try to get the damn thing from his hand. He slices it again, strengthening muscles and forcing me onto my back until he's above me.

"Put it down, Josh," I growl out, rage beginning to tip me over the edge of reason. He leers above me, chuckling as he shoves and grunts. "The fuck are you doing?"

"Canes take what they want," he mumbles, both hands managing to wrap round my one grip and power the blade down at my face.

My fingers latch onto the side of his head, ripping at his hair and heaving him with as much strength as I've got to get him onto his side. He crashes sideways, neither of us letting go of the knife, but then manages to knee me in the stomach and propel us the other way. It's a blur. Rage swells somewhere deep in the pit of my guts, reminding me of the man I used to be when killing was my life, no longer caring for brotherly loyalty. It forces momentum to rip through me, thumb sinking into his eye and relishing the yell that comes at the pain. My fist punches repeatedly, shoulder forging my hand into any part of him that I can get to, but he's filled with power I've not seen before.

"You're getting old, brother," he spits, his body rolling over mine and shoving me downwards. I blanch left, avoiding his fist. "All your fault." I push the blade away from me, trying to get him the fuck off me. "Always the favourite." I twist, still clinging to the blade, and manage to get my other hand to it only to have his head crash against mine. The room spins, my fingers losing their grip of the blade as I feel the back of my skull knock against the floor. I grunt as pain ricochets through me, making me struggle to focus on his face as he bears down on me again. "You never let me in." I blink and focus, lifting my hands to his face to get some grip, but I feel him knock them away and laugh at me. "Didn't think I was good enough, did you?" No, and he still isn't. "Should've done this years ago," he snarls. My hands raise again, hips trying to roll away from him, but he pins me with the blade at my throat before I get the chance. I widen my eyes, and shake my head, not knowing where the hell any of this has come from.

"The hell off me," I mutter as I reach around the floor for something to hit him with. He pushes the metal against me, inching it close enough that I feel the prick of it on my skin. Clarity comes racing back, his face becoming the centre of my fucking world again. I go lax in his hands, making him think he's got some ground on me.

"Who's in control now, huh?"

My eyes squint, fury beginning to find its base again at his words, and bring both my fists slamming into the side of his head. He falters above me, giving me enough room to shove the fucker off me and reel sideways from beneath him. I kick out instantly, my heel connecting with his ribs as he tries to stand. It gives me space to loom over him and kick twice more, ready to demolish what's left of the dick. I'm in fucking control.

He wheezes and curls into a ball, a choked sound coming from his fucking mouth. I glare at the noise, fury just holding me off killing him where he lies. Devious little cunt. How dare he try this fucking shit with me? All the years. All the times I've put up with his tantrums. All the protection I've offered, and this is what he gives me for thanks? Dick.

I scowl and back off a step, happy to let him dwell in his pain and remember who the hell is in control of this family. It's not him.

"Quinn?" Emily's small voice says.

I look across at her, watching as she stares at me and shakes. The fuck is all this? She shouldn't be here. She should be outside these walls, knowing a life away from the crap that Canes live in. I smile at her, trying to keep her focused on me and nothing else. She doesn't deserve any of me or my life in hers, let alone cunts like Josh trying to defile her good nature.

"You're okay," I say, grabbing at a blanket on the back of the sofa and starting towards her, snarling at Josh's balled frame as I go past him. "Let's get you out of here."

She doesn't smile back as I reach for her, she huddles further away from me, fear creeping through the blank expression.

"Sssh," I say, my arms slowing their movement just like they do with my mother. "I've got you. You're alright, Em." Her head shakes rapidly, fingers latching onto her top as she starts sobbing and tries to climb the wall behind her. I rise with her, staying in her vision to keep her away from the fucking mayhem around us. Her top falls open, showing the sliced material and small cuts to her skin, and I barely contain the need to turn and use the fucking blade on the dick who did it to her.

"It's not real, Quinn," she mumbles. "He was... And I was trying …" She looks at the wall, then floor, then back at me. "And you're like him. You are." She flails her body around, feet kicking her further into the corner. She starts crying to herself, doing everything she can to escape from me. Escape to freedom.

"Sssh, Em. It's alright now. I've got you. He won't touch you again."

Her eyes suddenly go wide, and she launches her lithe limbs sideways away from me. I follow, trying to grab her and calm her down before she hurts herself, but the weight of Josh crashes down on me from behind. My knees buckle, the force of him propelling me forward with no room to get away from his madness.

I turn, my arms wrapping around him in an attempt to force him off me, but he's all over me, and I feel the stab into my thigh before I've got a chance to move. My head digs into his shoulder, feet kicking me off the wall to get him the hell away from me before he does something idiotic, or I do, but the brawl carries on as I tackle him backwards. It's all brute strength and weight, two Canes battling to win a fucking war I didn't know was happening in front of my own eyes, and it'll carry on 'til one of us owns the end of it. Knife in my skin or not.

CHAPTER TWENTY-SIX

Emily

The gun vibrates in my hand as I struggle to keep it held up, the ringing still loud in my ears after the crack of it firing. I fired a gun. My right-hand aches from clenching the handle so tightly, and sweat loosens my grip, but I can't drop it.

Not yet.

Quinn and Josh stand motionless, and I don't know who I hit. I knew in my head I needed to protect Quinn. Josh was so mad, so angry that I didn't know what he'd do. I couldn't watch as he stabbed Quinn. My mind cleared and all I could see was Josh attacking Quinn like a madman.

The gun was at my feet, so I picked it up. My thumb pushed the safety back, and I held it out in front of me, just like Quinn showed me, my shaky arms offering little stability. They were apart when I shot. I winced and held my breath as my finger squeezed against the trigger. It stunned me. The jolt shook my whole body. And then everything froze.

I fired a gun.

My arms grow tired as I fall back down against the wall that was propping me up. Quinn slumps down on top of Josh but then kneels back up. His brother doesn't move, and even in the gloom, I can see a shadow spreading across his chest.

I push it all away. I close my eyes and focus on the song.

My song that has kept me from the edge for so long, but now I'm afraid that won't save me from my own mind.

I fired a gun and shot someone. I shot someone who's loved.

Tears stream down my face. They gather around the dried blood on my cheek. It stings, and I want to scrub them away. Everything hurts, everything aches. My fingers, my hands, my arms. They begin to fail, and my arm slumps, removing the gun aimed at Quinn.

He's pounding on Josh's chest, his grunts and murmurs barely registering. I see the fight replay in front of my eyes as I watch on, as if I'm a bystander to my own crime. Their bodies tangling together, tossing and wrestling. Quinn is winning. He was trying to protect me, help me, until Josh sunk the blade into him. I couldn't leave Quinn open and exposed. It was my fault he was here.

The recording in my mind plays on and I see me pick up the gun and pull the trigger.

An eruption of anger explodes from Quinn as he yells into the room. It shakes me from my introspection, and my eyes dart around, suddenly alert.

Blood. I see blood. Lots of blood. It saturates Quinn's hands as he presses them against Josh's chest. His face contorts his usual handsome features as he takes in what has happened.

My hands release the gun as if it's a hot poker, the thud heavy on the floor. *What have I done? What do I do?*

Panic rears up from inside again, and my breathing comes in short, sharp bursts. I killed someone. I shot someone, and he's lying in a pool of blood. I shot Quinn's brother.

The thoughts race through my mind faster than I can

process and it makes me dizzy. My head grows cloudy with visions the more I try to focus on anything. Everything blurs, a ringing in the back of my mind distracting me from concentrating on anything in front of me. My body shakes as I sit watching Quinn. He won't give up on Josh, but the pain I've inflicted is written across his face and in every move his body makes.

The blood continues to spill across the floor, the rug in front of the fire seeping it up.

"Quinn... I'm... sorry." I force the words out, each one lodged in my throat at first, but I don't think he's heard me, so I try again. "Quinn, I'm... sorry."

"I can't..."

"I couldn't... I didn't know what to do. He was going to kill you. He stabbed you." The words rush out, the need to explain overtaking me.

"Shut the fuck up!"

His bellow fills the room and turns me ice cold. If I thought Josh was mad before, it was only because I'd not seen Quinn in a rage like this. My lips quiver and I scrunch my eyes closed, shielding me from anything further. I filter through my mind to find the music sheets and start to sing. My hands come up and cover my ears, blocking out anything that will remind me of reality.

The song sounds flat, but it keeps me grounded. I concentrate on the notes, but images invade. Images of Quinn smiling, Quinn out in the sunlight, Quinn asleep on the bed we shared. The picture of him with his brothers. I've ruined everything. The nightmare isn't over; it won't ever be over. It's my life now, and I won't ever be able to outrun it or escape it.

"Stand up, Emily." The voice sounds far away, but that

doesn't make any sense. "Stand up." I still don't process what's being said.

Rough hands grab at my shoulders, and I'm hauled to my feet.

"Look. Look at what you've done." My face is forced next to the stony eyes of Josh. They're blank. Completely expressionless, as if made of glass. But I can still see the crazy in them when he took the knife to my skin. I close my eyes and try to break away from Quinn.

"No, leave me… I don't want to."

"You'll do as you're told. You think you can kill my brother and get away with it?"

I turn around and Quinn is standing over his brother, the gun I used to kill him in his hand, aiming right for my chest. I don't move. I don't flinch. Maybe this would be the most natural solution? It would take all the pain away. I won't be trapped by my feelings any longer. I won't have to miss Quinn, or battle with the shame I feel whenever I think of him and what he's done to me.

My lungs fill with air and I wait, holding my breath until my they scream for oxygen or I don't need to breathe any longer. Quinn's face is lined with aggression. All the evil and deceitful things he's done in his life now let loose and they're flowing around his body as fuel. He doesn't need two hands to hold the gun. He grasps it with the surety of someone who has killed without thought or remorse.

But as I accept my fate, I watch as Quinn's eyes soften. His jaw tenses, but he looks away, down to Josh before flicking back to me. He steps forward, bringing the barrel of the gun closer to my chest. He continues his advance until the gun is pressed over my heart.

"Why? Why you? Of everyone who could have killed my brother, why did it have to be you?"

I shake my head as tears start anew. I can't look at Quinn. It hurts too much. I turn my head and stare at the far wall. My heartbeat thuds in my chest, trying to push the muzzle of the gun away. The beats offer me something to concentrate on, the rhythm calming my thoughts. Lightness takes over and I grow distant as my mind relaxes.

"He did this to you."

A feather-like touch sweeps over my cheek and runs down my neck to my chest. The scraps of material that were my clothing still hang to the sides. I don't answer. It's clear that these aren't self-inflicted. "He did this and I wasn't here to stop him."

I try to cover myself, but Quinn stops me. He runs the pad of his thumb over the marks. His touch hurtles me back into the present and makes me remember the sensation of the knife in my flesh. It's what Josh did; he's doing what Josh did. But instead of fascination, I read confusion in Quinn's eyes. His eyes shimmer, the low light catching the moisture gathering in them. It breaks a part of my heart, shattering me into tiny pieces that I can't fathom ever being able to piece together again.

"Arghhh!" His thunderous roar fills the room, punctuated by rapid cracks of gunfire. The bangs make me jump in quick succession, waiting for pain to flare through me, for my body to give out, but it doesn't.

I turn back to look at Quinn and see he's emptied the chamber into the chair to the right of him. It fires my adrenaline and the urge to run scorches my limbs. I shouldn't be here. I want to escape. I need to escape. My hands cradle my head as I hide away, too terrified to look at the scene in front of me.

An acrid smell permeates the room as smoke floats through the air and forces me to stay in the present. My eyes land on the door and what that signals, but I can't look past Quinn. He heaves air into his lungs, his chest rising and falling in quick succession. I gasp, unable to breathe for relief. *He didn't kill me.* But as I think the words, I understand that I thought he might. The man I've fallen for, the man I've missed and wished for could have killed me. He stood over me with a gun once before. But that was play. His games. This is real. It's happening. How do I understand that? How can I?

"Quinn?" My whisper is so faint, but he turns to me. Confusion still mars his face.

He looks around the room and begins to pace around the body, his hands messing with his hair before he pauses and starts his pacing again. With each circuit he gets louder, his feet hitting the floor harder. The tension pulls all the oxygen from the room and I feel the pressure of his anger pushing me back into the corner.

He'll never let me leave now. He has the gun; he has the power. He always held the power. I couldn't ever say no to him. As soon as he touched me I was a puppet. He's taken the old Emily and shaped her into someone who can pick up a gun and kill someone.

He's a threat, front and centre, and instead of offering me help or support, all I see is another nightmare, one that I'll never be able to wake up from. Thoughts turn in my mind until all I can see is fear. A life of fear. Surely, I'll always need to watch for Quinn and what his revenge may be? I'll never be free. How can I be? People pay with their life for murder. Will

I pay Quinn with mine?

Tears soak my skin, falling and splashing onto my chest. My body trembles and shakes as I stumble along the side of the wall. My only way out is through Quinn, but I'm ready to collapse. I can feel the shake in my legs. My body needs to check out for a moment because I'm not sure that the grip on my sanity hasn't been lost.

He lunges to me, pulling me against his chest as I slowly give in to my body and let my subconscious pull me under. As I do, though, I don't miss the tenderness in Quinn's hold as he pulls me into his chest and down onto the floor.

CHAPTER TWENTY-SEVEN

Quinn

I travel the roads in the dead of night, unsure what the fuck I'm going to do with her as she shivers and shudders beside me. The fact that I've managed to get the buckle across her lap without her shredding my face is at least one problem solved. Every time I try to touch her she yelps, going into some crazy panic mode. The rest of the time she's zoned out, barely alive. It's two parts of her I don't like. Parts that remind me of myself all too often, my family's legacy, too.

The phone keeps ringing in the car, fucking annoying me that Shifty's not picked up quicker. Eventually, he does.

"Boss?"

"Go to the old place. Clean up the mess that's there."

"What, boss?"

"My brother, Shifty. He needs disposing of." There's an intake of breath that could eclipse the damn sun. I don't give a fuck for it. I'm still too wound up to care a shit for anything Shifty might think, and too confused about my own reactions to make any sense to anyone. All I care about is getting Emily away from the place before she falls into a madness I can't stop.

"Yes, boss. But how?"

"Burn him for all I care."

"Boss?"

The concern in his voice is evident. It's the same sense of concern I have, but mine's tainted with the fact that he did what he did to her, then attacked me. I sigh and look across at Emily, her fingers picking at her top, trying to wipe the blood splatters from it. It reminds me of my mother and her constant fidgeting, which makes me think of how the hell I'm going to explain any of this to the rest of my family. Mother included.

"Just get it cleaned up, Shifty. He's no different than any other problem that needs attention."

"Yes, boss."

That's enough of a confirmation for me to end the call, dispassionate about how he does it, or where the fuck my dead younger brother ends up. At the moment, and because of the continuing soft humming that's coming from my dirty little girl, I just care about her.

She carries on as I let the roads guide me, hoping they'll bring some sense of clarity. I don't know what I'm doing now. I'm just driving, unable to make a decision about what to do next. I wish I understood why he attacked either of us. I've given him everything over the years, fought everyone for him, protected him. Yet he tried to take something of mine, tarnish it. And then when challenged he attacked me like a rabid animal, ready to slit my throat. None of it makes any sense.

My fingers push at the wad of bandages I took from the kitchen before leaving, applying pressure to the stab wound in my thigh. It's not bad, just a few stitches needed. I'll do them when we get to wherever the hell I'm going. What's more rankling is that I should have shot her in there. I should have pushed the barrel into her goddamn head and pulled the fucking trigger, no thought to it. And I would have to anyone else on this planet, but I couldn't. She looked at me with those fucking eyes of hers, lips quivering around the words and told me she was protecting me. She did it for me. It's one thing to add to the list of my fucking regrets. Decent human turned murderer. She's been pulled as far under as we all are now, part of a broken system. One she never even knew of prior to me.

Some new generation.

I glance at her face as we head back into London, streetlights illuminating the gash on her cheek. It galls me as much as the sight of Josh's chest seeping blood onto the floor. More if I'm honest. Fucking idiot. Why? I'll never have an answer, never know what I did that was so wrong. All my power and I couldn't even look after him. And this woman here beside me, the one who still looks like she's fought for her life and is now barely part of reality, she killed him. Picked up my weapon and shot him. Dead.

By the time we end up pulling into the parking lot at my apartment, me not knowing where else to go, she's asleep. Or passed out through whatever catatonic state she's in. Either way, I've got blood coming from my wound, and she either needs a bath or a fucking doctor. Hell if I know, but she's not going to a damn hospital in this state. The nurses will ask questions, and with that comes cops, and then they'll ask damn questions—questions I won't let her answer. And they're questions I want nowhere near my business.

I carry her up through the back entrances towards the elevator, her arms draped around my neck and face tucked into my chest in case anyone sees us. Unsurprisingly, no one does. It's 4:00 a.m., barely anyone around as I walk through the small lobby and push the card over the keypad. And then I just fucking hover with her in my arms as the door closes behind us, my own knees almost giving in at the thought of my dead brother. It takes everything I've got to put one foot in front of the other and place her on the bed, a blanket tossed on her for warmth.

Fuck. My hand massages my brow, still trying to understand what the hell has gone down tonight. Yesterday she was miles from me and now I'm standing in London, her mutilated body in my bed, and my brother shot dead by the woman I love.

I need a damn drink.

I turn from the room and head to the bar, shedding my bloodied clothes into the basket as I go and gulping down the scotch the moment I reach the bottle. The liquor soothes its way down, calming the explosion that wants to trash every single fucking thing in this room. I stare at the lights outside the window, the skyline doing nothing to disguise the reflection of myself standing over it. Quinn Cane, gangster. I snort, near fucking lunacy taking over what should be rage. I couldn't protect anything for shit. Not my mother, not my brother, and now not even Emily. She's in there because of me, her mind in a billion fucking pieces because I did just what my father would do. I took.

Seems Josh wanted a fucking go at that, too.

The bottle falls from my hand, the crash bringing me back to the present and making me look at the liquid seeping into the carpet. It reminds me of blood, Josh's blood. It was everywhere. The floor, his chest, coating my hands as I tried to get him to breathe again, nearly reaching in through the hole to squeeze life back into his heart. Nothing worked. He was dead the second she shot that round into him. Straight shot. Aimed well regardless of her panic. How the hell she didn't hit me I don't know. Perhaps she's just lucky.

I remember my own blood is still pumping out of my leg. I twist to look at it, still able to feel the stab of the blade as it tore through my flesh. It's been a long time since someone cut me, and it'll be even longer before anyone does it again. I can't feel the pain. I'm too numb to give a damn. Numb because of her. Numb because of him, some semblance of normalcy settling in again now the night is finished. There's nothing to be done anymore. He's gone.

I rub the scar on my chin and head to the medibox, searching through it for a needle and thread. I could staple my leg closed, but I've got time to kill while she sleeps. I might as well make a neat job of it. I can organize what to do with her, work out how to make this situation safe again. Like it or not, she shot someone. A Cane. Nate should be good; he'll bend to whatever I say, and Mother and Father will just have to be told something vague to prove I've dealt with the issue. What the fuck that will be I don't know.

My feet end up dragging me back to her, medical supplies in hand as I hitch a chair and sit in the light of the bathroom. She hasn't moved. Her body's stock still beneath the grey blanket. If I didn't know better, I'd say she's pretending to be asleep, but she isn't. I know that because the humming has finally stopped. Whether it starts again the moment she wakes or not is anyone's guess.

"What the fuck did I do wrong with him, Em?" I ask, threading the needle in my fingers and then looking back at her. She's not listening. She's barely able to function let alone listen to me talk, but I need to get this out into the air, give it credence somehow. No one knows. Nate doesn't, and Mother barely registered him as alive most of the time. But she loved him so much, said he was her baby, and that I had to look after him.

'He's not like you, Quinn. Not strong and brave.'

She said that to me the night after my first murder. Made me promise. She stood there with her finger running over the line of my open wound and asked me to protect my family.

I did.

Until now.

"What the fuck do we do now, dirty girl? You killed my brother and yet I'm still in love with you."

It's another question I haven't got answers for as I clean the last of my bloodied leg up and begin pushing the needle through my skin. I hiss the first time, squeezing the opening together and pulling the suture through, but the second goes easier as my mind wanders off again. What do we do now?

"I should have left you that first night. Maybe called you the next time I was in town. We might have been better that way." I snort and look at her again, watching her chest rise and fall. There is no way we can be better now. She's complicit in murder, caused by me and my breed. The idea should turn me on. That any woman is ballsy enough to pull a trigger to protect her man should have me smirking, but it doesn't cause a smile of any sort. It hurts me inside. Makes me want to take that away from her and make her clean again. That's what she was to me. Dirty when I asked for it. Innocent the rest of the time. She was never meant to be pulled in this deep. "You wake up lucid again and I'll take you out for dinner, treat you properly."

She deserves that from me, not that I have a choice. The tables have turned. I'm in debt to her now. She saved my life, rightly or wrongly. I should give her my dice, have her spin them along a surface, tell me to call a number.

I finish up the rest of my sutures, spraying the wound, and head back to her with the rest of the supplies. She looks pretty, eyelashes fluttering as she sleeps, some colour coming back to her skin. That makes me smile. Probably the first one since I arrived in this country. I sit and brush her hair back, turning her face slightly to inspect the damage Josh caused. It's deep, but not too long. Cleaned up right it shouldn't scar badly.

It doesn't take long to wipe it over and lay some strips across it. It seems to take longer for me to wipe the tracked mascara streams that still line her face. They fucking annoy me more than the cut does. The thought of another man causing them infuriates me. Brother or not. I wipe at them some more until there's no makeup left at all, just her skin and the faint trace of a frown lingering while she sleeps. It feels good to soothe her and cleanse her of all this, rewarding somehow. She breathes easier as I touch her, her body seeming to fall deeper into sleep.

"I don't know when it all changed, Em. I tried to keep him out of it, but he kept pushing me. He wasn't supposed to get involved in this world. I just ..." I shake my head at myself, wondering why I'm talking at all, and stare at her as those eyes flutter again. "He was supposed to be like you. Away from it and living a good life. Kept safe. That's all I ever wanted for him. The youngest, you know? Fuck." He was. He was meant to be the one on the outside, never having to look in and deal with Cane, but at some point he became half invested. Neither in nor out. Probably too mixed up in the rights and wrongs to understand the principles of business. And now, because of that and my failure, she lies here damaged and he's gone. "And look at you here now. Fuck. None of this was supposed to happen. You weren't supposed to become a debt like the rest of them. You were just for me, Em. Just mine." I stare at her, watching another breath rise in her chest softly, still waiting for her to erupt into a nightmare like my mother does. "I watch my mother like you now. I've seen her do what you're doing now and then turn into a maniac because of what the Mortoni family did to her. What my damned father did to her." I snarl and blow out, closer to killing the bastard each time I think about it. But this in front of me isn't his fault, not this time. This is all me. "It wasn't him this time, though, was it, dirty girl? It was me. I did all this. I caused this whole fucking thing and there's not a damn thing I can do to rectify it now."

She rolls a little onto her side, lips mumbling something as I watch on and wait for her to come round. Nothing happens other than soft breathing. "You've got to be stronger than that, Em. You hear me? You've got to wake up and deal with this. Win your own damn fight and prove to me you're not screwed up like my mother. Fight me if you have to. Show me you're still alive in there." I half snort. Deal with it? How does an innocent deal with this shit and move on? Fuck knows. "It's a damn mess, Em."

Hours seem to go by and I watch the sun rise through the window, lighting up the room and bringing with it the realisation that she'll wake soon. I need something to give her, something to make it safe in her mind. Quinn Cane should be furious with her for killing his brother. I'm not, though. I'm relieved she isn't dead, too. I sip at my scotch, watching the sunrise and waiting for the inevitable words of apology to come from her again. "I'm sorry, Quinn." Fuck knows why they mean so much. It wouldn't have meant a damn thing from anyone else. They do from her.

She slowly stirs, legs curling up into herself. I've got nothing in my head but images of her in my bed at home, one she's never slept in. I want her in it. I want her there in the mornings, there in the evenings. Hell, I want her there every time the sun rises and every time it sets. The vision is as fucking infuriating as it is beautiful.

"Quinn," she mumbles as her fingers come up to her face. I smile and watch as she begins to come around. Soft movements, elegant whispers of touches across her skin as she stretches and pulls the blanket tighter to her. Her lips tip up, a flicker of a smile gracing bruised lips before she frowns and grimaces at some memory. And then the kicking starts, her body suddenly alive and fighting a battle that she's already won. I stare for a while, waiting to see if she'll fight her way out like my dirty girl always does. She's reckless like this, hands and feet clawing, strength coming from places she never knew she had before me.

It suits her as much as the vision I saw two minutes ago.

Eventually she settles and squeezes her eyes tight, shaking her head into the sheets and whimpering. It makes me realise she's pulled the trigger in her dreamlike state.

"I don't blame you, Emily," I say, smiling at the thought. She frowns but stills, her fingers loosening their grip on the blanket. "I just wish I knew why he did any of it in the first place."

Her eyes open slowly at that, immediately latching onto mine as she sighs out a breath. She lies there perfectly still, no movement other than her eyes blinking.

"I heard you last night," she whispers. "Some of the

things you said." I nod, not caring if she did or not and wondering which bits she did hear. "I felt you touching me, too." My brow lifts, comforted with the thought that she allowed my hands on her after last night. Her hands slide up to under her cheek, a small frown gracing her forehead as she touches the strips across her cut. "It's a damn mess, Em. That's what you said." I nod at that, too, a sigh coming from me as I wonder how to make it all right again. "He tried to rape me." I keep nodding, nothing else to say on the subject. He's dead now. She's had her revenge for the act. "You really don't blame me?" I shake my head and lift the bottle for more scotch, still unsure why I don't but assuming love has something to do with it. "He said he hated you. He said he was taking what was owed to him, that he always had your seconds and this time he was going to make the most of it." I scowl at the words, angry at the thought and trying to contain the rage that starts building. "He said he was tired of living in your shadow and that he deserved more than you allowed."

I stand and walk to the bathroom, too wound up and confused about the words to carry on listening. She should bathe, remove the rest of the night from her skin, and then she can go back to her life. I'll make some apology somehow, buy her studio and give it to her so she's set up right for her future.

"Quinn?" I don't answer. I turn on the bath to drown out the sound of her voice telling me things I don't want to hear. It's just reminding me that all of this, all this fucking mess is my fault. It's a fault I'm not letting her invest anymore time in. She should go and be free again, away from anything I thought I might be able to offer. I walk back out and point to the bathroom.

"Clean up. I'll call Shifty to come take you home soon."

She gapes at me, but then nods quietly and moves to sit up on the bed. I leave at the same point as her mouth starts trying to talk again. She needs time alone to realise that this isn't going to work. Whatever she heard me say makes little difference. My dirty girl needs to get on with the rest of her life without me in it, become who she once was again. Nate's right. She's not meant for this world, no matter how much she's suddenly become a part of it.

"Quinn, please," her voice says behind me. I turn to her and glare, warning her to stay away from the topic now. It's done. Over. "I need to talk about this, please. I just need …" The scotch bottle flies from my hand and crashes at the wall, desperation to stop the conversation taking over my calm demeanour. She quivers, her feet taking a step back from me. She's fucking right to. I just want her gone and safe. Away from me. "Quinn?"

"No. No more talking, Em. This is over now. Get cleaned up and then you can go."

"But I..." My blood boils as she keeps standing there, confusing me further. Part of me wants to pull her close and the other wants to make her disappear. "I think I... If you'd just talk like last night we could—"

"Why the fuck did you protect me?" I yell before I can stop it, the sound of the shot still so damn loud in my mind. She stalls her mouth, fingers coming up to it in fear. "Stupid girl." The vision of fear pisses me off more than the continued ring of the bullet. I sneer at it, annoyed that any of us are where we are now with no ability to turn back time. "Welcome to my world, dirty girl. You pulled a trigger. You've become one of the fucking damned." Because of me. She falters her feet backward, shaking her head at my scowl as I move forward into her. "Innocence finally shattered along with the rest of us."

She hovers there like a bluebird in the middle of chaos, no chance of finding her way out of the mess I've created for her. I stop four feet from her, desperate to tell her she'll be fine and unable to do so. She might never be fine again. She'll be changed for the rest of her life and the only thing I can do is repay a debt I never asked to be indebted to.

I sigh and calm my turmoil, my hand reaching for her regardless of the fact that I won't let my feet move. She'll stay there, away from me. She'll go back to being safe and manage life the best way she can. It's easiest that way. Better for both of us.

"I'll make sure the studio's paid off so you don't have to worry about money, set up a bank account. Hell, you want the house you live in? You can have that, too." She frowns and hardens her features, some thought flicking through her mind to change her from scared to irritated. "Whatever you need to get on with life, just ask and it's yours."

"Why would you do that?"

"Because that's how I pay my debts, Emily. The tables turned last night. You saved my life for whatever reason. This is all I can give you in repayment."

That's all I've got to give, because this love isn't worth her having. I'm not bringing her further into a world she's not meant for. She can go on without it.

Without me.

CHAPTER TWENTY-EIGHT

Emily

"A debt?" I whisper, my lips sticking together and hindering my speech. The weight of his words knock me back and I find myself back on the bed.

"Yes. Tell me what you want, and it's yours."

"Is that all this has ever been?" My voice breaks, the crack grating in my throat as I try to speak the words that are bubbling in my chest. So many feelings flow through me that my mind struggles to digest and understand each one. They all converge together, mixing into a soup of confusion and pain.

"I thought you were clear on that."

"Do you care about anything at all? Or do you see everything as what you're owed? The great Quinn Cane and his family. Untouchable."

"Clearly not, seeing as you put a bullet in my brother's fucking chest."

I blanch at his words. He's right. I took Josh's life. I have no right to be hurt at the way Quinn is treating me now. The old Emily, before Quinn, would curl up and let the guilt eat her alive. But the guilt weighs heavier than the shame I've struggled to understand. I might have been afraid, I might have been a mess, but I can't let everything consume me.

"No, not untouchable. I'm sorry."

"I know. You don't have to worry. There won't be any repercussions. You can move on with your life, free and easy."

"You think it will be that simple?" I look up at him, hoping to see some version of a struggle on his face as he answers my question.

"Yeah." He turns away as he responds, going back to pacing the room, unable to contain his agitation. I know he's not being truthful. I heard his words last night.

Despite everything that's happened tonight, somewhere, deep in my chest, I feel relief that Quinn's here. It's such a confusing feeling that it makes me want to collapse back onto the bed and switch off. But I can't. I have to face this head on, or I fear I'll never pull myself out.

Quinn needs to hear some home truths. He can hide behind words and threats all he likes, but I know him. I saw behind the gangster. I just have to reach him again. "I think you're a coward." They are the bravest words I've ever dared say. He swings his head back to me, a glare on his face. "What? No answer to that? Why are you even in London? To check up on Josh?"

"That's not your concern anymore," he mutters.

"It is, and you know it. You're more than a coward. You deceive people. You pretend to be someone you're not, and then when you get people to believe in you, you disappoint them."

"You need to watch your mouth, Em. I'm not fucking kidding."

"It's what Josh thought of you. All he wanted was to work beside you as his brother. He looked up to you, wanted to be you, and you pushed him away."

"Yeah, I did. And he still ended up dead." He stabs his

finger at me, his face scowling as his true feelings show.

I wrap my arms around my legs, pulling comfort from my core as I try to muster my strength. "Why didn't you shoot me, Quinn?" My voice sounds harder as I question him.

"You know, perhaps I damn well should have."

For once, my eyes narrow and harden at his words. They don't frighten me anymore. *He* doesn't frighten me.

"You're pushing me away. I know you see me as more than just a debt paid. You gave that up a while ago. You did the same in Chicago."

He dismisses my words by turning to pace the room, his body like that of a caged animal. My muddled brain may be struggling to comprehend all of what's happened, but it's clear on one thing, and that's making Quinn see the truth between us. No more false pretences, no lies, all the layers peeled back. "You wouldn't have come here if you didn't feel something for me. You would have killed me for what I did to Josh if I were anyone else. I need you to admit that to me, Quinn."

He scoffs.

"I think you're scared. Scared of what your life's become and of letting anybody close to you." He shakes his head, both hands rising to grab at his hair. "You live by the rules you've created through your business world, using your name as a shield and a weapon against anyone you want. But not me, Quinn. You let me in."

"I treat you like a whore, and you think that means something?" His frustration pours from him. He looks at me with so little respect I question my sudden clarity of mind, but know that I'll never truly be free of Quinn unless this is all out in the open.

"Then why didn't you share me with your brothers?

Isn't that what you do? Josh told me he always had your girls after you—that it was a Cane thing to share the skirt around." Silence greets my statement, his eyes narrowing at me. I've not moved from my position on the bed, and I've kept my voice calm and quiet. "You kept me away from Josh, Quinn. You did that for me."

"Don't read too much into anything, Em."

I pull the covers back and stand, my legs holding under my weight. "You stopped the Russian from raping me; you let me sleep with you, gave me free reign in the house, even took me on a bloody date." I keep up my list of evidence to show the man who holds a fragile piece of me that he might think he's a monster who lives in the dark, but he has something inside of him that is honest and isn't tainted by the world he runs.

"Shut up. Shut. Up." He turns to face me. "You want to know how I feel? My blood is itching in my veins to strangle the life from someone. I could pound my fists into faces until breath becomes irrelevant." He sneers, his body rigid as he gazes over me and glares again. "And here you are, Emily. The one who killed him." I try to stand firm, but my legs tremble under his stare. "Believe me, I'm doing everything I can not to take this frustration out on you." His jaw clenches as he grinds the words out, leaning into me. I hold my own and force myself not to react to his intimidation.

He scrubs his hands through his hair and storms towards the door. Before his hand can reach the handle, I call out to him.

"Why don't you then?" He doesn't move. "Come on, Quinn. You know how to do it. Get on with it."

His back expands, and I see all the tension vibrating

through his body.

"You carry on with your fucking mouth and I might."

I wonder if calling his bluff may be the last thing I do. He's so still, silent, and I fear all of his pain is going to erupt and need a target.

"I don't believe that." It's the truth. He won't hurt me. Not anymore.

My feet pad across to him and I stand behind him. My heart hammers in my chest as my body registers the danger. I reach out my hand, hesitantly, before finally placing it on his back, and turn around his imposing frame to get in his line of sight. I draw my fingers across his face and find his scar, trying to reach the man I know is behind it.

"You've made me do things I've never even thought about in my fantasies. You've turned me into someone I don't recognise, that I'm ashamed of when I think about it for too long. But I won't deny my feelings." He just stares. No words. Nothing to help me, as I draw my hand down his body. "They're dark and twisted, Quinn, but they all lead me back to you. To this." I push on his heart, feeling it pound in his chest. "For some reason, you built me up through all of this and made me stronger. Strong enough to kill, and I killed for you. Do you hear me, Quinn? I shot Josh to protect you." His brow rises slightly. "I wouldn't have done that if I felt nothing from you and I'm fed up of you shoving me away because you can't deal with your own screwed up feelings. Admit something, please. Anything. Explain it to me. Explain us." I gesture between us and leave my other hand resting on his chest.

His eyes watch mine, and I see the depth of emotion hidden behind the surface. Hope expands in my chest, rising like a helium balloon, that he might be brave enough to admit everything we've been through together and that things have shifted for him.

My fingers crawl back up his frame, finding that scar again, as I search his face for a sign that he'll relent. But all I see are stormy eyes, regardless of my hope. His shoulders bunch slowly, all stillness retreating as his chest puffs out to carry on with the lies. I'm sick of it, and I've got nothing to lose anymore. Quinn Cane won't crack; he's been honed into a man made of steel.

I pull my arm back and slap my palm across his cheek. It stuns him, giving me the time I need. My lips crush against his, determined to pull some reaction out of him. A second ticks by, the longest of my life, before I feel his fingers dig into my hair and his lips move against mine. The shot of lust diffuses the pain of his hold, and I show him the dirty girl he's shaped, my hands already clinging on for what's coming. But the fireworks and passion I want are taken to a slow and sensual simmer. His lips work against mine, overpowering me easily, and tenderly kissing and nipping at my mouth.

All of my words and all of the feelings I've needed are shown back to me in the dance of our mouths. It's the closest I've felt to Quinn since he let me go, and reminds me of why I've been so lost without him.

He pulls back, leaving me breathless for more.

"You still taste as innocent as when I first kissed you."

His words let the guilt back in, and my frown creases my brow.

"I'm not innocent anymore, Quinn. You stole that from me. You threw me into a world I only saw in films, and you won't even explain it all to me." His kiss might have slowed things down, but I still need answers. The gentle throb from my cuts is nothing in comparison to the storm inside my chest.

He doesn't answer, but runs his eyes over my face again and again, each time stopping at the mark on my cheek.

"I'm sorry that you'll always have to look at me and remember what I've done," I whisper.

"Always? Isn't that a bit premature?"

"I think you've ruined me for anyone else, Quinn. In every way possible."

"My intentions may have been fucked up in the beginning. I saw you as something I could take and enjoy. But you're right, things changed." He reaches into his pocket and pulls out those two cubes that seem to govern so many of his decisions. "That's why I gave you the choice. That's why you got to roll the dice." He sighs and looks away from me, a frown creasing his brow in thought. "You can let the dice decide again. They brought you to me and sent you away. Maybe they'll keep us together," he muses, sounding uncertain about anything.

"You'd leave that up to dice? Why? Why is it so hard for you just to say that you have feelings for me and that we'll try and work something out? I'm not asking anything more of you than the truth." He looks away from me towards the window. "My truth is that I've felt lost since I left you, that I don't think I can make sense of my life without you in it anymore. It terrifies me because I know so little about you. And a lot of what I do know chills me to the bone." Still he doesn't look at me. I drop my eyes to the floor and wonder why I'm bothering. "And I have all of that to deal with before I even consider my guilt and how you'll ever look at me without seeing the girl who killed your brother." I let my shoulders drop and step back, both annoyed and utterly lost. "I need you to make a decision for you, Quinn. Not leave it to fate, or have some screwed up family rule make the decision. You owe me that. You owe me a helluva lot more, but it can't be paid off like a debt."

"Emily it's not that fucking easy. He's dead," he seethes through gritted teeth. His comment infuriates me.

"Well, fuck easy. Nothing is easy. Do you think I found it easy when you tossed me at that Russian arsehole, or when you locked me in your room, or fucked me? It seems we're even on that bloody score. Why are you struggling with showing me any sort of honesty?"

"I don't want you drawn into my world. I'll be vulnerable with you. I can't afford that. This world is…" He shakes his head and backs away from me. "You're just not meant for it, Emily." His eyes are sad as he says the words. "You never were."

"So this is about you. You being vulnerable."

"Did you hear what I said about my mother?"

"Not all of it." I soften. "But I'm not like her." I reach for his face and make sure his eyes are trained on mine. "Perhaps in the beginning, but I can't describe just how different I am because of you. I'm not the same girl. Too much has happened, but that doesn't mean I'll crumble. Surely it means the opposite."

"No, Em. You don't belong with me."

"Well tough. Because I love you, and I think you feel the same about me. Which is terrifying in itself. But don't we owe it to ourselves to try to make something out of this mess?" I blink back the tears, determined to make him see the truth in my eyes. "Don't push me away. Don't do something you'll regret. There's been so much pain, even before me. I know you're better than all of this, or at least, that's what I hope." My fingers trace his cheek and I force a smile through the tears now falling readily onto my face.

My heart sinks when Quinn says nothing in response to my speech. Rejection stabs at my heart, and I add it to the list of burdens threatening to drown me. We stand, searching each other's eyes with no more words to say. They've all been said. At least from me.

"You're the only one who's ever stood up to me," he says quietly. "The fuck did you do that for?" The last of it muttered beneath his breath.

"If I didn't stand up to you, you'd have pushed me out, and I'd be left wondering what the hell happened. I wouldn't have coped with that."

He opens his arms and pulls me into his embrace. It's one of the first signs of affection he's shown and it increases the emotion leaking from my face.

We stand, wrapped in each other's arms for what feels like hours.

"Do we need to go to the police?"

"No. I've taken care of it." His voice is short and flat.

"What next?"

"Who the fuck knows, Em? Who the fuck knows?"

CHAPTER TWENTY-NINE

Quinn

"When are you coming back?" Nate asks, his voice as argumentative as it always is when he's out of his depth. "I'm not fucking telling him, Quinn. You need to get back here and face him. We all want to know what the fuck's gone down."

I frown into the phone, irritated with his damn tone and stare at Emily fucking around in this studio. I don't care a shit for facing my father or telling him where Josh is. He's dead. There's nothing else to say on the matter. How it hasn't happened before Emily is anyone's guess, regardless of my protection.

She walks past me into the back of the studio, tidying up some loose cables and beginning to pack her laptop away. Then she smiles as she comes out and wanders away from me again.

"When I'm goddamn ready, Nate." It's about the only fucking response I've got for him. Life is different here, interesting with her ass in my face all the time.

"Do you want some tea before we go?" she mouths as she pops her head around the corner, pretending to sip a cup of tea. The mimic is as fucking cute as she is.

I shake my head at her and stand, ready to take this conversation with my brother out of her earshot. I've barely talked to him about it since the morning after the event, not managing to find the right words to give context to the scenario. I just told him Josh had been killed. Gambling game gone wrong, and that I'd get the body back to Chicago soon. That was three days ago. Two of which I've spent with her trying to forget the whole fucking night. I just need to see she's good again. Then I can sort shit out. Deal with it all.

The door clatters as I head outside into the wintery weather and gaze at passing traffic, all the time listening to his grumbling about the fact that it's not his job to run everything. And that it's not his job to deal with Father. And that it's not his job to do anything but the damn numbers. He's right, it isn't, but it's also not his fucking job to question how I do run everything. From London or not.

"And who the fuck killed him, Quinn? What family? You've told us nothing." I narrow my eyes at the slow crawl of traffic around me and kick up some leaves beneath my feet, still unsure who should know the truth and who shouldn't. "The fuck's wrong with you? Why won't you talk?"

"It's not as simple as that, Nate," I mutter.

"The hell's not simple about it? He's our brother, Quinn. Cane's don't just die for no fucking reason. What have you done about..."

He carries on ranting, becoming more infuriated the longer I refuse to talk to him. It's not that I don't trust him. He'll do whatever I tell him to. It's more that he likes Emily and he might not after this. For some fucking reason, I care about that more than I thought I could.

She passes by the window, another small smile coming at me as she shrugs into her coat and starts switching lights off. She looks picture fucking perfect, framed by her own little empire.

"Emily shot him, Nate."

There's a hushed silence on the end of the phone. It's exactly what I expected. He's probably calculating the facts as smoothly as he does his numbers, trying to work out why and how without my explanation. One thing's for sure; he'll know why I've been so quiet now. He knows how I feel about her. He has since before I did.

"Why?"

"To protect me."

More silence comes after that, followed by a huff and the phone going dead.

I nod at the blank phone screen in my hand, acknowledging his need to go assimilate that information. I'm not sure what the fuck I would be doing if the situation were reversed, but I'd need the time, too, one way or another. He knows me well enough to know this has become far from a simple revenge kill.

"You ready?" she asks, her fingers turning the key in the lock.

"That security isn't worth shit," I say, instantly scrolling through my phone to find Shifty's number.

"What do you mean?" I don't answer her. Instead, I start us walking and send a message to Shifty to get the place secure. If she's going to be there alone, she'll have the best money can buy protecting her assets. "Quinn?"

"Give me your studio keys?" She does with no other questions as she drops them into my palm. "The guys will need two days to lock down the security for you. You'll have to close shop while they go in."

"What?"

"The studio. Unless you want another building instead?" She frowns and shuffles her scarf around, tipping her defiant little chin up into the air and still refusing any monetary help from me.

"I told you I don't want that." No, but I do. I'm fucking desperate to give her some of this wealth. I don't know why. Maybe it's because of the debt I still feel I owe her for saving my life, dead brother or not. "Besides, it's extortionate here. Have you seen London prices lately? It nearly kills me every month to pay the rent on this and the house."

"Why bother then?" She spins on me so quick I take a step back from her feisty little face, arching a brow at the attitude. "You don't need to. I've told you. You can have anything you want."

"It's mine, Quinn. I built it. I run it. Mine, do you understand? I'll pay the money myself." I chuckle and move around her, amused at her tone and loving her all the more for it. Shooting a man seems to have solidified whatever passion I knew was hiding there. My dirty girl's turned into a hellcat since that night. "Do you?" she asks again, her arm linking through mine as she catches up. "Because I have to be my own person, Quinn. You know that, right?" I nod and weave us through the crowds around Pimlico, heading for the restaurants and bars. "It won't work if you don't respect me." She has more of my respect than anyone has ever had. She had that the moment she shot my brother to protect me, and then again in my bedroom when she told me she loved me. Not that she needs to know, she owns every next fucking breath that comes from my lungs. Debt or not. "It's all about trust and respect, Quinn. Love is like that." Is it?

I frown and keep going, swiping at my phone as it buzzes

with a text from Shifty.

Boys set for starting security tonight, boss. Where shall I meet you for keys?

I send one back telling him to meet us in The Galley House Restaurant in fifteen minutes and asking if he's found Jenny yet.

Yes. She's being kept at the warehouse on Piermont Lane.

Good. I smile and flick the phone into my pocket, amused that the deceitful little bitch has finally been located. Shifty can have his fun for a while before I ask Emily what she wants to do with that information.

"So, where are we going?" she asks, her heels clacking the pavement as she starts walking backwards in front of me. "I've shown you some of London, but what else do you want to see?"

"I'm hardly a tourist, Em."

"I know, but this is nice. These past few days have been…" I catch her before her feet tumble her straight into the road, righting her back to facing forward.

"Your walking ability still needs work."

"I know. Thank you. Anyway, I was saying." She giggles, making my fucking hand slide into hers for some reason. "There are all these places you can't possibly have seen. Nice places. Places where no gangster stuff happens. Normal and…" I stop and push her against the nearest wall, smothering her mouth with my own before she forgets who she's fallen for.

Love or not, I am still a Cane. Life with me will never be roses and laughter. Half this damn city owes me something and my gun is still under this jacket. Always will be.

She gasps as I increase my pressure on her, my knee finding its way between her thighs and grinding into her as I tighten my hold. Then that damn whimper comes, the one that does all kinds of things to my dick. If we weren't out here on the sidewalk I'd fuck her where she stands.

I pull away eventually, too wound up to think about what the fuck I was trying to achieve in the first place.

"What was that for?" she asks breathlessly.

"Cane." She looks confused. It's not fucking surprising. I am, too. Have been since the night she killed my brother and I felt something other than hate because of it. "There will always be shit to deal with, Emily. Business doesn't stop because of you. It never will."

She nods, her face falling from the happy look it had minutes ago. Tough. I can do no more than I am doing for our future, my family's included.

"Always?"

"Always." In my lifetime, anyway.

A soft sigh comes from her as she wraps her arms around herself and looks away from me up the road.

"Isn't there a way out, at all?"

"No. Not for me."

The next generation will have that blessing, but not mine. We'll keep battling our entire lives regardless of my push for modernisation, always half in the shadows and wondering what old fucking ghosts will haunt us next. Maybe it will be less criminal in some ways, but I'm no fucking fool. Clean or not, we will still have to deal with our past.

She nods again and pushes off the wall, brightening her features and pointing along the crowds to our destination.

"We should make the most of our time, then." We should. She's right, because when I leave I'm still not sure if I'm coming back or not. "When are you flying back to Chicago?" Her voice is hesitant and I can hear sadness in it.

"When I'm ready." I'm not. Not yet.

"Okay. Well, do you like the cinema?"

I shake my head at her, wondering when the hell the last time was that I went to see a movie and take hold of her hand again.

"Do you?"

"Yes. Especially chick flicks, but not as much as live theatre or concerts. Have you ever been?"

We keep walking, part of me not listening to a word she's saying and another part fascinated with every damn word. She's like a breath of fresh air, untainted and yet one of us simply by her actions. Not that she did anything other than kill to protect. But I guess that's all I've done through these years. Protect what's mine and the things I love.

The restaurant comes into view a while later. It's one I've never been to, but the grapevine in London says it's the best. The first response when I called was that there wasn't availability. Money seemed to change that opinion. I told her I'd take her to dinner if she woke lucid, treat her properly. I meant it. Especially after she stood up to me and told me of a life that could be made to happen. That damned life might not be fucking perfect, but she'll get the best I can give until I work out how the hell to make all this fit together.

"Really?" she asks, her hands flustering around her clothes, as she looks up at the venue. "I'm not dressed for this,

Quinn. Couldn't we go…"

I've grabbed her arm and headed her for the door before she gets a chance to finish her sentence. This is what she'll have to damn well get used to, along with the heels she'll have to learn to walk in.

"Get used to it, Em. You're with me now." Maybe. I don't fucking know, but she'll hold her damn head high regardless. "Your clothes don't mean a damn thing." She trips over something, making me roll my fucking eyes. I snatch her up and nod at the doorman. "Your walk, however, does."

She giggles and runs her hand down to mine, crinkling her eyes as she smiles back and straightens herself.

We're shown to a table by the window, looking out over the hustle of the town. I smile at the view and wonder how long I can keep this going before I have to get back to Chicago. Marco's already emailing me. New deals to discuss. And Nate's now pissed, probably needing guidance on forward momentum.

"You need to go, don't you?" she asks.

"What?"

"Back." She lowers her eyes to the table, searching the menu. "I'm not stupid, Quinn. And this has been lovely, but I heard your tone with Nate. I'm sure he needs to know what's happened." I don't answer. I pick up my own menu and look at it, not ready to discuss anything other than food. It can all go to hell until I've had some time with her. Time to think. Time to make sure she's okay. "You can, go I mean. It's okay. We'll find a way." She frowns and takes a gulp of some water. "If you want to."

The whisper of her last words makes me reach across and grab her fingers, still unable to tell her the entirety of how I feel, but not wanting any hint of that frown on her beautiful face. Red scar or not.

"You still want me, and I'll come back, Em." She smiles and tightens her fingers in mine, a small nod at the thought. "You're right, though. There's business that needs dealing with. Nate's one of those problems."

"He'll hate me," she says, anguish clear in her eyes. No he won't. He won't hate anything I love, but it will take time.

A waiter arrives and takes our order, bringing with him a selection of wines. I choose one and send him away, wanting to keep the conversation private.

"So, cinema?" she asks, darting back to our earlier conversation and avoiding the harsher line of reality.

Fuck the movies. Fuck anything that has anything to do with me not being inside her in the next couple of hours. That's all I want. It's all I've wanted these last few days. Well, that and watching her smile as she tries to put what she did behind her. She still scrubs her hands too viciously for my liking. Still stares at her reflection for too long in the mirror, questioning herself. Trouble is, she'll never wipe that shit away. I haven't managed it yet either. Blood sticks, no matter the reason why you shed it.

"How about going home so you can suck my dick instead," I say, not caring about the date we're supposedly on.

She laughs, brightening up the damn room. It's a laugh I want with me for a long while yet. One I'll make a point of coercing out of her as often as I can, regardless of this world I live in, her too now. That's all I've got to give her to help her forget. "You can toss my dice, try and get those three fucking words you're after out of me again."

She will one day.

Not without trying my damn patience first, though.

"One day you'll answer a question of mine without me having to dig."

"Maybe, but we do have some business to discuss."

"Oh?" she pipes up, looking half anxious, half intrigued.

"I have Jenny locked up in a warehouse. What do you want to do with her?" She gawps at me, her mouth opening and closing. "Shifty's having his fun before you decide what she deserves."

"What she deserves?"

"Yes."

"Let her go," she snaps, tenacity hardening every feature she has.

I frown, not understanding what the fuck she's talking about. "Why would I do that?"

"I paid the damn debt, Quinn. You call Shifty now and tell him to release her."

"No."

She stands up and throws her napkin on the table, ass swerving the tables before I know what's fucking happening. I follow and have her back in my arms before she reaches the door, manoeuvring her along the hallway and into a quiet side room.

"The fuck was that?" She shrugs from my hold, hands on hips like she owns the goddamn world around her.

"You let her go or you can go to Chicago and not come back as far as I'm bloody concerned. I will not be complicit in this shit of yours."

She arches a brow back at me. The fucking venom that pours from her frame makes my dick stir. It's as arousing as the decency that comes from her on most occasions, making me want to do all kinds of shit to her.

"You want to let her get away with it?"

"Get away with what, Quinn? She's the reason we're here together now. Without her none of this would have happened. I love you. You think that's something I want revenge for? I'm not like you. My first thought isn't revenge. You might not be able to change, but I sure as hell won't for you. I've fallen far enough into your world."

The fucking decency of the words floor me, my own mouth not having any damn answers to throw at her no matter how much I want to argue my point. "You asked me what I want to do with her? I want to let her go, Quinn." She glares at me. "Let. Her. Go."

CHAPTER THIRTY

Emily

Minutes pass, neither of us backing down on the topic. Quinn gave me a choice. He asked me what I wanted to do, and there's no way I want him to keep her locked up like he did to me.

"Fine," he spits. His body turns away from mine, shielding the look of disgust I see cross his face. "Your choice."

He's visibly pissed off, but I don't care. I march past him back into the restaurant, satisfied that he's actually listened to me. I'm still amazed he'd think I'd want to seek out revenge.

He joins me at the table, and I wait for his next comment, my arms crossed defensively as I stare at him in challenge.

"Have you done it?" His eyes flash to mine, that spark of annoyance that's growing so familiar clear to see. "Now, Quinn," I prompt.

"You know what? Fuck this. This isn't what being a Cane is about. The sooner you damn well learn that, the better."

He grabs me from across the table and hauls me back outside. I struggle to keep up, and the heels just make the steps treacherous as I fight to stay standing.

"Slow down. What are we doing?"

"I'm taking you to Jenny," he snaps, aggression in his voice as he hauls me along. "You can't just dismiss this decision like you have."

"Excuse me?" I rip my arm from his grip as we hit the pavement outside, halting my walk immediately. "Dismiss the decision?" He spins back to me, a frown etched in as he stares.

"She set you up. Let you walk into a situation she knew wouldn't end well. Otherwise she'd have taken your place, wouldn't she? You're being too damn weak about this." Weak? Anger bubbles under my skin, along with resentment given everything he's put me through to get here.

"And then where would we be? Is that what you'd have preferred? Never to have met me?" I glare back, trying to give as good as I'm getting from him.

"Em, listen to me."

"Don't *Em* me." I turn away, ready to leave whatever he thinks this is about, but he grabs my arm before I've got a chance to move.

"You need to understand this. It's a part of my world, what I have to deal with. You've already seen part of it. You want us to have a future?" I stare at him, part infuriated and part knowing exactly what's happening here. "Well, this is part of me. You'll fucking deal with it if I have to force you to do it. Prove you can." His words echo the ugly truth I've been hiding from and trying to avoid. I thought the attack and consequences that happened with Josh was the lowest point— that I'd seen enough of the darkness of his world. I haven't, and this is yet more proof of what's coming for me going forward.

Quinn pulls me through the street without any other discussion, his other hand holding his phone to his ear. He's barking orders to Shifty, I guess. They're all words I don't want to hear as I try to push them away. Deal with it? I was dealing with it. I was dealing with it the best way I know how. Doing the right thing and countering this world he lives in. It seems that's not good enough for him.

Five minutes later, a car pulls up beside us, and we get in. I've not said a word to Quinn, understanding that this is something I have little say in. I might not agree with him, and I'm a lot more confident at standing up to him than I was, but I also know when to back down from his glare. This is one of those times.

We travel for around half an hour, silence thick in the car. He's kept my hand wrapped in his, as if trying to hold me together somehow. It's a comfort I need because I can't bear to think about what I'm going to walk in on when we arrive.

The car eventually pulls to a stop outside of a run-down building. It looks deserted. Quinn slides from the car, not letting go of my hand. Our feet crunch against the gravel leading up to an old warehouse. Shifty is standing outside the small door to the side. He kicks at the loose stones and chippings, digging his feet into the ground. As he hears us approach, he straightens up and nods towards Quinn.

"Boss," he says, opening the door for us to enter.

The metal clanks as he closes it behind us, the sound reverberating around the room. It's a cavernous space with only a few crates and storage boxes littered around one wall, a few pendant lights casting an ominous gloom over the space.

Quinn leads me across the hall and through another door. The irregular rhythm of my heels clacking against the cold concrete ring out loudly, building the anticipation stirring in my stomach.

Shifty opens another door into a smaller room, also lit to little effect. I can make out the shape of a woman sitting on a chair in the centre of the room.

Memories invade my mind—the cold, the pain and panic of not knowing where I was or what had happened to me.

"Quinn?" My whisper is so quiet as I cling to his arm, afraid of the rabbit hole I've found myself falling into. All the pain and darkness oozes through my veins, snuffing out any of the hope I ever managed to cling to.

"Em, you're humming." I stop my tune, not realising it was coming from me, and look at him as he brings his palm to my face and cups my cheek. He stands in front of me, crouching to get in my line of sight. "You're stronger than you know," he says quietly, a small smile gracing his lips. "You'll have to be to survive my world, no matter how much I try to change it." He smiles a little. "Deal with this."

His words snap me out of my panic, and I watch him step back towards the wall. I stare at him, still feeling his fingers in mine, and wonder how he felt the first time something like this happened for him. Fear, panic? Or maybe neither of those emotions crossed his mind.

He throws a switch on the wall, and a buzzing accompanies the yellow light that floods the small space.

"Emily!" Jenny's voice cuts through my thoughts and focuses me on the scene now illuminated in front of me. "Oh, thank heavens," she gushes at me.

I take in the image of her and can't help but note the difference between her and when I was in the same position. She's bound to the chair; her feet tied together with duct tape. Her lips look red raw, her hair a mess, her clothes are ripped but still covering her. There are no makeup tracks, though. No real panic in her face.

"Em, you have to talk to Shifty. Get me out of his place.

He's not told me anything, but I'm so pleased to see that you're here to help." She tries a version of a smile. It cracks her dry lips and a bright red spot forms on her top lip.

I let go of Quinn, remembering that she sent me to meet someone else and not Quinn himself. My feet close the distance between us and with every step, my confidence grows.

"You want me to get you out?" I ask. My voice is soft and quiet. Weak. But that's just what I want her to see me as. Weak. She doesn't know what I've had to do. What I *can* do, all thanks to her.

"Yes, yes. That's why you've come, isn't it? To explain that this has been a misunderstanding."

"What part has been a misunderstanding, Jenny?" I stop in front of her, intrigued as to her answer.

"This." She wriggles in the chair. "Keeping me here."

"Shifty, can we untie her?" It's like I'm in a daze suddenly, transfixed on the cold of the room, letting it surround me.

He looks towards Quinn, who nods, before coming back to cut Jenny's ties.

"Thank you, Em. Oh, god, I'm so pleased to see you. How did you… It doesn't matter." She stands and wraps me in a hug. It feels staged. Awkward. And a growing part of me wants to lash out at her, demand answers to all the questions that have flown through my mind over the last few weeks.

"Come on, let's go," she says, relief evident in her tone as she takes my hand. Metal scratches against my wrist, and I look down to see the charm bracelet that she stole from me. My grandmother's precious bracelet.

My mind flashes a kaleidoscope of visions in front of

me—all the blood, the gun, the fight with Quinn. All of it. It's all because of Jenny. Quinn asked me a question before he dragged me here. It seemed so easy to answer. An obvious choice to be decent in this world. But here, now, watching the expression change on her face as she realises she isn't going to get away with her actions and cheat me again, I'm not so sure it was ever the right choice to make.

Quinn said I need to be stronger. Well, I was strong for him. I protected him. I stood there and fired a gun to protect the man I love. I need to turn that around and make the same choice for me now, defend myself against her. He's right; this needs dealing with.

"Why has all this happened?" I ask, my fingers still latched onto hers.

"Come on, Em. I'll explain things when we're out of here."

"No, Jenny. Why?" Her whole demeanour shifts. She slouches into her body, the smile and falsity covering her face now dropped. "I want to know why, after everything you did, you felt it was your right to go back and steal from me? Wasn't it enough that I took on your debt? That I paid with my own blood, my own skin?" She drops my hand and backs away a step.

"Oh, don't be overdramatic, Em. It doesn't suit you. I needed the money. The cash you gave me didn't cover what I needed to pay." She sneers, as if now that the mask is gone she can't even stand to be close to me. "Besides, you never came home after your date."

"So you take my possessions? To gamble? That's your problem, right?"

"And what would you know of problems, Little Miss

Perfect?"

Her voice drips with venom, her arms crossing over each other as if she has every right to taunt me. The look sickens me, making my stomach swim with anger and betrayal all over again.

"What happened to you, Jenny? We were friends. Best friends." Seeing her like this makes me feel a bigger fool than I ever thought possible. It seems she's been playing me for a long time. The fact breaks a part of me inside, a part that kept the hope alive in the hours and days locked up with Quinn.

She laughs softly. Laughs. It makes tears prick my eyes, the thought of all those years wasted on her welling up inside of me.

"Well, I'll give you the short version, Miss Perfect. Betting was a thrill. And it was better than sticking a needle in my arm and shooting up. Certainly better than working in a shitty photography shop and wasting my life away like you do."

All the loyalty I felt for her diminishes with that last sentence, a part of me ready to walk out and let her rot.

"And you couldn't have told me that?" I snap, biting back the tears and refusing to show them to her.

"I didn't want to be a victim. It wasn't a big deal." She shrugs, as if all this is just another day in the life she leads. "Besides, I'd always found a way out before."

"And then when you couldn't, you just decided that I'd be your way out of the situation? That good old Emily could deal with the problem for you, make it go away?" My hands find my hips as my frustration and anger vent through me.

"You don't look too worse for it." She sneers again, as if she finds the situation amusing. "You seem fine."

Fine.

I look back towards Quinn, who's just standing in the shadows, his hands in his pockets and a frown on his face. He's rolling the dice in his fingers. I know he is. I can almost feel the animosity from him travelling across the space to me, as if he's ready to do what he believes needs doing with no other conversation.

Quinn's words—everything he's taught me—act to build my courage and conviction. Jenny's betrayal was devastating for me in the beginning. I couldn't understand why someone would do such a horrible thing to a friend. It's plainly obvious that she never considered me a friend in the first place. Or rather, not in recent years.

I turn back to her, my own frown matching Quinn's. "You don't know what your cowardly decision cost me, Jenny. How it's changed me." I snort lightly, suddenly assured in my own self belief of right and wrong. "You'll never know what you did. You're not even sorry, are you?"

"It's a tough world, Emily," she drawls, staring me down. "You have to look out for yourself first."

"Well, funny you should say that. Quinn gave me the choice of what to do with you." I see the shift in her eyes, trying to keep up with what I'm saying. "I wanted to let you go. Never see you again in my life. I didn't want to know why you did what you did to me. I'd rather have forgotten it and moved on," I say, smiling. "But Quinn doesn't work like that. He looks out for his family and *demands* what's right for them. I think it's about time I did the same."

"Who's Quinn?" she asks, her arms flourishing at me without a care in the world.

"Quinn Cane. The man you sent me on a date with," I

reply, tipping my head to him in the corner. "To pay off *your* debts. He's the reason you're still alive now, Jenny. The reason you're here. It's nothing to do with Shifty."

Her face pales, her eyes snapping to Quinn. "Actually, now I'm considering it, I suppose I'm the reason you're here now. *I'm* the reason you're still alive."

She gulps, an expression of clarity creeping over her features as she realises what's going on.

"You can still let me go, Em. You'll never see me again, I promise."

"It's too late for that, Jenny." I dig my fingers into her wrist and snatch the silver bracelet from her skin, making her face turn in shock at my harsh handling of her. Tough. "This is mine."

She's right; life isn't easy, but I'll never be walked over again. I turn and walk over to Quinn and put my hand out to him. He doesn't ask what I want. He doesn't need to. He just takes the dice from his pocket and hands them to me without a word uttered between us.

His eyes burn in the dark, and I feel the approval from him wrap me in a comfort that I need to keep me grounded.

"Jenny," I start, leaving Quinn and going to face her. "I want you to pick a number."

"What? Why?" Her eyes narrow at me, but I'm not going to give her the satisfaction of explaining things to her.

"I want you to choose a number between two and twelve. It's easy."

"Fine. Nine," she calls, sounding fed up.

"Well, let's see, shall we?"

I throw the dice, giving myself over to chance and letting fate make the choice I never thought I'd be capable of. Quinn was right. Some decisions are more complicated than simply saying yes or no.

The decision to pull the trigger wasn't one I was fully conscious of making. I shot Josh to protect Quinn. There was a reason behind it, but the guilt still sits heavy in my chest, infusing me with a darkness that I'll always carry. But every word from Jenny's mouth since we got here has eaten away at my first choice. Any shred of understanding or compassion has crumbled with each truth she's revealed, leaving nothing but the raw emotion that burns through me.

The two cubes skip over the floor and fall to a halt, landing on five. "That's a shame, Jenny," I mutter.

I turn on my unsteady heels and take Quinn's hand in mine, leading him through the door and away from all of this.

"Wait, what does that mean?" she calls after me.

"It means you're not my problem anymore. Shifty, she's all yours." I catch his eye, and he nods, a smirk attached to his lips.

My fingers dig into Quinn's hand as I force myself to stop shaking. I need to get out of the building before my legs give out. This show of strength will all be for nothing if I can't see it through and behave the way I intended.

As soon as we're clear of the warehouse I take a deep breath as if I've just surfaced from underwater, scared my next breath will be revoked somehow because of what I've done. "Quinn, I need to sit down."

"No, you don't. I've got you."

"I'm serious. I think I'm going…"

My words are interrupted by urgent lips, punishing my mouth and vanquishing any thought of dropping to my knees. Quinn's tongue demands entry, and I let him, opening myself up to him completely and in every way.

He backs off, his fingers holding my chin as he looks me in the eyes.

"Welcome to my world, Em."

EPILOGUE

Emily

One Year Later

"Quinn, you promised." I drop the camera down to my side and try my best version of a pout.

"You asked me when my brain was being ruled by my dick. Doesn't count."

"Come on, just one."

He offers a begrudging smile, not what I was hoping for, but I snap the frame all the same. I could do this all day, staring at his beautiful features. My eyes flick down to his scar, but it doesn't set my mind to turning anymore. I've seen everything behind Quinn, and it hasn't defeated me. I'm stronger for it, and that's the source of my courage to get up and press forward in our life every day.

My finger sets the shutter snapping as his slick smile resorts back to his usual hard line.

"When are you flying back?" I ask, backing off and walking alongside him through Hyde park.

"Tomorrow. Nate has a meeting set with Marco Mortoni. I need to be there, Em. You know I do. We've been working towards this for the last year."

"I know. I'm pleased it's gone according to plan."

My smile is genuine because this meeting will mark a milestone in his business. Quinn and Nate have been working to clean up the business and cut the criminal interests he used to rely so heavily on. When we'd settled into a kind of rhythm with each other he started to open up about the Cane world. It was shocking, enough so that I was terrified of what I'd gotten into at first, love or not. But then he told me of his future plans. It's taken a while, and it will be another year or two, if ever, before he's resolved everything, but it's another reason to hope for better. For safer.

"You'll be over on the weekend, though. The funeral is next week." Quinn's mention of the funeral sends a shudder through me. Quinn's father died nearly a month ago. He's been in London with me ever since, barely talking about it. He arrived back from Chicago, announced he was dead, and then moved onto the next topic of conversation.

I never met his dad, but he was always a presence in Quinn's life, a shadow casting him in the shade. And even though he's now dead, I still find myself hating him for what he put his family through. I might never know the entirety of what he did, but I understand enough.

Quinn has hardly ever spoken to me of him, always hiding his true feelings, and I know not to push him on the subject, but I want to. Maybe I will one day. I'll get deeper in and find the real reasons behind this empire he heads, but he gets the hard, stone-like gaze when I mention anything, building walls I can't get through.

So, for now, I steer clear and wait for the right time.

The funeral will mean I'll have to face Nate again. He's the only other person who knows the full truth about me and Josh and what happened that night. I was surprised at how calm he was the first time we met when I went back to Chicago with Quinn. It would have been easier if he'd shouted or got angry, but he's been stoic with me the handful of times I've seen him since. Less than happy, but not hostile at least. I'm hopeful that he won't be like that forever, though. Out of all three Cane boys, he always seemed the least affected by the family name, or the business he works in. I hate the feeling that I pushed him further into it through my actions.

"Will Angie be there?" I ask, moving around the flower beds to get to the far side of the path. He frowns at me, watching my feet as if I might fall any minute. Thankfully, I don't.

I know that realistically she can't be there. Quinn's mother hasn't made it out of her room for years, but I feel she should be there to see her monster of a husband laid to rest. Not that she really knows what he was like according to Quinn. Not anymore.

"No. But Maria reports that she seems calmer these last weeks." He pulls me back to him, linking our fingers. "I'm sure you'll be able to visit with her at Christmas. She liked you."

"That's just you trying to give me another reason to spend Christmas in Chicago." He smiles at that, making me raise my camera quickly. He pushes it away before I get a bloody chance at another shot, and keeps us walking.

I gaze up at the ominous looking winter clouds, thinking about her. I met Angela Cane a few months ago when she was, as Quinn calls it, having a better moment. She was like a classic theatre star, ready to tread the boards. I've seen the darker side of her as well. The state she finds herself in when her medication wears off, or when the demons take hold. It's a stark reminder of why I must keep strong in this world I'm now in.

"Anyway, I've been in London more than Chicago the last few months," he says. "All because of you. I can't be here all the time, Em. We've talked about that."

"I know, I know. It's just…" I let go of my camera and take his other hand, too, walking backwards to pull him along the path. "It's just that..." I sigh, feeling agitated that we can't compromise in our mixed-up life.

"This is fucking ludicrous." I halt, wondering what he's talking about. "I would have thought staying here would be harder for you. Chicago would be simpler all round."

I know what he's talking about—staying in the same city that I murdered in, a constant reminder of what I did. But for me, it's part of my penance. I've learnt to survive through the guilt. Quinn's shown me that I have to.

I turn and look up at the clouds again, wishing there was something to make this all seem as simple as he professes it to be. I killed to protect him, and I won't take that for granted. He's in my life, irrevocably connected, and I make it a personal goal every day to show him how we can make the best of both worlds—the empire he runs and is slowly forging a new path with, and my small business, capturing moments of happiness for all to see—but he's not content with how we are.

"I can't forget, Quinn. I've already conceded the house." We've been over this argument a dozen times.

It took Quinn one month half living in my house before he had me moved into a beautiful apartment, complete with garden. I didn't want to live in the apartment he already had. Too many bad memories and thoughts about the Quinn of the past.

"Moving to Chicago won't mean you'll forget anything," he says.

"I think the conversation of where we live is still open to negotiation."

We've not been able to agree, and while the shift in power and business direction takes place, I'm happy to stay in London. Quinn has other ideas, though.

"How about we negotiate now. I want you to come back to Chicago. I'm fed up of splitting our fucking lives in two." He looks at me and gives me a hard stare.

He's deadly serious.

"Hate to tell you, Quinn, but that's not how to negotiate." I shake my head at him and tug on his hand, wanting to continue our walk rather than get into another argument.

"It's how I negotiate, and no matter how clean the business is, I'll always get what I want in the end. Remember, you're helpless when I get my hands on you, dirty girl." He beams his full Cane smile, and I raise my camera to get the shot I've been after for weeks.

It's bittersweet, though, because I know he's not going to let the moving thing go.

"Quinn, please listen to me. I'm not ready to leave. I can't. My business is here, my parents..."

"Bullshit. You're afraid," he cuts in. "You've been afraid for a year, waiting for me to suddenly ask for my revenge or some shit. Tell you it's all been a lie. It's not fucking happening, Em."

"I can't just run away with you and live happily ever after. Not after what I've done." My voice is quiet and I scan the park around us to make sure there's no one in earshot.

"You won't let yourself forget what happened, no matter where you live. There are other counsellors you can see, other rehab facilities you can volunteer at. I don't even know why you're bothering. It's over, Em. Done." He backs away from me, frustration etched into his face. "And I'm getting damn tired of not being able to protect you."

"Protect me?" His statement confuses me.

"Protect me then. Do you think I enjoy living in the shadow of what my brother did to you? Hell, kidnapping you and locking you away has crossed my mind more than once, Emily." He huffs and stares out into the park. "I've fucking done it before." My brows rise at the comment. "I won't let anyone else I care for get hurt. Not again."

My argument to stay in London softens as I watch him look at the floor.

"You protect me just fine." I move in and steal a kiss, desperate to right this between us but unable to find a solution. "Can we talk about this later?" I take a few steps away, hoping he'll drop the subject and we can just enjoy the rest of the day. "Please? I don't want to waste the precious time we do have together arguing."

He tosses my hand away, still not letting the argument building drop.

"What will it take, dirty girl, huh? Do you want my name?" His name? "Will that help you take me seriously?" My eyes widen like saucers as I catch on to what he's saying.

"Your name? As in…"

"As in I fucking do. The ring. The name. Half of what's mine."

"You're proposing?" The shock in my voice is clear, shown by my hands flying to my face.

"Only if you move your ass to Chicago. That's my terms."

"You're giving me terms for our engagement?"

"More terms *of* engagement, I should think."

I can't keep up with this man. Marriage? My heart pounds in my chest, ecstatic at the thought of being bound to the man I love for the rest of my life. I assumed he'd never agree to marriage. It really isn't a Quinn thing.

"Should we roll your dice on the matter, too?"

He smirks, but doesn't reach into that pocket. "Everything is always on my terms. You should have learnt that by now." He doesn't move to close the gap between us. He won't. If I want physical contact from Quinn, I'll have to ask for it.

"Aren't I the exception to your rule?" The gap between us is now only a foot and I fight my urge to reach out and hug him.

"*You* are my only exception, Em. But not about this. You move your ass to Chicago and you can have the whole damn world."

I search his eyes and find his usual steely reserve. My mind rushes to go over all the possible reasons why this isn't a good idea, but my heart stomps them all out before they form into full coherent thoughts.

"I like the sound of that," I say, wrapping my arms around him and focusing all of my attention on him.

"Is that a yes?" He finally reaches his arm around my waist, providing the comfort I need from him right now. I love this man and everything he's working towards. And I knew that one day I'd have to make the decision to either move to Chicago or end things. I can't contemplate my life without him now, though. He's the other half of who I've become.

The man I love.

Living with Quinn and forging a new life together doesn't have to mean I forget the sacrifices made to bring us together. Wouldn't I be doing the exact opposite by walking away now? Dishonouring Josh's memory and all the pain we went through to reach where we are today.

I stare into his eyes, and watch a storm of emotion play behind them. He'd deadly serious about everything he's said, and I realise I haven't appreciated the situation from his point of view. I must be important to him. Quinn Cane simply wouldn't ask otherwise. Ultimatum or not.

Mrs Emily Cane, though?

ABOUT THE AUTHORS:

Rachel De Lune

Rachel De Lune writes emotionally driven contemporary and erotic romance.

She began scribbling her stories of dominance and submission in the pages of a notebook several years ago, and still can't resist putting pen to real paper. What ifs are turned into heartfelt stories of love where there will always be a HEA.

Rachel lives in the South West of England and daydreams about shoes with red soles, lingerie and chocolate. If she's not writing HEAs, she's probably reading them. She is a wife and has a beautiful daughter.

For every woman who's ever desired more.

Connect with Rachel

Follow her on Amazon -
www.amazon.com/-/e/B00ZS3RVKQ
Join her on Facebook -
www.facebook.com/racheldeluneauthor
Sign up to her newsletter -
eepurl.com/bckw0r
Join Rachel's Solace Seekers -
www.facebook.com/groups/RachelsSolaceSeekers/

Charlotte E. Hart

Charlotte is a Dark Erotic Suspence/Romance author living in the heart of the British countryside. She's lived all over the UK, but finally settled in a small town that still reeks of old school England.

Writing and poetry have become a revolution for the soul, and she cherishes every second that she's sitting at the laptop tapping her way into a new character.

When not writing she enjoys socializing with close friends and traveling cities across the globe. Travel has always been a constant companion to reading and it only increases her thirst for stimulation.

"Life is a torrent of differences, different needs and wants, and it doesn't always end that well. Yet we strive to find our souls final attachment, hoping for validation in our true desires." – Charlotte E. Hart

Connect with Charlotte

Follow her on Amazon-
www.amazon.com/Charlotte-E-Hart/e/B00PS8U5RW
Follow her on Facebook-
www.facebook.com/CharlotteEHart.author/
Follow her on Twitter-
www.twitter.com/CharlotteEHart1

Printed in Great Britain
by Amazon

Jane,

Enjoy the darkside
Happy reading

Rachel
De Lune